THE RAVEN'S WIDOW

A Novel of

Jane Boleyn

ADRIENNE DILLARD

The Raven's Widow:
A Novel of
Jane Boleyn

MadeGlobal Publishing
For more information on
MadeGlobal Publishing, visit our website:
www.madeglobal.com

PRAISE FOR THE RAVEN'S WIDOW

"*The Raven's Widow* is a ground-breaking portrayal of one of the most maligned marriages in Tudor history. Adrienne Dillard shatters the myths surrounding the Lord and Lady Rochford, offering, for the first time, a believable and complex account of a marriage struggling to survive the machinations of Henry VIII's court in one of its most fractious periods. Beautifully researched, empathetic and moving, Jane Boleyn is finally given the thoughtful and poignant story she has long been denied."

Olga Hughes, Editor - *Nerdalicious.com.au*

"Jane Parker Boleyn, Viscountess Rochford...vilified in the annals of history since her calamitous death in 1542. Everyone thinks they know her - but do they really? In this captivating novel, master storyteller Adrienne Dillard paints an entirely new portrait of Jane: one that is charming, sensitive, vulnerable, and altogether believable. Dillard's representation of Jane Boleyn has forever changed my perception of her place in the world of the Henrician Tudor court."

**Sandra Vasoli, Best-Selling Author
of the *Je Anne Boleyn Series***

"Dillard has a real and powerful gift for telling history through bringing alive the voices of the past. This richly and meticulously researched work not only gives us a fresh perspective of the Anne Boleyn tale through the eyes of her sister-in-law Jane Boleyn, but makes us see Jane anew as a woman trying her best to navigate a turbulent and dangerous world. A woman called 'wicked' and a major player in two terrible Tudor tragedies; Dillard constructs Jane in an

empathetic and sympathetic light in a novel also shining a loving light on her husband, George Boleyn. A story that tells poignantly of the frailty of the human condition and makes us wonder what we would do in similar circumstances, this novel depicts Jane as a woman who finds herself out of her depths, and swept deeper and deeper into the currents of Henry VIII's bloody reign. Forced to fight for her own survival, Jane loses hope and sanity until Henry VIII claims yet another victim."
Wendy J. Dunn, Best-Selling Author of *Falling Pomegranate Seeds* **and** *The Light in the Labyrinth*

PRAISE FOR COR ROTTO

"Cor Rotto is one of the most realistic, emotive fictional novels that I have ever read"
Sarah Bryson, author of *Charles Brandon: The King's Man*

"Fans of the Tudor period will truly enjoy Catherine's story, a woman who was smart, tenacious and feisty for the time. This author is a true historian at heart; I enjoyed how Dillard explained her research and how she blended fiction with fact."
M.J. LaBeff, author of suspense novels
Mind Games **and** *The Last Cold Case series*

PRAISE FOR
CATHERINE CAREY IN A NUTSHELL

"Meticulously researched, and it shows. A must-have book for all Tudor fans."
James Peacock, Founder of the *Anne Boleyn Society*

"Nicely filled in the little gaps of knowledge that I did not actually know existed."
Sarah Mueller, Reviewer from
All The Book Blog Names Are Taken

And if any person will meddle of my cause,
I require them to judge the best.
And thus I take my leave of the world and of you all,
and I heartily desire you all to pray for me.

Spoken by Anne Boleyn at her execution on May 19, 1536

This novel is dedicated to two people so rarely judged the best: George Boleyn and Jane Parker

History has not always been kind to these two ravens. This story cannot erase the damage done to their reputations, but perhaps it will shine a light on their humanity. I offer you a picture of two people who lived in a time much different than our own and lost their lives because of circumstances beyond their control. Two people who loved and lost; who made good choices and bad. Two who were once living, breathing people; may they forever rest in peace.

November 12, 1541
Journey to the Tower

THE RIVER was as calm as I had ever seen it. Ordinarily, the tide would have been wild by this time of year, and woe unto any man unfortunate enough to fall into the fierce currents of the Thames. Tonight the tides were still, and the surface of the water appeared glassy. When I peered down into the dark depths, I saw my tired, drawn face wavering in the reflection. I quickly turned away as I fought back a wave of nausea, frightened by the anguish I saw etched there.

I stared out across the water at the small patches of light in the distance as we drifted through the dense low-hanging fog. I could not prove the source of each hazy beacon, but in my mind, each one represented a home. The inhabitants of one of these homes invaded my thoughts, and I envied the present comfort they enjoyed. A mother, father, and their three children sat down to a small wooden table in the cottage of my mind. Curlicues of steam from a meat pie hovered around heads bowed in prayer. I noted a lack of fine tapestries and plates of gold as I took in the room around them; yet, a fire crackled invitingly in the hearth, and an air of joy permeated the dwelling.

I turned my attention away from the bare surroundings and returned to the family. They had finished the prayer. Their faces were now upturned, shining with delight. The children, two blond boys and a girl with raven hair, set about devouring the pastry before them. The man threw his head back in a hearty laugh at his children's exuberance, his dark wavy hair and gleaming amber eyes dancing in the candlelight. His familiarity caused my breath to catch in my throat. It was George – my George. I squeezed my eyes shut to ward off the tears burning behind them. I would not cry; I refused to show them my pain. I shook my head to clear my thoughts, and the family faded away like the ghosts they were and would always be. I would never have a family with George. Our children would never laugh at our table or scamper before our hearth. The life we should have had disappeared on a warm May morning, and now I was on my journey to the same stone fortress that had swallowed up our dreams. George was gone, and the agony of it ached within me.

I pulled my cloak tighter around my shoulders when a rash of goose pimples erupted beneath my velvet sleeves, but the bitter cold still ate its way through, chilling me to the bone. The stillness of the water and the sluggish pace of the barge made the journey seem interminable, and although I dreaded my arrival at the Tower, I was anxious to be out of the cold and cocooned in bed. I welcomed a sleep that could transport me from this doleful prison, and drown out the wails still echoing in my ears. Queen Katherine Howard's cries haunted me even after I was out of her company; only a steady slumber could quiet them.

"Only a few moments more, my lady; the Tower is just ahead."

The patience and sincerity in the guard's voice startled me. Perhaps I would be shown mercy yet. I choked back a polite response. I didn't trust my voice not to falter. Kindness or not, these were royal guards, and they were taking me to prison. Determined to maintain my dignity, I swallowed back the immense fear threatening to overtake my composure. I could not respond to their niceties, and I refused to weep at their solicitude. After all, they owed me their courtesy. I was still a viscountess, and the queen's sins were not my own. I could not be held accountable for Katherine's behaviour if I had simply been doing her bidding. My resolve stiffened, but deep down I knew my excuses didn't matter. I knew the king believed I had betrayed him yet again, and I would not escape with my life this time.

My stomach churned at the sight of the imposing prison that had formerly housed my husband and sister-in-law. It rose out of the gloom before me; its alabaster stone blaring against the dreary backdrop of the night. I waited until the barge docked before I stood up, drawing a deep breath to ward against the light-headedness threatening my balance. The kindly guard offered his arm to me, but I shook my head in response. He dipped a nod in return, then hurried to the dock where his captain was standing deep in conversation with Sir John Gage, the most recent Constable of the Tower. I knew Gage quite well from his time at King Henry's court, but it had been some time since I last saw him at the funeral of the king's third wife. On that day, I marvelled at the smoothness of the skin pulled taut against his fine jaw. I had longed to stroke the back of my hand against it to see if it was as silky as I imagined it was. Now that face was marred by the deep lines of age and worry.

After a brief exchange, all three of the men turned their eyes towards me. Gage merely frowned, but the captain's thin lips twisted into a sneer. Only a few words of his response drifted over the water, and they were not friendly. The guard ambled back to the dock, then stepped onto the barge as the captain yelled, "Oswin, tell Lady Rochford that she can get off the barge however she likes, but for all of our sakes don't let her drown." Oswin – the name sounded so familiar to me, yet so strange at the same time. It reminded me of a time long ago: the sweet tang of rotting apples, the dew on my feet and the warm sun on my face.

Oswin came towards me with an apologetic smile. "Please, my lady, allow me to assist you."

Too prideful to consent, I refused to give the captain any satisfaction. "Thank you, but your assistance is not required," I demurred again. The high timbre of my voice surprised me; it was strange and unfamiliar. The dutiful guard stepped back reluctantly, allowing me to sweep past him. I stopped short at the edge. Politeness dictated a timber plank be laid down across the barge and the stairs so passengers could easily step across, but I found no such comforts offered. Instead, I stared down at a ribbon of inky water between the two. It would be so easy to slip and give myself over to the murky depths below. No prison, no more despair, perhaps not even any pain. My brother told me once that drowning was an easy death if you could overcome your basic instinct to survive. I didn't know how strong my survival instinct was anymore. Would it be an easy escape?

Sensing my hesitation, Oswin quickly stepped off the barge and onto the stairs. He held out his hand, but I ignored it. I stepped forward, pausing momentarily with my foot dangling over the void. Before I could decide, a rogue wave washed against the side of the barge, knocking me off balance. The instinct I doubted only moments before surged through my body, and I lunged for the guard. Oswin's agile reflexes quickly righted me, but Gage and the captain noticed the disturbance, and they rushed towards us.

"That's enough, Oswin," the captain barked. "I will handle it from here." Oswin bowed, and then stepped back so that we could pass. I was grateful for his quick action, but my embarrassment kept me from meeting his gaze. Instead, I stared straight ahead, ignoring the men around me. I sensed the captain's fury and felt my own indignation welling up inside.

'*Of course, he wouldn't want to explain to the king why his prisoner had drowned,*' I shrieked inside my head. '*We mustn't allow anyone to escape the king's justice.*'

"Lady Rochford, you must know that not even pity from a failed suicide attempt could deliver you now. The king would have saved himself much trouble if he had only executed you alongside your deviant husband," the captain breathed in my ear. "Never fear, for you will be joining him in Hell soon enough." The foul sulphur scent lingering on his breath made me retch.

Gage stepped between us. "I can manage from here," he said, placing his hand on the captain's shoulder. The captain doffed his cap and shot me a parting glare before retreating to the barge. Gage cleared his throat as he offered his arm to me. "I'm sorry that man felt the need to humiliate you further, but I can assure you I do not agree with his sentiments." His candour gave me the courage to finally face him; the sincerity in his pale, cobalt eyes stirred a small measure of comfort inside of me. I took his proffered arm, and allowed him to escort me to his home and my prison.

The royal apartments were far meagre than I remembered them. The last time I had entered these rooms was the night before my sister-in-law's coronation. On that evening, light from a cosy radiant fire danced across the rich tapestries woven of fine golden thread hanging in Anne's bedchamber. We played cards above a table carved of warm mahogany on stools upholstered in cream coloured damask with falcons woven throughout while we toasted Anne's success with a spicy hippocras served in burnished gold goblets. George had been in France on embassy, so I slept with Anne in an immense tester bed hung with crimson velvet arras. A counterpane made of the softest claret silk I had ever felt warmed us against the chill. At the time I had wondered if I would ever feel anything quite so lovely and luxuriant against my skin again in my lifetime.

I kept pastime in comfort knowing that, although I longed for my husband in his absence, he would come back to me. George would return and beg me to tell him of all that he had missed. I would describe to him, in minute detail, all the ways in which the court had honoured his beloved sister; the envious way in which people stared at her. If I had known for one moment that all of that glory and all of that envy would have led to George's death, I would have returned it all in a heartbeat. I would have lived in a hovel for George if he had requested it of me, but George would have never desired a simple life. He relished the prestige his relationship with the king brought us.

George was as generous with his material wealth as he was with his affection, and I grew accustomed to the lavish lifestyle his position allowed us, but in the end it was hollow. When he died, I fought for my jointure and everything that was owed to me, but all I wanted was George. Those lands and properties funded the appearances I was required to keep up at court, but they never fulfilled the emptiness I felt. They also didn't save me from my own rash judgement. Now here I was, walking through the empty haunted halls of what had been and what would never be again.

Gage's boots squeaked across the bare stone floors. The queen's scandal was unexpected, and the constable hadn't anticipated any visitors. He had prepared nothing for my arrival. "I apologise for the musty smell. The rushes have not yet arrived, but I will be sure to have them laid in your room once they do," he said, reading my mind.

"It's quite all right, Sir John. I will cope, somehow, as long as I have my maid for company."

"Oh yes, Lucy is already here, my lady. We set up your former rooms, and placed a pallet bed in your bedchamber for her. The furnishings are mean, but you should be comfortable until…" his voice trailed off.

"Until I die, Sir John?"

His face flushed. "Until the king finishes his investigation is all that I meant; until we know his pleasure."

"I'm certain his pleasure will be to bury me with my husband," I muttered under my breath.

Gage swallowed, but said nothing. He knew as well as I did that any trial I might have would be a sham, but it was treasonous to say so aloud. I instantly regretted putting him in a difficult situation.

"I appreciate what you have done for me, Sir John. I'm certain that I shall be absolved of any responsibility for the queen's behaviour. My imprisonment is only temporary. I expect to be out soon and, perhaps, I shall return to Blickling to retire from court. I suppose I have served the crown long enough."

Gage's gentle smile failed to reach his eyes; the nicety was merely for my comfort. The odds seemed against my leaving the Tower alive; still I clung to hope and a sincere belief that I had done nothing wrong. I had escaped the disgrace of Henry's second queen, and I would escape the downfall of his fifth.

The king's secretary had removed Lucy from my service while I was confined to the queen's rooms, so I was pleased when she greeted us at the door. "My lady!" she cried, dropping into a low curtsey. "I am so relieved to see you. I panicked when they told me to pack your belongings for the Tower."

"Thank you for your concern, Lucy," I gestured for her to stand. "I am fine, and all will be well, I have faith." Lucy couldn't even muster a smile; her obvious anxiety unnerved me. I would have to maintain my confidence in my innocence to get through the next few days; I couldn't allow her fear to unnerve me.

Gage sensed my discomfort. "Lucy, would you please turn down Lady Rochford's bed and make sure my servants have put the warming bricks in it?" I turned to Gage, offering him a grateful smile, as Lucy scurried off to her duties. His took my hands into his own; their warmth soothed me. "Hold on to your faith, Lady Rochford, it will sustain you in your tribulations."

After the constable had excused himself, I wandered through the presence chamber I had occupied before Anne's coronation. Some of the very same furniture remained. I recognised a bench covered in vivid green silk beneath the window where I read a letter from George the morning before the procession. The cedar chest, where I placed my jewels for safekeeping while I slept in Anne's bedchamber, was propped open against the wall. These reminders of my former life left me bereft. I did not care whether my bedchamber was ready for me or not, I had to escape to my only comfort. Sleep released me from my torment. In sleep, I could forget.

MAY 1520
HALLINGBURY

THE EARLY spring dew had soaked through the layers of my gown, dampening the linen underneath, but I minded little the nuisance. My father, Lord Morley, was translating Plutarch's *Life of Aemilius Paullus* and had honoured me with a copy of his work thus far. It was a very early draft, and it was streaked with black stains crossing out errors and revising interpretations, but my father's favour felt thrilling, and I treasured his generous gift. I roused myself at dawn before the rest of my family stirred, then hurried out to the apple orchard with a small loaf of manchet to immerse myself in the old stories of the ancient Romans in the peaceful early sunlight.

By the time I had finally emerged from the tale long enough to notice how much time had passed, the bread was gone, and the gurgle of my stomach reminded me that the mid-day hour approached. The sun had melted away the last of the snow weeks ago, revealing the rotted remnants of our bountiful fruit season. I gazed longingly at the sad worm-eaten remains of a lone apple lying on the ground near me, before turning back to my manuscript. I became so lost in my story that I didn't realise I had company under the tree until I heard a giggle.

"I never knew you to be so much of a scholar that you would ignore the likes of Master Wyatt," Margaret teased.

"What do you know about Thomas Wyatt?" I retorted, tossing the desiccated apple lying beside me just hard enough to land it near her miniature leather slippers.

"I know he's with our brother at the fish pond catching trout for supper and bitterly complaining of his upcoming wedding to Elizabeth Brooke. He's even written a rhyme about it. I think he has his eye on someone else, a dark-haired beauty," she wistfully sighed. "Is love always so dramatic?"

I pursed my lips to hide my smile at the dreamy rapture on my younger sister's face. Margaret was only eleven, but she was already enamoured with the idea of romance. She desperately hoped our father would make her a love match. As unlikely as that possibility was, I knew the man she married would at least fall in love with her beauty, if not her penchant for theatrics. I leaned against the coarse bark of the tree to hoist myself upright, and then I straightened the rumpled fabric of my skirt, brushing off the dirt and clippings that had accumulated on it. Margaret blanched at the dark spot near my bottom where the dew had soaked through. "We can avoid the pond if you like. I'm sure you want to clean up before Harry, and his companions return."

"Actually," I replied with a wink. "I don't think I will. Why would those boys care how I look?"

Appalled by my lack of propriety, but still overcome with curiosity, Margaret doggedly followed me to the pond. She never missed an opportunity to display her contrived coquettish manners, and our brother's compatriots always happily encouraged her with compliments and attention. As silly as I found her behaviour, it was, I reluctantly admitted, a very good exercise in preparation for the courtly games she would play if she were ever called to serve the queen. Our father grew up in the household of Henry VIII's grandmother and was looked upon favourably by the monarch. So far, only Harry had spent any significant time at court, but Margaret and I expected that we would find places in the queen's household eventually.

We picked our way across the field, through the tall grass, to the small pond we kept stocked with fish throughout most of the year. The peaceful spot was surrounded by trees that gave just enough shade to escape the sultry heat of the mid-summer sun. Harry and I spent many lazy afternoons splashing in the cool water during the warmer months, followed by skating across the ice when it got cold enough to freeze over. The modest pool had provided many hours of entertainment over the course of our childhood. I would miss its beautiful simplicity when the time came to leave home.

Thomas Wyatt made Harry's acquaintance at a Yule banquet shortly after my brother earned a place at court. Our father had a reputation as a man of letters and served as one of the king's translators, so he was already acquainted with the witty and intelligent Wyatt. The budding poet often shared his pieces with Father and in return, Lord Morley conversed with him on the classics. He developed a paternal rapport with the young man; he introduced him to Harry in hopes that they would become friends. They bonded rather quickly, and Wyatt often tarried at Hallingbury when our brother came home to visit. In addition to his brilliance and charm, Wyatt was striking in his appearance. He walked with a grace that belied his muscular stature, and he tailored his clothing in the most fashionable style. General adoration of this boy on the precipice of manhood assured a small coterie of loyal companions in his retinue; many of whom trailed along when they called upon us. Two of those friends appeared to have joined them at our pond.

"You've got it, Hugh; we'll land it yet!" My brother shared a toothy grin as he clapped a young man I didn't recognise on the back in excitement.

While Wyatt lounged beneath one of the trees with his long legs splayed out on the grass, a slight, dark-haired boy sat on the ledge of the pond with his feet in the water and a fishing pole made from a carved willow tree branch in his hands. The young man next to Harry braced himself, and tugged carefully on his line. The sport of fishing was a test of patience and control, for if the angler jerked too quickly, he ran the risk of losing his catch and scaring off the rest of the fish. He made no sound as he slowly drew his line in and I found myself holding my breath, muscles tensed in anticipation. I could not move for fear of startling him. The moment he landed the fish, I released my breath, mesmerised by the silvery body dancing in the grass.

"Would you all mind keeping your peace? I'm creating something magnificent over here," Wyatt boomed, breaking the hushed silence.

Harry groaned over his shoulder. "Oh, hold your tongue, Thomas. You haven't even quills or parchment. You're likely to forget your masterpiece the moment a pretty face passes you by."

Wyatt winked playfully at Margaret, who I had completely forgotten was still standing beside me. "You're right Harry! These fair ladies have caused me to forget all about my miserable story before I've even had a chance to write it down."

Harry turned around in time to catch the blush enflaming our sister's cheeks. We both knew, embarrassed though she may have seemed, Margaret relished the attention. She flashed Wyatt a coy smile, then granted him a deep curtsey before flouncing off in the direction of the gardens. Harry and I exchanged a meaningful glance. "You really shouldn't tease her so Thomas," I chided. "It only encourages her."

"That girl needs no encouragement from me. Besides, it's good practice for court. Those fair looks she shares with her elder sister will assure her many admirers and envious stares."

"Thomas!" I exclaimed in mock irritation. I feigned indignation at his flattery, but privately it pleased me. I knew Wyatt used his charm as currency to create goodwill, and his compliments were often meaningless, yet I still derived a secret pleasure from feeling desired.

My brother interrupted before Wyatt could charm me further. "Jane, these are my friends, Hugh Wynter and Oswin Danvers." The young fisherman had been kneeling in the grass with his back to me, tending to his catch, but at his name he jumped to his feet, turning to face me; he held the fish triumphantly above his head.

"Well, I know you are Hugh so that one must be Oswin," I pointed to the boy still seated with his feet in the water.

Hugh Wynter's boyish grin coaxed a small dimple in his chin. "Give the lady a prize! Harry, you said your sister was intelligent, but I didn't know she was brilliant." The remark was harmless, but hearing it from a stranger annoyed me. Before I could stop myself, my hand connected with Hugh's chest, and he flew over backwards, the dead fish soaring through the air. He landed in the pond with a tremendous splash. My brother stared at me, eyes wide and mouth agape, while Wyatt shrieked in laughter, slapping his hand on the ground. Oswin scrambled away from the edge of the water in terror that he would be next. Utter mortification of my unexplainable act of impetuousness burned a crimson heat of shame across my face. Hugh resurfaced after what seemed like an eternity and spat a stream of water from his mouth. "I think you scared the fish away!" he shouted.

Wyatt was, by this time, gasping for air, and my brother's astonishment had finally given way to a hearty belly laugh. Only Oswin was fit to help Hugh clamber, sopping wet, out of the pond. Once on dry land, my brother's friend gingerly approached me with his hands extended in a gesture of surrender. "Peace, my lady, peace. 'Twas only said in jest."

I plucked up the courage to meet his gaze. I anticipated seeing anger or at the very least bewilderment there; instead, I was met with a pair of cool sapphires twinkling in merriment. He obviously found my impulsive reaction, and resulting embarrassment, quite amusing. "My deepest apologies, Master Wynter," I muttered, backing away slowly, eager to make a quick escape.

Hugh grasped my hand before I could slip away. "Stay with us, Mistress Parker, I promised your mother trout for supper. We have some fish to catch," he said with a grin. "I'm certain your brother will be a better chaperone from here on out." I acquiesced, against my better judgement, and allowed him to lead me back to the pond.

I spent the rest of the afternoon under the dappled shade of the trees with my brother and his friends. They invited me to partake in their feast while they prattled on about people they knew at court, and which ladies in the queen's service were prettiest, as they devoured sun-warmed crusts of bread and sharp smoky cheese. They compared athletic prowess and contemplated what it would be like if they ever had the chance to participate in the king's military exploits, while they traded witty barbs and guzzled wine from a bottle they had packed along. I listened in wonder to their romantic tales of chivalry, feeling a pang of wistful jealousy at the camaraderie they shared. I hoped that I too would find such close companionship when it was my turn to go to court.

We gathered up the fishing poles, baskets of food and fish, then ambled towards Hallingbury Manor as dusk settled over the land and daylight slowly faded away. The soft glow of candlelight flickering in the windows and the savoury scent of roasted meat wafting across the yard warmed our stomachs, welcoming us home for supper.

Alice Parker, Lady Morley, was not an overly warm or emotional woman. Physical affection from her was a rare commodity fully cherished by her children when she chose to dole it out. Neither was she given to fits of anger or rage. She never dealt in physical punishment, finding that a frown of disapproval was often more than enough to get her point across. Lady Morley's lack of tenderness would seem to make her an unkind or distant parent, but that couldn't have been further from the truth. My mother was always kind to her children and deeply involved in our education. She demonstrated her love in the generosity of praise and the quiet way in which she encouraged our curiosity and ambition. Lady Morley was also very charitable and led by example in her hospitality to the visitors that the men in our family often brought home. It came as no surprise when she greeted us at the door with one of our servants trailing behind her, balancing a tray of gold cups filled with warm spiced wine. "Welcome back, gentleman. I trust you had a successful day at the pond, and I see you've brought Jane with you. How kind of you to include her in your diversions. Please, take some refreshment."

I had always thought my mother beautiful, but the rosy glow the fire cast on her skin and the way the shimmer from her emerald jewels enhanced her eyes took my breath away. I resisted the urge to touch one of the tendrils of flaxen hair framing her heart-shaped face.

Wyatt gave my mother an impish grin as he grabbed a cup from the tray, "Believe me, Lady Morley, it was a privilege to have your lovely daughter with us. She provided us with endless hours of entertainment."

"Yes, she was quite lucky as well! She helped us fill our baskets!" Hugh chimed, lifting the lid of his basket to show her the bounty.

"Even if she had to encourage Hugh to swim after them!" Harry guffawed.

My mother shot me a curious glance as the four young men melted into hysterics at my brother's wit. I could do nothing, but shake my head in response. "Well," she said with a smile. "Shall we eat?"

My father and sister sat at the long trestle table in the hall where we took our meals. Margaret picked at her food like a bird, fingers darting furtively between her plate and her mouth, while Lord Morley appeared to be absentmindedly cramming a roll of bread in his gaping maw. His plate sat to the side while he hunched over a book laying open next to it. The pinched face he always made while he was deep in thought was hidden behind a curtain of wavy brunet hair. Whatever he was reading had captured his attention, and he was oblivious to the group of visitors that had entered his home. My mother offered an apologetic smile as she glided over to my father. She placed her hand on his shoulder, then bent down to whisper in his ear. Lord Morley sat up quickly, taking in his surroundings with a look of surprise.

"Oh yes, my apologies Harry. I forgot you had visitors. Please, come sit down," he commanded, gesturing to the empty chair beside him. I watched my mother deftly slide the book off the table, away from my father's reach. Her actions did not go unnoticed by him. "Careful with that book Alice; do not lose my place," he barked over his shoulder.

I settled into the seat opposite Margaret so she would feel less self-conscious about eating in front of Harry's friends, but instead of appreciation, she shot me a look of annoyance. I knew by her petulant pout she would have preferred to have Thomas Wyatt in her sights, even if it meant she was too nervous to eat. I was too distracted by this silent redress to notice Hugh had slid into the empty chair next to me until I heard him ask, "May I pour you some wine?" His voice startled me, and I turned too quickly, nearly knocking the bottle out of his hands. "You are determined to ruin my best jerkin aren't you?" he scolded with a shake of his head.

With blood rushing into my face, I silently cursed my ineptitude, while my father turned the conversation to the king's plans for his upcoming trip to France. Father told us that Cardinal Thomas Wolsey, the king's Lord Chancellor and Archbishop of York, was determined to join the most powerful Christian nations in a treaty of diplomacy for everlasting peace. War was expensive, Wolsey reasoned, avoiding unnecessary military campaigns would be the best way to maintain the king's treasury and the goodwill of the people. They were much more likely to admire and respect the king if he wasn't taxing them out of their homes. Wolsey encouraged our sovereign over the last year to make overtures for a meeting with King Francis, now it appeared that the summit would finally happen.

The aim of the meeting may have been for diplomatic negotiations, but King Henry was still determined to dazzle the French King and his court with a retinue filled with the powerful elite of England. He invited along everyone with money, to show off their good fortune. Our family was far from rich, but we still had more than many; most importantly, my father had a title. He could barely contain his satisfaction when he informed us that we would be joining the king. Margaret perked up at the news, her bright eyes glittering in excitement, and a shiver of anticipation crawled up my spine. This was an excellent opportunity for our family. We would be travelling with the king, in the grandest style, to mingle with one of the most fashionable courts in the world. Here was my chance to show the queen that I had the skills necessary to serve in her household. Wolsey's purpose may have been to join England and France in a holy alliance, but I was resolved to manoeuvre a successful marriage alliance. My fortune hinged on making a shining debut at court.

The remaining rays of sunlight had long disappeared, and the Heavens shimmered with the golden points of light embroidering the clear night sky. The heat of the day was gone, replaced by a cool breeze that danced across my skin in its place. The courtyard was empty and quiet, the perfect place to digest father's announcement and gather my thoughts. I closed my eyes as I leaned against the solid brick wall. Excited as I was, I also felt terrified. I was certainly intelligent enough for service to the queen. My father had hired excellent tutors, and all of his children were well-read. My mother taught me to sew and play cards, but I was not as musically inclined as she had hoped. I struggled with the lute, and I could never quite capture the correct notes with my voice, but I could dance. I studied the galliard and the pavane and could perform both with ease. I was well-prepared for service to the crown, so why was I so scared?

"You certainly are the most reckless of all the Parker children. What are you doing out here in the cold? You'll never get to France if you catch your death." Hugh's compact form slowly came into focus when I opened my eyes. He had removed his cloak, and held it out in an offering to me. I hated to admit that he was right, so I held my tongue until he shrugged it back on. "Whatever suits you," he replied, turning back towards the manor.

"Wait!" I called out, regretting it the moment it I saw his look of satisfaction.

"Changed your mind then?" Hugh sauntered back towards me, pulling off the offending article. I stepped away from the wall so he could wrap it around my shoulders. The supple velvet shimmered in the same pearl grey colour as the doves that nested in the trees on our land. The cloak felt silky against my exposed collarbone, and it instantly warmed me against the chill.

"Thank you. It is rather cold out here," I admitted reluctantly.

"There is no need for obstinacy, Mistress Parker. I have no ill designs on you," he said with a grin as he leaned against the brickwork of the wall next to me. "I would expect Harry to extend the same courtesy to my sister if she behaved as madly as you."

The embarrassment of my stunt at the fish pond came flooding back. I feared I would never overcome my mortification, so I just held my silence, even though I was screaming a rebuttal inside my head. I was obviously deluded about any grace I thought I had before today.

Hugh read my thoughts, "You will do fine once you overcome your uncertainty. You may refine your practical skills all you like, but self-assurance only comes with experience. The ladies that serve the queen will teach you to carry yourself with elegance and dignity. By the time you return home to exchange vows with your future husband at St. Giles' Church, you will be a changed woman."

"And do you expect that you will be the one waiting for me at the altar of St. Giles?" I teased.

"You truly are delightful, Jane!" Hugh howled in amusement.

"I wouldn't want you anyway," I retorted, my feelings stung by his churlish response.

"You're probably right" he replied with a sigh. "Unlike most men, I have no desire to father any children. That makes me less than enticing as a suitor; unless we wait until you are a rich old widow, of course."

"Well, Master Wynter, I want an army of children so our union would be unsuccessful, but I will certainly help you find a wealthy widow." I replied with a laugh, but then I quickly turned sober. "Why don't you want children?"

Hugh pushed away from the wall, "I'll tell you when you are older and far more graceful," he replied as he trotted away. His remark stirred my curiosity. Why didn't he want children? Or, at the very least, an heir? His behaviour was certainly puzzling, but I saw his kindness, even if it came in the form of bravado; it comforted me to know I had a friend waiting for me when I arrived at court. However, I was starting to believe that my new friend had wholeheartedly deserved his swim in the pond.

Summer 1520
France and
Greenwich

Whispered murmurs of excitement flitted through the air around me. Not even the intolerable heat, or the dust cloud kicked up by our march towards Guînes, stifled the anticipation crackling through the air. The melodic jangle of the silver ornamenting all of our horses set my heart racing, and my bottom lip burned raw from the nervous way in which I ran my tongue across it. On any other day, the rhythmic sashay of my palfrey's movement might have lulled me into a daydream, but today I was alert and perched on the edge of my saddle. The muscles in my thighs throbbed at the tension, but relaxation felt impossible.

I glanced over at my mother for reassurance. Lady Morley held her head erect; eyes forward and with perfect posture. She kept her expression passive and her bearing refined, but the bead of perspiration I saw trickling down the tender skin behind her ear comforted me. As always, she hid any trepidation she felt underneath a cool veneer, but even she sweltered under the oppressive sun. An image of my sister, Margaret, back home at Hallingbury coalesced in my mind. Her exclusion infuriated her, but the cost of travel had been far too prohibitive to include her. The king had already spent a small fortune on his accommodations; he would not be contributing to the board of any of the nobles accompanying him.

The timing of the historic meeting between the monarchs was a happy coincidence for me. I celebrated my fifteenth birthday in early spring, attaining the preferred age for an appointment to the maid's position at just the right moment. My mother had several new gowns tailored just for the occasion to make a vital lasting impression on both the king and queen. Unfortunately, my debut at court was forgettable, even though I was beautifully attired and well-prepared. I arrived at Greenwich only a week before we set off for France. The preparations for our journey had begun a few months before, but as the day of our departure crept closer, anticipation grew and so did the chaos. My first day in the queen's chambers passed unremarkably and, rather than being disappointed, I found myself a bit relieved. The older noble ladies paid little attention to me. They were far too busy coordinating their wardrobes and travelling trunks to show much consideration for the meek daughter of Baron Morley. I quickly realised I would need to make myself invaluable to secure a permanent place at court. I vowed to keep my eyes and ears open for any opportunity to be of service.

The train of bodies came to an abrupt halt at the front of the bridge marking the entrance to a stately tawny and russet coloured castle. Two stone turrets flanked the entrance and three more rose up from behind the imposing brick walls. The cannons mounted on the side belched plumes of grey smoke as they bellowed out their greeting. Behind the castle, a labyrinth of tents had been erected to house the royal retinue. Opulent fabrics of the deepest crimson and brightest gold flapped in the warm breeze. A soft snort from my horse broke the spell of my amazement. I leaned forward and rubbed my hand on her sweat-slicked shoulder. The small movement relieved the tension in my muscles, and I indulged myself with a quick stretch. I longed to leap off the constraining saddle and exercise my legs, but no one would be permitted to dismount until the king was ready.

A small contingent of riders, led by Cardinal Wolsey, broke off from the main group, riding ahead to announce our arrival to the King of France. Once they received their orders and galloped off into the distance, the rest of us continued our trudge into the castle. After the king settled in, the horde of travellers broke away from the main group to claim their lodgings. My family spent the first evening in Guînes unpacking our trunks and organising our temporary living quarters, while I assisted the other ladies in doing the same for the queen. When I arrived in Queen Catherine's rooms, I was set to work with another young woman; a doe-eyed maid called Mary. Our task was to manage the unpacking of the spruce chests that held the queen's clothing and bedding. Eager to finally be of service, I took to my task with great zeal.

The hanging locks securing the chests were difficult to open and I felt triumphant when I managed to wrest the first one from its hinge. Before I could prop the heavy lid up against the wall, it slammed down hard on my hand. Mary heard my yelp of pain and rushed over to help. "Oh, Mistress Parker, that must have hurt!" she exclaimed, taking my throbbing hand into her own." She trailed her finger across the angry red welt forming on the back of my hand. Her touch was soft, her skin warm. "Please let the servants do that. We need only make sure that they put everything in their proper place."

"I'm sorry, I just thought…" I trailed off wistfully, feeling stupid for being so careless.

Mary tucked her finger underneath my chin, lifting my eyes up to meet hers. "Don't ever be sorry, contrition will not fix your mistakes, and it will make you an easy target. Be ever watchful; listen and learn. Always do as you are bid and be mindful of whom you trust." The gravity of her words contradicted the smile on her face. I wondered momentarily if she was attempting to scare me, but the kindness in her eyes appeared sincere. Before I could muster a reply, she called out over my shoulder to a servant who had just entered the room with his arms full of indigo sarcenet fabric. "Those hangings go in the queen's bedchamber."

Once the trunks were unpacked and all of the beautiful furniture had been settled in, Mary and I were excused to sup with our families. Mary properly introduced herself as we traipsed through the lush green field to the small city of tents. Her father, Thomas Boleyn, served as an ambassador to the king; he had spent the past few years representing Henry's interests at home and abroad. Mary was eager to reunite with her younger sister, Anne, who presently served in the court of the French Queen, Claude. She had not seen her sister since her return to England in the train of King Henry's sister, the Dowager Queen of France, when the young queen completed her mourning period after the death of the late French King, Louis XII. "It was quite the scandal," she whispered, though I was certain no one else could hear us. "Queen Mary returned in disgrace, having married her brother's closest friend, the Duke of Suffolk, without royal permission." Mary, herself, had been married this past winter to another of the king's companions, William Carey. "It isn't the most illustrious match my father could have made, but William is considerate and gentle, and he comes from good stock. He may not be wealthy or titled, but he is related to the king. I suppose he is the best I could expect as the daughter of a mere knight," she remarked with a tinkling laugh. "I suspect Anne will be much harder to please."

"It sounds as though Master Carey has many admirable qualities. My father has yet to discuss any man he has a mind to match me with, but I hope that whoever he chooses will be as gracious as your husband."

Mary paused to pull the gabled hood from her head, loosening her hair in the process; the golden brown tresses cascaded over her full bust. "That's much better," she sighed. I was taken aback by the intimacy of the action; I had never even seen my mother with her hair down. Mary's sensuality, the ease in which she inhabited her skin, drew me in. When she caught me staring, I felt the heat rise to my face. She brushed off my shame with a careless flick of her wrist. "I've become accustomed to it," she said, as if she expected the attention. "I take comfort in the body God has blessed me with and I don't mind emphasising my gifts." She then told me that she had been accused of moral lightness while she was at the French Court and she found it quite hypocritical that they would judge her so. "Some of the most shamefully behaved men and women I have ever seen!" she crowed. Rumours of a liaison with the French King followed her since her time in his kingdom, but she assured me that it was only idle gossip borne out of jealousy. She appeared unconcerned with the malice shown to her reputation, but I sensed a touch of sadness. How lonely it must have been to be the subject of such envy. I understood now the meaning of her warning earlier in the queen's rooms.

Mary perked up at the sound of a young man calling out her name from across the field. "My brother, George," she indicated with a smile. "I look forward to seeing you tomorrow. Enjoy this glorious evening." The sun's descent blazed a brilliant golden arc across the sky as the air cooled to a much more tolerable warmth. My mind raced from all I had experienced during the day, and my new friendship made me feel giddy. It truly was a glorious evening, and I was thrilled with the knowledge that this was only the beginning.

We filled the long days in France with one wonder after another. During mild weather, we crowded into the tiltyard to cheer on the joust until great gusts of wind made it too difficult to balance a lance. When that happened, we settled for daring displays of strength and agility as the men wrestled and competed at bowls or tennis. When the evening dusk settled over the camp, the queen and her ladies moved indoors to feast and entertain the French King, while our king received the same reception at the French camp.

Since I was the newest and the youngest of the queen's ladies, I took it upon myself to help wherever I could. I fetched stockings and ribbons and helped the senior ladies into their costumes for the masques. I performed every task the other ladies asked me to do, in the most efficient way possible, while wearing an unwavering smile upon my face. My dedication meant that I had very little time for socialising, but I hoped that my efforts would eventually be rewarded.

Finally satisfied my duties were complete, I retreated to an empty embrasure to observe the festivities going on around me. I felt a twinge of jealousy when I spied Mary and another girl huddled across the room in a corner. By the way they traded secrets and covert smiles, I soon guessed at the girl's identity. Mary had found her sister, Anne. As silly as Margaret could be, I found myself mourning her absence; sorry she was unable to join me in all the merriment. To make myself feel better, I took in the beauty surrounding me so I could share all the details with her when I returned. I was so deeply entranced by the music and the vivid colours of silk and damask swirling across the dance floor that I didn't notice the raven-haired young man making his way towards me, until he tapped me on the shoulder.

"Are you Jane Parker?"

"I'm sorry, who are you looking for?" I inquired, hardly hearing him over the rhythmic thud of the drums.

He leaned in closer; his breath, thick with the crisp scent of mint, warmed my ear. "I'm searching for Jane. Are you her?"

"What do you want with Jane Parker?" I asked, tossing him what I thought was an imperious glare. I knew I had failed miserably when he laughed in reply.

"My sister said I should ask her for a dance."

George Boleyn had been too far away for me see in great detail when he had called out to his sister in the field, but now that he was in front of me, I could see how handsome he was. His amber eyes were almond-shaped and flecked with gold; they flickered like fire when he curved his full sensual lips into a smile. I did my best to ignore the nervous flutter in my stomach and I offered him my hand. "Well, I suppose if Mary suggested it, it would be rude to refuse."

"Yes, quite rude, indeed," he replied with a grin. He carefully wrapped his hand around my fingers, before leading me out into the crowd of courtiers.

George was an accomplished dancer, and I enjoyed the graceful way in which he guided me across the floor. Though he was much taller, I had little problem keeping up with his long stride. When the players struck up a volte, I easily moulded into his strong embrace. After we finally parted, several dances later, I noticed the envious stares directed towards me. My partner sensed my instinct to flee and pulled me back into his arms. "Don't look at them, look at me," he commanded. I moved my head so that he was the only one in my line of sight, and the discomfort I felt at the unwelcome attention slowly slipped away.

Ensnared by his gaze, his ferocious confidence seemed to sooth my nerves. I could not resist his request for one more dance.

I was so wrapped up in my duties during the remainder of the journey that I had no further opportunities to seek out George, but he often occupied my thoughts. A few days after our meeting, we embarked on our return voyage home, spending a few weeks at the Calais garrison, before heading back across the English Channel. One day during our stay, my father accompanied the king to Gravelines to meet with the queen's nephew, the Holy Roman Emperor, Charles V. Relations between the Emperor and the French King were tenuous at best, and the successful meeting between the two monarchs caused him some consternation. Lord Morley was honoured by the invitation to attend the king on such a delicate matter.

The queen summoned me to her privy chamber shortly after our arrival at Greenwich. I checked my reflection in the mirror before leaving our rooms to make sure that every hair was secured in place beneath my heavy gabled hood, then I smoothed out the wrinkles marring the pale rose silk of my gown. I had to appear beyond reproach if I wanted to secure my place here at court. I followed the queen's page into the hushed quiet of the privy chamber, dropping to my knees before her royal presence.

"Thank you, Mistress Parker; you may stand." I carefully rose to my feet, but kept my head down, eyes averted. "We were very impressed by your diligence over the last month," the queen continued in her thick Spanish accent. "We can see that your mother has trained you well, and your dedication has not gone unnoticed. Would you like to stay on here at court as one of my maids?"

A wave of elation swelled in my belly. I had prepared for this moment for so long, knowing that a place at court meant a successful future for me. This offer meant I belonged with the most prestigious women in England, and their acceptance was something for which I desperately longed.

"I would love it more than anything," I whispered, hardly daring to breathe.

"Then it is done. My porter will arrange a bed for you in the maid's dorms. The Mother of the Maids will see to it that you are informed of your duties and provide you with your wardrobe requirements. Your mother has always been a pleasure to have in our service, and we hold a very high regard for your father's intelligence and loyalty. We anticipate that you too will maintain the same standard."

I dipped into a deep curtsey, profusely thanking the queen for her favour, and assuring her that I would behave in a manner befitting my new position. Somehow, I managed to swallow my joy and maintain my air of dignity until she dismissed me from her presence.

November 13, 1541
The Tower of London

THE CRUEL winter-tide sun, piercing the thin gossamer curtains surrounding my bed, dragged me from a tortured slumber. Sleep had always been my escape during the lonely nights while George was on embassy, and my refuge after his violent death. Last night, I greeted it like an old friend, but it did not return the favour; sleep did not spare me from the pain I now felt. Dreams filled with the blood and screams of all who had ascended the scaffold on the frost-crusted lawn just beyond my lodgings haunted me.

My initial wave of relief upon waking from the dreadful scenes slowly playing out in my head ebbed away when the barren stone walls of my prison reminded me of the harsh reality of my situation. Heavy despair sank into my body, crushing the breath from my lungs. I pushed what remained through my parched lips with all my might, then constricted my throat, refusing to draw the air back in; my stomach clenched tight at the effort. I stared at the canopy over my bed, watching the wrinkles in the sheer fabric twist and writhe in a macabre dance. I watched until the world around me faded away, my lungs burning at their deprivation. *'Only a few moments more,'* I thoughtfully reassured myself.

"I've come to break your fast, my lady."

My body took advantage of my mind's alarm at Lucy's abrupt entrance, and I inhaled the sweet breath of life, before I could stop myself. Lucy's intrusion infuriated, yet relieved me. I would face the shadow of death soon enough; there was no need for me to hasten it along. Besides, taking my life would only condemn me to eternal damnation and suffering without hope of reuniting with my beloved husband.

Lucy strode purposefully over to the table by the window, placing the tray she balanced in her arms on top of it. She removed a loaf of bread, a small wedge of cheese, and a pear that had been skinned and sliced from the tray, laying it out on a small pewter dish. She started to place a knife next to the dish, but then her hand stopped just above the table. She looked over her shoulder, considering my unmoving form for a moment, turned back, and used the knife to slice the bread herself. She returned the knife to the tray, then carried both from the room. Had I been so obvious even my maid didn't trust me with a sharp object?

My stomach growled in hunger, but I turned away from the food laid out for my breakfast. I couldn't imagine enjoying a meal ever again. When Lucy bustled back into the room, she found me on my side, legs curled into my chest with my arms wrapped around them. She tilted her head to meet my gaze. "No appetite?" She waited a moment for me to respond, and when I didn't reply, she sighed. "There is no point in starving yourself. It is only a matter of time before you are released. The king will see that you have no blame. We've only to wait until they gather enough evidence for the trial; it is only she, Culpeper, and Dereham who are culpable."

The names of Queen Katherine Howard's lovers fell upon me like a lead weight; they had put my life in mortal danger. I couldn't abide her former lover, Francis Dereham, or his arrogant temper. I bristled at the audacity he displayed with his demands for the queen to accept him into her service. I found him insufferable. I warned Katherine against taking him in when she told me of their history together. I knew it was only a matter of time before the truth about their relationship got out. Dereham's lust for her still burned, and he demonstrated jealous rage when he finally came to the realisation that another man had replaced him in Katherine's affections. I knew he would be Katherine's undoing. I only wished that I had suspected that he would also be mine.

The queen's most recent lover, Thomas Culpeper, had swaggered about the court for quite some time. I knew him long before Katherine arrived from Lambeth, but I'd paid him no great attention until the queen commenced her relationship with him. I saw him as merely one face among the many roaming the halls of the king's palaces. I never understood what Katherine found attractive in him. I only knew that if any of us deserved to die, it was him. At least Katherine's liaison with Dereham happened before she became the king's wedded wife. Dereham may have been detestable, but his efforts to win back the queen were ultimately unsuccessful. He committed his sins long before she wore the crown upon her head. I hoped that Lucy was right about my impending release, but a small voice in my head scoffed at her optimism. I remembered my sister-in-law's disgrace well. She truly had been innocent of the charges laid against her, but that mattered not. Her bones rested in the nearby chapel along with those of my husband.

"George," I whispered under my breath.

Lucy eyed me hopefully. "Perhaps if you eat and give the constable little trouble, you will be allowed to visit the chapel."

I had never been allowed to visit my husband's grave, and all traces of George had been wiped away after his death, leaving me with nothing to aid my grief. I sometimes felt as if I mourned for a man who never existed. George's grave offered proof of his life; seeing it could help me find closure. Perhaps Lucy was right. I supposed that it didn't hurt to ask Gage if he would allow it. The worst he could do was say no. I heaved a deep sigh as I uncurled my body from its protective pose, then I threw off the heavy counterpane, gingerly swinging my feet to the floor. Without the rushes, the frigid stone floor froze their soles. Under Lucy's watchful gaze, I crept to the table, and sat down to the meal she had prepared.

Though my insides burned with hunger, the sight of the food repulsed me. Regardless of my distaste, it was clear I would have to force it down. Juice from the overripe pear clung to my fingers, flavouring each piece of bread I consumed, and the pungent scent of the cheese burned my nostrils; it was far too strong for my taste. My stomach lurched with every bite, yet I defied the urge I had to throw it back up. I persevered, calling for a finger bowl to cleanse my hands, after I swallowed the last bite.

"Was that so terrible?" Lucy asked, placing the pewter bowl and linen napkin next to my plate.

I managed to ignore the temptation to heave the food from my belly while Lucy worked quickly to remove the remains of my meal, then she returned to dress me for the day. I saw no point in getting out of my nightgown; I was a prisoner, I was not expecting guests. However, Gage would be alarmed if he came to my rooms and found me still abed, so I obediently allowed my maid to drape me in one of the drab black gowns that had become my usual attire.

"There," she said, pleased that she had coerced me into appearing presentable. "I am going to find Gage and see if we can get those rushes in here. I've laid a book on a stool near the hearth in your presence chamber if you care to read. I will return shortly." I dismissed her with a wave.

The presence chamber was warmed by a flickering fire dancing in the hearth. When I had arrived last night, the room was lit by only a few candles, so this was the first opportunity I had to see it clearly in the light of day. I noted the same bench and cedar chest I saw the night before, but the rest of the room was sparse. Just as Lucy said, a stool sitting near the hearth held a book on top of its russet-coloured cushion, but beyond a matching cushion on the floor and an ornate desk in the corner, little else decorated the room.

So great was my apprehension, I had no desire to read. Instead, I ambled over to the window, and perched on the edge of the bench. I rested my forehead against the cool glass as I stared out into the bright November morning. A cluster of ravens gathered around the decaying body of a small rodent on the browned grass below me. It occurred to me at that moment that my mother had once taught me that the correct name for a group of these sleek onyx birds was an 'unkindness' of ravens. I watched them pluck and pull the meat, while I mused at the irony. Only a few short months after learning this word, I officially joined the queen's court of ravens, and learned of my own capacity for unkindness.

March – May 1522
Greenwich and York Place

THE PAGE shifted nervously from side to side while Mary contemplated her response. The king had been relentlessly pursuing a relationship with the olive-skinned beauty for a few months, and this present was just one of many returned to her impassioned suitor. I imagined the servant was not especially keen to return the gift to his master with the trinket still safely wrapped inside. Mary tossed me a salacious smirk, then grabbed the box, squealing in excitement at its contents. Her hand dipped inside, re-emerging with a gold chain entwined in its fingers. The blood-red ruby dangling from it glittered in the sunlight. She admired the bauble for a few moments, then tucked it back into the box before handing it back to the page.

"Please tell the king that his favour greatly overjoys me, but I find myself very undeserving. As a married woman, I simply cannot accept such tokens of affection. I sincerely hope he understands," she simpered.

The page's face fell; her refusal assured him a sound beating upon his return to the king. He reluctantly retrieved the gift from Mary, before fleeing the room with his head hanging in displeasure. Anne and I could contain our amusement no more, and we fell into gales of laughter at the page's misfortune.

"Sister, you know you are only punishing that poor page," Anne gasped. "The king is going to be livid once he sees you've returned yet another trinket."

Mary collapsed onto the bed. "You know, as well as I do, the king will inevitably get his way, but I don't want to seem too eager. William's terribly upset, but what does he expect me to do? Besides, he's hardly touched me since our wedding night."

"What do you mean he's hardly touched you?" I asked, hardly bothering to mask my disbelief. Why would a lusty young man want to neglect his pretty and charming wife?

"His Grace requires constant attendance, Jane. It is not enough for William to spend every waking moment in his presence; there are times he even has to sleep in the same room! The rare spare moment my husband does have is spent entertaining any nobleman who might bolster his prestige. William certainly has ambition…" Mary's voice trailed off as she stared at the ceiling. After a few minutes of silence, she broke the tension with a dry laugh, "Perhaps I shall see my husband more often if I do become the king's mistress!"

I would have been stunned by Mary's uncaring attitude towards her husband when I first arrived at court, but I had become jaded. I was once naïve about the romantic entanglements between men and women, but the last year had changed me. I had learned that there was merely a thin line between courtly flirtation and true affection. More often than not, the former slipped very easily into the latter, regardless of one's marital status. Rather than being shocked by Mary's situation, her indecision exasperated me.

"Just give in already, Mary. In a few days, the Lenten season will begin, and there will be no more pleasures until after Easter," I cajoled. "Give him a few moments of joy to comfort him during this sad season of deprivation," I added in a low cheerless voice, working my face into a frown. I ducked into the closet in time to avoid the pillow she threw at me.

"What are you wearing for the joust tomorrow?" Mary's younger sister interrupted from her perch on the bed. "I want to make sure we all have different colours, since we have to match for the pageant." Anne tailored all of her gowns in the most fashionable French style; even the most beautiful maid appeared dowdy next to her. Our greatest concern was making sure she never outshined the queen, which was an impossible task.

I groaned at Anne's remark, digging deeper into the trunk holding all of the kirtles and gowns I had collected over the last year. Every event for my first year had required a new and fashionable garment, so I managed to amass enough pieces to create different combinations, always appearing to be in something fresh. At the bottom of the trunk, my hand brushed across extraordinarily soft velvet. I pinched the fabric between my fingers, then dragged it to the top of the pile. When I held the cloak up, a wave of guilt washed over me. I stared sadly at the plush, grey fabric, contemplating how to return it, until the concern in Mary's voice pulled me from my thoughts. "Jane? Are you all right in there?"

"Be out in a moment," I replied, shoving the cloak, and my guilt, back down to the bottom of the trunk.

We spent the days leading up to the Lenten season in decadent indulgence. Nothing was too good to eat or too pleasurable to do. We enjoyed ourselves to the fullest extent in preparation for all that we would be denied in the coming weeks while we mourned Christ's death. The celebrations began on Sunday afternoon after mass, when the court headed out to the tiltyard for the Shrovetide jousts. A chill nipped the spring air, and the clouds overhead warned of possible precipitation, so Mary, Anne, and I took our positions in the gallery with the queen, rather than risk a brisk shower.

The spectacle commenced with a parade of knights. One by one, they strutted before the gallery, showing off their beautifully crafted armour on prancing steeds, caparisoned in the most brilliantly hued trappings. When the king arrived, I was struck by his sheer size. He was a regal tower in flashing silver armour. The ivory courser beneath him was draped in plum-coloured velvet trimmed in cloth of silver, and embroidered with the French motto *'elle mon coeur a navera'* – *She has wounded my heart*. Anne's audible gasp at the king's declaration earned her a swift elbow to the ribs from a flustered Mary. I glanced sideways at the queen to gauge her reaction, but her face remained impassive, as always. King Henry liked to keep most of the liaisons outside of his marriage covert. He never flaunted his mistresses and, unlike the French King, he did not have an official paramour. However, gossip ran rampant among the courtiers, and the identity of the king's latest sweetheart was always hotly debated. Queen Catherine could never escape the reality that her husband enjoyed the company of other women, but she was not required to acknowledge it. Her lack of reaction to the king's choice of motto came as no surprise to me. The longer I spent with the queen, the more I began to admire her strength of character and her ability to rise above the fray; Queen Catherine rarely revealed her emotions and kept her counsel. I was more like the king; every emotion I felt danced across my face.

The combat commenced at the trumpet's blare, and I turned my attention back to the spectacle on the field. My heart leapt into my throat at every strike of the lance. No matter how many jousts I had been privileged to watch, the amount of pain the king's closest friends were willing to inflict upon themselves for his amusement astonished me. I worried that each charge brought them within a breath of death.

Sir Nicholas Carew and Charles Brandon, the Duke of Suffolk, two of the king's most treasured boon companions, were the last to compete before the winner challenged the king. The competition between the two most accomplished athletes at court was fierce. Though it was an even match, the duke managed to best Carew with a direct hit to his helmet. I winced at the sickening sound of the wood scraping against steel. Once poor Carew limped off with his head in his hands, the king trotted onto the field to face Suffolk. I felt a tug on my hand and looked down to see Mary gripping it in her clenched fist. Suffolk always pandered to the king, so it came as no surprise when His Grace soundly beat him. The king's sister, Suffolk's wife, raced onto the field to embrace him the moment he dismounted his horse. At the king's triumph, Mary finally released her tight grasp on my hand. By some great miracle, the rain held off until after the prizes were awarded and we all ambled back to the palace for the banquet.

I awoke early on Shrove Tuesday morning unable to shake off the anxiety that had plagued me through the night. I packed my costume for the evening's revels before crawling into bed, but upon waking, I dug through the small trunk again to reassure myself that I had remembered every piece. Once I accomplished that task, I called in a maid, and set about preparing myself for the day before the rest of the ladies stirred from their slumber. I slipped my arms out of my linen nightgown, allowing the fabric to fall in a heap around my ankles. The chambermaid brought me a warm cloth soaked in rose-scented water to wash the perspiration from my body. Once I was clean, I ran my fingers through my hair to release the tangles, then rubbed my tresses with a linen cloth to smooth them down.

I slid a nude-coloured chemise over my head, while the maid stood by with a kirtle the colour of charcoal and a pale blue over-gown. Finally, I went to the mirror to put on my hood. I admired the way the sleek French version of the headpiece emphasised Anne's beauty, so I requested a few of them to be made for myself. It was now the only style I preferred. My lips curved into a satisfied smile when I saw how perfectly the angle of the hood emphasised the contour of my cheekbones in the mirror's reflection. The hue accented my pale skin, colouring my hair a brighter gold and my almond-shaped eyes a deeper grey. For a fleeting moment, I felt beautiful.

Once the ladies were up and ready, we made the trek to York Place, one of Cardinal Wolsey's opulent residences, where he was entertaining the Imperial envoys. The sky had brightened since the Sunday jousts, and the journey down the Thames River was smooth. The cardinal waited on the privy landing for the arrival of the royal barge, his rotund body clad in deep crimson robes encrusted in ropes of gold and jewels. I bit back a laugh when I noticed how his jowls shook at the enthusiasm in his greeting. We trailed behind the royal couple as Wolsey led them on an endless tour of his grand estate that, to our great delight, finished on the bowling lawn. Anne and I could not resist when William Brereton and Sir Henry Norris challenged us to a match. I scanned the crowd for Mary while I awaited my turn. My eyes swept over the sea of jaunty feathered caps and jewelled hoods, hunting for her familiar face. I found her standing by the king. She leaned into him, listening intently to his words, with a coy smile on her face. Perhaps the king's declaration at the joust had accomplished its purpose.

"Jane, are you ready?"

When I turned back to the game, one of Norris' bowls had come within mere inches of the jack waiting on the other end of the green. "How am I supposed to beat that?" I cried, preparing to launch my bowl. Brereton and Norris tittered as my ball rolled slowly towards its target. It curved as I was ready to concede defeat, stopping just short of kissing the jack. "Well done Mistress Parker!" Norris smiled as he relinquished his silver coin.

The sight of Wolsey's great hall took my breath away. Rich emerald green arras embroidered with threads of gold decorated the walls, while miniature torches dangled from elegant willow branches hanging from the ceiling. At the opposite end of the hall, three lofty towers covered in a dark green moss were erected to represent the Chateau Vert. Three waving banners announced the theme of the masque: three red hearts torn in two illustrated the first flag, the second depicted a lady's hand gripping a man's heart and the third showed a lady's hand turning a man's heart. If the court had not inferred the state of the king's heart based on his motto at the joust, they were sure to understand it now.

The king's sister climbed to the top of the middle tower first. She would lead the masque as the womanly virtue of *Beauty*. The rest of us, clad in gowns of cream-coloured satin, followed behind to take our positions on the two flanking towers. We replaced our hoods with jewelled bonnets and cauls with the names of the virtues we represented worked on them in gold. Mary played the part of *Kindness*; Anne showed *Perseverance*; I represented the virtue of *Constancy*. The Countess of Devonshire joined in as *Honour*, while Mistresses Browne and Dannet portrayed *Bounty* and *Mercy* respectively. The virtue of *Pity* ascended the tower last.

The young men of Wolsey's choir were trussed up in brightly-coloured cauls depicting the womanly vices: *Danger, Disdain, Jealousy, Unkindness, Scorn, Malebouche,* and *Strangeness*. They defended us against the vicious assault on our castle by the male virtues of *Amorous, Nobleness, Youth, Attendance, Loyalty, Pleasure, Gentleness,* and *Liberty;* all led by His Grace as *Ardent Desire*. When the king, dressed in brilliant crimson satin embellished with gold flames, charged into the great hall with his army, the court met him with a roar of enthusiastic applause. Guns sounded as the virtues rushed the castle and the vices fought them off with rose water and sweet candies. The men responded in-kind with a hail of dates and oranges to entice our amorousness. Once the vices were run off, the king and his companions rescued the virtues. *Youth* and *Loyalty* led *Beauty* and *Honour* from the tower while the king came for Mary; *Attendance* liberated me.

I focused on the honey brown eyes behind the mask, but they gave little indication as to the identity of my rescuer. I gamely took the man's proffered hand, allowing him to place the other on my waist to help me off the tower; we followed the rest of the dancers out onto the floor for a stately pavane. My partner was slight, his body lean, and he led me with unexpected grace. I felt comfortable in his embrace, so I darted a furtive glance around the hall. During one of my spins, I caught sight of George Boleyn paying court to Mistress Margery Horseman. He whispered to her, as she leaned back against the wall, a look of bemusement fluttering across her face. I felt my heart plummet into a fire of jealousy, ignited in the pit of my stomach. When the dance called for me to turn back to my partner, *Attendance* pulled me in close. "My brother-in-law isn't worth your sighs, Mistress Parker. He is quite like the king, very fickle in his affections," he whispered.

At the realisation that it was Mary's husband hidden beneath the mask, I was struck by a surge of remorse for encouraging her surrender to the king. Having spent so little time in William Carey's company, it seemed I had developed apathy for his feelings on the matter. The sadness in his eyes indicated that, ambition or not, no reward from the king was enough to share his wife's affections. When the music came to its rousing conclusion, the gentlemen stepped back and offered their partners a bow before revealing themselves. Master Carey removed the gold visor concealing his features, but his face still wore a mask of geniality. He offered me a superficial smile, along with his hand, and we both paid reverence to the cheering audience.

Before slipping away, Master Carey leaned in to kiss my cheek, and offer one last piece of advice. "Cherish the ones you love, Mistress Parker. You never know when they might be taken from you."

The Master of Revels cleared the castle to make way for the kitchen servants bustling into the hall with their arms full of platters and trays piled high with delicacies. My self-pity over George was so great that I had little appetite, and merely picked at the lavish offerings. Instead, I spent the evening drinking wine and dancing. When the world began to spin around me, I ran out into the cool evening air to anchor myself, and dry my sweat. As the sun went down, a low mist rolled in from the river, bringing with it a light drizzle of rain. I leaned against the wall, tilting my head to feel the drops on my face. I closed my eyes and opened my mouth, relishing the fresh water on my parched tongue. The music throbbed through the windows above my head, but I stayed against the wall until my composure returned and the light-headedness passed. When I turned to walk back towards the door, the sound of a familiar voice gave me pause.

"It is on dreary evenings such as these when I find myself yearning for a warm velvet cloak."

I turned to face my visitor, curved my lips into what I hoped what a convincing smile, and replied, "Yes, Master Wynter, that would be nice, wouldn't it? I think I have left mine inside."

Hugh smirked at my feigned ignorance, inching a few steps closer to me. "Have I done something to offend you, Mistress Parker? I can't recall any specific instance, but you've done such a wondrous job evading me that I cannot help but wonder if I have wounded you in some way."

I had forgotten how forthright he could be. My reasons for eluding Hugh Wynter had more to do with my self-preservation than for anything he had done. I didn't know why, but there was something about him that always caused me to fumble. When I danced with him at the revels in France, I tripped over my own feet, moving so awkwardly the other maids had subjected me to endless mockery. I hated looking like a fool, so I rebuffed his friendly overtures, avoiding him at all costs. To his great credit, Hugh continued to be gracious each time I fled his presence, but my brother was furious with me for my mistreatment of his friend, treating me to bouts of silence on more than one occasion. "I'm not sure what you mean, Master Wynter. My duties have just so consumed me..." Hugh raised his hand to stop my meaningless excuses.

I felt my face redden with embarrassment, infuriating me further. "I haven't been avoiding you. You're Harry's friend, not mine," I seethed through clenched teeth. "Don't you have some wealthy old widow to bother or are they sick of you too?" I turned on my heel to flee, and found myself face-to-face with George Boleyn.

"Jane? Is everything all right out here?"

I should have been happy he had followed me out into the courtyard, but when I saw George, the image of him whispering in Margery's ear came to mind, further inflaming my fury. What was he doing out here? Couldn't they see I just wanted to be left alone?

"I'm perfectly fine; I just needed some air," I spat out. "Now if you will excuse me, I must be getting back inside."

George flinched at the force in my response, his eyes widening in surprise. "As you wish, my lady; I only sought you out for a dance."

I wanted so much to take his hand and follow him back inside, but I was too stubborn to admit it. I also knew I would only think of Margery, wondering if he truly wanted to be in her company instead of mine the entire time we danced. No, I couldn't dance with George tonight, but I didn't know how to refuse graciously. I looked to Hugh, but his face was stone. He would not help me.

I turned back to George; he stared at me with one eyebrow arched in curiosity. A dozen excuses raced through my mind, but I could not mould even one into a coherent response, so strained silence hung in the space between us. After what was surely only a moment that seemed like an eternity, I felt Hugh's muscular arm curl around my own, and the heat from his body, as he sidled close to mine.

"My apologies, Master Boleyn, Jane has already agreed to dance with me. Perhaps next time," he gently replied before escorting me back inside, leaving a stunned George to stare after us.

Hugh led me across the dance floor in silence. He held my gaze, but refused to speak a word to me. With my mind so absorbed by what had happened outside, my self-doubt had no opportunity to creep in, and I danced just as gracefully as I ever had with any other partner. After I made it to the end of the second song without tripping or stumbling once, I finally worked up the courage to thank him. Unfortunately, my words failed to move him, and after one last bow he said, "You may

keep the cloak. Farewell, Jane; I hope you have a wonderful life."
With a parting curtsey, he retreated into the crowd.

I blanched at the scarlet rose of blood blooming on the soft
linen cloth I held against my tender fingers. When I gingerly
pulled the cloth away to survey the damage, I saw angry red welts
gashed across my skin. "You will soon become accustomed to the
discomfort. If you play enough, you may even develop a callus,
then you will feel no pain at all; like me." Anne proudly held
out her hand to display the hardened white skin on the pads of
her fingers. After only a few weeks of lessons, I was uncertain if
I would ever enjoy playing the lute enough to tolerate the pain
now throbbing in my fingertips. I shoved the linen back into my
palm, making a fist to keep it in place.

Anne rose from the cushion, carefully placing her instrument
in the cedar chest next to her bed. With a clean cloth gripped
in one hand, she lifted the lute I had propped against my knee
with the other, then sat down again. She ran the cloth down the
strings, wiping away the last traces of my blood, polishing the
smudges I left behind on the glossy wood. "The oils from your
skin will cause irreparable damage," she explained. "You must
always make sure to wipe away all traces when you finish."

I possessed little desire for these music lessons, but Anne was
an adept lutenist and saw my lack of skill as a personal failing, so
she took it upon herself to teach me. I was a difficult pupil and
complained bitterly about the amount of time she demanded
from me for practice, but she was optimistic I would come to
love the instrument as much as she did. I felt less than confident.
I got to my feet, tossing the blood-stained linen aside, as I strode
over to the window. My attention was drawn to the fountain
where a group of laughing young men splashed water at each
other in the brilliant hot sun. After a few moments of watching
their carefree play, my longing to join them dissipated when I

realised that the group consisted of my brother, Thomas Wyatt, and Hugh Wynter.

Satisfied she had removed all traces of me from her lute, Anne returned to the chest, where she reunited it with the other, then she sidled up next to me at the window. The scent of rosewater that had been so faint during our lessons enveloped me. I closed my eyes, inhaling the sensual musky tones. When I reopened them, her lips were twisted into a satisfied smirk. "That is precisely what I am hoping Henry Percy will do."

"Anne! He's already spoken for!"

Anne wrinkled her nose in contempt, "Promised is not the same as married. If that were true, I'd be married to James Butler instead of standing here with you staring at three fools." Her piercing stare dared me to contradict her words.

"Are you calling my brother a fool?" My own eyes met hers in intensity, and I arched my brow for added effect.

Anne turned back to the window and began trailing a finger down the leaded pane of glass. "Perhaps…He does keep company with them."

I used my sleeve to wipe away the streak her touch left behind, then I moved towards her bed, perching myself on the edge to gaze at her. "Thomas Wyatt is no fool and, for that matter, neither is Hugh."

Anne tossed her long dark hair over her shoulder as she turned to lean against the window frame. She folded her arms against her chest, fixing me with an angry stare. "Thomas Wyatt is the biggest fool of them all. I cannot be rid of him no matter how hard I try. He is constantly writing me poems and letters knowing that I will only toss them into the fire. I used to be amused at the way he trailed after me, but now it is infuriating. I can never be anything but a mistress to him. Does he value me so little after our long friendship? I would have gladly pledged my troth to him, but his father found him a more suitable match while I was in France. There is little point in carrying on as though things haven't changed."

Her outburst took me by surprise. In all the time I spent with Anne and her sister, I had never once considered that Wyatt's presence had more to do with Anne than my brother. Harry was often in our company, and I always assumed that was why the poet hung around. Margaret's words in the orchard at Hallingbury about Wyatt's love interest came rushing back to me, and I bit my lip to suppress a laugh. "You're the dark-haired beauty?"

Anne's face contorted with fury, the sweltering sun no match for the heat coming from her stare. "I know not what you refer to, but I don't find it amusing in the least," she huffed.

"Oh, never mind, Anne. It was only something silly my sister said," I replied as I threw myself back on the bed, stretching my arms out wide. I watched a lone fly hum across the ceiling, artfully dodging the cobwebs blocking its path. I decided to change the subject, "Tell me about Henry Percy. Has he promised you marriage?"

At the mention of Percy, Anne's demeanour changed just as quickly to joy as it had to anger when I spoke of Wyatt. She relaxed from her defensive posture and joined me on the bed, where she spread out her arms, entwining her fingers in mine. When I closed my fingers around hers, she rubbed the slick surface of my nail with the pad of her thumb.

"We've been meeting in secret," she confessed, breathlessly. The other maids made much chatter about the fact that the lanky heir had been roaming the queen's rooms more often than usual since he partnered Anne in the Chateau Vert pageant, but they had been discreet, and I was quite unaware of their furtive trysts. "Oh, don't look at me that way. It's all quite innocent," she continued. "Percy's told me that he plans to repudiate his match with that Talbot girl."

The daring romance of Anne's proposed secret elopement stirred a taste of jealousy in me; it sounded both tempting and wonderful. It was completely reckless, yet a small piece of me wished that I too had a secret paramour. I thought of George for one brief moment before allowing my scepticism at the very idea to sweep his face from my mind. No, George would not be interested in plain Jane Parker.

Anne leapt from the bed and started pacing the room while she told me her plan to tell her father of her relationship with Percy. When she got to the window, she paused for a moment to gaze out, before turning to me with a quizzical look on her face. "Jane, who were you watching out there?"

I bolted upright. "I wasn't watching anyone. I was merely gazing at the gardens."

"I've never seen anyone gaze at roses in that way; I know you certainly weren't looking at your brother with that longing." She tried desperately to hide the snort of derision with her hand. When she recovered she finished, "You are a terrible liar."

I threw a scowl at her. "I wasn't looking at anyone with longing. I was looking at someone with guilt."

"Guilt? For that boy who embarrassed you in France? Why would you ever feel guilt over him? He should feel remorseful for making you look like a fool," Anne replied with a disdainful stare.

My jump from the bed disturbed the rushes on the floor, kicking up the crisp scent of rosemary. "Don't speak of him that way. *I* embarrassed *him*. To make matters worse, I was unforgivably spiteful to him when he showed me nothing but kindness."

Anne's eyes darkened while she considered my response, then I saw a light creep into them as she pursed her lips into a tiny rosebud. "Jane," she asked evenly. "Are you in love with this boy?"

I had to ask myself the very same thing before I could respond. Did I think of Hugh in that way? I was certainly fond of him. He was handsome and courteous, but he was my brother's friend, and so I had not truly considered him as anything other than that. I knew my feelings for George were romantic, and this felt different. No, it was not ardour that caused me to act so strangely in his presence. When I thought of the hurt and confused look in Hugh's eyes the last time I saw him, I was reminded of how candid he had been every time we spoke. I realised then why he made me anxious. Hugh was so honest and sincere that I never had to pretend to be anyone other than who I truly was. He made me face the things I hated about myself: my hesitancy and self-doubt. I hid those things well from others, but not from him. I recoiled from vulnerability, so I pushed him away.

Instead of revealing my true feelings to Anne, risking her ridicule, I scoffed at her question. "Don't be ludicrous. Hugh is much too old for me. Besides, my father would never think he was a suitable husband. I don't even know if he reads; I've only ever seen him fish." Anne dissolved into laughter at my grimace of disgust. I joined in her merriment but felt sick at my behaviour.

The queen's nephew, Charles V, journeyed across the English Channel at the end of May to grace us with his presence. Queen Catherine's parents, Isabel and Ferdinand, great rulers of Castile and Aragon, united their kingdoms in marriage, embarking upon a quest to rid their land of the heretic Moors. Their son and heir, Juan, died young and the baby his wife carried in her belly refused to thrive, following him to the grave. The next in line, Joanna, was believed to be mad so she was refused her father's kingdom of Aragon. Her son, Charles, was chosen to ascend the throne in her stead. Having been recently elected Holy Roman Emperor, he ruled a great swath of land covering territories in the Low Countries, including parts of Italy and Burgundy.

The Emperor constantly warred with France and His Grace's alliance with the French King continued to make him uneasy. For him to undertake the gruelling and costly journey of coming to England, it was obvious that King Henry had not convinced him of his loyalty during their visit in Gravelines. The king honoured Anne's father with a request to accompany him and his retinue to Canterbury to greet the Emperor upon his arrival from Dover. As treasurer of the king's household, Thomas Boleyn had continued to rise in eminence since my arrival at court. Both he and George were, very recently, the recipients of valuable offices and manors once belonging to the Duke of Buckingham. Buckingham's treasonous words and bold declarations of his claim to the English throne won him a swift decapitation by the executioner's axe. The Boleyns were not the only family to benefit from the duke's downfall, but much envy accompanied their bounty. Some courtiers muttered that Thomas owed his success to the fact that his daughter warmed the king's bed, but I didn't believe that to be true. Thomas was an exceptional diplomat with a keen eye for the king's interests. His Grace prized Thomas' knowledge and skill, and he handsomely rewarded him for it.

My father was not among the other barons at Canterbury and, instead, waited back at Greenwich with us to attend upon the queen. We traipsed out onto the wharf with the remaining courtiers to await His Grace's arrival. The king had every ship in his navy docked from Greenwich to Gravesend in a proud display of England's military might. The crisp snap of the Tudor green banners whipping in the breeze greeted the Emperor's arrival, and the heart-stopping clap of ordnance thundered down the Thames from each ship.

The court entertained the Emperor and his enormous retinue with several banquets and pageants held in his honour. The normally solemn queen delighted in hosting the son of her elder sister, taking great pains to assure both his comfort and enjoyment. The young maids serving Her Grace were trotted out to perform elaborate masques for the benefit of the Spanish visitors. Anne and I relished the attention, but the king was reticent to parade his mistress before the queen's kin, so Mary was shunted to the side in favour of the other beautiful women populating her rooms. While the youngest of the Boleyn sisters enchanted the future Earl of Northumberland, I avoided the dimpled, blue-eyed compatriot of my brother. I had not yet worked up the courage to apologise or return the cloak still stuffed in the bottom of my clothes chest.

November 13, 1541
The Tower of London

Lucy bustled into my rooms with two young servants dutifully following behind her. The boys trailed a small wooden cart behind them filled to the brim with river rushes and straw. As they moved around the room, Lucy followed along tossing rosemary and lavender on the floor behind them. I leaned back against the window and inhaled the perfume. The faint citrusy scent, usually so calming, did little to sooth my raw nerves, but I found a small measure of comfort in it. Satisfied with the work they had completed, my maid shooed the servants from the room with orders to return with more wood for the fire.

The constable arrived at my door appearing even more haggard than the night before. I knew by his exhaustion, I was not the only prisoner of means in the Tower that night. The titled expected far better treatment in prison than the poor; they were much more demanding on Gage's time and resources. I took pity on the man even though I was the one facing punishment. How many deaths would he see before my time here was over? How many deaths would he see before *his* time here was over? Truthfully, he was just as much a prisoner as I.

The corners of Gage's tired eyes crinkled when he offered me a warm smile. "I know it isn't quite what you are used to, but I hope you are finding your accommodations adequate," he intoned with a gesture at our surroundings.

I couldn't bring myself to return his smile, but I rose from my chair to show him courtesy. "I think I've received far more than I deserve. I appreciate your hospitality, Sir John."

Gage nodded before shifting his gaze to Lucy. My maid acknowledged him with a nod of her own, then busied herself at the hearth. The constable seemed as though he wanted to make sure I was ready for what he was about to tell me next. He cleared his throat, "I've just been informed that the king's secretary, Master Wriothesley, shall arrive this afternoon to take your statement. Would you prefer to have your supper before then or after he departs?" Gage's question at the end of his announcement led me, for a brief moment, into believing that I still had choices, and that life would continue as it always had. A small ray of hope unfurled itself in my stomach. If the constable thought I would have an appetite after my interrogation, then perhaps my situation was not dire. Perhaps I would, again, see the world outside the stone walls of the Tower. This hope gave me the courage I needed to ask a question of my own.

"Oh, I do not think my nerves will allow me to eat anything before Master Secretary throws his questions at me. I do, however, have a request. I am certain your response will be an unfavourable one, but I do still hope you will take it into serious consideration." Gage's piercing blue eyes unnerved me, but I had come this far. I had nothing to lose by asking, and everything to gain if he gave his assent. I stepped away from the chair, and moved closer to the constable. Taking his worn hands in mine, I offered him a tentative smile. No doubt curious as to my desire, his eyes urged me on. I pushed the words out of my parched lips before I had the opportunity to reconsider, "May I go to the chapel to visit George?"

My words wounded him the moment they tumbled from my mouth. This was something he could not; *dared* not give me. Of all the things I could have desired, of all the things I could have requested, I asked for this one impossible thing. Gage could not give me what I wanted, and I realised too late how callous it was of me to ask knowing that, in satisfying me, he risked the king's displeasure.

Gage maintained his dignity despite my audacity. He wrapped my hands into the warm cocoon of his own, squeezing them reassuringly. He needed no words, only a perfunctory shake of his head. No, he could not grant my request. The king would never allow it. I swallowed back the ray of hope that had been slowly, hesitantly, making its way from my stomach into my heart. I pulled my hands away, then returned to the bench by the window. I drew my knees to my chest, burying my face in the crevice between them. To overcome my sadness, I thought of how angry I was when my father told me that I was to spend the rest of my life with George. If only I had held on tightly to that anger. If only I had never allowed myself to fall in love with my husband, perhaps I would be shielded from the pain I now felt. George and I had never been so close, and yet so far away at the same time.

MAY – JULY 1523
GREENWICH

DURING THE early weeks of May, Harry and I retreated from the court at Greenwich. A few months prior, my brother had been betrothed to the daughter of our neighbour, John Newport. Sadly, Master Newport was gravely ill; his imminent death meant that eight-year-old Grace would soon come into her inheritance. Because our father was eager to bring those lands into our family, he sought a special dispensation to push the wedding ahead, despite Grace's young age. Once permission arrived at the end of the restrictive Lenten season, a minister at the local parish church of St. Giles performed a short, perfunctory service. Neither celebration, nor dancing, was held to honour the couple; only a small, simple meal awaited us at the manor when we returned home.

Grace cowered in her seat during supper. She curled her body inward, making it as small as she could on the wooden chair, and pecked at her food. She avoided eye contact with everyone at the table for most of the meal, but when the time came to put the couple to bed, she finally trained her wide, fearful eyes upon my brother. Our mother instructed me to accompany the young bride to Harry's bedchamber first, so I could explain to her in private that the ceremony was merely for show due to her youth. I assured her that she need not fear her husband because he would be kind and gentle with her.

In the morning Grace appeared much calmer and, no doubt, relieved when she emerged from Harry's bed with her maidenhood still intact. She even attempted a shy smile when Margaret and I invited her out to the fish pond for a swim when the heat from the afternoon sun became unbearable. She continued to say very little during her early days with our family, but by the end of the first week, she had latched onto Margaret, and they were inseparable.

However, when word arrived that Master Newport had indeed succumbed to his illness, she became inconsolable. My brother made arrangements to stay behind, while I returned to court.

George was the first to greet me upon my arrival at Greenwich. I found him preparing his chestnut courser for a late afternoon hunt when I rode my palfrey, Avalon, into the stable. I ignored his friendly overtures, working quickly to stable my horse. Once I was satisfied that Avalon had been properly groomed and fed after our journey, I tried to make my escape. I had only taken a few steps out into the sunlight when I felt a hand grasp my own.

"Well, aren't you going to face me, Jane?"

A few years ago George's touch would have made me tingle, but now it made my skin crawl. Over the last year, I noticed that everything the young man did was so considered, so measured, so perfect, the mere sight of him inspired a slow-burning fury within me. He was accomplished at everything he tried. I could find no fault in his flawless dancing, his articulate speech, or his masterful diplomacy. His perfection moved the other maids to simpering affection, and they happily trotted after him in a besotted daze. However, it did nothing but remind me of my own imperfections, causing me to despise him.

I closed my eyes and took a deep breath, counting to ten before pushing the breath from my lungs through pursed lips. I coaxed them into a smile before turning to face George. "My apologies, Master Boleyn, but I am in a hurry…" I trailed off, hoping he would release his grip so I could make my escape. The gold flecks in his eyes in his eyes danced merrily as he considered my feeble excuse. When he ran his tongue across his bottom lip, my stomach quaked. The arousal I felt immediately repulsed me. *'Stupid Jane!'* I silently berated myself. I tried to pull my hand away, but he held it firmly in place.

"Ah, so George is no more. Am I to be Master Boleyn now? You truly are the strangest creature, Jane Parker."

"Seemed the most respectful way to address you," I shot back. "Now, what do you want?"

"She raises me, yet wounds me in the same sentence. Does your charm know no bounds? I never know which way the wind blows with you. One moment you gaze upon me with desire and the next, you rebuff every advance I make. I do wish you would make up your mind about me, for I've grown quite weary of your antics."

I narrowed my eyes; any fleeting lust I felt moments ago flitted away on that very same wind. George finally released my hand when his smile failed to charm me. "Fine, Jane, you may go. I only wanted to give you a message from my sister, Mary. She has some wonderful news to share and asked that I direct you to our family rooms."

I received no response when I knocked on the heavy oak door leading to the Boleyn accommodations, but since George had directed me there himself, I assumed I could let myself in. The presence chamber appeared empty, but I heard muffled sounds coming from Anne's bedchamber. The door was ajar, and I saw a flash of yellow damask bustle past the open space. When I pushed the door open, the sharp, pungent odour of vomit assaulted my senses.

Anne startled at the sound of my entrance, but she gestured for me to close the door with her one free hand. The other hand held a pewter bowl as far away from her body as possible. Mary, still clad in her nightgown, sat on the bed, hunched over with her head between her knees. When she finally deigned to lift her face, it was a shocking shade of green. I rushed towards the bed to comfort her, but she held me at a distance, "I will be fine. This will all pass soon enough."

"Perhaps in nine months' time," Anne chimed from behind the door of the close stool. She returned to the room with the empty bowl, just in time for Mary to begin retching again. I pulled Mary's hair back from her face, then rubbed my hand across her sweat-slicked back. She heaved until she collapsed backwards onto the bed in exhaustion. I looked to Anne for help, but she merely rolled her eyes to the ceiling. "Looks like the king will have himself another bastard," she replied with a shrug of her shoulders.

"I don't know that, Anne," Mary cut in with a groan. "This baby could just as easily be William's. It is not as if he has let the king have me all to himself. I am still his wife. Besides, I love him, and I want more than anything for this child to be his."

I climbed up next to Mary, then used a linen handkerchief I had tucked in my gown to wipe the perspiration from her brow. "Have you told the king yet? Is he overjoyed?"

"You are so simple, Jane," she huffed. "Of course he's not. Even if he is the father, it doesn't matter – the child will bear the name Carey."

"But if it is a boy…Look at Bessie Blount's son; the King has provided well for him."

She pushed my hand away from her face, which was finally returning to its usual rosy colour. "That was very different; when Bessie was the king's mistress she was unmarried. Please just forget the matter. This is not the happy occasion I had hoped for." I threw my arms around Mary, holding her tight even though the scent of her sweat and vomit made my stomach churn.

SEPTEMBER – DECEMBER

1523

GREENWICH

MARY'S GRIEF and ever expanding belly grew as the months passed. Many of the women who served the queen with us chalked Mary's drastic mood swings up to the dolefulness that often accompanied mothers through their pregnancy, but Mary suffered from the sorrow of a broken heart. One morning as we sat near a window in the queen's presence chamber sewing New Year gifts in the golden autumn sunlight she confessed to me that, despite her better judgement, she had fallen in love with the king. His Grace's favoured treatment of Mary only added to her plight. We had all expected him to put her aside; instead, he treated her even better than before. He no longer called her to his room at night, because intimacies during pregnancy could harm the child, but he continued to lavish attention upon her and even sent one of his personal physicians to tend to her health. Mary erupted into tears when I pointed this out.

"I do not deserve such kindnesses," she gasped between heaving sobs. "I've behaved so shamefully. My heart should belong to my husband, not the king. Worse still, I don't even know which man fathered my child."

"But, Mary," I interjected. "The king gave you no choice; he would have summoned you to his bed regardless of William's opinion on the matter."

"True," Mary sniffed. "But, it is one matter to share the king's bed and quite another to fall in love with him. I chose to give him more of myself than necessary at a great cost to my husband, and now William will always wonder if the child is his. If the baby looks like the king will it hear their Lady Mother called a whore? How do I explain that?"

I understood Mary's sadness, and in all honesty, I could not blame her for falling for the king. It was easy to get swept up in the attention of a man as charming and powerful as Henry Tudor. William Carey was kind, but he was not overly affectionate, nor could he ever afford the gifts the king had showered upon Mary over the last year.

"I feel even worse knowing how Godly and pure the queen is. Every time she kneels at her prie-dieu to pray for a son, I feel a knife in my womb," she muttered.

"Mary, you cannot live in the mistakes of your past," I cajoled as I grabbed the blanket she was sewing from her hands. "It is never too late to redeem yourself and move forward on a different path. See this?" I set her blanket on the cushion next to me, then held up the cloak I was embroidering. "I was very unkind to someone who asked for nothing but my friendship, and I have regretted it ever since. It is only now that I have worked up the courage to make amends, and it may be too late. Perhaps he shall laugh in my face, but I think this may be the only way I can forgive myself. You, too, need to find a way to forgive yourself."

Mary's round eyes glistened with unshed tears, but she offered me a small hopeful smile. "I hope one day I can, Jane."

During those autumn months, Mary's sister faced her own relationship troubles. The secret meetings with Henry Percy finally led to the marriage proposal Anne so desired. However, when Percy approached Wolsey for his help in forwarding the matter, the cardinal soundly berated him in front of the other servants. The Earl of Northumberland was commanded to court from his lands in the north to correct his son's behaviour. Regardless of Anne's noble blood lines, they did not consider her a suitable bride for the heir to the most powerful earldom in the realm. Rather than giving in to sorrow, as her sister had, Anne became enraged. She unleashed her fury in a torrent of curses on Percy, calling him weak and spineless. Displeased as she was, there was nothing to be done about it. Their reckless gamble failed, sealing Percy's betrothal to Mary Talbot. Anne would be fortunate if the incident didn't besmirch her future marriage prospects.

Anne held tight to her resentment, but her animosity cooled as Percy spent less and less time at court. With Christmastide creeping ever closer, she turned her attention to the needs of her pregnant sister. Mary's ever changing moods caused minor sisterly bickering, but at the end of the evening, Anne always sat with her, strumming calming lullabies on her lute, in the low candlelight. Ever the accomplished needlewoman, Anne finished her New Year gifts well before we did, so she spent many afternoons sewing bonnets and slippers for her niece or nephew-to-be.

Just as they had in the most recent years past, the Yule celebrations were held at Greenwich. I loved Christmas, and I couldn't wait to see the castle decorated in all its glory. Each year the Lord Chamberlain decked the palace out in the splendid greenery of ivy, mistletoe, and holly with the deepest crimson berries full to bursting. The Master of Revels planned the most elaborate dances and mummeries, and after Christmas Eve, we all ate until we could hardly move. I held high hopes that the cook would again prepare a turkey. Last year, I was permitted only a taste of the newest addition to our traditional feast and my mouth watered just thinking of the tender, juicy meat.

My mother informed me that Father would be home in time for them to attend the celebrations at court. The news filled me with joy. Almost four months ago, the king had sent my father to the Continent to present Archduke Ferdinand of Austria with the Order of the Garter. The mission was a great honour, but also a treacherous one. In his last letter home at the end of October, Lord Morley reported that they were passing through dangerous country and had been compelled to beg safe conduct from the Lieutenant of the Duke of Cleves.

The court also eagerly anticipated the return of another of the king's loyal servants. The Duke of Suffolk returned from campaigning as the first winter snowflakes began to fall. Charles Brandon had been sent on behalf of His Grace to wage war with the French for the Emperor at the end of May. Much to his chagrin, aid from the Emperor and his compatriot, the Duke of Bourbon, failed to materialise, and Brandon was left in Paris without reinforcements or supplies. Winter arrived early in France, decimating over half of Brandon's force. The men were lost to frigid temperatures and the plague. The Duke returned battered and broken, yet lauded for his fortitude.

Apprehension tempered my excitement for the season. I made the decision to apologise to Hugh and ask for his forgiveness shortly after my return to Greenwich in the summer. I regretted the way I had treated him, refusing to return the cloak he had given me after it had been wrinkled and buried at the bottom of my chest. I decided to make him a new one for New Year. I saved up my earnings, before haggling with my mother's tailor for a good price on a deep grey velvet fabric. I chose a bright azure blue thread to compliment Hugh's eyes, and set to work sewing a new cloak with elaborate embroidery. I hoped he would graciously accept my gift and my apology, but I prepared myself for the inevitable rebuke.

My parents arrived with both Margaret and Grace, their eyes sparkling and cheeks aglow, as we headed to the chapel for Christmas Mass. It was their first time attending the celebrations, and neither could hide their delight when they saw the king and queen glide down the corridor dressed in sumptuous cloth of gold attire, topped with velvet robes of rich scarlet. The jewels in the ornate crowns atop their heads winked in the flickering candlelight of the tapers we carried as we followed behind them. We came together for a grand feast in the great hall after the mass. Just as I hoped, the kitchen served a plump roasted turkey, dressed in its own feathers, during one of the courses. After gorging myself on all of the savoury dishes and pies sent to my table from the queen, I refused the sweet confections my sister and Grace gleefully crammed past their rosy cupid bow lips.

Anne stood, resplendent in an emerald-hued damask gown trimmed with white rabbit fur over a pale grey kirtle, in the corner with Henry Norris. She threw her head back in laughter at something Norris said and gracefully slid her dainty hand down her slender white neck. She aimed a pert smile my way when she caught me staring, then beckoned me over with one elongated finger. I ambled over slowly, picking my way through the throng of courtiers. "Anne…Master Norris," I said with a slight curtsey. "Happy Christmas to you both."

Norris brought my hand to his lips in greeting then replied, "Happy Christmas to you as well, Mistress Parker. You look as though you are in need of a dance partner."

"Is that an offer Master Norris?" I inquired with a coy smile.

Norris' eyes widened in bemusement, but Anne was having none of it. She pinched the sleeve of his velvet doublet hard enough to make him wince.

"Henry, you're dancing with me."

"Yes, my lady, I did promise," Norris replied with a laugh. "My apologies, Mistress Parker."

I brushed him off with a wave of my hand, then turned my attention to my friend. "What can I do for you, Anne?"

Anne flicked a strand of silky hair over her shoulder before informing me that she and Norris were planning to join her brother and some of his friends for an evening of cards. "Would you care to join us?" she asked.

When my stomach lurched, I wasn't sure if it was the overabundance of food or the prospect of spending the evening with the ever perfect George causing my discomfort. Luckily, I had a perfect reason to excuse myself. "I am so sorry, Anne, but I am going to have to decline your offer. I would like to spend as much time with my family as possible before they return to Hallingbury. I'm sure you understand."

Anne shot me a resentful pout, but accepted my refusal, "Oh, go enjoy your evening. I shall see you tomorrow in the queen's rooms."

I skittered out of the hall before her mood soured, but slowed my pace once the door slammed shut behind me. The torches lining the corridor threw a soft glow on the festive evergreen boughs draped over the windows. I pressed my face against the cool glass of the one nearest me to watch the snowflakes dance in the moonlight. Carol music drifting out of the great hall enhanced the scene with an aura of holiness. I inhaled the moment of peace deeply, wishing I could hold on to it forever. When the draft from the window began seeping through my sleeves, I stepped away from the divine scene, and continued towards the maids' dorm. I wanted to change into something warmer and less constricting before I went to my family's temporary apartments for the evening. As I rounded the corner, I saw Hugh Wynter's familiar profile in the light of a torch. He was deep in conversation with one of the king's grooms. I stepped back for a moment and waited for the opportunity to approach him. Once the groom scurried away, I quickly called out Hugh's name, before I could change my mind. Our fortuitous meeting meant that I needn't involve my brother in the delivery of his gift.

"Mistress Parker, I must admit I'm rather surprised to hear you use my Christian name. I don't know if we continue to have the familiarity that permits that anymore."

I felt the heat creep into my face, but I stepped forward into the light despite my discomfort. "That's true, Master Wynter, and I have no one but myself to blame. However, I am hoping that the Christmas Spirit will move you. Would it be too bold to kindly ask you to escort me to my room?"

Hugh studied me carefully, as if to determine whether I played some deceitful trick. He squared his shoulders, crossing his arms in a posture of defence, while he considered his response. I bit the inside of my cheek and nervously shifted my weight as I awaited his reply.

"Jane, I really don't think…"

I threw my hands up to stop him. "Please? I just…well, I…I have something for you," I stuttered.

"Very well, but I only do this out of my loyalty to your brother," Hugh answered with a sigh.

The journey to the maids' dorm was so silent that I was certain Hugh could hear the erratic pounding of my heart. I restrained myself, several times, from fleeing down the corridor before we reached our destination. When we arrived at the door, I motioned for Hugh to wait outside while I went in for his gift. I pulled the cloak out of my chest, brushing the supple fabric against my cheek for just an instant, before carefully tucking it under my arm. When I opened the door, Hugh was leaning against the stone wall with his arms crossed. He straightened at my appearance, smoothing down his doublet with nervous strokes.

"Happy Christmas, Master Wynter," I murmured, holding out the cloak in offering.

Hugh gaped at me in wonder, his eyes wide with disbelief. His stunned silence filled me with dread and sent my thoughts racing: the fabric was cheap, my stitching was poor. Why had I insulted him with such a paltry gift?

"Did you make this?" His voice sounded incredulous as he held the cloak up to inspect the swirls of embroidery.

"I lost yours so it was the least I could do." The lie tasted bitter on my tongue, but I wasn't ready to admit how I had mistreated the one he gave me. "I'm very sorry about my behaviour; I had no reason to treat you that way. I hope you can forgive me and we can renew our friendship."

Hugh gazed at me apologetically when he finally lowered the cloak. "Jane, I am leaving Greenwich in a few days' time. I am to marry after Epiphany."

"That's wonderful, Master Wynter," I feigned a cheerful reply. "I wish you both nothing but happiness." I quickly dipped a small curtsey, then slid back into my room before the tears burning behind my eyes began to fall.

April 1524
Greenwich

"JANE…JANE…WAKE UP Jane!" I launched myself from the warm cocoon of my bed the moment Anne's frantic voice pierced the veil of my dreams.

"What is it? Are you hurt?" I panted as I struggled to catch my breath; I thought my heart would leap from my chest at any moment. The appearance of my dishevelled friend in the maids' dorm alarmed me. Anne lodged in her parents' private rooms, and she avoided the dorm at all costs. Things must be terribly amiss if she was willing to appear here in her nightgown.

Anne grasped my shoulders, shaking them in excitement. "Mary is having the king's baby!" she cried. I threw my arm around her, clasping my hand over her mouth. The stillness of the quilt covered mounds of the other maids in the room reassured me, but my bedfellow, Elizabeth Dannet, stirred beneath our counterpane.

I arched my brow at Anne in contempt before pulling my hand from her mouth. "Mary is having *a* baby; paternity yet to be determined," she whispered. I shoved her aside with a groan of irritation, then ran to my clothes chest for a dressing gown and cap.

A flickering sea of candles chased the early morning darkness from the presence chamber of the Boleyn apartments, but the screams of pain coming from Anne's room dampened the cheerful glow. I hesitated when she pushed the heavy oak door aside, but swallowed the dreadful lump in my throat before she beckoned me inside. Mary was curled into a tight ball of misery on the bed, while her mother perched near her head, smoothing the matted hair from her face and shushing her through pursed lips. A midwife busied herself in the corner preparing the cradle.

"You've arrived just in time, Sweetheart," Elizabeth Boleyn murmured in hushed tones. "Help me move your sister to the chair."

With the midwife's help, the three of us moved Mary into position on the birthing chair next to the bed so she could begin the arduous task of pushing the child out into the world. Mary set her teeth, straining with all her might; only the grunts and groans of her struggle and exhaustion punctuated the apprehensive silence of the room. As the first rays of the morning sun crept through the curtained windows, the indignant cry of the newly born tore through the air.

Once she was bathed and dressed in a clean linen shift, we propped Mary up on the bed and placed the squirming infant into her arms. The baby's pale eyes fluttered open, drinking up the loving countenance upon her mother's face. Anne and I exchanged a worried glance over the wisps of red hair escaping from under the tiny bonnet the midwife had placed on her head, but Mary just heaved a contented sigh as she smiled down at her daughter. "I think I shall call her Catherine," she said.

William Carey arrived later in the morning to pay a visit to his wife. When he lifted the infant from Mary's lap, the bonnet slipped off, exposing the shock of russet hair. He tenderly smoothed it down with his thumb, then brushed his lips against the silken skin of her forehead. "My mother once told me that red hair runs in my family," he told us with a smile. I knew then that it mattered not whose blood pumped through Catherine's veins, William Carey would always claim it was his own.

I stumbled back to the maids' dorm, so drained and exhausted, the quiet comfort of my bed seemed a delicious and forbidden treat. Fortunately, the room appeared empty when I arrived. I quickly returned my dressing gown to my trunk, then padded over to my bed. I didn't notice the piece of parchment, until it fluttered to my feet, when I turned the counterpane back. Thinking it was for Mistress Dannet, I picked it up with the intention of flinging it over to her side of the bed. I realised then it was addressed to me. I contemplated leaving it until I had taken some rest, but my curiosity got the better of me so I slipped my finger under the seal, cracking it open. The note was from my father requesting my presence in his rooms, at my earliest convenience. I hesitated for a moment, staring longingly at the inviting hollow of my bed, but I eventually gave in to my sense of duty. My father stopped at court only to report to the king after his recent trip to Calais, so I knew he would be eager to return to his books at Hallingbury.

Lord Morley failed to rise from his chair when I entered his apartment. He merely held up a finger in greeting, then he continued reading the heavy book that lay open on his lap. I waited patiently in the doorway for him to finish his thoughts and invite me inside. The moment he closed the book, a groom hurried over to take it from his outstretched hands. Before beckoning me inside, he motioned for another groom to stoke the fire in the hearth. "Are you ill, Jane? You look miserable."

I straightened my spine, attempting to appear alert. "My apologies, Father, I was with Anne Boleyn all night. Her sister has just given birth to a beautiful baby girl. I'm afraid I'm quite tired from the evening's excitement."

"Well, that's wonderful news indeed. I'm glad you've nurtured such a close bond with your future sisters," my father replied with the hint of a smile.

A dry yelp of laughter escaped my throat, "I'm very sorry, Father, but my mind must be more overtaxed than I thought. I thought for a moment you called Anne and Mary my future sisters."

"No, you've followed the conversation quite well, Jane; you always were a very good listener."

I shook my head, desperately trying to clear the cobwebs and cling to a coherent thought, while his words tumbled around in the fog of my confusion. My brother, Harry, had already married so a match with Anne was out of the question. Did he mean to marry my younger sister, Margaret, to George Boleyn? No, that was unlikely. They would certainly settle the matter of my marriage before they turned an eye to Margaret's prospects. As I struggled through my exhaustion, father waited patiently for his meaning to finally become clear to me. "I'm to marry George?" The words left me cold and bereft.

"I've opened negotiations with Thomas Boleyn regarding your jointure," he replied, his smile widening to a grin. "By this time next year, Mary could be attending *you* in childbirth... well... perhaps preparing you for it at least, that might be a bit premature."

No! No! I threw out my hands as if to stop his words from slamming into me. "I can't marry George. Please don't make me do this."

The grin slid from my father's face as he fixed his eyes upon me with a stony glare. "Don't be absurd, Jane. Of course, you will marry the Boleyn boy. Why ever would you disagree to this match? He far exceeds his peers in both intelligence and wit and his relationship with the king all but assures his bright future. I'm no great judge of appearance, but George is quite seemly, and I think most of the young women in your position would be glad of his attentions."

"Ha!" I barked bitterly. "They all receive his attentions!" My hands flew to my mouth, but they were far too late to stop my indignant response slipping out.

Lord Morley finally rose from his chair. "That is quite enough. It's obvious to me that you are far too easily influenced by the light behaviour abounding in this court. The daughter I raised would never speak to me in such a tone, let alone disobey my express commandment. You *will* marry whomever I see fit without comment, and you *will* modify your behaviour to one that is more becoming of the education I have invested in you."

When I bit the inside of my cheek to hold back my response, I tasted the warm brine of blood on my tongue. I saw no point in arguing. My father ruled his heart with logic; he was indifferent to an emotional response. It wasn't that he was cold or spiteful, he just didn't understand. I knew his anger stemmed from confusion over my reaction; his mistake in expecting me to be overjoyed irritated him. I knelt into a deep curtsey when he finally excused me and kept my eyes on the floor as I fled from his room, broken.

November 13, 1541
The Tower of London

I RUBBED my face against the heavy fabric covering my knees to wipe away the salt crusted tracks left behind by my tears. What started as a weak pulse at the base of my skull had grown to a painful throbbing that spread up to the crown of my head. I felt as if a vice was tightening around my ears and I could do nothing to stop it. I swallowed back the tendrils of bile creeping out of my stomach and up into my throat. The acute pain caused a film of sweat to bead across my forehead. Unseen fingers loosened the ties of my hood, pulling it off my head. The tension was alleviated for a brief, sweet moment, but then the throbbing returned, only slightly lessened in intensity. I heard Lucy shuffle away, even though I kept my head buried in my knees.

"It will be awhile yet before Master Secretary is here so I see no reason for you to have any more discomfort than necessary."

Lucy had been in my service for less than a decade, but in that time she served as a beacon of comfort through some of my darkest days. She always had an innate sense of everything I thought or felt; she probably knew my body almost as well as I did. Ladies and their maids shared an intimacy that often surpassed that of husband and wife out of sheer necessity. I would have been helpless without her, and I was thankful that she was with me now. It was a great courtesy, and mercy, that the king allowed her to accompany me to my prison. When my sister-in-law was here, she was surrounded by women who hated her. It was little wonder that she succumbed to fits of hysteria; there was no one there to console her.

Anguish speared my chest at the thought of Anne. Her body rested with George's in the chapel outside my lodgings, but were either of their souls at rest? Since their deaths, I often wondered if anyone, besides me, ever offered prayers for their salvation. I doubted if their father did. Not because he didn't care, but because I suspected that he did not believe in Purgatory. In his eyes, God had already received his children in the Kingdom of Heaven. I didn't feel as certain. The Boleyn family believed in the reformed ways of the church: one made their way to Heaven by the justification of their faith; there was no need for intercessions from the church. In my terror of the unknown, I clung to the old ways. What if they were wrong? What if there was more to it than faith? I just couldn't risk it. The sacraments and rites of Catholicism consoled and assured me, and I could never fully give them up.

After George died, I prayed fervently for the delivery of his soul. I gave from what little I possessed to priests so they would pray for him as well. If Purgatory did exist, I didn't want my beloved there for long. George would be infuriated to know I did this; religion was one of the few things we bickered over. He spent many nights patiently explaining his reasoning and reading to me from books we were forbidden to have. I desperately wanted to tell him I believed as he did, that I was ready to enter this new world; but I just couldn't bring myself to do it. He believed I would eventually give in, but the executioner cut short our time together. With George gone, I gripped those traditions even closer to my heart.

From the swirl of my memories of George, a terrible thought emerged. Who would pray for my soul? If the jury found for the king, sentencing me to death as a traitor, would there be anyone who loved me enough to ask for God's intercession? Surely someone from my family would? Or would they be too scared? My heart thudded wildly within my chest, and I could not slow the breaths that came shallow and fast. I abruptly pulled my face from my knees and swung my feet around and off the bench. My muscles screamed in pain after having been cramped in one position for so long, but I ignored the discomfort and vaulted towards the prie-dieu in the corner. I fell to my knees, gripping my hands together so tightly that my knuckles faded to white. My lips formed the prayer that they knew so well over and over again, "Lord Jesus, I commend my soul unto you."

I instinctively turned when I felt a heavy hand press against my shoulder. My whispered prayers fell away when I opened my eyes. My beloved George stood before me, strong and handsome as ever, with a smile etched upon his face. When I reached out to touch his faltering image, my fingers closed around nothing but space, then the encroaching darkness swallowed me whole.

September – December 1524
1524
Hallingbury and Grimston

I MET George at the door of the St. Giles Parish Church on a crisp late autumn morning as the golden sun began its daily ascent into the clear blue sky. The heat of the summer was long past, and the harvest had dwindled to a close. The icy fingers of winter were beckoning the world ever closer to the season of howling winds and glittering snowflakes. The silk-lined furred mantle that covered my shoulders was warm enough to keep the chill out, but small puffs of smoke hung in the air with every breath I exhaled.

I still resented my father for yoking me to a man whose accomplishments and grace seemed, to me, to be otherworldly. My self-regard had grown very little over the last year and, though many of my peers remarked upon my comely appearance, I did not believe myself to be beautiful or refined, and my insecurities waged an internal war as the negotiations for my marriage got underway. Difficulties beset my father in his dealings with Thomas Boleyn. The two thousand marks he demanded for my jointure was well over the amount that my father could afford and much of the property offered in return was, in truth, owned by Thomas' mother. If anything happened to George while his grandmother still lived, I would remain unable to claim the rents from my manors.

I waited patiently for the contract to fall apart, granting myself a small sliver of hope each time my father returned, angry after another meeting with George's father; but when the king stepped in with the additional funds to cover my dower, I knew it was a fait accompli. Resigned to my fate and resolving to trust in my father's decision, I made the short journey from Greenwich back to my home at Hallingbury, where I spent the next few weeks making preparations for my new life as a wedded wife.

I arose before dawn, and after a warm bath before the hearth, my mother's maid eased me into a velvet gown the colour of claret wine, then my sister set about weaving fragrant rosemary into a braid that crowned the flaxen waves of hair cascading down my back. After my wedding, I would no longer be allowed to wear my hair loose in public, so I savoured the weight of it against my shoulders while I could. Once the rest of my family had donned their best formal attire, we set off in solemn procession to church. My parents had baptised me at St. Giles and, today, I would be married there. I hoped that someday my own children would be baptised there as well.

I felt a catch in my throat at the sight of the elegant, lithe young man leaning against the sturdy oak door waiting patiently for me arrive with my family so we could exchange vows. I thought George handsome since the moment I first laid eyes upon him, but it seemed like he had grown into something so much more during our long betrothal. He became taller and leaner; confidence and assurance replaced the arrogance with which he had previously carried himself. The deep crimson of the velvet doublet stretching across his broadened shoulders emphasised his dark hair and the golden flecks in eyes that never failed to mesmerise me. His family flanked him on either side; Thomas and Elizabeth Boleyn stood to his right while Anne propped herself against the stone wall of the church to his left.

Happiness stirred inside of me at the sight of my dear friend. Anne returned home to Hever shortly after the birth of Mary's baby, and many months had passed since we were last in each other's company. She ran to greet me the moment my coterie appeared, her arms wide in welcome. I threw myself into her embrace, and buried my face in her silky hair, inhaling the creamy scent of vanilla and cinnamon. It reminded me of Christmas. "Good morrow, Sister," she whispered in my ear.

We embraced briefly, parting so I could continue my march to the church door. At my approach, George leaned forward in a bow of reverence. When he came back up, he brushed the waves of hair from his eyes, disarming me with a lopsided grin. I shared a tentative smile in return, taking his offered hand. Moments later the priest emerged and commenced the ceremony. We exchanged vows and rings, then entered the church for a blessing and the nuptial mass. It felt so strange to stand at the altar as the centre of attention in this holy place where I had only ever blended in as one in a congregation of many. I often dreamt of my wedding during the quiet moments of the ceremonies I witnessed here in the past, and now I found myself performing those same rituals. I always hoped that it would be someone I desperately loved standing next to me, but I knew that would have had to be a happy coincidence of luck. My hostility towards George had cooled somewhat since I resigned myself to the prospect of being his wife, but I felt nothing close to love for him. The priest asked us to turn towards each other and, when I gazed into the golden pools of George's eyes, I recognised sincerity in them. Had I merely ignored it all this time? I didn't love George now, but perhaps I would grow to in time. This would be the new dream to which I would cling.

We spent the afternoon celebrating our wedding with an abundance of food, music, and dancing. My mother asked the cook to prepare a special meat pie I favoured, and we had a course of sugared sweets in addition to the elaborate bride cake. After the meal, I wondered if the rumbling in my stomach was from the richness of the food or nervousness for what was to come next. When dusk settled over our party, my mother took me by the hand and led me to my room to prepare me for the ritual that sealed my marriage. Lady Morley and her maid removed my heavy velvet gown, but left my silk chemise undergarment in place. In a nod to a tradition passed down in my family, we tied a small carnation inside of it for George to find. Once I was wrapped in a new silk robe, and the servants had been in to lay out the bride-ale and an assortment of dried fruits and cheeses for later, George entered the room in his bedclothes with the priest.

After the bed was blessed and the last of the witnesses shuffled out of the room, I closed my eyes tightly, bracing myself for George's eager pawing. I stood in expectation for a moment or two, but when the lecherous groping never came, I dared a peek from under my long eyelashes. My new husband merely gazed at me with a slight grin on his face. "I don't know what you've heard about me, but I don't make it a habit of throwing myself upon unwilling maidens," he said with a laugh.

"I haven't heard anything about you, and I'm not an unwilling maiden, I'm your wife," I huffed as my cheeks burned in embarrassment.

"Even more reason why I wouldn't want to harm you. I know it's my right to take you as I wish, but I would prefer something a bit more romantic. My father taught me to have a little more grace than that."

I felt relieved, but still abashed by my presumption. "Thank you," I managed in a soft voice. George waited for my nod of approval before carefully removing my robe. He leaned forward, placing a warm kiss on my bare shoulder as the silky fabric slid away from my skin. The tender gesture surprised me and sent a surge of anticipation through my body.

"I'm going to find your flower now if you are ready."

I swallowed hard but gave him an encouraging smile, so he dropped to the floor and lifted the hem of my chemise. The flower was easy to find, but we had tied it rather high, so it took him some effort to retrieve it. The sight of the ever graceful George fumbling beneath my undergarment caused a ripple of amusement, and I repressed the urge to laugh. He emerged victorious a few moments later with his hair dishevelled; he had a tiny posy pinched between his fingers.

"I daresay you've earned your reward, husband."

George pulled down the counterpane so I could crawl into bed, then he walked around to the other side. After he slid under the covers, he propped himself up on his elbow so that he could gaze down at me. "You are quite beautiful, Jane."

"You don't have to say that, George," I replied dispassionately. "You don't have to charm me."

"I know," he said before he put his lips on mine.

My mother tried to prepare me for my wedding night in her reserved way, but I assumed that George would be a seasoned lover, and there would be little for me to do besides lie there. Pretty maids always surrounded him, and he wouldn't be the first of his peers to have shared the company of one or two before his marriage, so his inexperience came as a surprise and a welcomed relief to me. His touch was tender, if hesitant, and, after a few clumsy starts, we came together as one. I anticipated the pain, but was completely unprepared for the flood of emotion that overtook me. George was turning out to be nothing like the person I thought he was.

Once the festivities were over, the Boleyn family returned to their home at Hever, and we set off to Grimston to set up our household. Our new home had come to George by grant of the king, in honour of our wedding. We spent the next few weeks unpacking our meagre belongings and growing accustomed to each other's habits and daily rituals. Before George and I could cultivate a peaceful existence, we were summoned back to the court at Greenwich for the Yuletide celebrations.

DECEMBER 1525 – OCTOBER 1526 GREENWICH, GRIMSTON, AND HEVER

THE FIRST year of our marriage swirled by in a whirlwind of activity. I continued to serve in the queen's rooms, but I no longer slept among the maids. George and I were given rooms on the king's side of the palace and, though they weren't as luxuriously appointed as his family's rooms, they were far more splendid than I could have imagined. George remained one of the king's closest companions; he was in constant attendance upon His Grace. They occupied their days hunting stag in the nearby parks or taking their hawks out for sport. George developed a keen interest in the enormous birds, so he never missed an opportunity to play games of chance with the king in the hopes of winning one for himself. When the king excused my husband from his duties, George headed off to the countryside to manage his recently granted properties.

The king brought his son with a former mistress, Bessie Blount, to Bridewell Palace before we set off on the summer progress for a spectacular ceremony. He elevated the little boy to the peerage, granting him the dukedoms of both Richmond and Somerset. He honoured my Boleyn family as well, creating my father-in-law as Baron Rochford at the same event. The court seethed with gossip about what this favoured treatment of the king's illegitimate son implied. A few of the queen's Spanish ladies declared, with indignant disgust, that the king intended to groom the little duke for the throne and bypass his legitimate daughter's claim. Their attempts to engage the queen into open opposition against the king failed miserably; Instead, His Grace summarily dismissed the lot of them for their efforts.

We escaped the confines of the city as an outbreak of plague settled upon it. Princess Mary was sent to Ludlow in the Welsh Marches to escape the sickness and establish her household, while the rest of the court went on progress. The queen cried as she was parted from her beloved daughter, but I'm sure she knew it was the order of things. With no male heir to inherit the throne, the princess needed to be properly educated and prepared for the eventuality that she would rule. Reports of illness plaguing the city had not dissipated by the time the mild autumn months arrived so, rather than returning to Greenwich for the Advent season, the king and queen fled to their palace at Eltham and sent the rest of the courtiers home for the remainder of the year. George and I kept our first Christmas at Grimston. It was a quiet affair, but we both enjoyed the much-needed respite.

The king returned to Greenwich at the end of Yuletide and held a revel to whip the court into a frivolous cheer, but soon afterwards, a pall descended. Cardinal Wolsey brought to Greenwich a new ordinance for the running of the king's household. Many of the monarch's favourite courtiers were stripped of their positions within his intimate circle, and a strict order of rule was instituted to clamp down on the king's spending habits, weeding out those whom Wolsey deemed a base influence. Wolsey must have felt his power waning to have instituted such sweeping changes. I was surprised that the king didn't chafe more at the tight rein in which his leading churchman had roped him.

Though he maintained his cool demeanour publicly, my husband was livid. Wolsey removed George from the king's direct service, demoting him to the inferior position of cupbearer. I reminded him that he would still attend upon the king when he dined outside of his private rooms and that Wolsey had given him a significant increase in his wages, but I knew none of that compared to the privileged position he had occupied only weeks before. Being so privy to George's personal disappointments had begun to erode the view I had of his perfection. His frail humanity started to shine through. It also gave me an opportunity to be at my very best. I gained a measure of poise in the role of confidante and consoling helpmate.

As George's eminence at court slowly ebbed away, his sister's began to climb. When Anne returned, plump and freshened by the country air at Hever, she caught the eye of the most important and least eligible man at court – the king. The initial indications that the king's favour had fallen upon my sister-in-law were almost imperceptible, but as the warmer weather coaxed the flowers into uncurling their bright blooms, the attraction he felt for her blossomed into something demanding a public statement of his affections.

The Shrovetide jousts at Greenwich served as the stage from which the king declared his love for his new paramour. Dressed in a shimmering doublet of cloth of gold and silver embroidery, the strident king rode into the tiltyard with his new device: a man's heart in a press engulfed in crimson and amber flames. His new motto: *Declare Je Nos – Declare, I Dare Not –* an ironic motto for such an obvious message. If the image of the king's flaming heart wasn't enough, the costumes worn by his challengers underscored his point. They came trotting out behind him, garbed in rich green velvet doublets with matching hearts aflame. Their design also included a shapely feminine hand holding aloft a pot of water raining down silver droplets to cool the lusty fires of desire.

Anne was beside herself with rage at the king's flagrant display. "What is he thinking?" she seethed as we sat watching the tournament from the queen's gallery. "I will not follow the path that my sister so brazenly blazed before me. He must not think much of me if he believes I will lie on my back and give him more bastards…And for what? Mary was lucky to have a man like William Carey, but I want something more for myself. I won't be anyone's spoilt goods, not even the king's."

Not wanting to cause a scene in the presence of the queen, I seized the opportunity to change the subject quickly. "How does your sister fare?" I asked. "I haven't seen her since she went into confinement. I'm sure William happily anticipates his first natural child."

"More than anticipation! It's all William has spoken of since Mary felt the quickening," she replied with a tinkling laugh. "I do hope he gets a little boy. William has been a good husband to my sister and an even better father to Catherine, even though he's had no cause to be. He deserves a small measure of happiness."

Anne and I left talk of Mary and her family behind us and turned our attention to the action on the field as the jousts got underway. George would not be jousting at the tilt, but I still held my breath at each break of the lance, praying he would avoid the showers of jagged wood from his position in the lists. The competition was fierce, and many of the contenders limped away after a brutal unhorsing to lick their wounds. A lump of dread had taken up residence in my throat since the tournament began and I couldn't shake my sense of unease.

"Oh! There's my cousin!" Anne squealed. She pointed towards Sir Francis Bryan as his jet black destrier strode onto the course. Sir Francis was one of the most accomplished jousters and his participation always ensured a great show. I looked across the field to see who would be challenging him, but I didn't recognise the armour. I felt pity for whoever it was because he was sure to come out worst in the contest. Anne and I held our breath as the two contenders charged towards each other, bodies taut, bracing for the blow. The sickening crack of the lances made my stomach lurch. Sir Francis' armour muffled the sound of his scream, but it was loud enough that we knew something had gone terribly wrong. A fearful muttering rippled through the crowd when three men ran out to drag the lifeless body from the muddy field. The challenger tentatively removed his helmet and revealed the bewildered face of Sir Henry Norris.

"A terrible, terrible accident," George moaned later that night in our bedchamber. "A sliver of wood went straight through his visor, blinding him! The blood was streaming from his eye in such a repulsive manner that I could barely look at it. He's going to be like Sir John Russell with his bloody eye patch. His jousting career is over, and to Norris of all people."

I had always been fond of the friendly and gracious Norris, so I felt compelled to come to his defence. "Norris is a fair jouster; it is no shame to lose to him. It's not as if he meant any harm to Sir Francis."

George turned away from the fire and gave me an inquisitive look. "Does my wife harbour a fondness for the king's new Groom of the Stool? He gains a bit of power and rises higher in your favour? Have I declined in your eyes since my demotion?" My husband's face betrayed no signs of anger, only impudent curiosity, but his accusation stung me all the same. I had never given George any reason to believe that I craved power, and his insinuation insulted me.

"How could you say such a thing? Have I done nothing but encourage you for these past weeks?" I held George's gaze until he turned back to the glowing flames dancing within the hearth. An uncomfortable silence hung in the air, but I refused to break it. He could stew in his jealousy for all I cared. I tucked my hair into my linen nightcap, crawling into bed without bidding him good night.

I rolled away from the blinding morning sunlight streaming in through the open window when I awoke the next morning, expecting to find George sleeping soundly with his arm thrown over his face like he always did, but his side was empty. In the soft dent he usually occupied, I found a long-stemmed carnation and a slip of parchment with '*I am sorry, please forgive me*' written on it.

The king's amorous pursuit of Anne intensified into the late spring. Each day brought a new excuse to visit the queen's rooms. When he couldn't manoeuvre himself close to Anne without drawing undue attention, his eyes caressed her body from across the room. Every night, he sent George to the Boleyn family rooms with some costly trinket for his sister. The costliest of these gifts, a set of four gold brooches, were engraved with symbols of love. The brooches, along with everything else, were always returned upon delivery with a gracious refusal from Anne.

Upon returning from his third march back to the king with a rejected gift in hand, an exasperated George plopped down on a cushion in front of his sister with groan. "Mary already employed this tactic. It didn't work then so what makes you think it will work now?"

"I know," she replied tartly. "That is why I'm returning to Hever for the summer. Once I am out of his sight, he can shift his attentions to someone more welcoming of his affections. There are plenty of other maids who would be more than satisfied to warm his bed."

At the time, Anne's reasoning seemed sound. The king's affairs were relatively fleeting events; he usually tired of them once he fulfilled his conquest. The fact that he had held Mary in his graces for so long surprised all of us, but even she was duly set aside when her pregnancy ended and the baby was born a girl. We all anticipated the king moving on once Anne retired to the country, but her absence only seemed to stoke his desire even more. I spent the sultry evenings of the summer in an empty bed while George travelled between Hever and the various palaces we repaired to during the annual progress, delivering messages of love between his sister and the king.

I was thrilled to see George when we finally arrived in the Kent countryside for a few days repast at the Boleyn manor. Though we had already been married for over a year, my courses continued to arrive consistently each month. It was hardly surprising I had yet to conceive; George and I had not spent many nights together in the past few months, and the opportunities to come together had been sporadic. However, the separation was frequently a blessing in some ways. My affinity for George had grown, but I still found myself shying away from his affections. It's true I stopped seeing him as a boor, but more effort was needed to overcome our past. I hoped fulfilling my most important wifely duty, and providing George with an heir, would be a momentous step forward. Perhaps this time together was all that we needed.

Any hope I had for intimacy with George faded away when I saw how exhausted he was. Feeling ragged from so many days on the road, my husband collapsed into bed and drifted off into a deep slumber on our first night together. The journey made me restless so, while he peacefully slept, I perused his personal library. George treasured books, and he kept them in pristine condition; they were all lined up perfectly on shelves like little soldiers. I ran my fingers across their soft leather spines looking for something light that might tempt me to sleep. One manuscript bound in red leather titled *The Book of Gladness* caught my eye; I pulled it from the shelf, then tumbled onto a cushion near the fire.

The book was a French translation and refutation of a poem written centuries ago satirising marriage, but as I read further, I realised that it was more of a treatise in defence of women. The author argued that women were worthy of man's love and unfairly criticised as a whole for the actions of only a few. Above all, he denounced physical and sexual violence against women. As I read the words of Jehan Lefèvre, I thought of the first night I spent with George and how insistent he was at receiving my permission before claiming his conjugal rights. My husband had obviously taken Lefèvre's words to heart, and now that I knew his actions were honest and not some veiled manoeuvre of seduction, it endeared him even more to me.

When my eyes finally began to droop, I rose from the cushion and took the book back to the shelf, careful to leave it just as I had found it. Before padding over to my side of the bed, I knelt beside George. I brushed my lips against his supple cheek in a tender kiss, inhaling the spicy musk of his sleep, then I climbed in next to him, moulding my body close to his.

The torrents of rain plaguing the progress thus far seemed to pass by Kent, so George chaperoned Anne during romantic walks with the king in the orchard, and thrilling hunts in the surrounding parks. I found my husband's devotion to his family admirable, even though was drained by the time he returned to me. Thomas Boleyn spared little expense hosting the king, treating us to the richest foods and the best wines during our stay. Even Mary, recently churched after the birth of her son, gleefully joined in on the fun. While Anne and the king kept George busy, I occupied myself in the nursery. Mary rocked baby Henry while I played on the floor with Catherine. The little girl's shock of red hair had grown into a halo of golden strawberry curls and her eyes had darkened into the deep amber colour of her uncle's. Mary closed her eyes as she rocked her baby boy, basking in the warm sunlight from the window. She appeared more content than I had ever seen her.

"Are you happy, Mary?" I asked, redirecting Catherine to a wooden horse when she attempted to jam her saliva streaked thumb into my mouth. Mary's humming quieted as she curled her lips into a satisfied smile. She didn't even open her eyes to answer me.

"Yes."

Anne remained at Hever when the court returned to the city. The king had been unsuccessful in his quest to make her his official mistress, but his efforts did not go totally unrewarded: my sister-in-law had finally softened in her stance. Anne refused to be his mistress, but she agreed to accept his gifts and promised that she would not only read, but also respond, to his letters. I knew this meant that George would have to continue to be their intermediary, but this time, I would have Mary to keep me company while he was gone.

December 1526 –
February 1527
Greenwich

WE OBSERVED the Advent season at Greenwich in high spirits. Queen Catherine appeared overjoyed by the return of her daughter from the far reaches of the Welsh marches, and the king was thrilled to finally be receiving encouragement from Anne. The season was particularly special for George and me for the best reason of all, we had finally conceived.

It wasn't until mid-November that I realised I had not felt the cramping and discomfort of my monthly courses in quite some time. I ran directly to Mary's rooms to share my joyful news when the meaning of its absence dawned on me. While George was away at Hever, we formulated a plan to tell him, enlisting the help of William to accomplish our task. Mary told me of the ancestral ivory horn her father had inherited from the Ormonde side of his family. It was tradition to grant it to the heir and Thomas eagerly anticipated passing it along to George, but was reluctant to do so until George had an heir of his own. It would take some convincing on Mary's part, and I was hesitant to share my pregnancy with my father-in-law before enlightening George, but I knew that presenting him with the coveted horn would make my announcement all the more meaningful. William eagerly accepted his mission. He arrived at Hever, with a letter from Mary, just after George returned to court. Thomas was hesitant to part with the relic; he wanted to be the one to present it to George. Fortunately, his wife and daughter took up my cause, badgering him into submission. When William returned victoriously, Mary tucked it away until the timing was right.

On the eighth day of December we celebrated the Feast of the Immaculate Conception, a solemn and holy remembrance of the conception of the Virgin Mary, mother of Jesus. George and I returned to our room after supper in the great hall; both of us feeling subdued after spending most of the day in the chapel, hearing masses and offering prayers. I quietly followed George through the doorway to our presence chamber. He removed his cap, casually tossing it onto the bed, then he started to pull his doublet off. I held my breath, waiting for him to notice the small ivory horn I had paid a servant to slip onto the table next to his side of the bed while we were out.

"Jane?" He called out in a wavering, uncertain voice.

"Hmm?" I quickly turned my back to him, pretending to busy myself with the ties of my clothing. Within minutes, I felt his breath caress my neck and his arms wrap around me; I saw the horn clasped tightly in his hand.

"Is it true?" he whispered, his face alight with joy. He carefully placed the family heirloom on the mantle above the hearth, returning to embrace me, his lips crashing against mine.

After the traditional gift exchange, Cardinal Wolsey staged an elaborate feast for the New Year. During the masque, he set loose a boom of cannon fire, sending the royal lap dogs skittering out of the room. George and I waited in blissful anticipation for the quickening of our child, but I never felt the overwhelming nausea that Mary cautioned would come, nor the early fluttering she described. I tried not to worry overmuch because each pregnancy progressed differently, but I couldn't rid myself of the sense that things were not happening as they should. I realised my fears when a rip of pain in my belly tore me from my dreams in the dead of night on the eve of Candlemas.

"What is it, Sweetheart?" George asked when my cry of agony brought him stumbling out of his dreams. His voice was groggy, thick with sleep.

"It hurts, George!" I shrieked through my sobs. My womb was rent by such a sharp pain, I was certain that it had cleaved in two.

George hurled himself from the bed; his eyes were wide and his hair wild. He yanked the counterpane from the bed, revealing a crimson stain spreading across the sheets. The sight sent me into a frenzy; my husband could do nothing, except hold me as I screamed my throat raw.

MARCH – AUGUST 1527
GREENWICH

GEORGE DUTIFULLY mopped up the blood after I calmed down, then wrapped me tightly in his arms while I sobbed, but he was beside himself with this new display of emotion from me. I had always been so stoic and reserved in the past, and I loathed showing him any vulnerability. He was attentive and kind, but the loss of our child rendered us both helpless. When it seemed that I only grew more bereft, he sent me to my mother at Hallingbury.

Lady Morley knew all too well the devastation of miscarriage. "You're fortunate that the babe had barely begun, it's far worse when they come only a month or two before their time; after you have become attached to the flailing butterfly inside your womb," she said. "Have no fear, darling daughter; healthy children will come in time."

I tried to take solace in her words. My mother had suffered several miscarriages in the past, and George had once informed me that not all of his siblings had thrived, but both of our mothers had three healthy children grow into adulthood. Surely my miscarriage was only a chance occurrence, not an omen for the future.

I returned to court in April after my recuperation in time to celebrate a new treaty, signed between His Grace and the French King, negotiating the release of the Dauphin. The heir of King Francis, along with his brother, had been held for ransom in the custody of the Emperor since their father was defeated at the Battle of Pavia two years past. Francis had yet to secure the freedom of his sons, so he called upon our king, who was now in the unenviable position of taking sides against the family of his wife. The fact that King Henry had enlisted Cardinal Wolsey to investigate the possibility that his marriage to the Emperor's aunt,

Catherine of Aragon, was invalid served to make the situation even worse.

His Grace welcomed Anne for the May Day festivities in grand style. She would no longer reside in the apartments her family occupied because he had gifted her with her own sumptuous rooms. When I arrived to greet her, she dragged me through each doorway, gushing over the intricate tapestries hanging on the walls and shoving me into chairs covered in fine damasks dyed in the richest hues of emerald and indigo.

"I have to be truthful with you, Anne," I said, trailing my fingers down the gorgeous new sleeves adorning her gown; yet another gift from the king. The delicate seed pearls sewn into the cloth of gold felt smooth to the touch. "I am clean amazed you gave in to the king's demands."

Anne shot me a heated look. "I did no such thing," she replied, yanking her arm away.

"But all these gifts…What else could they mean?" I gestured at the luxury surrounding us.

Anne strode angrily towards the window overlooking the Thames. The river was awash in the brightly hued banners that rippled atop the noble family barges making their way to the palace. "I thought you would be pleased," she huffed, crossing her arms protectively across her chest. "I didn't do anything wrong. I merely did what I promised, I read his letters. Through them, I realised that I had misjudged his intentions, just as you are misjudging mine."

I slid next to her sulking form in the embrasure. She stiffened, but didn't ask me to move. We stood in stony silence, staring at the rainbow of barges stretched across the river. When she finally relaxed, I gently pushed my elbow against her. "You know I only want you to be happy, Anne. You seemed so set against this from the beginning and I am just surprised at your change of heart."

Anne brushed a tear from the corner of her eye. "The king changed my heart," she said. He has made me happier than I ever thought I could be. In time I hope I can return the favour he has shown me by giving him something the queen cannot – a son."

Son – the word inspired a hollow ache within me. I slumped against Anne, fighting back the tears burning behind my eyes. "Oh, Jane," she soothed, rubbing her hands briskly across my back. "I truly am sorry. I didn't mean anything by it, I promise. It was awful when George came back to Hever to return that cursed relic to Father; we were all incredibly heartbroken. Your son will come, Jane. He will come, and he will be a credit to the Boleyn name, just have patience with God."

That night, I cornered George when he returned to our rooms. "Why didn't you tell me Anne was Henry's mistress?" I demanded, my hands balled into fists at my hip. How could he have withheld this from me? I was his wife!

George shot me a puzzled look, then sat down to remove his riding boots. He pulled off the first one, stretched his toes, and then looked back up at me with a sheepish grin. "Anne is not the king's mistress," he replied with a chuckle. "Anne is going to be his wife."

The king wanted to marry Anne? Impossible! The king already had a wife. His lie incensed me further. "Are you mad?" I spat at him. "Don't let anyone hear you say that!"

George's brow furrowed. "Why are you so upset, Jane? I swear on my honesty. The king promised Anne he would marry her, once the Pope concedes that his marriage to Catherine was unlawful."

"When did we start calling our anointed queen by her Christian name? I don't believe any of this."

George drew himself to his full height. He placed his cool hand against my hot cheek, probing my eyes with his own. I longed to pull away from his touch, to reach out and slap the look of patronising concern from his face.

"Jane, I apologise. I wanted to tell you – truly I did, but you were terribly distraught after the baby, and I couldn't bring myself to do it. You still grieved, and I respected that."

"Didn't you grieve, George?" I sniffed.

He pulled me closer, enveloping me in the earthy scent of leather and oak. "Of course I did, Jane – of course, I did," he murmured into my hair. He held me for a moment, and when he pulled back, he tucked my hair behind my shoulder. "We have to move forward, Jane. I'm devastated, but I cannot give in to self-pity and neither can you. Anne needs our support, and she deserves your loyalty. Catherine will not go quietly. His Grace is in for a fight he may not win. He thinks it will be easy, that it is just a simple matter of Biblical Law. But Catherine is proud, and she comes from a very powerful family who will not look kindly upon her mistreatment."

His words filled me with fear. I adored the queen; she was kind and beloved, pious and generous. How could the king do this to her? How could I do this to her? Anne was my family now, and I loved her as well. I wanted her to be happy and knew she had the potential to be an admirable queen, but I would have to betray the woman I had faithfully served for almost a decade.

"Are you certain there is no other way?" I whispered in a daze.

"Come, Jane," George gently guided me to the bed. Rather than call my maid in, he carefully loosened the laces on my stomacher, then helped me out of my layers of clothing. He carried them all over to the closet and returned with a linen nightgown. I raised my arms so he could slip the cool fabric down around them, then allowed him to tuck me into bed. "A new world is coming, my love. And it will be greater and brighter than you ever imagined," he breathed.

My Love – it was the first time my husband had ever called me that.

George had already gone by the time I awoke the next morning, so I stayed under the quilt and savoured the quiet emptiness of the room until my chamberer bustled in. When she threw open the curtains, the brilliant morning light chased away the darkness. I broke my fast with some dried fruit and manchet, followed by a swig of small ale. My maid entered a few moments later to dress me for the day. I met Mary and the other maids in the queen's chambers, then we all solemnly processed to the chapel for mass and morning prayers. After our devotions, we traipsed out the tennis courts for an afternoon diversion. When Mary and I took our seats in the queen's viewing gallery, it felt discomfiting to see Anne set apart from us.

George was a keen tennis player, and quite pleased that the king had chosen to partner him in a match against Thomas Wyatt, who had just returned from the embassy in Rome, and the Duke of Suffolk. I felt a surge of pride watching his agile form hustle across the court, and I hardly dared to tear my eyes from him. The competition was fierce, and it was obvious after only a few rounds that both the duke and the king were getting winded by their exertions. Never one to accept defeat, the king continued the match until one wrong step sent him sprawling to the ground.

The crowd held its collective breath waiting for an explosive reaction, but it never came. Instead, the king released a great bellow of laughter. "'Tis nothing! Merely a scratch!" he cried, waving off the pages anxiously crowded around him. Once he managed to hoist himself up from the ground, he threw his hands in the air to show us all was well, offering up a humble bow. "Master Carey," he called out, beckoning William onto the court. "Please finish my game. Don't let those two scoundrels win." He clapped Mary's husband on the back with a wink, then limped out of sight.

Despite the king's injury, the sporting events continued the next day in the tiltyard. Rather than dance on a swollen and painful ankle, His Grace joined the queen and her ladies in the viewing gallery, playing gracious host to the French ambassadors while he watched the tournament from his throne. After Nicholas Carew won the day, we all gathered together at the new banqueting house, where the angelic choir voices of the Chapel Royal greeted us. Not since the meeting in Guînes had I seen anything quite so luxurious or awe-inspiring as the king's new pleasure house. Lilies wrought of golden thread blossomed down the crimson silk carpeting the floor beneath our feet, and a painting of the world as seen through the eyes of the king's artist, Hans Holbein, stretched across the ceiling above us.

The wonderment of the evening continued with a lavish banquet, during which bowls of the rarest exotic spices were passed around to tickle our noses. Later, I floated across the floor in the arms of my husband, while glimmering stars and the constellations of the zodiac swirled across the transparent cloth suspended above us. We celebrated throughout the night, lost in the heady pleasure and hazy glow of the torches, until the rays of the early morning sun crept through the painted windows. The spell we had all fallen under broke when a page burst in with the devastating news that the Emperor had sacked Rome and taken the Pope as his hostage.

The king waited until Anne had returned to Hever after the last of the May Day celebrations to deliver a blow that shook the very foundation of his queen's world. The news that he was embarking on an investigation into to the legality of their marriage came as a shock to everyone but Mary and me. Everyone knew the king was unhappy in his marriage and that he entertained the idea of an annulment, but no one truly believed he would set aside a woman as esteemed as Queen Catherine. The fact that her powerful nephew continued to hold the Pope under his sway made the idea seem all the more preposterous. In all the time that I had served Queen Catherine, I never once saw her give into her emotion, so the sight of her extreme distress unsettled me to the core.

George attempted to comfort me when I returned to our rooms that evening tense and on edge from the scene I had just witnessed, but he didn't understand why I was so angry. He believed it was all for the best. With Anne as Queen, our family would be in a far grander position, and she would give the king an heir to secure the realm. Catherine was far too old now, her chances of pregnancy diminishing with every passing day. His platitudes merely served to make me feel worse. I, too, aged with every sunset, and our union was proving even less fruitful than the royal marriage. George winced as though I had physically struck him when I asked if he would also set me aside for failing to give him an heir.

"Jane, there is no need to be quite so dramatic. We've hardly spent enough time together; that's all. There is no reason to believe that you won't conceive again. I would never leave you, and I'm rather insulted that you think I would."

George appeared so sincere, but how could I believe him? Queen Catherine was being sent away because of his sister. Was I so wrong to worry that I could be as easily expendable?

AUGUST 1527 TO AUGUST 1528
BEAULIEU, RICHMOND, GREENWICH, WINDSOR, AND WALTHAM ABBEY

DURING THE annual summer progress through the countryside, I saw just how isolated I had become. When Wolsey's New Year ordinances revoked my brother's position at court, he had returned to Hallingbury to manage the family lands, and many months had passed since I last visited our parents. George's family was the only one near, and I realised rather quickly that since I had spent all my time with his sisters, I'd failed to form relationships with any of the other women in the queen's service. I grew increasingly nervous without any outlet to confide my fears. I hid my angst from George, but he wasn't a fool. My affection for him seemed to be waning, and my failure to respond to his touch only added to my discomfort. The more I rebuffed George's advances, the further the likelihood of conceiving a child diminished.

The cardinal sailed off to France on a mission to garner support from their king in July. Anne joined us on progress at Beaulieu in August for a month of merriment with the king. The couple awoke each morning at the break of dawn to ride out on the hunt. During the evening hours, George and his father supped with them in the privy chamber, no doubt strategizing the king's nullity suit with the Dukes of Norfolk and Suffolk. Anne continued on with us to the next stop at Richmond, where she sat in audience with the king as he welcomed the cardinal back from his journey.

Thrilled with the French King's pledge of support, King Henry dispatched a party of nobles to France with a collar and habiliments to induct him into the Order of the Garter. When the French knot embroidered cloth of silver mantle and collar of the Order of St. Michael arrived in return, we entertained the French ambassadors once again in the pleasure house at

Greenwich. After an extravagant banquet, they moved on to the disguising chamber which had been decorated with two silk trees, one each of hawthorn and mulberry, representing England and France. A fountain wrought of marble and gold sat nestled between the trees, ringed by benches trimmed with rosemary entwined golden braids. Mary and I, along with six other maidens costumed in gowns of silver tinsel and cloth of gold, served as pretty decoration upon the benches while we observed a great play extolling the virtues of the cardinal in his efforts to free the Pope and the sons of the French king from the tyranny of the Emperor. The king made a hasty exit during the masking that followed so he could return, richly garbed and accompanied by a jubilant band of his favourite courtiers, to rescue the maidens and lead us off on a merry dance.

Queen Catherine sat nestled in her grand throne throughout the entirety of this spectacle designed to insult her nephew with a beatific smile on her face. The king may have made his intentions known, but until approval arrived from the Pope for the annulment, all appearances must be kept up. King Henry insisted it was merely his conscience and nothing else moving him to question the validity of his marriage. If his conscience could be satiated, he had no intention of setting aside his wife. Until then, he played the diligent husband, even as his servant, Dr Knight, quietly hurried back from Rome with the dispensation allowing him to marry Anne once he was free. In keeping with tradition, Queen Catherine also presided over the upcoming Christmas festivities while the fierce and bitter winds of winter blew Anne and her mother back to Hever.

My quiet footsteps were accompanied by the lilting notes of George's lute spilling out into the darkness of the corridor. When I finally arrived at the door to our rooms, I stood quietly for a moment, listening to the rise and fall of two baritone voices singing in harmony. My eyes were watering, and my hands throbbed from the strain of having spent much of the day embroidering shirts in the queen's presence chamber, so the prospect of a visitor was less than appealing. I whispered a silent prayer that whomever George entertained at this late hour kept him occupied so that I could retire to bed early.

I saw Thomas Wyatt lounging against a cushion in front of the bright hearth when I cracked open the door. He closed his eyes and tilted his head back for the mournful tone easing from his throat. An empty bottle of wine and two pewter cups rested near his hand. My husband reclined in his favourite chair. He had one long leg dangling over the side, and the other stretched out before him. At my entrance, his hands stilled against the strings of the lute sitting in his lap.

"Good evening, Jane," he greeted, with a lazy grin. Looking down at Wyatt, he declared, "Thomas, isn't my wife looking rather beautiful tonight?"

"I've yet to see her when she hasn't," Wyatt murmured without opening his eyes.

I dismissed them with a wave before bustling towards the bedchamber. "I think you've both had too much wine. Goodnight, George, I shall see you in the morning."

In my haste to flee, I forgot to call for my maid. I contemplated going back out into the presence chamber but doubted I would succeed in escaping so cleanly again. No, I would just have to manage on my own. As I started loosening the ties holding my stomacher in place, I heard Wyatt muttering to George through the cracks of the closed door. "Whatever have you done, George? I don't think the coldest breath of winter could chill as much as that greeting."

George responded too low for me to hear, but they both burst into gales of laughter after he said it. Determined to ignore them, I struggled out of my layers of clothing and into my linen nightgown. Thankfully, the chamberers had been in before I arrived so a cheery fire already danced in the hearth and the bed was cosy from the warming bricks. I climbed beneath the turned down counterpane, eager to sleep away the rest of the evening. I ignored the noise outside my bedchamber, but snatches of their song slipped, unbidden, beneath my door. The first lines of the song sounded innocent enough: *My lute, adieu, perform the last labour that thou and I shall waste and end that I have now begun; for when this song is sung and past, my lute be still, for I have done.*

'*Yes, please be still lute, for I have heard enough,*' I groaned to myself, burrowing deeper under the blanket to drown out the sound.

Then the lyrics turned a bit more personal: "*My song may pierce her heart as soon, should we then sing, or sigh, or moan… The rock doth not so cruelly repulse the waves continually, as she my suit and affection.*"

Was George singing about me?

"*Proud of the spoil that thou hast got; of simple hearts, thorough loves shot. By whom, unkind, though has them won; Think not he hath his vow forgot, although my lute and I have done.*"

He *was* singing about me! I had never forgotten his vows. If anyone had forgotten them, it was him. While I was alone, he did everything he could to help the king set aside his wife. Did the promise to love and cherish a wife end when she failed to give him a son? If that were true, it would only be a matter of time before George found someone to replace me. I fought back the urge to charge out and confront him in front of Wyatt because no good would come of it. His words infuriated yet tormented me at the same time, but I could do nothing. I slipped out of bed, plodding across the room to the closet, then dug through the pile of fabric until I found the familiar grey cloak I had buried so long ago. I held the supple velvet against my face, crying as I thought of the man who gave it to me. I had never felt more alone; I desperately needed a friend.

The court retired to the palace at Windsor in March so the king could hunt in the nearby park. Anne and her mother arrived from the countryside shortly afterward to join us. The king was so happy to see his sweetheart that he spent every available moment with her. One particularly lovely day, after a morning hunt with the new greyhound the king had bestowed upon her, Anne invited George and me to join the lovers for a picnic in the park. We toasted a successful hunt with the finest Gascony wine, then dined on a supper of cold lamb and pheasant. Anne appeared so blissful and content when she closed her eyes and held her mouth open for the king to feed her sugared almonds during the dessert course. I yearned to feel the same joy and excitement, but the guilt I felt for Queen Catherine dampened my spirits. The remorseful look George aimed at me made me feel even worse. The rapturous way in which Anne and the king behaved only served to make the strain in our marriage even more obvious.

While Anne was at court, I learned to balance my time between my duties with the queen and stolen moments with the woman who was to replace her. George never told his sister of our disagreement, nor how I reacted when he broke the news to me of her intended marriage to King Henry, so it was easy to pretend that everything was fine. Anne included Mary and me when His Grace entertained her, and we both plied her with words of admiration over the beautiful tokens of love that George often delivered to her rooms on his behalf. Anne's collection of jewels grew significantly over the tenure of their courtship, and I felt envious of the sparkling diamonds and brilliant gemstones she used to trim her already sumptuous gowns. Mary and I dutifully echoed her contented sighs each time she held out her hand to admire the glimmering emerald betrothal ring that graced her long, tapered finger.

Passion enhanced Anne physically. She had been quite thin and angular for as long as I had known her, but the rich foods she consumed with the king nourished the soft curves she began emphasising in her apparel. Her cheeks were full and permanently rosy, and the hint of a smile always played across her dainty blush-coloured lips as though she were hiding some marvellous secret, of which only she was privy. Anne's gleaming black eyes had always been beautiful, but now they sparkled in perpetual delight. George's sister was as joyful and as beautiful as I had ever seen her. I felt torn between resentment for the way Anne had somehow slipped between the king and his wife, and desire for inclusion in this new life she had made. When that desire welled up inside me, I always met it with disgust; disgust with the king and disgust with myself for wanting any part of it.

A blustery sodden spring tempest brought with it an outbreak of smallpox and the perennial threat of plague. Thomas Wyatt's mistress, Elizabeth Darrell, was the first to complain of a sharp pain in her head. Growing ever more restless as the day went on, she was dismissed to the maids' dormitory to recover, shortly before supper. By the next morning, a mass of angry red lesions had erupted across her ruddy skin. Within hours, two maids more complained of torturous pain, accompanied by dangerously high fever. The outbreak of smallpox abated within weeks only to have an eruption of the dreaded sweating sickness replace it. There was no way to predict who the deadly disease would target, but it struck quickly and indiscriminately. Once infected, a man could be dead in mere hours. Nothing could cure it and very little could be done to prevent it. Any illness mortified the king, no matter the severity; news that his dear sweetheart had been exposed to the sweat by the death of her maid sent him fleeing the city in alarm. Only the most indispensable servants were chosen to accompany him in order to contain the threat of infection. As cupbearer, George was included in this select band. William Carey's presence was deemed unnecessary, so he and Mary retired to their property at Plashey, while Anne and her parents fled to the Kent countryside. I dutifully followed along in the queen's train. If George was going, so was I.

George was inconsolable when word arrived that Anne had fallen victim. The king sent his personal physician, Dr Butts, to Hever to care for her, but even that failed to soothe my husband's worried mind. George ate very little, and fretful dreams haunted him at night. I tried to console him, assuring him that Dr Butts wouldn't let Anne die, but he became even more distraught to learn that his father had also succumbed to the disease. When he returned from the king's privy chamber complaining of a headache, I felt the sharp knife of dread pierce my heart.

I tested my husband's forehead for a fever, but his skin felt cool to the touch. George insisted he wasn't hungry, but I sent my maid for hot broth anyway, then stood guard as he meekly slurped the steaming liquid. Satisfied that he had imbibed enough, I stripped him out of his doublet and hose, then eased him into bed. As George drifted off to sleep, my maid prepared me to join him before slipping quietly around the room to blow out the candles.

When I awoke in the night, disoriented and drenched in perspiration, my hands searched my face for the tell-tale burn of fever. My skin felt moist, but not hot; however, the consolation of that discovery disintegrated into a panic when I realised that it was George covered in sweat. I vaulted out of bed, tearing the counterpane off in the process, as I ran to my husband's side. His face shined slick with perspiration, his cheeks burning bright with fever. "George! George! Wake up!" I cried, shaking him desperately. George merely groaned in his sleep, turning from me. "Please, George," I begged. "I need you to speak to me. I need you to wake up."

I searched the room for anything to fight the fever and spied the jug of water that my maid brought in for washing the previous morning. I ran over to the table where it sat, and shoved my hand inside of it. To my relief, it was still half-full, and the water had chilled overnight. I grabbed the linen rag next to it and dunked it in. Goose pimples spread up my arm as the cool water splashed across my skin. Water slopped from the jug when I dashed back to the bed to wipe the sweat from George's face. The heat from the fever burned through the linen to my hand after only a few brief moments against his forehead. My strong, robust husband seemed to have shrunk overnight. Pain caused his body to curl inward, and a new spate of sweat spread across his grey skin. I didn't know how to save him, so I bolted from the room in search of help.

"Help! Someone, please help me!" I shouted hysterically, my cries echoing down the deserted hallway. "Anyone – please I need a doctor!" I pounded my fist on every door down the corridor.

At the end of the hall, I turned back around, running headfirst into Cardinal Wolsey's secretary, Sir Brian Tuke. He stepped back carefully, placing his hands upon my shoulders. "What is it, Mistress Boleyn? What is the matter?" Lines of concern etched his face.

"It's George," I cried. "He is burning up and soaked in sweat. I don't know what to do. Please, please fetch me a doctor."

Sir Brian patted my arm. "Everything will be all right, my dear. I will find someone to help you." Several doors flew open, my cries having woken the entire wing from their dreams. "No one panic," Sir Brian intoned in an authoritative voice. "Master Boleyn has caught the sweat. Stay in your rooms and guard yourselves against the disease. I will get the doctor, and all will be well."

I was grateful Sir Brian had taken control, but his words didn't fill me with great confidence. If George had the sweat, all would not be well; while I stood helplessly in the corridor, George laid in bed on the precipice of death. Sir Brian turned his attention to me once the others scurried back into their rooms. "Jane, you must go. Since you've already been exposed, you must stay away from the king and queen. Do not go back to your room, the threat is far too great."

What was he saying? Leave George? No, I would never leave George, especially not now. I pushed Sir Brian away. "Please just call for the doctor," I pleaded. Sir Brian shook his head, then ambled down the corridor.

George was curled up in a ball of misery by the time I returned to our bedchamber. I rushed over and wrapped my arms around him. "Please don't die, George. Please don't leave me, I need you." Tears streamed from my eyes, mixing with the beads of sweat that pooled on his face. The regrets of the last year flooded my mind as I held his limp, lifeless body.

I'd behaved terribly towards him for something he could not have helped. He had done nothing to make Anne and the king fall in love, and they concocted their plans for the future without his help or inducement. My husband bore no ill-will for Queen Catherine, and I couldn't fault him for seizing the opportunity to provide a more stable life for us. George continued to be nothing but kind to me even as I spurned him. He was devastated when I had confronted him over the song he composed with Thomas Wyatt. I completely disregarded his explanation that he and Wyatt composed it together when Wyatt complained to him of his unrequited love for Anne. He'd seemed sincere, but I had refused to forgive him so easily. I was cold and disdainful to him, and now he was caught between life and death. "Please God," I prayed silently. "Don't let him die. I promise I will change, please just let him live." I knelt against George until I felt strong hands pulling me away.

"Jane, you must go. Get out of here," muffled voices instructed while I flailed from their grasp.

"No, I won't leave! You will have to drag me from this room!" I screamed. The hands came around my shoulders, and I felt myself being pulled across the floor and out into the presence chamber.

Sir Brian handily threw me into a chair near the darkened window. "Jane, you must do as I tell you. Dr Butts cannot help your husband if you are under his feet. If you refuse to leave, then promise me that you will stay out here until he has finished." I nodded meekly, bringing my knees to my chest so I could wrap my arms around them against the chill. Noting my discomfort, Sir Brian sent for a chamberer to relight the cold embers in the hearth.

Time stood still as I rocked back and forth in the chair, waiting for Dr Butts to come out of the bedchamber with his diagnosis. Sir Brian stood guard to keep me from bursting in on him. I nearly leapt from my chair when the physician finally shuffled out with a look of resignation. "George's fever still burns unabated, but he's lost a lot of sweat, so that is promising. I've wrapped him tightly to keep the sweat going. We must make sure he stays in his binding; we can't risk him catching a chill," he counselled. "If you insist on putting your health in jeopardy, then I am going to need you to listen to me. His sister went in much the same way; these next few hours are critical."

"Anne? Please tell me she's not...dead." His words filled me with horror. For the first time, it occurred to me that Anne suffered the effects of the same disease. Her distance from us made her illness seem unreal, and now my vibrant and charismatic friend was gone. No, it couldn't be true. My mouth filled with saliva before I vomited onto the floor. Dr Butts waited until I stopped heaving before correcting himself.

"I'm sorry, Mistress Boleyn, I misspoke. I meant to say that his illness came on in the same way as Anne's. She has recovered quite nicely, so there is hope yet for George," he said. "You must be strong for him, he needs you. In fact, he's been moaning your name in there."

I flew past Dr Butts into the bedchamber. Just as the doctor said, George was tightly bound; only his face was visible under the mound of quilts. I grabbed a clean linen rag from my clothes chest before approaching the bed to wipe the sweat from his brow. His eyes flew open at my touch, and I lost myself briefly in the dark pools. His lips were white and appeared painfully chapped, but he managed to open them long enough to say my name. "Jane," he croaked.

"Hush, George...Sleep now and everything will be better in the morning, I promise."

My promise revealed false when George's condition had not improved by daybreak. His fever continued to rage, and he could do little more than moan in agony. When Dr Butts checked on him, I begged him to do something, anything, to take away his misery. The doctor merely shook his head and reminded me that there was nothing to do but wait. I stayed with George, hardly daring to snatch even a wink of sleep. Instead, I rubbed my rosary as I paced the room, praying silently. I finally gave into my weariness as the sun sank out of sight and dragged in the chair from the presence chamber so I could rest. A tingle ran down my spine as I plunked down on the plush cushion and relaxed my body. I closed my eyes, losing myself in the sweet release. My eyelids felt heavy, and exhaustion threatened to overtake me. When I managed to pry them back open, I saw that George was finally coherent and staring at me. "Have I ever told you how beautiful you are, Jane?"

I scrambled to George, throwing my arms around him. "Only every day," I replied as I covered his face in kisses, grateful that God had chosen to give us another chance.

My husband grew stronger with each passing day, but others were not as fortunate as we were. The sweat stole the lives of not only the king's closest companion, Sir William Compton but also my brother-in-law, William Carey. Mary was now a widow with two young children to care for on her own. William Carey was a good man and a loving husband and father, but he was not wealthy, and all of his offices were soon snatched up by the greedy men scavenging the court. Mary had to come to terms with the loss of both her husband and her way of life. God blessed me by sparing my husband and saving me from a similar fate.

November 13 & 14, 1541
The Tower of London

MY THOUGHTS were hazy, and I could not quite recall what I was doing before the world fell away from me. Was I still here in this stone prison or was I dead at last and finally past my pain? I felt disconnected from my body as though floating high above it somehow, observing everything below me on a gust of wind.

"She hasn't slept much since she arrived. I heard her thrashing about in the dead of night, muttering George's name. She's struggling to keep her wits together for your sake, but being so close to the place where her husband died has resurrected her grief. I'm sure she will recover once she's rested."

The weight of Lucy's whispered words tugged on the invisible tether that tied me to my body, pulling me, unwillingly, back down to the earth. I sank heavily into my shell and laid there quietly as their words wash over me.

"I hope you're right, Lucy, right now she is in no condition for Master Secretary's questioning. She's not thinking clearly, and he will do everything he can to get her to incriminate herself and Katherine. She is more vulnerable than ever."

"Is there anything you can do, Sir John? Maybe if you let her visit George, it would help?"

"I absolutely cannot, Lucy. I fear that would make her even worse. I'll see if I can stall Wriothesley a while longer. He knows I am overwhelmed by all the new prisoners they've brought in so I think I can buy us a few hours. I'll send a messenger over. He won't be pleased, but he will wait." Gage's footsteps faded away while Lucy's shuffled closer. I felt the cool back of her hand rest briefly against my cheek, then her fingers brushing away a strand of hair from my forehead. Maybe she was right; perhaps

I just needed some sleep. I would do anything to chase away the terrified desperation haunting me since I first entered the Tower.

I saw the flicker of candlelight reflected in the darkened windows of the presence chamber when I finally opened my eyes. Bright sunlight had bathed the room when I heard the whispered conversation between my maid and my gaoler so hours must have passed since I fell asleep. To my great surprise, I noticed almost instantly that my body felt buoyant. The heaviness weighing down my shoulders had disappeared; the pain around my head had gone. I felt light and airy, invincible even. Perhaps the deep slumber truly had been all I needed; it seemed to have awakened in me a renewed sense of purpose. Surely this was the best time to call Master Secretary, now that I was ready for him.

"Lucy," I called out hesitantly before easing myself from the cushion on the floor. I couldn't remember how I had got there; Gage must have somehow guided me there in my stupor. Lucy bustled into the room just as I got to my feet. Her eyes sagged with weariness; her face was pale and drawn.

"My Lady, is everything all right? Can I get you something to drink? Perhaps something to eat? You must be famished," she fussed over me.

I held out my hand. "I'm fine, truly – I will be soon, anyway. You look exhausted, Lucy, how long have I been asleep?"

"It is almost day-break, my lady. You've slept the entirety of the day away. I was so nervous you would wake up, I haven't yet slept," she stifled a yawn. "Are you certain I can't bring you something?"

"My poor Lucy, I would love some ale if you can fetch it and would you please let Sir John know I am ready for Wriothesley? When you return, I insist that you retire for a few hours. Wriothesley won't allow you in the room during my interrogation in any case."

Lucy's eyebrows jumped, her eyes widening in surprise. "Are you certain my lady? You've had a terrible shock. It may be better if…"

I cut her off before she could finish her sentence, "Lucy, I am certain. I feel as assured as I ever will be. I am ready for this to be over…and for me to be free. It must be done." Lucy frowned in disapproval, but she dipped a low curtsey, then hurried off to find the constable.

If the tide was good, Wriothesley could be here in an hour or two, depending upon the palace from which he left. I couldn't remember where the Yeoman said the king had headed before Katherine was dragged off to Syon Abbey, but I was certain it wasn't far. He wouldn't leave the city until things settled and things wouldn't be settled until all of the witnesses had been questioned, especially the most important witness – me. I was the only one present during Katherine's stolen moments with Culpeper. Besides the two of them, it was me alone who could say for certain what went on during those secret meetings. As far as the king and his secretary were concerned that was the truth, but in truth, I knew no more than anyone else. At least that is what I told myself.

I escaped whenever Katherine met Culpeper, always straying just far enough that they slipped out of sight. I knew not what happened during the whispered words and breathy sighs behind the closed door, but I had a fairly good idea. I, too, once knew the love of a man and remembered well what caused those sounds. But *hearing is not seeing*, I reminded myself. The fact that I heard it wasn't proof that it happened. I had mere hours before Wriothesley would be here to take my statement so I needed to decide what I would tell him. Which answer assured a lighter sentence for both Katherine and me? Did it even matter? After what happened to George and Anne, I didn't believe that any answer would exonerate either of us, but I had to try. I stumbled over to the window and stared out into the darkness as I formulated my defence.

April – June 1529
Greenwich

I GREETED Anne with a new sense of appreciation upon our return to court at the end of the summer progress. I had spent so much time being angry at my dearest friend that I had missed out on sharing in the wonderful events happening in her life. I would have never forgiven myself if she had died. In October, when the king set her up at Suffolk House after the Papal Legate, Cardinal Campeggio, arrived, and I begged leave from Queen Catherine's service and left court to serve Anne there. His Grace insisted upon removing any indications that his request for an annulment had to do with anyone or anything other than his conscience. If Campeggio even suspected he had a replacement wife in mind, it would stain the king's case. Hidden away from the eyes of the court, Anne whiled away the days with all manner of frivolity in the company of her family and closest friends. She was served with such great estate it was as though she had already become a queen, and we were grateful for any diversion that kept her mind from Wolsey and the upcoming trial. The longer it dragged on, the more impatient she became.

Campeggio's first order of business, upon shuffling his old gout-ridden bones to London, was to attempt a reconciliation between the king and his wife. Anne suspected that Cardinal Wolsey instigated the preposterous idea, so His Eminence quickly became a despised subject in the Boleyn family. Neither Anne nor her father believed he was doing enough to further the king's suit, and they knew he had counselled the king to consider a French match to strengthen the foreign alliance rather than marry one of his subjects. The plodding pace of the Papal Legate only added to Anne's restlessness.

A frigid winter squall soon blew away the russet and gold leaves of autumn, and the court moved on to Richmond for the

Yuletide festivities. While the rest of the court feasted on steaming meat pies, roasted birds, and sumptuous sugared subtleties at a banquet presided over by Queen Catherine, Anne hid away in her private apartments. George and I headed to her rooms every night to share in laughter and games before the roaring fire as dainty crystal flakes of snow fluttered past the leaded windows. On New Year's Day, in addition to the gifts we exchanged and the ones received from the king, I gave George one more – tidings that I was once again with child. Jaded from the humiliation of having to return the ancestral horn, I disclosed my news with far less fanfare. George's reaction, however, was just as ecstatic as before.

My husband also had an announcement to make. In addition to his promotion to Esquire of the Body, the king had granted him the keepership of his manor at Beaulieu in Essex, a perquisite once belonging to William Carey. For now, the king used the manor as a royal residence, but we would eventually have the privilege of residing there. The prospect of making our home in such a luxurious setting overwhelmed me. Having stayed there for a month on the previous progress, I knew how sumptuous it was – even its name, Beaulieu, meant beauty. The keepership in Essex, along with the annual pension of fifty marks that George began receiving, meant that we lived comfortably; yet, my happiness was tinged with the sadness I felt for his sister. The benefits George received as the keeper of Beaulieu had once belonged to her dead husband, William.

Though Mary slowly recovered from her grief, her financial affairs remained dire. I wasn't sure why Thomas Boleyn refused to help his elder daughter, but he was adamant against it, and it was only because of the king's influence that he eventually gave in. Angered by her father's refusal to help her sister, Anne wrote to King Henry pleading Mary's case. His Grace stopped at nothing to give his sweetheart anything she desired, so he made sure Thomas followed through with financial support. I slipped Mary a handful of coins at every opportunity to mitigate my remorse for advancing at her cost. Her Boleyn pride chafed at my charity, but I was certain Mary thought of her children's future every time she accepted the handout.

As the Thames began to thaw and the Lenten season drew to a close, Cardinal Campeggio was finally forced to accept his failure to resurrect the royal marriage. Queen Catherine was told to prepare her defence, and a trial date was officially set for June at Blackfriars. The king again sent Anne from court. This time, he rented a private residence for George and me in nearby Greenwich so we could be close by for support. The house was small but cosy, and there was room for a nursery.

"George," I whined. "Can I please open them now?" George pulled me closer and brushed his lips against my neck, keeping his hand pressed tightly against my eyes.

"Not yet. You must be patient, my love," he whispered in my ear before pulling away long enough to call out to some unseen servant. "That's perfect. You can leave it right there."

I listened intently for any hint as to what George's surprise was, but I heard nothing. I half expected to hear barking. George had recently become Keeper of the King's Buckhounds and taken it into his head that we needed a dog. I was less enthusiastic about the prospect, but if that was what George wanted, I would happily abide it. I shifted nervously in my husband's embrace, waiting for the moment when he would reveal his surprise.

"Are you ready, Jane? I'm going to remove my hand now."

When I felt the weight of George's hand pull away from my face, I cautiously opened one eye, then the other. I drew a sharp breath at the sight before me. In the middle of our presence chamber, the most gorgeous cradle I had ever seen sat in a beam of sunlight. It was fashioned out of oak the colour of honey with a lion rampant carved into the headboard. A pale yellow quilt embroidered with prancing grey foxes was folded carefully inside.

"George, it's beautiful! When could you have possibly had this made?" I exclaimed as I knelt down to stroke the satiny finish, mesmerised by the way it gleamed in the sun.

"Never mind about that," George laughingly replied. "Tell me what you think of it. Are you pleased?" George's face was a mixture of excitement and anticipation. I leapt up, burying my face in the plush velvet of his doublet. I felt his chest heave in merriment. "I'll assume that means yes."

I pulled back for a moment so he could see my smile, then I pushed myself up on my toes to plant a kiss on his lips. They still tasted of the citrus fruit he ate earlier. "Of course, I love it, George, it is wonderful." I looked back down and moved my hand between us, pressing it against the small curve that had only recently begun to develop on the lower part of my abdomen. "You don't think it is too soon do you? I am scared of it all going wrong again."

George tipped my chin up to meet his eyes. "Have faith, Jane. Perhaps that baby was not truly meant to be. Everything has changed between us, and we conceived this baby because of that. I know how frightening this is. I too was worried when you first told me, but now I'm more certain than ever we shall have a beautiful babe in time for Christmas."

He seemed so confident and assured, but I could not claim to feel the same way. True, the symptoms of my pregnancy were much different this time. Every morning, I awoke with terrible nausea and my womb expanded at a steady pace. A few weeks ago I rejoiced when I felt the child's quickening. My mother assured me these were all excellent signs, but I refused to indulge myself with hope because I knew that God could call this little one back at any moment just as before.

George was right about the change between us. Those horrible days at Waltham Abbey when I feared for his life made me realise how much I needed him and how wrong I had been about him. I'd never truly believed him when he complimented me or declared his love; what reason would he have to love me?

I'd felt insignificant in comparison, for I had nothing to offer him. If I couldn't even carry his children, what use could I be? My grief blinded me and fed my already present insecurities. I found my strength in caring for him during his illness, and that was when I finally found my self-worth. George's infirmity changed the way in which I saw him. He was not perfect, nor was he invincible. He was just a man, like other men. He had talent and charisma that often surpassed our peers, but he was just as human and as frail as they were. Only a few hours of sickness could have snuffed out his life, just as it had William Carey's.

"I think if we have a girl, her name should be Anne," George murmured, startling me from my reverie.

"You want to name our baby after your sister?" I softened my jest with a playful smile.

He threw his head back with a laugh. "Of course not, I want to name her after our future queen!"

"You are ever the optimist aren't you?" I teased. "Perhaps it will be a boy, and we can name him Henry."

George wrinkled his nose. "I think I prefer the sound of George much better."

"You're so vain," I scolded as I tweaked his nose. "Of course, you like that name. Well, George, it will be, and he will be witty and intelligent just like his namesake."

"'Tis no wonder that I am vain when you flatter me so," George said, planting a kiss on my forehead. "Anne or George, it is no matter to me as long as the babe doesn't come before its time."

George's words haunted me when I awoke the next morning with a dull ache at the base of my spine. I tossed and turned, trying to get comfortable, but the pain continued to throb unabated, so I finally raised myself into a sitting position on the edge of the bed. There was no use lying there, being miserable.

"What is wrong, my love?" George asked sleepily. I gazed over my shoulder at the form of my husband twisted up in the quilts. He appeared peaceful, so I hated to disturb him.

"Have no fear; it's only a slight discomfort. Go back to sleep, George."

I quietly slipped out of the room, gently pulling the door shut behind me. The sun was shining through the oriel window in the presence chamber, while a cheery fire danced in the hearth. I smiled at the sight of the cradle in the corner and gave my belly a comforting pat. The discomfort still felt confined to my lower back, and there was no sign of the cramping I felt during my first pregnancy, perhaps all would be well. I spotted a mound of white fabric on the floor next to my chair, remembering I had discarded a shirt I was mending the day before in haste when George came in with his surprise. I gingerly bent down to pick it up, then eased myself into the chair. Finishing the shirt was the perfect way to distract me from the pain and Anne would be thrilled to add another one to the pile. My sister-in-law intended to surpass Catherine in every way, including her reputation for generosity during the Easter season. For now, there was no role for her to play in the traditional royal customs, so she took it upon herself to create an opportunity for benevolence. Always eager to use her considerable talents, she decided to put her skills with a needle to good use mending shirts for the poor. At Anne's instruction, Mary had combed through the remains of William's clothing while I collected George's cast-offs and, together, we spent the frigid winter months mending the holes so that they could be put to better use warming the city's destitute. The shirt in my hand was the last I had left to mend; if I finished soon, I could hand it, and the rest, over to Anne later in the afternoon.

I had finished my mending by the time George ambled out of the bedchamber to break his fast. He knelt beside my chair, caressing my cheek with his lips as I held the shirt up to examine my stitching. "It appears expertly done, as always," he intoned with a smile. "Anne will be pleased."

"I'll find out soon enough. With Holy Week upon us, I know she is anxious to distribute them.

George tenderly brushed the hair from my eyes, then cupped my chin in his hand, skimming the pad of his thumb against my lower lip. "Jane, you will make such a wonderful mother."

Anne rushed forward to grab the mountain of fabric I struggled to manoeuvre awkwardly through the door. "Jane, what a goodly belly you have!" she exclaimed, pulling the pile from my outstretched arms. "It seems to have popped out overnight. I only saw you two days past, and it was hardly noticeable."

"Thank you so much for taking those. They truly were not all that heavy, but I'm not feeling well today," I groaned as I gratefully handed over the bundle.

Anne strode to a bench by the window, placing the shirts she had taken from me into a pile she had already begun with her stores. I ambled over to a chair by the hearth and plunked down on the feather-stuffed cushion. I hoped that I would find relief by getting off my feet, but the pain only seemed to intensify.

"You look very pale, Sister. Are you eating enough?" Anne's brow furrowed in concern as she searched for the source of my discomfort. "Perhaps you should rest for a while."

I closed my eyes and shook my head. Even if I attempted to lie down, I knew I wouldn't get comfortable enough to sleep off the pain. Instead, I offered her a smile through clenched teeth. "I'll just have to sew right here."

"Don't have your baby in that chair!" Anne teased me with a sly grin. "You know it's my best one."

"That would be all the better – I demand only the best for your niece or nephew," I replied, forcing a strangled laugh.

Anne settled into a plush velvet cushion at my feet, then picked up a shirt she had been working on when I arrived. I shifted forward and rubbed my hand gently across her shoulders, winding my fingers through the silky cascade of her dark hair.

"Next year it will be you performing the Maundy Thursday giving."

Anne heaved a great sigh. "If only Catherine would listen to reason. She knows Henry needs an heir so why does she persist in her stubbornness? Henry would reward her beyond her imagination if she would just agree to go into a convent."

"The queen...I mean – Catherine," I quickly corrected myself. "She was borne of one of the most powerful families in Christendom. Her mother was a warrior, Anne. She could never give up so easily. The only way she will accept defeat is by a Papal pronunciation, and that will come in time. You must have patience."

Anne stopped her needle and reached back to squeeze my hand. "Thank you, Jane."

I huffed in exasperation. For what did she have to thank me? I had done nothing, save resent her cause.

"I know this hasn't been easy for you," she continued. "I know you feel as though you've compromised yourself by abandoning Catherine, but your loyalty means everything to me. Catherine will always have supporters, but if this trial does not go in our favour, I fear I will have none."

"Anne, please don't speak that way." I tried to lean forward to kiss her hand, but I couldn't manage; the discomfort was too great. "You know your family will always support you, regardless of the outcome." Before Anne could respond, her maid entered the room with sewing supplies for me, and two cups of ale.

Anne and I spent the remainder of the afternoon in the dappled sunlight discussing her plans for the future while we mended the last of the shirts. Strangely, I found myself nodding off as she chattered on. The heat from the sun warmed my face, and the lilting tone of Anne's voice seemed to lull me into a daze. It wasn't until the shirt I was working on slid off my lap, hours later, that I realised I had fallen asleep. I scanned the room for Anne, but she had gone, having abandoned her sewing in the empty cushion at my feet. I rocked forward and put my weight on my feet, but as I raised my pelvis to stand, a jagged pain tore through me and sent me back into the chair as it ripped the breath from my lungs. I sat still until I could control my breathing, then I called out for Anne. The only response I received was the deafening sound of silence.

I stayed seated for a moment longer, hoping one of Anne's servants had heard me, but when no one appeared, I knew I had to push through the agony if I wanted to stand up. I braced my hands against the arms of the chair, set my teeth, and then very carefully raised my body up from the cushion. Droplets of sweat streaked down my face at the effort. I immediately felt a gush of warm wetness rush down my leg when I finally got to my feet. I twisted back to look at the chair and stared in horror at the brilliant crimson stain streaked across the creamy damask upholstery.

"No!" I cried out, choking back the rising panic in my throat. Why was this happening again? Why did my body betray me? "Anne! Anne! Please help me!" My heart thudded hard enough to burst from my chest.

I remained hunched over; the pain was so fierce, I could hardly bear to stand. I let go of the chair and gripped my hands against the curve of my belly. The throbbing ache in my back was now accompanied by a stabbing pain deep within. I stumbled away from the chair, calling for help as I pushed my trembling legs forward. Where had everyone gone? Why had they abandoned me? I felt my hysteria rising while the world spun around me. I leaned against the wall to catch my breath, and before I could move again, the door flew open; Anne strode in with flushed cheeks, a grin stretched across her face. When she saw my pitiful state, the grin fell away, and the bouquet of brilliant blossoms she gripped in her hand dropped to the floor.

"Jane? What is wrong?" Anne rushed over and wrapped her arms around me. I heard a guttural moan escape from her lips when she peered over my shoulder. There was no point in looking back; I already knew that there was stream of blood trailing over the rushes behind me. The sound of Anne's distress drew two pages in from the kitchen as Anne's maid, Bess, bounded in through the front door. "Go get George! Do it now!" she screamed at them.

"I called for you, Anne," I whimpered against her neck, my tears streaming salty, wet tracks down her fine silk dress.

"Hush now, Jane, try not to worry," she whispered as she rubbed broad strokes down the damp curve of my back. "Come, let's get you cleaned off. Bess will get some water and meet us in my bedchamber."

With Anne's support, I shuffled down the corridor to her room, each step sending a jolt of pain through my womb. I took no comfort in her words. The likelihood of my child's survival seemed impossible now. I had lost so much blood that my hopes dimmed with every passing moment. Bess charged into the room behind us carrying a pail of hot water and a stack of linen cloths. Together they carefully undressed me, wiping away as much blood as they could, then Anne pulled a silk nightshirt over my head. Bess cautiously eased me into Anne's bed, and my world turned dark as I finally succumbed to my weariness. By the time I awoke, George had arrived with a midwife. He perched on the bed to comfort me when the agony returned as I delivered what remained of our son. I cried out at the sight of his delicate lifeless body, so tiny and perfectly formed. I cradled him in my arms, praying to feel his heart beat against mine. I screamed at the midwife as she pried him from my arms, then threw myself at George, crushing my face against his chest. He stroked my hair and whispered words of comfort in my ear, but it did nothing to relieve the raw pain in my heart. I had failed my husband yet again; worse, I had failed our innocent child. I was not strong enough to keep him alive.

June – December 1529
Bridewell, Greenwich, Westminster, and York Place

I RETURNED to our private residence once I was strong enough; it was there that I hid away, grieving for my son, during the Easter festivities. George stayed with me a few days before he was recalled to court when Anne caused a scandal. Unsatisfied by what she saw as a meagre donation of shirts to the poor, she took it upon herself to also offer them cramp rings that she had blessed. The anointed queen traditionally blessed the rings, so the move was seen as an act of arrogance on Anne's part, and the common people were in an uproar. The furore continued into the mild days of June when the Legatine Court summoned the king and queen to Blackfriars to hear evidence for Henry's nullity suit. Hordes of spectators welcomed Catherine to the proceedings with shouts of support and encouragement.

Having healed physically from my miscarriage, I journeyed to Bridewell Palace to join Anne in her seclusion during the trial. Mary and I attempted to distract her with card games and idle gossip until evening when their father and George returned with news of the day's events, but her nerves could not be tamed. Anne's anxiety wasn't for naught; Catherine had been magnificent in her defence. Even George was unable to hide his awe as he told us of her act of supplication to the king. The sight of such a noble woman on her knees before the throne reduced many in attendance to tears. When she swept out of the courtroom that day, with her loyal women behind her, she took with her any hope we had for a swift decision.

The cardinals found Catherine in contempt of court for her act of defiance and ordered her to return to Blackfriars four days later. When she failed to show, the trial continued in her absence. Though King Henry's lawyers put up a spirited case, Catherine's refusal to return to the courtroom stalled the final ruling. To

Campeggio's relief and Wolsey's chagrin, the Pope revoked their legatine authority and remanded the case back to Rome. To add further insult, the Papal Curia adjourned for the summer months; there would be no hope of resolution until late autumn at the earliest.

The king's fury was palpable. "I will not be made a fool of!" he railed during supper in Anne's apartments. "Am I not the King of England? Am I not ruler in my own lands? This decision will not stand." He was so blinded by rage that he missed the almost imperceptible nod traded between George and Anne when they locked eyes. Spurred on by her brother's encouragement, Anne took a swig of her wine, then tossed her hair over her shoulder.

"You need not abide this insult, Your Grace. False councillors have misrepresented your interests; one of them in particular who holds something dear to me."

Candlelight danced across the diamonds encrusting the king's collar as he shifted angrily in his seat. "What has that knave stolen from you, my own dear sweetheart? I will not fail to have it returned to you immediately."

Anne reached across the table, taking his hand in her own. She lazily trailed a finger down his arm, then worked her lips into a pout. "Oh, it is nothing of great importance. 'Tis merely a book, but it was given to me as a gift, and I've sorely missed it."

"How could Wolsey have come into possession of your book?" The king asked, clearly baffled that his most powerful minister would have taken the time to confiscate something so insignificant from his paramour.

George came to the table and refilled the gold cups nestled between them. "Anne lent it to her maid, Nan Gainesford, and it fell into Master Zouche's possession, where the Dean of the Royal Chapel promptly swiped it," he called out over his shoulder as he returned the wine to the oak sideboard.

Anne pressed the king's hand to her lips. "The whole episode frightened poor Nan," she told him. "I could not bear to be angry with her. I'm sure he wanted to keep it from falling into your hands. How could Nan have refused such a powerful man?"

The king indulged her with a smile. "Fear not, Sweetheart, I shall have it retrieved at once. When it is in my own hands, I shall read it myself. If it is important to you, then surely it is imperative that I read it to know your mind further."

Anne leapt from her chair and sank to her knees before the king. "You are far too good to me, Your Grace," she declared.

I could not shake my unease at the way Anne had manipulated the king. I didn't recall her lending a book to Nan, but I had been so consumed with grief over the past few months, I was not surprised that it had slipped past my attention. She and George were such keen readers, they had countless shelves lined with books, so I would never have been able to keep track of them all anyway.

"George?" I asked as I climbed into bed later. "Who gave Anne the book she spoke of this evening? She never told me that Wolsey had taken it. Surely he wouldn't have confiscated anything he didn't have cause to take."

George clambered in next to me, pulling the counterpane over us, then he leaned over and kissed my cheek. "Of course, he had reason to take it. He would never want the king to read what is in that book. It is forbidden even to have it. Anne has risked her very life asking him to retrieve it for her."

"What do you mean it is forbidden?" I asked in alarm as I struggled to sit up. "Why does she have it? Where did it come from?"

"Jane," he groaned in exasperation. "I'm far too tired to discuss this with you right now. Can we please talk about it in the morning?"

"You've just told me that your sister is risking her life! How can you expect me to sleep? How can you sleep? You know I hate secrets, George."

George inhaled deeply before raising himself up against the wooden headboard; his bare shoulder brushed against mine. "I can sleep, dear wife, because I know the king. Once he reads that book, he will fall over himself in appreciation that we have handed him the ammunition he needs against the Pope. The book will expose the trial for the sham that it is, and the king will declare his marriage invalid himself." He turned his head, catching my eyes with his own. "I have no secrets from you, Jane. You need only ask, and I will always tell you the truth."

"Can he do that? Does he truly have that power?" How could the king overrule the Pope? George seemed certain, but I didn't understand. What he spoke of was heresy.

He arched his brow, then shrugged his shoulders. "William Tyndale says he does."

"George!" I gasped. "Tell me that book has nothing to do with Tyndale. How can you be so calm? That book is dangerous. Where did it come from?"

"Jane, hold your peace," he scolded. "You can't go around screaming that name. My father brought the book back from the Continent. It is dangerous, but only when it falls into the wrong hands. Wolsey has told the king lies, so he doesn't realise the power he has. If King Henry knew what was actually in those books, there would be no more cardinals in England. Wolsey is only protecting himself and his power and it is our duty to inform him of that."

"George, you'll be the death of Wolsey. How can you sacrifice him like that?" Was my husband so cold? Wolsey had done little to endear himself to Anne's cause, but he had not acted against her. Or had he? I had been so removed over the last weeks that my judgement of Anne's actions seemed suspect now. There was so little I knew.

George cast his eyes down to the counterpane and curled one of his long fingers around a loose thread. I watched him sever it from the fabric with a quick tug. "It is not personal, Jane," he said with a mournful sense of finality. "It's become all too clear that Wolsey has no interest in the king's annulment. If we don't stop him, he will end us and all of this will go away."

I could live without the fine furnishings and sumptuous clothing; it was the peace and security that came with Anne's success that was critical. She and the king had already gone so far in their quest there was no turning back now. If the Pope ruled in Catherine's favour and the king was forced to take her back, we would all be banished. Catherine and her adherents would do everything in their power to quash Anne and her family. George's lands and offices would be stripped away leaving us with nothing. Moving against the cardinal felt callous, but it was far crueller to risk the inheritance of our future children – if God would ever see fit to grant them to us.

"I'm frightened, George. The Lutherans are dangerous. Why would your father bring such a book home with him? Doing so puts us all in jeopardy."

"Oh, Jane," George replied with a deep sigh. "Tyndale is not a Lutheran. He doesn't want to destroy the church; he merely wants to reform it. We are so insulated on this island that no one sees just how corrupt Rome is. The priests do nothing but fornicate and count their gold as their parishioners starve and flay themselves for penance while worshipping at the feet of idols, which – I might add – the Bible expressly prohibits."

"Surely the priests do not fornicate!" I squawked indignantly. "And those *idols* provide a great deal of comfort to many people. Why would you want to take that away from them?"

"As a matter of fact, Wolsey has already had a child by his whore. He thought he could cover it up, but we all know the truth. Those people you speak of should derive their comfort from God's Holy Word, not statues of stone. Even worse are the pig bones and shards of firewood that are passed off by the priests as saint's remains and pieces of the True Cross. Those things do nothing to bring the faithful closer to God. It's a true disgrace these things are allowed in His name."

George's claims stunned me. Wolsey had a child? Impossible! How could George believe that these holy people would betray so many? Pig bones, indeed. It was my husband who was deceived to believe such vicious lies.

"George Boleyn, what you say is heresy and treason and I won't be a party to it." I wanted so much to slap him across the face that my hands trembled. His words alone could get us killed and, now, he and his sister had alerted the king to their ownership of a forbidden book that disseminated such lies. How could they do this? It would be our undoing.

George pushed the counterpane away as he swung his legs off the bed. He strode across the room, disappearing into the closet before emerging with a book bound in calfskin in his hands. He approached my side of the bed, holding it out to me in an offering. "Please, read this. If not for yourself, do it for me."

I briefly hesitated, searching his flashing eyes for anger or malice, but I found only earnestness. Rather than judging me, he appeared intent on educating me. I sighed, grasping the book from his hand; the cover felt smooth and supple against my skin. I gingerly opened the cover, expecting the worst. My breath caught in my throat when I realised that I was holding a Bible and that the words inside of it were not written in Latin. "Where did you get this?" I gasped.

George allowed himself a smug smile. "I can't tell you that."

"But you said I need only ask…"

He stopped me short with a shake of his head. "Jane, for your own safety, leave it be. I will not tell you where I got it, but I will tell you that I've hidden it here, and I encourage you to read it. You will see that men like Tyndale are right."

A sense of unease settled over me as I carefully turned the delicate pages of the book. I couldn't even begin to imagine what would happen if anyone found out that we were in possession of it. The idea was so terrible and frightening and the mere thought of it sent a shiver down my spine. Worse still, I was now involved and just as liable as my husband. Overtaken by fear, I quickly closed the book, shoving it back into George's hands. "Please just put it away, George. I can't look at it anymore."

He breathed a deep sigh, but acquiesced to my demand. This time, he was empty-handed when he re-emerged from the closet. "I know you are frightened, my love, but I am confident that the king will rejoice that we have brought this to his attention. He is furious with the Pope and Wolsey's ineptitude. If we ever want him to take action, we have to do it now. Besides, Tyndale says that the king is the final authority in his kingdom, beholden to no one. Not even the Pope. How can His Grace disagree with that?"

I shifted restlessly, but allowed George to take me in his arms. "What if that's too much power?" I whispered. "He could do anything his pleases. What if he reads it and still wants to punish you or Anne for having that book?"

George pressed his lips to my temple and trailed kisses down to my neck. "Anne has so besotted him, he would never even think of doing that," he murmured. He dragged his hand down my arm, then across my breast before he pressed his lips to mine. We kissed deeply, and when he pulled away, he whispered breathlessly, "Just as you have besotted me. Please don't worry Jane, I will always protect you."

"I can't tonight, George."

George tucked a loose strand of hair back under my nightcap, then gave me a comforting smile. "I understand, perhaps another time," he said as he kissed my cheek. I slid down under the covers, and he curled up behind me. I wrapped his arm around me and snuggled into his body. I had no doubt George would do his best to protect me, but there were dangers even he could not defeat. I whispered a silent prayer asking God to give me guidance and protect us from the troubles ahead.

George's prediction came true. The king was so delighted by the words of William Tyndale that he declared, upon finishing it, "This is a book for me and for all kings to read!" He became even more daring in his disobedience to Rome. At the end of the month, when we headed out on the annual summer progress, the crowd of courtiers travelling the countryside was significantly smaller because Catherine and her household were left behind at Greenwich. Instead, Anne sat triumphantly astride a fine white palfrey in her place. She and the king spent their days hunting and hawking in celebration at their freedom from the dour stare of the queen.

In a show of appreciation for George's part in bringing Tyndale's book to his attention, the king took him hawking at Woodstock, then charged him with a diplomatic mission. He and Dr John Stokesley would go to France in the autumn to relieve the resident ambassador, Sir Francis Bryan, of his duties and use the opportunity to wring support from King Francis for the annulment.

"This isn't permanent is it?" I worriedly asked him when he ambushed me with the news.

"Of course not, my love, only long enough for Bryan to sort his affairs. This is truly a wonderful opportunity for me to learn from Dr Stokesley," he assured me.

We moved on to Grafton the second week of September. When Cardinal Wolsey arrived a few days later with Campeggio, the king granted him a chilly reception. He gave Campeggio private rooms, but he found no such accommodation for his own minister. George told me later that Wolsey visibly winced when he, much like Jesus' mother, was informed that there was no room at the inn. Ever a gentleman, Sir Henry Norris offered up his own rooms to the cardinal, to Anne's great annoyance. "The king was trying to make a point," she seethed later in private. George tried to rationalise with her.

"Anne, of course Norris is going to be gracious. Wolsey is still Lord Chancellor and Archbishop of York and the king may have even asked him to do it," he reasoned.

"He would not!" Anne crowed indignantly. "Why would he do that? Wolsey has done him no favours."

"He is merely reminding Wolsey that it is he who rules; he only wounds him to show his power. It is not in the king's best interest to completely destroy the cardinal until he finds some other way to get his annulment. Leave this matter in the king's hands, Sister. He knows what he is doing."

The weather turned colder towards the end of the month, so George and I spent the quiet days together huddled by the window in our rooms at Windsor watching the rain trail down the leaded glass. When night fell, and the winds picked up, we made love before the fire. I clung tightly to George as the day of his departure crept ever closer. He was certain that his time there would be brief, but the previous ambassador had been gone for quite some time, and I dreaded the idea of him being gone for so long. Though I still desperately longed for a child, I began to dread the day that I would miss my courses. I was torn between a desire for intimacy with my husband and fear of another pregnancy. What if I discovered I was pregnant while he was gone? I couldn't go through another miscarriage without him.

The king knighted George in a private ceremony days before he set off. Instructions were sent ahead of him to France that he was to be met with all due honour. Anne reminded him in no uncertain terms how much she depended on his success, but he knew what was at stake. The French Court had a long history with both Anne and her father, so George was certain he could convince King Francis to pledge his support to their cause. I kept quiet about my worries. George already carried the heavy burden of expectations upon him; I need not add any undue pressure. I awoke with him in the early morning hours before his departure and sent him off with the taste of me on his lips, the scent of my skin lingering on his body.

Cardinal Wolsey's world cracked open soon after, threatening to swallow the man whole. The Dukes of Norfolk and Suffolk stormed in upon him as he took his supper in the gallery at his home in Westminster and reclaimed the Great Seal of the King. The triumph was the culmination of an unholy alliance the two adversaries formed to take down the weakened cardinal. Norfolk came from a long line of nobility and had always looked down on Suffolk for earning his title by the king's benevolence, but they saw fit to put aside their differences and work in conjunction, though Suffolk cared little for Norfolk's niece, Anne. Once the seal was passed on in great ceremony to the new Chancellor, Thomas More, the king commanded Wolsey to his parish in the far reaches of York, then set about taking an inventory of all he had stripped from the cardinal. He took Anne and her mother by barge to inspect his new prized possession: Wolsey's palatial estate, York Place.

While Anne made plans for sumptuous private rooms at her new palace, I visited my father in Westminster, where he had been called to attend Parliament. "It is so wonderful to see you again, my dear daughter," he said as he patted my head, then kissed me in greeting. He shuffled back to his great oak desk, gesturing to a chair across from it. He placed the book he held in his other hand down and inserted a slip of fabric between the pages where his finger had marked his place.

"Good day, Father," I said, arranging myself carefully in the stiff-backed chair. My father had it designed that way to discourage visitors from lingering. "It has been far too long since I saw you last. How is my Lady Mother? Are Harry and Margaret doing well?"

My father settled in the chair across from me, then heaved a great sigh. He leaned back and rubbed the bridge of his nose before answering me. "All and sundry are well. Your mother is making preparations for Christmas at home this year. Harry and Grace will be there. Margaret grows taller every day; soon I will need to set about finding her a good husband. I'm pleased to see that you've finally settled into your marriage. I never quite understood why you were so distraught over it."

"I'm sure it was just youthful theatrics, Father," I replied with a light chuckle. Now that I had come to love George, I almost didn't understand my initial horror either.

Lord Morley arched his eyebrow as he inhaled deeply. "Hmm…" he murmured. "You were never one for melodrama, so it did seem rather odd at the time. In any case, I am happy to see that you are well, and that your husband and his family are growing in prominence with each passing day. I do, however, find it unfortunate that it comes at the expense of so great a lady as the queen. Sadly, it seems your sister-in-law will only be satisfied when she wears Queen Catherine's crown."

I could think of nothing to say so I stared down at my lap where my hands were clasped tightly together. I felt great pity for Catherine, she was a good woman, but what could I do to help her? I was insignificant. Besides, I was tied to the Boleyns now; in a marriage that my father had instigated. Did he think that I should sacrifice my future to save her? "Are you asking me to do something or just trying to make me feel guilty?" I probed.

My father's piercing grey eyes pinned me back. He stared long enough to make me uncomfortable. "I'm merely thinking out loud. I would never expect you to compromise your safety. It makes no difference anyway; the king is set upon having all or nothing now. I merely wanted to make sure you knew the cost of your elevation."

"Trust that I am well aware, Father," I said as I stood up. "Give my regards to everyone at Hallingbury. I hope you all have a very joyful Christmas." I dipped into a curtsey, then made haste towards the door before my tears spilt over.

"Jane," my father called out. "Don't be discouraged. Healthy babies will come in time, and I am certain you and George will have a vast legacy to leave them."

I wanted to laugh out loud; a vast legacy, indeed. It would be a vast legacy that my father obviously found tainted by Queen

Catherine's mistreatment. My father matched me with George because he knew that the Boleyns were a rising family. He certainly treasured my success, but he would never allow himself any connection with it if it sullied his reputation. In one short exchange, Lord Morley let me know that if the Boleyn's fell, I could be on my own.

I stayed at court with Anne and Mary while my family spent the Yule season at home together. Early in December, the king elevated Thomas Boleyn to the Earldoms of Wiltshire and Ormonde in an elaborate ceremony held in the rooms formerly owned by his recently demoted minister. George was still on the king's business in France, so he missed the ceremony, but the promotion meant that he inherited his father's previous title. We were now Lord and Lady Rochford.

November 14, 1541
The Tower

WHEN LUCY returned with my ale, I took it over to the window, curling up on the bench to watch the sun rise over the Tower walls. I stared in awe as the brilliant rays stretched across the clear sky, wondering how many more I would see. I didn't think I ever appreciated one quite as much as I did at that moment. Having sent Lucy into the bedchamber for a brief respite, I enjoyed the quiet stillness of the presence chamber where the only sound I heard was the pop and crackle of the fireplace. I sat on the bench, gazing out the window until my back became stiff, forcing me to move. I swung my legs around to the floor, set my empty cup beside me; then I stood up, stretching my arms out wide. I felt a nervous energy course through my veins from my belly into my fingertips.

Five years had passed since the dreadful hours I sat across from Thomas Cromwell while he peppered me with questions about George and Anne. He could take any statement I made and twist it to fit his purpose, so I had been terrified of saying the wrong thing. It was only because of George's preparation that I was able to escape the scaffold. Cromwell's quest to dig up evidence against Anne was stealthy, and he made every attempt to catch her ladies unawares, but he miscalculated when he made the decision to question my brother's wife, Grace, before he questioned me. If not for her dire warning and George's quick thinking, I would have found myself in these very same rooms much earlier. Now, having spent so much of those last five years in grief and distress, I wondered if Grace's loyalty to me was a blessing or a curse. It seemed God saved me from his cruelty only long enough to deliver a much harsher blow.

There were no warnings for me this time. Grace was dead and rotting in her grave; her life unfairly snuffed out during the rigours of childbirth. None of the other women in Katherine's service cared for me. I was older than most of them, and they resented the fact that Katherine singled me out to be her closest companion. What many of them didn't know is how much that suited her purpose; as an outsider, I was less likely to betray her secret. They were jealous the queen took me into her confidences, but I was envious of them. My relationship with Katherine was strictly for her benefit, not mine. I received no greater treatment or reward, and I often had less liberty than her other ladies, for Katherine liked me to be near at all times. No, Margery Morton and Kat Tylney would not stir one foot to help me like Grace. My present state surely overjoyed them.

A brief rap at the door startled me from my thoughts. I expected Lucy to hustle past me towards the door, but then I remembered that I'd sent her to bed, so I ran to answer the knock quickly before the noise woke her from her much-needed sleep. Gage appeared surprised at my greeting. "Lady Rochford, is everything all right? Where is Lucy?"

I brought my finger to my lips, hushing him. "I've sent her to rest, Sir John. Everything is…well…it's as fine as it can be. Please, come in." I pulled the door open, stepping aside so he could enter.

The constable doffed his cap, then dipped a quick bow. "I've come to tell you that I've sent for the king's secretary," he said as he straightened. "He's only down the river, so I expect him at any moment. He is keen to make his final report to the king so I would advise against putting him off any further."

"I have no intention of that, Sir John. I know not what happened yesterday, but I am confident that I have sufficiently recovered."

Gage eyed me wearily, but nodded his assent. "Is there anything I can bring you, my lady?"

"Perhaps you have some bravery to spare?" I asked, offering him a terse smile.

His face softened as he reached out to pat my arm. "If I could, Lady Rochford, I would give you every last ounce of courage I possessed."

I turned away, shifting my gaze to the window that faced out into the confines of the Tower grounds. "Thank you, Sir John." Satisfied that I had regained my senses, the constable took his leave of me to prepare for Wriothesley's arrival.

My mind raced as I thought of my defence. What could I say to absolve myself? I paced nervously across the floor. The third time I passed before the hearth, I paused by the stool that held the book Lucy mentioned earlier. When I lifted the cover, I realised why it looked so familiar to me; it was one of Anne's Bibles. Overcome by sadness, I wrapped the book in my arms, nestling it next to my heart. Through my tears, I heard Anne's voice repeating the words of the Apostle John: *And the truth shall set you free.*

There was no need for me to panic; there was no need for despair. All I needed to do was tell Wriothesley the truth. I was tired of hiding Katherine's secrets. Besides, the king would leave no stone unturned; everything would come out in the end. If I were honest from the beginning, then perhaps His Grace would be more lenient on us both. As I breathed a deep sigh of relief at my moment of clarity, I heard another knock. This time, Gage opened the door without waiting to be let in. I quickly dropped to a deep curtsey when I saw who was behind him. When I stood up, Thomas Wriothesley fixed his cool blue eyes on me. "I have some questions for you, Lady Rochford."

MARCH – NOVEMBER 1530
YORK PLACE AND THE
SUMMER PROGRESS

"HE SAID what to our father?" Anne's face contorted with fury as she leapt up from her cushion and threw her sewing to the side. George had just wandered into her rooms with the latest missive from their father who was on embassy in Rome with the cleric, Thomas Cranmer. Wiltshire and Cranmer had been sent to entreat the Pope and the Emperor to support the king's annulment, but the response was not as favourable as we had all hoped. Wiltshire's letter indicated the Emperor's continued obstinacy, telling Wiltshire that he, as Anne's father, had no business in the matter.

"How dare he insult us?" Anne continued. "It is the Emperor who should take no part in the matter; what business is it of his? I don't know why Henry insists on his approval. The Emperor can mind matters in his own lands."

I shot a helpless glance towards George who was trying, unsuccessfully, to contain his amusement at Anne's fiery indignation. As of late, he had begun to believe that her increasing emotional outbursts did nothing to help her cause and only served to rile her further. He brought his hand to his lips to hide his smile, clearing his throat before responding. "What did you expect, Anne? The Emperor was never going to support us. We all knew that before Father left to meet him. Besides, His Grace has no need for his approval; we must convince him to release the French King's sons so that King Francis' letter to his theologians demanding their support can finally be presented. You know I worked very hard for that," he finished with a pout. His mission in France had been to return with favourable opinions from the top theologians at the University of Paris in support of the divorce. This tactic was engaged at the urging of Cranmer who said the debate was theological, not legal; everything hinged on how a passage in the Book of Leviticus was interpreted.

"Oh yes, you laboured extremely hard for that, didn't you?" Anne sputtered. "I can only imagine how tiresome it was to take part in all the delights of the French Court. Feasting and dancing with the king while you were both entertained by beautiful, lusty women. Tell me again how you withstood such appalling conditions?" Anne tugged on the gold chain dangling below George's neck, "He even made you a necklace to commemorate the memory of your debauchery."

The smile fell from George's face as he pushed his sister's hand away. "Anne, that is enough, you go too far. You know that isn't true." When I looked up from my sewing, I saw that, though George was speaking to his sister, his gaze fell upon me.

Despite assurances that the University of Paris would return with favourable opinions, the academics responded with a list of signatures refuting the divorce. Rather than accept defeat, George followed the French court to Dijon to persuade the king to intervene; the monarch was hesitant to throw his full support behind King Henry because the Emperor still held his sons as hostages in punishment for his defeat at Pavia four years ago.

George had very little diplomatic experience, so no one truly believed he would be successful in convincing King Francis to enter the fray. Anne spoke of the licentiousness swirling about the French court, warning me that George might engage in the illicit liaisons taking place there. What better way to earn the merry monarch's support than by joining him in his sport? When word arrived that George had indeed secured the letter of support from the French King, I assumed the worst. The idea that my husband could have, at any given moment, entertained an alluring French courtesan in his bed caused me to retch for days on end.

Anne dropped the chain with a sigh. "I'm sorry, George; that was unkind." She paced the floor as she continued. "This is taking too long and my youth is almost spent! By the time this is resolved, my childbearing days will be over, and there will be no hope of an heir! Everything will be spoiled."

"I understand, Sister, but there is no need to take your frustration out on me. Father and Cranmer are doing their best, and we will be successful. You will feel better once they return, I'm sure of it," George replied. "There is no need to impugn my reputation; some people might not realise you are jesting," he continued with a frown.

I set aside my sewing as I arose from my cushion, then I strode over to George. I brushed my lips against the rough stubble of his cheek, "I'm sorry I was so eager to believe the worst of you, George. You don't have to continue pleading your fidelity to me or anyone else. I'm proud of what you accomplished in France, and I know His Grace is grateful."

"George is right, Anne," Mary piped up from her cushion. "We must remain united. Any dissension between us will be exploited by those who wish to undo you. We must keep our council and let no one know of our frustration. I've noticed the new Imperial Ambassador, Eustace Chapuys, lurking about, and I'm sure he would be thrilled to report any of our weaknesses back to his master."

Anne gazed at us helplessly. "I know all of this…and I try. I do, but sometimes I cannot help myself. The best part of my life is slipping by, and I can do nothing to stop it. I tried to extend an olive branch to Wolsey, but he returned the favour by working against me. Suffolk hates me and his wife refuses to come to court because she can't bear the sight of me. I feel like the only one who wants me here is Henry."

Mary pushed herself up from the cushion, joining George and me at Anne's side. She grasped both of Anne's hands in her own and squeezed them tightly. "Have faith, Sister. The pain will all be worthwhile when you fill the royal cradle with a handsome prince."

Cardinal Wolsey languished away in his diocese while the court romped across the lush gardens at his former home. Matters in Europe were not progressing in the way that King Henry had hoped, so he submersed himself in all manners of frivolity to divert his attention. George, now a member of the Privy Council, eagerly joined His Grace on the bowling lawns and at the archery butts. My husband prided himself on his athletic prowess, refusing to allow anyone to beat him. When he and Master Weston played the king at tennis, they won four games, pocketing a tidy sum from the royal coffers.

While we were on summer progress, escaping the pestilence running rampant throughout the city, we learned that King Francis had finally presented his letter to the Doctors of Theology at Paris and, in return, they issued verdicts supporting His Grace's arguments. They determined it was unlawful for a man to marry his brother's wife and that the Pope had no authority to issue a dispensation excusing it. The king celebrated by hunting and hawking across the countryside, but his victory was empty. Both the Emperor and the Pope ignored the findings of the French universities; the Earl of Wiltshire returned with nothing but a citation from the Pope commanding His Grace to present his case to the Papal Curia in person – in Rome.

To crack down on heresy, the king's new Lord Chancellor, Thomas More, staged a bonfire at St. Paul's Cross in order to burn forbidden books. He took particular relish in destroying every copy of Tyndale's Bible he could find. Though I had not seen it since he showed it to me, I knew George still owned a copy. It was now hidden away in a locked chest in our home at Grimston, but I still feared its discovery. The king may have chafed at the Pope's authority, but he still hated anything that stank of Lutheranism; he fully supported More's attempts to stamp it out.

As the warm season faded away, whistling autumn winds blew the remaining ashes of Cardinal Wolsey's influence and reputation away. In a sweet twist of irony, Anne's former paramour, Henry Percy – now the Earl of Northumberland – was sent to the cardinal's home at Cawood to arrest him for treason. I wondered whether the earl felt any satisfaction at being the one to carry out this final insult. As Anne had approached the throne, Northumberland's father shunted him into a miserable marriage. A marriage that he could have avoided had Wolsey thrown his support behind Percy's relationship with Anne. Northumberland found a broken man at Cawood. The cardinal was deathly ill and in fear for his life. The trauma of his arrest was too much to bear, and his body gave out near Leicester. The once all-powerful cardinal was vanquished forever.

December 1530 – June 1531
Greenwich,
York Place, and
Grimston

AFTER YET another year of hiding away while Catherine presided over the Christmas revels at Greenwich, Anne re-emerged more determined than ever that she would be the one to command the attention of the court during the next Yule season. The king's impulse to shove her aside for the sake of appearances scraped her pride, and she responded like a wounded animal would. When one of Catherine's ladies asked her when she would put her vanity aside for the sake of her mistress, Anne lashed out in fury. "I wish to God that all the bloody Spaniards were rotting at the bottom of the deepest sea. I care nothing for Catherine, and I would rather see her hanged than acknowledge her as my mistress."

The death of Cardinal Wolsey signalled a change. Anne's father, and the Duke of Norfolk, were now a force with which to be reckoned. As leaders of the new guard of men surrounding the king, they took it upon themselves to host a dinner for the French ambassador, Claude La Guische, at Wiltshire's home on the Strand. I stayed behind at Greenwich with Anne, but George attended. When I returned to our rooms that night after supper with Anne, I was surprised to find George sprawled out, brooding, in his chair.

"I wasn't expecting you home so early," I called out as I untied my hood, removing it from my head. I loosened my hair, groaning in relief as I felt it cascade down my shoulders. Sauntering over to George, I wrapped my arms around him as I leaned over the back of his chair. I buried my face in his neck and inhaled the spicy scent of him: wood smoke, rosemary, and sweat.

George rubbed the limbs I had draped across his chest, placing a tender kiss on my hand. "A dull thing it was," he replied with disinterest.

"Since when are you bored with politics? That doesn't sound like my husband," I placed a light kiss on his cheek before pulling away. I dragged a plush velvet cushion over and wedged it between his feet, then I plopped down, and leaned back against him. I closed my eyes against the heat of the sparking flames crackling in the hearth.

"Yes, I know," he replied with a deep sigh. "Perhaps I am merely tired. I haven't slept well these past months."

"You have seemed restless. What is troubling you, my love?"

"I am sure I worry for nothing. It's just that – well – the cardinal was so powerful, and so beloved by the king, even up until the very end. And yet…" George's voice trailed off. I let the silence linger between us while he gathered his thoughts. "There was a masque at my father's house tonight for the entertainment of the French ambassador. He hired a company of players to act out Wolsey's fall and at the end of the play, a score of men dressed as demons came out to drag the cardinal down to the depths of Hell."

"How gruesome," I shuddered.

"Yes, it was, and I am not the least bit surprised that it was not well-received. To say that La Guische was displeased would be – well – I'm afraid that much wooing will be needed on our part to repair the insult."

"Why would they do such a thing, George? It sounds so callous and distasteful. Your father is a seasoned diplomat; surely he knows better."

"He does know better, Jane, but Uncle Norfolk…The cardinal's disgrace has filled him with glee. He designed the masque and my father went along with it. I, too, am relieved that Wolsey is no longer in power, but…God's Blood! I served the man in my earliest days at court, and I still admire him and all that he accomplished for England. I certainly don't relish his death." He paused for a moment, carefully choosing his next words. "Whatever Anne thinks, this battle is far from over, and

I'm not certain that we won't face the same fate as the cardinal at the end of it."

I shifted onto my knees, turning to face George. "Please don't say that," I beseeched him. "The king loves your sister. We will never end up like Wolsey."

George tucked a strand of hair behind my ear, and trailed his thumb slowly down my face. "I hope you're right." He tilted my chin so his mouth could meet mine, then murmured in a husky voice, "I don't want to talk about Wolsey anymore, Jane." The taste of his lips sent a tremor of pleasure rippling through me. As he gently laid me back on the cushion, he trailed soft kisses down my neck. Deft fingers unlaced my gown and explored the soft curves hidden below.

I ran my hands down the length of George's body, savouring the weight of it upon mine. When he dragged his lips away, jagged and breathless, I purred softly, "I love you George."

His golden eyes shimmered in the firelight. "Let's go to bed."

"If Norfolk wants to make an impression on someone, he would be better served to impress upon his wife the danger lying ahead if she continues to support that prideful daughter of Spain," Anne cursed as she threw a bolster pillow across the room. "And when, in God's name, will it ever stop raining?"

"I think it's lovely," I replied as I traced the trickle of water careening down the chilled glass of the ornate oriel window. "It's only been two days, Anne. I've thought the weather rather fair this winter."

Anne grimaced at me, throwing herself back on the counterpane. "I cannot believe the nerve…My own aunt! It's an utter disgrace."

"If you truly wanted to get under her skin, you could ask Norfolk's mistress to serve in your household when you become queen."

"Jane!" Anne gasped.

Even I was taken aback by the callous words dripping from my lips. Anne's dark humour had begun to affect my own. "Never mind that foolish suggestion."

Anne popped her head up with a wicked smile. "It's actually quite ingenious," she replied in awe.

"Anne Boleyn, don't you dare!" I cried, instantly regretting my jest.

She shimmied up against the headboard, and pulled her knees to her chest, wrapping her long arms around them. She chewed her bottom lip thoughtfully, then ran her tongue across her teeth as she nodded. "Yes, I just might invite Bess Holland to court," she said gulping back hiccups of delight. When she finally calmed her merriment, she sighed and wiped the tears from her eyes. "Now I just pray that Parliament finally recognises Henry as Supreme Head of the Church."

Parliament discussed the legal ramifications of the king's supremacy while the Convocations of Canterbury and York met to determine the spiritual ones. If the bishops recognised His Grace's authority in spiritual matters, he could finally declare his marriage to Catherine invalid and my sister-in-law would get her heart's desire. The last few weeks had been fraught with turmoil while we waited for both to make the decision that would ensure Anne's future success. Though Parliament and many of the bishops agreed to the king's demands, there were still holdouts refusing to allow him all of the power he craved. The Bishop of Rochester, John Fisher, was the most recalcitrant, arguing at every turn. If the act naming the king as Supreme Head failed, it would be due to Fisher's obstinacy.

Although George was not a Member of Parliament, he was now a part of the Privy Council, and it was he who was sent to persuade Convocation of the monarch's right to supremacy, using the scriptures and religious tracts from the king to make his case. He took great pride in the honour and confidence that the king had bestowed upon him in giving him this important duty, and he continually practiced his delivery well into the night in the days leading up to his appearance. The senior bishops were irritated that the king would send someone they deemed of so little importance to address them, so they sent a member of the lower house to appeal directly to His Grace, but King Henry merely rebuffed the envoy and sent him to our apartments to deal with George.

As the proceedings carried on, the French ambassador, previously so insulted by Wiltshire and Norfolk's masque, was feted in the grandest style. After attending mass in the cathedral, King Henry brought him to see the lords amassed at Parliament, where they gave the ambassador a lavish reception. He was even invited to dine with the king and the Dukes of Suffolk and Norfolk at the great table. It was imperative that any stain remaining from the supper at Wiltshire's house on the Strand was wiped clean. During Shrovetide, we invited him to feast with us in Anne's private chambers. The king honoured him with a special toast and assured him of the everlasting friendship he desired. Though he had the findings he wanted from the French theologians, he still needed the support of La Guische's master, King Francis.

Parliament's ruling came down before the month was out, striking a blow to the king's pride. Henry would be Supreme Head of the Church of England, but only as far as the law of Christ allowed; adding the restrictive coda had been the only way to convince Bishop Fisher to give his assent. During a break in Parliament, the bishop returned home. A few days after his arrival, a batch of pottage made for his household's consumption was spiked with poison. The bishop refrained from the meal and narrowly escaped, but his servants weren't quite so fortunate. Nearly all fell ill, and two of them died. The king's recent displeasure with the bishop cast a shadow of guilt over both Henry and the Boleyn family.

His Grace took the accusations in stride. "Of course, they would blame me," he said with steely calm when he came to inform Anne of the rumours. "They think I have nothing more pressing to accomplish. Rest assured that if I wanted to punish Fisher, I would do it properly, not hire some inept cook to do my bidding."

The suspicion eviscerated Anne. After the king's hasty departure to meet with the Privy Council regarding the cook's penance, she crawled over to my cushion and laid her head in my lap. "Jane," she whimpered. "They think I had something to do with it. How could they believe me capable of such evil?"

"They don't know you, Anne," I soothed as I brushed her silky dark mane from her face. I pulled a linen handkerchief from my girdle and used it to catch the fat teardrops that fell from her eyes. "Surely this isn't completely unexpected. You've been the target of much harsher animosity since you have been with the king. Where's your spirit?"

"How much longer do I suffer this indignation?" she sniffed. "Henry assures me that he no longer loves Catherine, but her spectre looms ever present in all that we do. I am not like my sister; I cannot have three people in a marriage."

The empathy I felt for Anne had begun to overshadow the pity that I felt for Catherine. I was certain that both women suffered in equal parts for far different reasons, but I was no longer privy to the former's distress while Anne's despair grew every day that I spent with her. With only Mary or me for company, she was not the same vivacious girl that had charmed the king. Fear brought out her worst characteristics, and she often lashed out at those most undeserving of her wrath. Recently, an innocent chamberer bore the brunt of her outrage when she discovered that he was taking a pile of Henry's shirts to Catherine for mending. The king couldn't understand why she was so upset; they were only shirts after all. From Anne's perspective it was yet another slight reminding her that, at least legally, Catherine was still his wife.

"I wish I had an answer for you. I know you're tired of the constant refrain reminding you to have patience, but look at how far you have come. The king is now head of the church," I reminded her.

"Until it's time to make a ruling on the marriage," Anne muttered. "The bishops need only claim that the 'Law of Christ' binds his hands. We are no better off than we were before."

Anne received a brief reprieve when Catherine removed herself to Richmond Palace to visit her ailing daughter. Catherine begged her husband to accompany her, but His Grace was steadfast in his refusal; Catherine could go wherever she liked, but he would stay at court. As glad as I was for Anne, I found the king's neglect of his child shameful. It was not her fault that the brothers Catherine bore for her died. Nor was it her doing that the Pope refused to rule in her father's favour. Her only crime was that she existed as the physical representation of a union the king was determined to destroy. The passage in Leviticus said that an impure union would be childless; her very existence hindered the king's argument for his annulment. Catherine returned to court after Parliament recessed, further irritating the two lovers who found no satisfaction from the obstinate bishops.

On St. George's Day, the annual chapter of the Order of the Garter was held at Greenwich. The vacancy left behind was filled by the Earl of Northumberland. No doubt it was a reward, not only for his hand in Wolsey's arrest but for throwing his support behind the annulment. Northumberland's appearance at the celebratory feast was the first that we had seen of him since he was banished to his properties in the north to conclude his marriage to Mary Talbot. I was surprised and genuinely troubled to see how sickly he had become. His miserable marriage, a mountain of debt, and unrelenting warfare to secure the northern borders had severely undermined his health, and the strident young man was merely a shadow of his former self.

"Have you noticed?" Mary Boleyn's whisper tickled my ear. "Anne can't take her eyes off Henry Percy."

As nonchalantly as possible, I dragged my eyes across the sea of courtiers filling the great hall, daring only a fleeting glimpse of my sister-in-law. She was perched prominently beside the king, dressed in a resplendent crimson gown dripping with glittering diamonds. I expected her to appear cheerful and triumphant; instead, she looked regretful and unnerved.

"Anne truly loved Percy," I replied under my breath. "She would be heartless not to feel pity for him. Look at how pallid his skin is; he is so thin, it's practically hanging off his body. Time has not been kind to him."

I was taken aback by Mary's subsequent question. It was one that I had asked myself over and over again, never having the courage to vocalise it to anyone else. "Do you think she is happy, Jane?" Her deep blue eyes stared at me expectantly, but I had no answer for her. True, Anne's status grew far beyond anything we could have imagined, but it came at a steep price. Old alliances were ripped apart, lives overturned, in the king's pursuit to make her his wife. Sadly, four years of destruction had not brought him any closer to dissolving his first marriage. If asked, Anne would of course insist that she was joyous, but she became increasingly anxious over the delays and often lamented over how much of her youth had passed.

"I'm certain Anne believes she is happy and, perhaps, that is all that matters," I replied truthfully. "What of your happiness, Mary? Is your mourning period for William over?"

A blush rose to Mary's round cheeks, but her eyes watered with unshed tears. "My family is not concerned with my marriage prospects," she replied with a frown. "I have little in the way of a dowry and my father barely tolerates keeping me fed and dressed appropriately. He is not keen to offer anything more on my behalf. Anne gave me a small sum of money to set aside in exchange for a beautiful ruby the king gave me years ago, but it's not enough to make a good match. It would have to be an exceptional man indeed who sought my hand."

"I have no doubt that your time will come again, dear sister. Once Anne is married to the king, we will have to beat your suitors away with a stick," George roared with laughter as he came up behind us, startling us both. My husband's eyes glittered in the torchlight, his face flushed with too much drink. He held his hand out to me and, with a wink, commanded me to join him in a galliard. I wrapped Mary in a quick embrace, kissing her hot cheek, before I followed him out onto the dance floor.

George had always been a nimble dancer, and he was exuberant as we followed each other in a *cinq pas* across the floor. I felt as light as a feather when he pulled me in tightly, lifting me high in the air during a *lavolta*. I caught a few disapproving stares during the intimate step, but George carried on, oblivious. We danced until the music trailed away and we were breathless with the effort. George made reverence to me with a deep bow once the dance was over, but before I could offer a curtsey in return, he dragged me through the crush of dancing courtiers and out into the gardens.

The pungent fragrance of the lilac bushes greeted us when we stepped out into the encroaching dusk. Even as the light was fading, the vivid violet of the blooms stood out against the pale sky. I kept a tight hold onto to George's hand, following him into the yew hedges that bordered the knot garden.

"What are we doing out here?" I asked with a giggle once we had hidden in the garden.

George twitched his lips into a smile. "Acting like love birds," he said before he swept me into his arms, throwing me back with a kiss. "I have something for you," he whispered as he pulled away. The dip and ensuing passionate kiss left me dizzy, and I momentarily stumbled when he righted me. Once he made sure I was steady, he dug into one of the pockets of his indigo silk doublet and pulled out something that took my breath away. Dangling from his finger was a gold pendant wrought in the shape of a lover's knot on a delicate satin ribbon strung with pearls.

"It's beautiful," I breathed. As I reached out to touch it, I asked, "Where did you get it?"

George ambled around me, lifting the ribbon over my head so he could tie it around my neck. "I had it commissioned with my winnings. I carried sixty pounds off the king at shovelboard."

"George!" I exclaimed, fingering the silky pearls around my throat. "Please tell me you didn't spend it all on this."

"Don't concern yourself with that, my love," he said, punctuating the statement with a kiss. Hand-in-hand, we walked deeper into the garden until we came upon a bench where George could sit down while I burrowed under his arm for warmth. We sat huddled together in the quiet stillness of the night as the bright stars marched out across the sky.

As the breezy spring months warmed in the summer heat, so too did Anne's temper. Catherine's mere presence chafed at my sister-in-law and, what she saw as the queen's continued manipulation of King Henry enraged her. Anne lashed out with such intensity she began to alienate some of her most ardent adherents. George grew anxious when Norfolk rescinded his support and began to speak in reverent tones of Catherine's courage to the Imperial ambassador, Chapuys.

"He thinks that we know nothing of the treachery between them," George whispered to me when we passed the two deep in conversation during the May Day feast in the great hall. "But we see and hear everything...and we remember."

To lighten his sweetheart's dark mood, His Grace loaded Anne and her mother onto his grand barge, *The Lyon*, and took them down the Thames to inspect the on-going construction to refurbish York Place. Anne immersed herself in the plans for the palace, which would house her very own private apartments rivalling any of Catherine's, and looked forward to the moment when they could move in. While Anne spent those early months shuffling between the king's homes at Windsor, Greenwich, and Hampton Court, George and I retreated to our country home at Grimston. All of the furniture that decorated our cosy apartment in Greenwich had been moved in April, when the king paid the final rent due on the property. I had not seen the beautifully carved cradle since my miscarriage, when George hastily bundled it into the empty nursery, locking the door behind him. Seeing it again at Grimston was a bleak reminder that I still had yet to fulfil my duty to provide my husband with an heir.

George reassured me when my courses arrived, as expected, at the end of the month. "Jane, you will make yourself bitter with grief if you continue to believe that your only value to me is as a brood mare."

"But you are the heir to an earldom; of course you want a son to pass it along to," I argued emphatically in exasperation. "Why am I the only one that seems to care about that?"

George grasped me by the shoulders, probing my eyes with his own. "You are not the only one who cares and, I think, you know that. I merely refuse to allow my anger to control me," he intoned carefully. "Would it make you feel better if I screamed at you? How about if I broke the cradle to pieces? What if I cursed at God? I will not do any of those things because none of them will help you conceive. They will only serve to make us both miserable." I knew he was right, but I was so resentful of his ability to remain calm, I pulled away from his every attempt at affection for the entirety of a week.

The quiet solitude of life at Grimston was a far cry from the hustle and bustle of the chaos at court. In the mornings, George and I rose early to break our fast with a simple meal of pottage and fruit in the dining hall. If the weather was fair, we took the horses out for a ride in the nearby hunting park. George was keen to keep his archery skills sharp so, more often than not, we returned with a stag for supper. In the afternoons, I retreated to the solar to sew and read or I ventured out to the gardens to enjoy the blossoms that had already exploded into a riot of colour. I knew very little about the flowers and plants that grew at Grimston, so I often trailed behind the gardener while he patiently explained to me how to harvest the choicest vegetables and when to pluck the ripest berries from the vine. While I explored every corner of our property, George hid away in his library for hours at a time. He hated to be bothered while he was reading, so I avoided disturbing him as much as possible. I was never sure of what he got up to during his seclusion, but everything was soon to become clear.

I saw the cloud of dust from my perch in the garden before I heard the staccato of hoof beats. We weren't expecting any visitors, so I sent one of the servants to investigate before troubling my husband, then turned back to my prayer book while I awaited his return. I was searching for a particular prayer known to help with conception. I had just found the words I was looking for when I heard the servant call out to me, "Masters Henry Parker and Hugh Wynter are here to see you, my lady."

When I looked up from my book, the familiar forms of both my brother and his closest friend were bent low in identical bows. "Harry!" I squealed in excitement. "Get up! Get up! Both of you! No need to bow for me. What are you doing here?" I placed my prayer book on the bench, then ran to Harry, throwing my arms around him in a warm embrace. Hugh offered me a sincere smile when I peered at him from over Harry's shoulder. After a few moments, I stepped back so that I could take in their appearance. My brother was as tall and strapping as he had ever been. The only difference I could see was a fine down of tawny hair now covering the lower half of his face. Hugh had the same dimples and boyish grin, but his shoulders had broadened, and he was much thinner than I remembered. I could tell by the crinkle of the lines around his deep-set eyes that he marked the passing years of his life with much joy and laughter.

"I thank you for the warm welcome, Sister," Harry replied with a grin. "While I am always thrilled to see you, I've come here today to speak with your husband. Is he at home?"

This new development perplexed me. Why would my brother be here to see George? "Of course he is here, but I don't understand. What business do you have with George?"

Harry took my hand, placing a dry kiss on the back of it. "It is nothing that concerns you, dear Jane, so please don't trouble yourself with worry. We won't stay long, but I would be greatly appreciative if you would entertain my companion while I speak with George. You remember Hugh Wynter, right?"

"Of course, I remember Master Wynter. Although I must confess, I almost failed to recognise him in dry clothes," I confirmed wryly.

A short burst of laughter escaped Hugh at my mockery. "How refreshing to see that you've grown so saucy, Lady Rochford."

Harry snickered, shaking his head at us in disbelief. "Well then, I will leave you to it," he said as he trampled off behind the servant in search of George.

Hugh and I stood staring awkwardly at each other, both waiting for the other to initiate a conversation. After a few moments, I turned away and began stalking off towards the vegetable garden. "Well, are you coming?" I called out over my shoulder. I heard the rustle of Hugh's feet behind me, but I refused to turn around until I reached the patch of dirt. "I need onions for supper," I explained stiffly, dropping to my knees to pull the plants from the ground.

"Do you not have servants to do this?"

"We can sew if you like," I replied with a frown. "Or we can pray. I was just about to do so when you arrived."

"Onions it is then," he replied with a chuckle, then bent down to help me dig the roots out of the ground. "You don't have to do this, Jane."

"Do what? Dirty my hands in the garden?" I asked, leaning back to wipe the sweat from my brow. "I don't mind a little toil. It reminds me of all that my servants do for me, so that I always treat them with kindness."

"You know that's not what I meant. I was referring to this posture of defence that you've always taken up around me. I'm still not certain what I've done to deserve it."

"You ran off and got married!" I shouted as I threw a clod of dirt at him, then I groaned in disgust. Why did I say that? I wasn't even angry about that. In fact, I genuinely hoped he had a peaceful marriage.

Hugh leaned to the side to avoid the dirt, but a piece hit him square in the chest. "I wasn't even aware of your interest. How could I be? You always behaved so unpleasantly towards me," he said brushing the crumbs of soil from his jerkin.

"I know, and I regret that," I replied meekly. "I wasn't…I mean… I didn't want to marry you. That isn't what I meant. It's just that – well – first you left, then Harry did. I felt abandoned."

Hugh dropped the onion to the ground before scrambling to his feet. He held out his hand to help me up, "I'm sorry you felt that way, Jane, but perhaps it was for the best. Harry tells me that you are very close to George's sisters. If we had been at court, you would have used us as an excuse to avoid them. Instead, you were able to lean on each other during a time of turmoil. Has it ever occurred to you just how lonely Anne must have felt? Her life changed the moment the king chose her; Catherine's ladies saw her with nothing but disdain from then on. You were there to show her kindness in a way that her family never could. You showed compassion even when you didn't have to. When she is queen, you will be one of her most trusted companions."

He was right of course, it had been for the best, but it took him saying it for me to recognise its truth. Besides, I was tired of holding on to my bitterness; it was time to let go. When Hugh offered his arm to me, I took it and led him back towards the house. "How is your wife anyway?" I asked reluctantly.

"I think she's quite lovely," Hugh replied with a grin. As we made our way across the lush green grass, he told me about the widow with three grown daughters. Her first husband died of an arrow wound almost two decades ago when the Scottish King, James IV, was routed at the Battle of Flodden. Her second died during an outbreak of the plague. She was a survivor who made good marriages for her children; all three were now mothers themselves. Her monthly courses stopped naturally, if a bit prematurely, by the time they married so they had no children of their own and that suited Hugh perfectly.

"So am I mature enough to know now?" I teased when I asked him again why he didn't want children.

"You don't forget a thing do you?"

Hugh told me he was the product of an affair between a Prior and one of his poor parishioners. His mother died when he was very young, so the Prior had placed him in the care of a noble family who lived nearby. They raised him as their own and sent him to court to serve their eldest son as a page. Though he was grateful for all that the family had done for him, he had always believed that he had nothing to offer and never wanted to subject his children to the abject poverty he had once faced. He also said he felt ashamed his existence was the result of a man of God abusing his power.

"Don't you see, Jane? That's why I am here. Those holy houses are supposed to provide comfort and guidance to the followers of Christ, but my father desecrated it. He turned it into his own personal brothel," he groaned with disgust.

"I don't understand. What does George have to do with your father?" Only after the words were out of my mouth did the truth become clear. I answered my own question with an awed whisper, "You are working with George to reform the church."

"Yes," Hugh replied with a dip of his head. "Well," he continued thoughtfully. "Your brother is helping George reform the church. I am merely smuggling in their Bibles.

I led Hugh into the house with a heavy heart. If their secrets were found out, they would be imprisoned or even worse. Lord Chancellor More would have them burned at the stake for what they were doing. Sensing my unease, Hugh squeezed my hand. "I apologise. I should not have told you, Jane."

I tried to be reassuring, but my voice faltered when I replied, "Not at all, Hugh. Thank you for your honesty. I will pray for your safety."

When Harry and I exchanged our farewells after supper, I resisted the urge to be anything but kind. I wanted to scream at him for being reckless, but I dared not betray Hugh's trust. Besides, Harry would never heed my warnings; once he was convinced he was doing the right thing, nothing would deter him. My husband was not spared my wrath. I waited until after my maid prepared me for bed and hastened out of the room before delivering a stinging rebuke. "What are you thinking, George? You've put us all at risk!"

"No, I haven't," George replied calmly as he pried open the window to let in the cool evening air. The breeze blowing through the curtains danced across my skin and sent a chill down my spine. When he turned back to me, he continued in earnest, "Don't you see how necessary this is? Not just for Anne, but for all of us. The Pope has allowed the slithering serpent of vice into his church, and it is our duty to expel it once and for all. Don't you agree that it is time God's Word was available for all to read and take comfort in? Men like your brother and Hugh will create a new church free of idolatry and greed."

I collapsed onto the bed, overtaken by a wave of emotion. I saw the necessity of reform, but I didn't understand why they were willing to risk everything to cure the masses of an illness they refused to recognise. If Anne's tribulations taught me anything, it was that the people of England loved the Catholic Church and the man at the head of it. They didn't care that men like Cardinal Wolsey hoarded their gold or kept mistresses and sired bastard children. They would gladly give their last shilling to any priest who promised them everlasting grace. If even the king couldn't reform the church, how did George expect that he could? I clenched my eyes shut to hold back the tears, but I felt George's presence as he crawled onto the bed beside me. He brushed the hair from my face and kissed my cheek. When I dared open my eyes, I saw him gazing back at me; the gold flecks in his dark eyes flickering with the candlelight. "Everything will be well, Jane. Have faith in me."

July 1531 – August 1532
Hampton Court,
Windsor,
Durham House

WE RETURNED to London the first week in July, joining Anne and the king at Hampton Court Palace. While George entertained His Grace at the archery butts, Anne and I strolled through the gardens. The roses were in full bloom and the thick scent of their perfume hung in the air. Anne told me of all the work that had been accomplished at York Place as we walked. The renovations were taking longer than she anticipated, but she was not upset; the plans for her apartments were very detailed and boasted every luxury, she was pleased that the builders were so thorough. She expected that we would all be able to move in by this time next year. Additionally, the king had shared with her a bit of news that was even more pleasing. "Next Friday, Henry is taking me to hunt at Woodstock and leaving orders that Catherine is to vacate her rooms and leave court before we return," she confessed.

"That's wonderful news," I replied, marvelling at the change in her. A woman of calm assurance had replaced the one I left behind, teetering on the edge, only months ago. "Does this mean that your marriage will happen soon?"

Anne paused at a rose bush covered in plump yellow blooms. She reached out with deft fingers to pull the stem closer, despite the sharp thorns guarding it. Dipping her nose into the heart of the blossom, she inhaled deeply. "Lovely," she purred. "I really must have a perfume made from those." She let go of the stem and watched it spring back to the bush with a smile before continuing, "Oh yes, I hope to be Henry's wife by the end of the year."

On the morning Anne left for Woodstock, I followed her down to the stables so she could show me the saddles the king had made for her while we were gone. The Master of the Horse, Sir Nicholas Carew, was in the process of fitting one on when we arrived. It was designed in the French fashion, and the plush black velvet with silk and golden fringe emphasised the slate colouring of Anne's palfrey. She took great care in approaching the horse quietly to avoid spooking it and when she was certain it was safe to do so, she nuzzled her face against the animal's neck. "My dearest Artemis," she cooed.

"Goddess of the Hunt," I mused. "How very clever, Anne." I turned to Sir Nicholas expecting him to nod in agreement, but he merely grunted as he carried on with his work. In addition to the saddles, Anne's new riding gear consisted of harnesses with buckles of copper and gilt, white fustian pillions stuffed with down, and velvet covered footstools to match. She didn't yet have the title of Queen, but His Grace made certain she travelled like one.

While Anne and the king chased their quarry through the countryside, George and I stayed behind at Windsor. Mary and I stood by in awe as the former queen's possessions were carried from the palace and loaded into a train of empty carts to be taken to the More. Catherine's new home was large enough to house a great many of her servants, but those who were not absorbed into the king's household were sent home. The former princess' lodgings were emptied as well, but her belongings were sent on to Richmond. Both ladies put on a courageous façade, but anyone could see how painful it was for them to be separated. I watched the princess bid farewell to her mother with tears in her eyes and found myself tearing up alongside her.

Having left her own daughter behind at Hever, Mary sympathised. "I would not wish this wound on even my greatest enemy," she whispered to me as Catherine swept down the corridor, with her head held high, to the litter waiting to take her away.

George showed little compassion for Catherine. "Their marriage was never legal," he said with a shrug. "She will be treated to every comfort she deserves as Princess Dowager to Arthur. Who are we to question His Grace? He will do right by his brother's widow."

Once they were certain that Catherine had gone, the happy couple returned to court for a few days, before moving on to Berkshire, Ashridge, and Ampthill. The only thing marring the joyful summer progress was an incident during the hunt in Hertford when Anne's greyhound killed a cow. She paid a tidy sum to satisfy the outrage of the farmer, but she still felt as though it left a black mark on an otherwise perfect experience. When the hunting season drew to a close, the business of populating Anne's new establishment finally began. She had already appointed an almoner, John Skypp, but there were many more positions she needed to fill. It was vital that the women Anne chose to serve her behaved loyally and beyond reproach. To get away from the noise of the court, we took a boat down the Thames to Durham House to sup with my mother-in-law and discuss Anne's choices without distraction.

"Your aunts, the Ladies Derby and Fitzwalter, must be appointed," Lady Wiltshire commanded before taking a sip of her wine. "My brother, Norfolk, has distanced himself from us far too much. Appointing our sisters will go a long way towards placating him."

Anne's face brightened in the soft sunlight bathing the hall where we dined. "Oh, my dear Jane already has a wonderful plan for making the great duke happy," she remarked with a giggle.

I felt a hot blush rise to my cheeks as Anne's mother eyed me curiously. "I would love to be privy to it," she replied.

Before I could respond, Mary reprimanded her sister, "Stop it, Anne." Lady Wiltshire's gaze travelled from one daughter to the other, waiting for one of them to divulge the secret. The eldest sister broke the silence first with an exasperated sigh, "Jane told Anne, in jest, that she should appoint Norfolk's mistress, Bess Holland."

Lady Wiltshire broke into a broad smile. "Well, that would certainly please him," she said with a laugh.

The door to the hall swung open, and we turned our attention to the handful of servants marching in with trays of steaming meat pies, roasted birds, and a baked apple tart. The savoury scent of lamb made my mouth water. Once the servants filled our plates, we tucked into our meal while a maid refilled our cups with rich Burgundy wine. We ate until our stomachers grew tight, then continued our discussion while we digested the satisfying meal.

"Lady Lisle would make an ideal companion," Anne mused thoughtfully. "I've always admired her intelligence and the way in which she commands her household. Better still, she is married to the king's cousin."

Both Lady Wiltshire and Mary nodded in agreement at Anne's shrewd choice. Honor Lisle's husband was the illegitimate son of Edward IV, making him not only a cousin to the king but one of the last living members of the Plantagenet family. He would never be a threat to the throne, but it would assure his loyalty if Anne promoted his family as much as possible. Mary added yet more cousins to the list: the Shelton sisters and Mary Howard. I sat listening to their suggestions, quietly shoring up the courage to make my own. I wasn't certain if Anne was seriously considering Bess Holland or if she was mocking me, so I was hesitant to give any names. Unfortunately, Lady Wiltshire noticed my reticence and turned her attention to me. "Jane, who do you think should serve Anne?"

"Well," I started, haltingly. "My sister, Margaret, is old enough to come to court now."

Anne frowned at the mention of Margaret's name. "No," she replied, shaking her head. "Henry mentioned that Lady Shelton had asked for her. She is to be married to her son, John. Did you not know?"

I silently cursed my brother for neglecting to mention it when he had been at Grimston, but feigned a smile, "Of course, how silly of me." The thought of my brother brought another suggestion to mind: his wife, Grace.

"That is a wonderful idea!" Anne exclaimed when I mentioned it. "I've heard that she has a very sweet disposition, and George is quite fond of your brother."

A dull thud against the window sent a breathless page scurrying into the hall. "My lady," he panted. "A mob has begun to congregate outside. They are screaming obscenities and calling for the Lady Anne; you must flee this place now."

Anne's face went ashen with panic. "Do something!" she cried to the page as she leapt from her chair and away from the window. Lady Wiltshire and Mary exchanged a worried glance, before pushing away from the table, following Anne from the room. I traipsed behind them, filing up the stairs, to survey the scene from safety.

From a second story window, we saw a crowd of women storming towards the house, pelting the windows with rotten fruit. "Come on out and face us Nan Bullen!" They screamed in anger. One woman jeered, "Go back to France, Whore!" and a cheer rose up when another cried, "Long Live Queen Catherine!"

"Anne, we have to leave now before they have us surrounded," I cried, pulling her away from the window. "Come, let's go."

While Lady Wiltshire stared at us hopelessly, Mary ran to the closet to fetch a cloak. "Put this on," she commanded as she threw it across the room. I grabbed Anne's hand and dragged her back down the stairs. The view from the second floor had shown me that the back entrance used by the servants was still clear. I tossed the black cloak over Anne then shoved her out the door before she could protest.

The emotion outside felt raw and terrifying; enraged women came at us from all sides. I swallowed the lump of fear in my throat and continued to lead Anne down to the river. The spectacle was so chaotic, we were nearly to the boat before they realised that the object of their outrage was underneath the cloak.

"Quick, into the boat," the ferryman ordered as he hurried us down the dock. A wave caught us as we pushed away from the shore and sent the boat down the river before the mob could catch up. A woman cried out after us, "Bring that concubine back, you traitor!" I wrapped the cloak tighter around Anne, pulling her in close to me as her body trembled with fear. Hot tears splashed down her flushed cheeks as she took big gulps to catch her breath.

"You're safe now," I whispered, gently rubbing her arm. I felt a tremor of guilt for lying to her. Anne may be safe from the mob, but I feared that she would never be safe on the throne. The king was glad to be rid of his first wife, but the people were furious. They adored Catherine of Aragon and would never accept Anne in her place. We were fortunate to have been warned early enough to escape this time, but would we be as lucky if it happened again?

November 14, 1541
The Tower

WHEN THE constable dragged the desk to the middle of the room, the grinding screech of wood against stone set my teeth on edge. Secretary Wriothesley paced the room, impatiently waiting for Gage to finish so that he could start. He approached the desk when the constable finally closed the door behind him and began laying out items he'd carried in with him: a glass inkwell, a quill, and two rolls of parchment. He made himself comfortable in the chair behind the desk, then he rolled out one of the pieces of parchment. I heard him mutter to himself as he went over the instructions one last time. I sat across from him on the cushion with my hands underneath my thighs to keep them from fidgeting and quietly waited for him to address me. I felt a lead weight resting in my gut.

Wriothesley's eyes narrowed in irritation when he finally looked up at me. He inhaled sharply, considering me for a moment before lowering his eyes back to the parchment before him. He dipped his quill into the pot of ink, scribbling a few words at the top of the page before returning the quill to its holder. He then placed the holder on top of the parchment to keep it from rolling and streaking the ink. He pushed the chair back abruptly and jumped to his feet, finding that it pleased him more to look down upon me rather than remain at eye-level. "Lady Rochford, you know why I am here, don't you?"

He didn't appear to expect a response, so I gave none but maintained eye contact as I waited for him to go on. He rocked back on his heels, then continued, "If I recall correctly, this isn't the first time you've assisted one of the king's wives in their illicit affairs is it?"

It was a trap. If I said no, I admitted that Anne was guilty, and I had helped her; if I said yes, I admitted that I helped Katherine.

I incriminated myself no matter how I answered. "I'm not sure I understand the question," I ventured bravely.

Wriothesley's lips twisted into a sly smile. "You're very clever, my lady. Obviously, you learned from your previous interrogation under my predecessor." I inwardly scoffed at the secretary. He would never be half as effective as Thomas Cromwell. Cromwell was a masterful manipulator who always hid his true feelings and allegiances, while unfailingly portraying himself as the king's most humble servant. Wriothesley's arrogance betrayed him. He was too overconfident in himself, and it was apparent to everyone. He had never been adept at reading the king's changing moods. "Tell me, Lady Rochford," he continued. "How did you come to be in service to Katherine Howard? Was it at the instigation of her uncle, the Duke of Norfolk? Were you placed as his spy?"

"The Duke of Norfolk has barely spoken a word to me since the death of my husband," I replied. "His family believes that I gave evidence against Anne and George, so why would they ever trust me to keep their secrets? My father and Thomas Cromwell were kind enough to sue Queen Jane for my return to court. My experience in the queen's household earned me a position serving Anne of Cleves and Katherine requested that I stay to serve her once she married the king."

"So as Katherine's friend you knew of her time in the household of the Dowager Duchess? She told you of Henry Manox and Francis Dereham, yet you never came forward? It was her secrets you were keeping then, not the duke's."

It was yet another trap. I never said I was Katherine's friend; I said that she requested that I serve her. "I kept no one's secrets, my lord. I know nothing of any Manox and, as for Dereham, I did not know of their relationship until his arrest."

Wriothesley sneered at my response. "Ah, but you did keep secrets, my dear Lady Rochford. Master Culpeper gave you up as the instigator of his meetings with the queen."

I lost my composure at this revelation. "He said I was to blame?" Tears sprung to my eyes. "He lies! He has told you nothing but lies!"

I had given the king's secretary exactly the reaction he craved. He gave me a satisfied smirk, then took his seat behind the desk. He removed the quill from its stand, dipped the nib in the inkpot and scribbled a few notes. When he finished, he replaced the quill, then leaned back in his chair. "If Culpeper has lied to me, then tell me the truth. What do you know of his relationship with the queen?"

I shifted nervously in my seat. Every instinct I had told me to lie, but I had to tell the truth; it was the only chance I had to save myself. "Truthfully, Master Secretary, I know very little," I confessed. "The queen asked me to accompany her to her meetings with Master Culpeper, but I was never privy to their conversations."

"And why not? Were you not in the same room with them?"

"I was, but I stayed as far away as possible. They spoke in hushed tones so I only ever heard snatches of conversation. For instance, during one meeting, I heard them speak of Bess Hervey."

Wriothesley consulted his parchment, then looked back at me. "The same Bess Hervey who served Anne of Cleves?" he asked. "I was not aware that she was at court."

"She hasn't been for some time, but she and Culpeper had a flirtation prior to the queen's coming to court. He treated her poorly, and when I reminded the queen of it to warn her of his reputation, she took pity on Bess and sent her a damask gown to compensate her for her trouble." In truth, I believed Katherine sent Bess the gown because she felt guilty. She had replaced Bess in Culpeper's affections when Anne of Cleves was on the throne, long before she even caught the king's eye. It was only after her own elevation that she had the funds to offer such a reparation.

"Tell me about the summer progress. Did the queen meet with Culpeper during this time?"

"Yes, they met several times. I kept watch at the door while they met at Pontefract. They stayed near the stairs so Culpeper could slip away should anyone appear."

Wriothesley arched his brow, then made another notation on the parchment. "Am I to assume you were not privy to their conversation?" he asked without looking up.

"I was not," I confirmed.

"Were you privy to any of their conversations, Lady Rochford?" the secretary asked with a deep sigh.

"No, I was not. In fact, I was asleep when they met at Lincoln."

Wriothesley barked in glee, his eyes widening in disbelief. "It seems most incredible to me that you heard nothing that passed between them. The very idea that you slept through their meeting stretches the imagination."

"It's true," I insisted. "Although I'm not sure how I managed it, worried as I was." Wriothesley's eyes narrowed as he waited for me to go on. "I waited with the queen for Culpeper at the back door near eleven of the clock at night. A watchman startled us, so we hid from sight. When he locked the door behind him, the queen assumed her sport was spoiled so we went back to her rooms. Culpeper arrived shortly thereafter when he had his man pick the lock. I left them in my bedchamber and waited in my presence chamber for them to emerge. In that time, I fell asleep. I was only awakened when the queen sent me to answer Mrs Lufkyn."

Mrs Lufkyn was the mistress of Katherine's maids. She never caught the queen during any of her trysts with Culpeper, but it was not for lack of trying. I would have thought she had her hands full with young maids Katherine kept about her, wild things that they were, but she kept a close eye on their mistress as well.

Wriothesley placed his quill back in the stand, then shifted in his chair. He considered me, his eyes roving my face as if to assess the truth of my words. Finally, he asked the question he had been turning over in his mind, "You were closeted with the queen after

Dereham's arrest. Did she say anything about Culpeper during that time?"

"Yes," I confirmed with a nod. "The queen asked about Culpeper daily. She begged me not to say anything about their meetings. She believed that, since her relationship with Dereham occurred before her marriage, she would be safe as long as His Grace didn't know about Culpeper."

Wriothesley rose from his chair, and then walked towards the window. He stood there for a moment, watching the ravens fly past the streaked glass. Without looking at me, he asked his final question. "If the queen begged you not to tell, then why are you sharing this information with me? It has come freely; I have not tortured it from you. In fact, you have answered quickly and with little hesitation. Why have you betrayed her confidences?"

I felt the bile rise in my stomach as the words bubbled from my mouth. "I believe that Culpeper has known the queen carnally and that they have betrayed the king. I'm hoping that, in his graciousness, the king will look favourably upon my honesty and regret and show us mercy."

When Wriothesley finally turned to me, he had a reptilian smile plastered on his face. "I thank you for that sincerity, Lady Rochford. You've been most helpful, and I feel rather terrible for what I must do next."

My heart sank at his words. I had gambled everything and lost. The truth would not save me; it would only make it easier for them to punish me. What had I done? I swallowed back the vomit in my throat. "What must you do now, Master Secretary?"

"I'm going to need to take your maid, Lucy, with me. Mistress Tylney has implicated her in your crimes."

JUNE – OCTOBER 1532
GREENWICH,
THE SUMMER PROGRESS,
AND CALAIS

WITH CATHERINE rusticated at one of the king's lesser houses, Anne found it easy to slip into the role of queen. Though she did not lead the festivities during the Yuletide celebrations at Greenwich as she had hoped, her rival's banishment from court pacified her, for the time being. Our New Year gifts to the king were, by far, the costliest yet and a testament to the comfortable life that George's grants provided. To show his deep appreciation, my husband presented His Grace with two gilt daggers purchased at the price of almost a month's rents. For my part, I spent weeks crafting four black caps made from the finest velvet and satin. I trimmed two of them with heavy gold buttons. Not to be outdone by us, Anne's gift was a set of beautifully decorated boar spears crafted in the Biscayne fashion.

The mood at court was more subdued than in years past, but everyone appeared light-hearted and only one brief moment tainted the festivities. I was not there to see it, as the king's gifts were always presented privately in the presence chamber, but George witnessed first-hand the king's anger when Catherine's messenger presented her customary gift of a gold cup. He said His Grace raged at Catherine's presumption and sent the man scrambling in fear from the room. Once they were able to calm him, he relented and allowed the messenger back in to avoid the possibility that he would attempt to deliver the gift again in public. King Henry stuffed the cup, unceremoniously, into the pile of gifts until he could send one of his own messengers to return it.

The protest at Durham House had been a mere taste of what was to come as Anne's prominence grew. It was not only the common people who expressed their distaste for the king's great matter, but his bishops and councillors rebelled as well. During

Easter Mass, William Peto of the Observant Friars preached a resounding condemnation of the king's relationship with Anne. He compared His Grace to King Ahab, calling Anne his Jezebel, and prophesied that when he died, the dogs would lap up his blood. The king's cousin, Reginald Pole, exiled himself in Rome and spoke out against the annulment and even his very own sister, the Duchess of Suffolk, sparked a lethal altercation between her husband's retainers and those of the Duke of Norfolk with her inflammatory words against Anne. As the king edged closer and closer to a clean break with Rome, his most trusted companions grew ever more distant.

The clergy was finally forced to recognise the power they had bestowed upon the monarch when he made them sign a submission indicating his control over Convocation. This defeat challenged the principals of the conservative Thomas More, and he tendered his resignation as Lord Chancellor. When The Great Seal of the office was delivered back into the king's hands in the garden at York Place, I finally relaxed. More's increasing determination to root out heresy kept me in fear of his discovery of the actions of George and my brother; I'd bitten my fingers to shreds each time they met in secret to discuss the spread of their humanist ideals on the Continent. With Thomas More retired from public office, Hugh's career as a smuggler became more lucrative as demand increased for the forbidden materials espousing these beliefs.

These public displays of antipathy served to erode the tenuous confidence Anne had gained. She feared that the king would give in to these displays of rebellion and set her aside to improve morale. Rather than temper her mood to act in a more conciliatory manner, she became haughty and disdainful, further fanning the flames. We all looked forward to the commencement of the summer progress when we could retreat from the scorching fire of emotions at court. The French Ambassador, Giles de la Pommeraye, joined us as we made our way through the countryside. Along with a gift of two fine greyhounds from his master, he came with a proposition: The French King wished for a personal visit from his most entirely beloved friend and royal brother.

Anne was ecstatic at the prospect of returning to the country where she had spent so much time as a maid; her presentation as the king's intended bride would be a great triumph. To show her appreciation for such a welcome invitation, she presented the ambassador with a hunting cape and hat of her own working along with a horn and a sleek greyhound. The excitement for the upcoming journey became all encompassing, and the hunt was soon forgotten as planning got underway.

"Oh, Mary, could you have ever imagined it when we were in France? I'm going to return, not only as Henry's betrothed but as a peer in my own right. I became so overcome with joy when he told me that I almost fell to my knees in front of his entire household," Anne's face shined a beacon of joy as she informed her sister and me of her upcoming elevation to the Marquess of Pembroke. "Of course, it will be a hereditary title so our son can inherit it and that makes me the first woman to receive it in my own right. See how much he loves me? I don't know why I was ever so worried," she continued breathlessly.

Mary beamed a sincere smile as she poked the needle she wielded back through the crimson satin, pulling the thread tautly. "Anne, you've always worried far too much about what others think," she said. "The king does not need to grant you titles to show you how much he cares for you. It is quite obvious to everyone that he is just as besotted with you as he ever was."

"That is why everyone is so angry," I interjected with a laugh.

Margery Horseman approached, as we melted into a fit of giggles, with an armful of Cypress lawn and a scowl. "Here are the tabards you requested for the maids at Calais," she said as she attempted to hand over the aprons to me.

"Thank you, Mistress Horseman, please take them to the tailor so they can be packed away properly," Anne directed with a smile. "When you return, you and the others can get started on the cloth of silver embroidery. These masking costumes will be the finest that King Francis has ever seen, don't you think?" Margery merely nodded her assent, before slinking off in annoyance. Anne shook her head as she watched her walk away. "She has never gotten over George's marriage to you. I'm sure it stings even more now that he has a title."

Margery was jealous of me? I still remembered the sting of envy I felt when I saw George whispering in her ear at the Chateau Vert pageant. It seemed, in some ways, as though it had happened only yesterday and yet, so much time had passed. I marvelled at the idea that it could have been Margery in my place. Margery who carried and lost two of George's babies. Margery adorned with jewels bought by George's grants. Margery who made her home at Grimston.

"She's not much younger than us, Anne," I said, trying to shake away the unsettling thought that perhaps Margery was better suited to my life than I was. "I suppose she worries over her marriage prospects. When you are Queen, you should see that she makes a good match."

Anne nibbled on the tip of her finger as she thought about my suggestion. "You know, she often reminds me of myself… particularly when she is cross!" she exclaimed with a chuckle. "I can certainly sympathise with her predicament, and it wouldn't hurt to have her loyalty. I may just do that."

Mary looked up from her sewing and caught her sister's eye. "Don't do it for her loyalty, Anne. Do it out of kindness."

The hurt look on Anne's face compelled me to her defence. "Like it or not Mary, Anne must take these things into consideration; she doesn't say it to be unkind. Every benefice she makes will be questioned; every cause she takes up scrutinised. She has a responsibility to wield her power wisely."

Mary shrugged, turning back to the costume in her lap. "Just don't lose your capacity for compassion. The power you have here in this world will mean nothing when death comes for you."

She offered a sobering truth. The more George taught me about the new religion, the more sense it made. No matter how much wealth and power we had, we could not buy our way into Heaven. Perhaps the church merely taught us that so they could line their coffers. Maybe delivery truly did come by our faith alone. Still, I hated that every word Anne said seemed twisted against her, even by her own family. She had shown kindness and compassion quite often during the time I had known her; I had no doubts that her generosity would continue, regardless of her title.

In the days leading up to Anne's elevation, we worked our fingers bloody with all of the sewing needed for the ceremonies abroad. I stayed up late most nights stitching by candlelight until long after George retired for the evening. When I finally crawled into bed, I tucked myself in next to his warm body and tumbled into dreams of silk and jewels. The sheer number of precious gems that Anne accumulated during her time at court confounded me. It seemed that every time I closed my eyes, their glittering images danced in my head.

When we awoke on the morning of Anne's investiture, George pulled the covers tight against the crisp autumn air creeping in through the window we had left cracked open and snuggled closer to me. The first cool dawn of the season was clear and bright; it almost seemed a harbinger of the glorious days to come. George's warm breath on my neck sent a tingle down my spine and the gentle stroke of his fingertip down my arm raised a trail of goose bumps. I brought his hand to my lips, pressing them into his palm.

"Be careful, Lady Rochford," he murmured. "There is much to accomplish today, but if you continue in this manner, I may not let you leave this bed."

I rolled over to face my husband, pulling him closer to me. "Don't tease me," I whispered in his ear.

George leaned back to survey my face. He caressed my cheek with his hand, before his lips sought mine. I surrendered myself to his deep kisses, feeling the surge of arousal course through me. His deft fingers drew my silk nightshirt up, and I leaned forward so that he could pull it up over my head. I drew a sharp breath against the frigid air crawling across my skin. George pushed himself into me, and we came together as one. When we finally pulled apart, breathless, I weaved my fingers through the dark, wavy hair at George's temple, probing his eyes with my own. I wanted to remember every gold fleck in their rich amber pools. I needed every detail of his face, from the line of his aquiline nose to the cleft in his square chin and every freckle in between, seared into my memory.

I sent George off in his finest doublet and hose, before calling my new maid in to help me dress. Lucy came highly recommended from my sister-in-law, Grace. She had a sweet countenance and radiated kindness. I knew instantly upon meeting her that she would be a pleasant companion, and I had yet to be disappointed. After she had trussed me up in layers of white linen and dusky blue damask, I traipsed to Anne's lodgings to help her do the same. When I walked through the doors of her bedchamber, I saw that her maids had garbed her in a gown of decadent crimson velvet trimmed with plush ermine. Her loose hair cascaded down her back in a curtain of black waves. She stood erect, with her head held proudly aloft, under the weight of the glimmering gemstones encrusting her gown.

"Jane, you're finally here!" she exclaimed, her voice bright with excitement. "Would you please let the Garter King-at-Arms know we are ready for him? Mary has gone on ahead to the king's presence chamber; she waits for you with George."

I planted a quick peck on Anne's cheek and shot her a wink as I backed away towards the door, "Anything you desire, my Lady of Pembroke. We shall meet again shortly."

A scene of solemnity greeted my arrival at the king's presence chamber. A handful of nobles huddled around His Grace, waiting in hushed anticipation, for the arrival of the royal sweetheart. George caught my attention from across the room and gave me a smouldering look that set my heart thudding against my chest. I crept quietly through the gathered courtiers and took my place next to my husband. Without turning his gaze from me, he reached for my hand to give it a squeeze, and whispered, "You are beautiful, as always."

The Earl of Wiltshire stood behind George. At the sound of the trumpets heralding Anne's arrival, he clapped his hand on his son's back. "This is merely the first moment in a series of triumphs to come."

Anne entered the room flanked by the Countesses of Derby and Rutland, then the Garter King-at-Arms conveyed her and her cousin, Mary Howard, who carried her crimson and ermine mantle and a golden bejewelled coronet to the king's presence. His Grace stepped forward, leaving the Dukes of Suffolk and Norfolk behind him, as Anne knelt at his feet. The Bishop of Winchester, Stephen Gardiner, read out the patent conferring upon her and her future children the title of Marquise of Pembroke as the court and the French ambassador looked on. The king's lips pursed in pleasure when he took the coronet from Mary Howard and placed it on Anne's head. With a deep sigh of satisfaction, he draped the mantle carefully about her shoulders. When Gardiner finished reading the patent, the king took it from him and gave it to Anne, then he offered to help her to her feet. Before she let go, she brought his hand to her lips for a chaste kiss. "Thank you, Your Grace," she said in a reverent tone before retreating from the presence chamber.

We followed a jubilant King Henry to the chapel for mass once the ceremony concluded. After a rousing service conducted by Gardiner, His Grace and the French ambassador swore to the terms of their most recent treaty before the court and made an official announcement of the upcoming journey to Calais to seal their mutual amity. We exited the chapel to the sounding chorus of a *Te Deum*, moving on to the great hall to celebrate with a magnificent banquet.

Two weeks before Anne's elevation, William Warham succumbed to his old age and infirmary on a visit with his nephew and passed from this life into the next. The Bishopric of Canterbury was now vacant and the terms of the clergy's submission allowed the position to be filled by royal appointment. In the days following the investiture ceremony, Thomas Cranmer was appointed to the position and a royal decree was sent to him in Italy where he was serving as the English ambassador to the Imperial Court. This low-born cleric had been the architect of the king's break with Papal Authority and, as such, developed a very close relationship with the Boleyn family. When the Earl of Wiltshire went to Rome to sue for the Emperor's support, it had been Cranmer who had travelled with him. Anne was overjoyed at the appointment of one of her most ardent supporters, and she could hardly restrain her glee when she confessed to Mary and me that this meant that the thing she had so longed for would finally be accomplished in France. It wasn't a wedding to which Anne referred. She would finally give King Henry everything he desired. He already had her heart and soul; now she would give him her body.

Disappointment tempered the royal couple's excitement for the journey across the English Channel. The first blow came when the king sent for Catherine's collection of royal jewels. She brutally rebuffed the king's page with a harsh message: her conscience would not move her to give up her jewels to adorn the *'Scandal of Christendom.'* Her temerity enraged him. How dare she disobey a direct command? Even worse, she used his own argument against him. If she had been forbidden to send him things, then how could she return the jewels? Anne remained undaunted; eventually, the jewels would be hers, she need only wait Catherine out. The strategy had been successful thus far, what were a few months more?

Anne expected Catherine's insubordination; it was the insult from King Francis that wounded her the most. When she served at his court, she had been beloved of his wife, Queen Claude, but a poor constitution and successive pregnancies had taken her life far too early. Now, the French King was married to a sister of the intransigent Emperor. Even if Queen Eleanor felt amenable to meeting Anne, King Henry would never agree to it. Anne requested, in vain hope, that Francis's sister, the Queen of Navarre, receive her. Marguerite was sophisticated and elegant; she had been highly educated and supported those who wished to reform the church. Her consent to receive Anne as her equal would be seen as a great boon. Sadly, it was not to be, and to Anne's great dismay, Marguerite pleaded some indisposition. If that did not disappoint her enough, Francis's solution to the matter was to suggest that his official mistress receive Anne. In spite of the indignities lodged at her, Anne persevered. She would take her ladies and hold her own court at Calais while Henry met with Francis at Boulogne. When the two monarchs returned, she would entertain them with a grand feast.

We left for Dover in the early hours of a crisp October morning. The dense fog obscuring the dirt-packed road before us forced the winding train of the king's retinue to move by slow stages until the sun burned off the low-hanging clouds. Avalon, my beloved companion on so many previous journeys, had been recently retired, so I sat astride a new chestnut coloured palfrey. The horse was a gift from my husband, and he had outfitted her with the most beautiful tawny leather saddle made especially for the visit. In keeping with my taste for Arthurian names, I named her Morgana. At Anne's request, George and I rode near the head of the procession so that we could keep her company on the long march through the countryside. We arrived at the manor of Stone as the sun began to dip below the tree line.

The king sent the rest of the party ahead and we settled in for the night at the home of Lady Bridget Wingfield and Sir Nicholas Hervey. Lady Wingfield was an intermittent attendant at court. She was with us on that first visit to Calais so long ago, when she served as a maid to Catherine. She attended upon Anne when she could, but she had recently given birth to a son so she would not be joining us this time. Our gracious hosts treated us to a feast of roast suckling pig served with savoury puddings and a venison pasty. After supper, we sat before a cosy fire and played a round of cards as we laughed and talked about the goings-on in London. During the second round of Primero, Lady Wingfield excused herself to see how her infant was faring. I asked if I could come along and she welcomed me wholeheartedly.

A nurse was quietly rocking in the corner with the baby suckling at her breast when we crept into the sweet scented nursery. Lady Wingfield stopped the nurse when she moved to bring the baby closer. "We can wait until he finishes," she said with a smile. I gazed around the room as we waited and took in the bright, woven tapestries hanging on the wall. They seemed to contrast with the gloomy portrait of a dour ancestor standing sentry over the carved wooden cradle. "That is my father, Sir John," Lady Wingfield whispered. When the baby was satiated, the nurse eased herself out of the chair so that Lady Wingfield could sit down, then she carefully placed the bundle in her arms. Mother and child cooed at each other for a few moments, then Lady Wingfield brushed her lips against her son's forehead. I furiously blinked back the bitter tears that burned behind my eyes. "Would you like to hold him, Lady Rochford?" she inquired.

I wanted more than anything to cradle the infant in my arms, but I feared that sadness would render me useless, so I quietly demurred. "Oh, I don't know if I could, Lady Wingfield, but thank you so much for asking. I would like to see his face, though." I inched closer when she beckoned me, peering at the miniature features hidden beneath the layers of fabric. I traced my little finger down the bridge of the baby's plump nose, marvelling at the softness of its supple skin. When I pulled away, his tiny fingers grasped my own and held on with a fierce strength. "Oh!" I exclaimed.

"My George is already a strong boy; he will do his father proud," Lady Wingfield tittered.

George – My stomach lurched at the name. If my husband's namesake had lived, he would now be three years old. My breath caught in my throat. "I have to go, Lady Wingfield, I am so sorry," I sputtered as I backed away. I had to escape before bursting into tears.

"Is everything all right, Lady Rochford? Did I say something wrong?" Her voice was filled with concern, but I could say nothing in return. I fled from the nursery before I could humiliate myself further. Ignoring the light-hearted cheers coming from the hall, I hurried to my bedchamber where I threw myself on the great tester bed, burying my face in a pillow to cover my sobs. I had thought myself ready when I volunteered to accompany Lady Wingfield to the nursery, but my emotions were still too raw. Would I ever have the chance to hold my own child? I felt ashamed of my failure. My prospects dimmed with each passing month that my body betrayed me. What had I done to deserve such pain? My chances of conceiving seemed hopeless.

I was so distraught that I failed to notice George, until he had his arms wrapped around me. "Lady Wingfield said you looked like you had seen a ghost when you fled the nursery. I knew why when she showed me baby George. I'm very sorry, my love. I should never have let you follow her."

"It's not your fault. I thought all would be well, but it wasn't. I feel poorly for having embarrassed you and myself," I sniffed.

George hugged me tighter. "Jane, you didn't embarrass anyone. Lady Wingfield has lost two children of her own, she understands. Please don't cry."

I tried to choke back the tears, but they continued to stream down my face, soaking the pillow. "Do you hate me, George?"

"Of course, I don't hate you. Do you hate me? Hasn't it occurred to you that our failure to conceive could be my fault?"

"Why would you say that? How could it be your fault?" The mere thought struck me dumb.

"We're rarely together anymore," he murmured. "I'm always with the king. If I'm not sweetening ambassadors or addressing Parliament on his behalf, I'm playing tennis or shovelboard to entertain him. The few moments we have together are fleeting, and we are both so exhausted from our duties…"

Everything George said was true, but other couples were able to manage. Lady Wingfield and her husband were often apart and yet still conceived a child. Why couldn't we? Our positions had made it possible to build a secure legacy, but we had no children to inherit it. It felt cruel and unfair. "I feel so defeated, and I don't know what else to do. Should I go to Our Lady of Walsingham to beg for her intercession?"

I felt George's body stiffen at the mere suggestion of a pilgrimage to the shrine. "No, Jane. We have no need for the idolatry of those shrines. God will grant us children in due course. Now is the time for rest, we still have a long journey ahead. I will send Lucy in and bid our hosts good night."

After a fitful night of sleep, we arose in the early morning hours to break our fast and continue the journey to Dover. Lady Wingfield and Sir Nicholas Hervey sent us off with full bellies and their best wishes into the mists of a fine drizzle. The roads had not yet turned to muck, but the inclement weather still slowed our pace. By the time we reached the home of Sir Thomas Cheyney, the rain had seeped through every layer of my clothing, chilling me to the bone. The Lord Treasurer fed us a hot meal and kept us warm and dry for the evening; we set off for our last stop before Dover at daybreak. Christopher Hales and his wife, Elizabeth, eagerly greeted us upon our arrival at their home in Canterbury, but I was less enthusiastic. Like Lady Wingfield,

Elizabeth had also given birth in the last few months. I avoided the nursery this time, but every sharp cry that drifted past its doors pierced my heart. I found no peace until we finally made our departure.

The sky was still dark when the mast of *The Swallow* rose into view. The wooden tower stood sentry over a calm sea against a pitch black backdrop alight with the pinpricks of a thousand stars. The porters loaded the carts and our horses onto the ship while we made ourselves comfortable and prepared for the voyage. A fair wind carried us swiftly across the channel, and we arrived in France before the sun reached its peak in the sky. We disembarked at Calais to the thunderous peal of cannon fire. The Mayor and the Lord Deputy met us with a company of knights and soldiers in great ceremony, before we were taken to the Church of St. Nicholas to hear mass. At the conclusion of the service, we were finally able to retire to our lodgings at The Exchequer.

Over the past months, The Exchequer had been refurbished and enlarged to house the mass of courtiers coming across the Channel, but it was still relatively small in caparison to the houses we usually occupied. To accommodate Anne's suite of rooms, George and I were allotted only a bedchamber. Though it was a bit cramped, it was all we needed; we spent our leisure hours in the company of Anne and the king. Indeed, the next ten days at the garrison were filled with great feasts and all manner of entertainments. When the weather was fair, the Master of the Mews brought out a pair of majestic white gyrfalcons for the royal couple and a few smaller birds for their companions. I had always been a spectator any time the court went hawking, but George adored the sport, and he delighted in the opportunity to teach me what he knew. When George lowered the bird onto my wrist, the weight of it surprised me. His supple leather glove protected my skin from the sharp claws of the goshawk, but they gripped my arm with a strength I had not expected. He expertly removed the hood and loosened its jesses, releasing the bird to hunt for its prey; it returned soon after, bearing a dead hare in its beak.

When it was too wet for hawking, the household huddled indoors and engaged in more artistic pursuits. One of the king's newest companions, Marc Smeaton, was an expert musician, and he thrilled us all with his smooth falsetto and deft handling of the lute. My brother's wife joined us in Anne's rooms to teach a few dances of her own creation. Grace was no longer the skittish mouse I remembered. She moved so gracefully, her feet appeared to glide across the floor. A broad face now framed her bright almond shaped eyes and pert nose. She was a whisper of sweetness among the maids, and I was pleased Anne had taken my suggestion to place her in the position.

While the ladies danced, the king and his men inspected the defences along the coastline of the garrison. The matter of the annulment encouraged the threat of invasion from the Emperor and his supporters, so it was imperative that England's arms were always ready to defend a siege. After ensuring our military might, the men resorted to card and dice games for entertainment. George won a small fortune off his uncle, Norfolk, on a particularly stormy day.

Two days after we received word of the French King's entry into Boulogne, His Grace rounded up a retinue of almost two hundred men, and made his way towards the Calais Pale. From there, both kings processed into Boulogne, where the French court entertained our king at the Abbey of Notre Dame. George and his father were among the men in the monarch's suite, and I looked forward to his tales of the luxurious accommodations he saw there. During their absence, we rehearsed the masque Anne had commissioned for King Francis' entertainment. It was simple yet elegant and played to Anne's strongest suits of flirtation and grace. The clap of gunfire heralded the coming of the monarchs to Calais four days later. That evening, the Provost of Paris presented Anne with a gift from the French King to signify his friendship, a glittering table diamond; the largest I had ever seen.

On Sunday, we moved onto the Staple Inn to see a bearbaiting. Anne remained closeted until after the feast when we were to appear in the hall as a stunning course for the senses. My ragged nerves hindered my appetite, so I merely picked at the delicacies. I was eager to taste a baked porpoise sent by the Grand Master of France, but my stomach was too agitated to brave it. At Mary's signal, Ladies Derby, Fitzwalter, and Wallop, Honor Lisle and I beat a hasty retreat from the hall to join Anne in preparing for the masque. We reappeared in the hall draped in flowing layers of cloth of silver elaborately embellished with gold laces. Margery Horseman, Grace, and two other maids trailed behind us in blood-red crimson satin covered by Cypress lawn tabards. We beguiled the two kings with a sensuous dance while Anne enticed Francis and his gentleman to join us. When the music stopped, His Grace marched proudly onto the floor and pulled the ribbons that held Anne's mask with a flourish, revealing her identity to a stunned French King.

The next day King Henry honoured both the Grand Master and the Admiral of France with the Order of the Garter. A wrestling match was held to celebrate, and we all cheered when the English wrestlers soundly beat the French. We feasted Francis and his court one last time before King Henry accompanied him back to French soil. Though an ominous beginning threatened to derail the visit, the meeting had ultimately been successful. The alliance of the two kings was strengthened by the friendly atmosphere of the entertainments and King Francis was reminded of the admiration the king's future wife held for his country. Most importantly, he agreed to approach the Pope in support of King Henry's annulment. It was now more certain than ever that Anne would be queen.

January – June 1533
York Place,
Greenwich and
the Tower of London

"I DON'T understand why this all has to be so secretive, George. After all they've gone through their wedding should be celebrated for all to see. Keeping it hidden only gives Anne's detractors even more reason call their child a bastard. How could Anne allow this? George? George, are you even listening to me?"

The only thing I could see through the valley of my husband's hunched shoulders was a tangle of dark curls. The quill grasped in his long fingers scribbled across the parchment, halted long enough for him to collect his thoughts, then rasped out another sentence. His effort completed, he finally turned his dark eyes to me. "I'm sorry, Jane. What did you say?"

The sight of his rumpled nightshirt and tousled hair melted away my irritation. "When was the last time you slept? How can you even see through those swollen pockets under your eyes?"

"I think it's been days, sweet wife," he answered with a chuckle. "How could I sleep with that infernal racket you make? It's like that time Norris and I chased a wild boar through the underbrush at Hatfield."

"I do not snore!" I exclaimed as I grabbed a bolster pillow from the bed and aimed it at his face.

George's eyes widened in alarm. "Jane, don't!" He barked, throwing his hands out to stop me. "You'll knock the inkwell over and ruin it all. It was only a jest."

He appeared so panicked that I couldn't help the bubble of laughter that escaped me. I made to toss the pillow at him, but stopped before it could fly from my hands. His face crumpled into a scowl. "You're going to pay for that you crazy woman," he admonished, launching himself at me.

The weight of his body knocked me back onto the plush mattress on our bed. His knees held my arms to my sides, and lithe fingers danced across my skin. "Stop! Stop!" I cried breathlessly, squirming against a tickling sensation that bordered between pleasure and discomfort; it was sweet torture.

George pulled his hands away, then leaned back to free my arms. "That should teach you," he intoned with a sly grin. "I may not be quite so lenient next time. I do hold keys to Bedlam you know." Without saying a word, I grabbed the collar of his nightshirt and yanked him closer to me, stopping his lips with a kiss.

"Must you go back to France?" I asked with a pout when we finally tore ourselves apart from each other. "Can't someone else go this time?"

"Of course, I must go, Jane. Who better to tell King Francis that Anne is now queen and carrying the heir of the kingdom, than her brother?"

"By that logic, wouldn't it be far more appropriate for her brother to attend her wedding? Instead, Norris and Thomas Heneage will be there. It is insulting enough that Anne will be attended by Mistress Savage rather than Mary or me, but you should be invited at least after all you've done for them," I sniffed in indignation.

"But we were there in Dover as witnesses when they pledged their troth, and that's the ceremony that matters. The burgeoning curve of my sister's belly makes it quite plain they consummated that union. As far as I am concerned, that was their wedding. This service is merely a formality for the king. He wants the marriage consecrated by a bishop for his conscience. He chose the witnesses, not Anne."

He hadn't entirely mollified me, but he did have a point. The ceremony at Dover had been an intimate and joyous affair, even if it was quite spontaneous and sudden. Officially, Anne conceived after Yule celebrations at Greenwich, but I knew better. A torrential squall kept us holed up in The Exchequer for the better part of a month. It was during those days spent snuggled together for warmth, while the wind howled and a hard rain pelted against the window, they finally gave in to their desires. Anne couldn't have known that she would soon carry the heir in her belly when we crossed the Channel back to England in the midnight fog, but with the physical barrier between them finally destroyed, she recognised it would only be a matter of time. When our feet touched English soil, hasty arrangements were made, and troths were pledged. Anne fell pregnant before the first snowfall.

"I am surrounded by babies, George," I lamented, channelling my irritation into gloom. "I will be an aunt twice over this year." It was difficult enough when Grace informed me of her pregnancy while we were in France, but I felt stricken when Anne confessed that she too was with-child a few weeks ago. It was a stark reminder that my own womb remained empty.

"Well, we will have to work harder to add our own child to the bunch," George murmured as he leaned forward again, covering my torso with his. "The translation for the king will have to wait; I have something much more pressing to finish first."

"Thomas Wyatt! How kind of you to grace us with your presence. Perhaps you would accompany us on a walk in the garden," Anne proffered her hand when the poet rose from his bow.

"I would be most honoured, my lady. Though I must insist, the blooms are no match for your beauty. Your skin seems to glow in the most wondrous way today," Wyatt replied with a smirk. Anne did not fool him with her pretence of innocence. He had been among the first she chose to goad with her proclamation of an insatiable craving for apples. Wyatt knew Anne from birth and was well aware of her distaste for the fruit.

"You never cease to flatter us do you, Master Wyatt?" Anne teased, then she turned to us. "Jane, Grace, come along. The other ladies can stay here and prepare for the ambassador."

"She's using the royal *we* now I see," Grace whispered as we followed them down the corridor. "When do you suppose they will officially announce her pregnancy? She can't hide it for much longer." I suppressed a wave of jealousy when her hand caressed the curve of her own burgeoning belly.

"Perhaps they never will. What would be the point now? Everyone already suspects and they have all but confirmed it."

Anne and the king took great pleasure in dropping hints all over court as to the state of their matrimony. It was beginning to seem almost as if it were a game to them; how much could they reveal without showing their hand? I had grown tired of the charade, and I resented Anne's coy behaviour. I hated that George was going back to France without me, but I looked forward to the end of the farce. Once King Francis was informed, Anne's coronation would proceed, and there would be no more time for games.

Grace and I followed our mistress out of the palace and into the garden. The last of the snow had finally melted away, replaced by a blanket of the white blooms that bore the same name. I looked forward to Candlemas every year because I knew that the hardy snowdrops would soon start poking up out of the frozen ground. Their beauty and persistence made them my favourite flower. I focused on the signs of spring unfurling in the garden while Anne tittered about the preparations that were going on at the Tower for her coronation. Wyatt, however, graciously indulged her. He listened patiently, exclaiming in appreciation at all the right moments, but I found myself wondering how much of it was sincere. There was no doubt Wyatt had been besotted with Anne at one time. Did he still feel the same? How much did it sting when he learned she was carrying another man's child? I shook Wyatt's misery from my mind. I had enough of my own residing there; it was far too crowded to allow for anyone else's.

Grace's plaintive apology startled me from my thoughts, "I'm truly sorry, Jane. I can't begin to imagine how hard this is for you. If it would help, I will gladly ask your brother if I can return home for my lying-in early." Her doe-eyes surveyed my reaction.

"Don't be silly, Sweet Grace," I replied with a smile. "I am delighted for you. You shall make an excellent mother. Besides, I need you; you are one of the few people here I trust."

"Never be afraid to tell me if your mind changes. Your kindness comforted me when I came to Hallingbury, so timid and afraid. I hope to repay the courtesy one day," Grace said as she squeezed my hand.

That evening, Anne invited King Henry and the Privy Council to sup in her rooms while they entertained the French ambassador, but the event was a calamity from the beginning. An abundance of wine coloured the king's mood and raised his amours, causing him to ignore almost every soul in the room save his sweetheart. He became belligerent and incoherent at times; at one point nearly deafening the Duchess of Norfolk, who sat beside him, while shouting, "Has not Madame la Marquise a grand dowry and rich marriage, as all that we see belongs to her?" The Duke of Suffolk seethed in the corner, his eyes lodging arrows at Anne. The atmosphere continued to remain unsettled long after the servants cleared the feast away. Though the royal couple had wedded and bedded, the question of the king's first marriage had yet to be answered. How could they recognise Anne as queen while Catherine still lived?

George received his instructions two days before he left for France. He appeared nervous yet optimistic when he shared them with me the night before he left. "His grace did precisely what he told King Francis he wouldn't do by marrying my sister so quickly. The official explanation is that I am there because I am Anne's brother, but the truth is that he wants me to be the one to inform him because of the close relationship we developed when I was there before."

"Ah yes, the Brotherhood of the French Whores," I snidely interrupted him.

George ignored my barb and carried on, "Once I tell him of the wonderful news, I am to encourage King Francis to withhold his consent to the marriage between his son and the Pope's niece until he issues a ruling in His Grace's favour. To do that, I am to convince the French King that the Pope is usurping His Grace's authority by demanding his presence in Rome. If he can trample our king's royal dignity in that way, what is to stop him from doing the same to him? He's even prepared a letter for King Francis to sign and send to Rome."

I climbed onto the bed and knelt behind him, kneading away the tension radiating across his broad shoulders. "I have full faith in your success. If anyone can convince King Francis, it would be you."

He groaned in pleasure, arching his back against my fingers. After a moment of silence, he said, "Well, I did convince you to love me."

"You vain, arrogant man," I replied with a playful shove. "I'm still not convinced."

Anne's first appearance as queen came on the Eve of Easter. We arrived at the chapel for mass, heralded by the sound of trumpets. The crowd stood by in silence as Anne, draped in expensive cloth of gold frieze adorned in a rich array of rubies and emeralds, glided in to take her place next to the king. The crowd of courtiers drew a collective breath when she dropped into the chair of estate reserved for the queen. From my perch behind the royal couple, it appeared as though the enormous gilded chair swallowed her whole. I scanned the upturned faces of the congregation; I recognised the sneer of disgust on more than I cared to admit, but for the most part, many appeared merely confused. The silent prayers I offered up concerned their behaviour. '*Please don't let them make a scene. Please make them sulk in quiet,*' I begged God. I couldn't see Anne's face when the preacher offered up prayers for her as queen, but I desperately hoped that she remained unmoved when her detractors rose from their seats and fled the chapel. The preacher's face fell when the tide of courtiers ebbed out the door. Plans for the coronation continued unabated by this admonishment. His Grace insisted Anne would be crowned queen regardless of any protestations.

The day after Archbishop Cranmer pronounced on the validity of the royal marriage, we processed down the Thames on the newly refurbished queen's barge from Greenwich to the Tower of London. An excessive formation of barges dressed in all manner of brilliant colours surrounded us as we trailed through the water behind a monstrous dragon belching fire from its jaws. The sight of it sent a delicious ripple of horror through my belly, and I couldn't help but jump at the barrage of cannon fire and scattered pop of fireworks that accompanied it. The people on the banks stood agape in wonder at the spectacle floating passed them. Both the Constable and Lieutenant of the Tower greeted us upon our arrival at the court gate just outside the imposing Byward Tower. They led us through the walls of the great stone fortress to the king who then glued himself to Anne every step of the way to the royal apartments. I thought it was charming that he plied her with so much tender affection, but I involuntarily flinched each time he caressed the curve of her belly.

"Jane, quit frowning," Grace whispered as we made our way through the crush of bodies. "I know it hurts, but you must endure it. Be strong." I knew she meant well. The others wouldn't understand my unhappiness; they would think me angry about Anne's elevation. I couldn't have rumours swirling about my loyalty to my sister-in-law.

"Is Harry nervous about tomorrow?" I swiftly changed the subject. "A Knight of the Bath; he must be thrilled."

A bright smile spread across Grace's face, the sunlight glinting off her perfect, even teeth. My brother could not have chosen a more comely wife. Fortunately for him, she was just as beautiful on the inside. "Beyond thrilled, Jane. He shall do us all proud."

The king led us on a merry tour of the grand lodgings prepared for his new queen before we moved on to the hall for supper. There was a sort of calm weaved through the celebratory spirit of the evening's proceedings. The day's events had exhausted Anne, and she complained of the swelling in her hands and feet, so we retired after the void course. The strong Rhenish wine muddled my mind, and I easily slipped into a deep slumber. The next day, eighteen baynes were prepared in the long gallery for the ancient rituals that accompanied the creation of the Knights of the Bath. After being supped by the king, my brother and seventeen other men bathed together in the filled tubs. While they spent the night holding vigil in the chapel, Grace and I entertained Anne in her lodgings.

The sight of my two sisters-in-law, full with child, crammed into the window embrasure stung me. I stared at them as they gazed out into the courtyard, marking every curve of their bodies. I grew jealous of their engorged breasts and the way their gowns hugged the swell of their bellies. I desperately longed to join their company. Anne noticed the distraught look on my face when she turned away from the window. "You look lonely, Jane," she remarked with a tender smile. "George will be home soon; I'm certain of it. Why don't you stay with me tonight? I would be honoured to share your company."

I accepted the kindness knowing full-well she offered it with sincerity. There was no denying Anne could be prideful and haughty when under extreme pressure, but she also displayed grace and benevolence. We spent the evening playing cards and sharing laughter before a roaring fire that chased away the chill of the draughty Tower rooms. Sometime during the early morning hours, we tumbled into the immense tester bed drunk on hippocras and cheer. I snuggled close to Anne's warm body underneath the creamy silk counterpane and lost myself in dreams of my husband.

June – October 1534
Hampton Court and
Woodstock

THE AFTERNOON sunlight filtering through the oriel window chased shadows across the vellum pages of the Bible I held in my hand. The crimson feathered linnet in the corner trilled an airy tune, but I was too absorbed in the story of Elisabeth to follow its notes. The words of the mother of John the Baptist filled me with so much hope that the desire to physically touch them overcame me. God had fulfilled the angel Gabriel's promise to her husband; after years of childlessness, she finally conceived. I felt the warmth on the page as my fingers trailed across the raised letters. *The Lord has done this for me. In these days He has shown His favour and taken away my disgrace among the people.*

I'd never ceased praying for the Lord to take away my disgrace, but He had yet to see fit to answer those prayers. When I first picked up one of the English Bibles Anne kept in her presence chamber, my wavering faith had been nothing more than a breath away from being snuffed out. I worried that the words inscribed on the leather bound pages had lost their power in translation; for I had always derived comfort from the repetition of the words in Latin, even if I didn't truly understand them. I needn't have concerned myself with such trifles. The teachings of our Lord came alive when written in English; every word felt meaningful, palpable. I found solace in the stories of barren women given the gift of conception long after they believed it was impossible: Elisabeth, Hannah, Sarah, and Rebekah. I finally understood why George had risked everything to keep that Tyndale Bible safe.

"Jane, what did it feel like when you lost your baby?"

Anne's question pulled me from my thoughts. How could I possibly explain the torment I felt knowing that my children had died inside of me? I had no knowledge of the correct words to describe my despair. With a deep sigh, I closed the Bible and set it on the table beside me, then turned my attention to the tester bed. Anne was propped up against the oak headboard, surrounded by pillows. Her lithe fingers trailed lazy spirals around the arched contours of her belly. "How can you ask me such a thing when your child grows so steadily? You'll bring yourself bad luck even imagining it."

Anne nibbled on her lip, then let her arm go slack beside her. After an interminable silence, she turned to me, "I can't remember the last time I felt the baby move."

"I'm certain everything is fine," I replied with a confidence I had never felt during my pregnancies. "I'll get you some strawberries. He always seems to kick when you eat those. He's like his father; he has a taste for sweetness." Anne's eyes darkened at my thoughtless remark. The king had taken an interest in a new maid at court, Joan Ashley. Mistress Ashley arrived after New Year with Mistress Jane Seymour, a maid of honour turned out of Catherine's household when King Henry moved her to a smaller house at Buckden. Having served in the Lady Mary's strict household, Mistress Ashley was unaccustomed to our sumptuous feasting and promptly gorged herself to puking on sugared comfits during Shrovetide; the episode earned her a new title from Anne.

"I pray God this one's a boy. Perhaps that will distract my husband from the tedious Mistress Marchpane," Anne mused sarcastically.

The year that had passed since the halcyon days, when Anne received St. Edward's crown, had been marked with one disappointment after another. In the weeks following the coronation celebrations, news came that the Duchess of Suffolk had lost the battle against her illness; King Henry's beautiful sister slipped gracefully from this world into the next, wrapped in the arms of her beloved husband. His Grace kept up appearances, but his swollen red eyes revealed his pain. In the midst of his mourning, my husband returned from France with tidings of devastation: the Pope's final ruling on the annulment favoured Catherine. If the king did not set Anne aside and return to his wife, he would be subjected to worst punishment the Church handed down, Excommunication. "Norfolk fainted when he heard," George confided to me on his first night home. "Don't tell my sister until after the baby is born." When the time came, I didn't have the heart to tell Anne about her uncle's reaction.

"Anne, that healthy baby girl sleeping in the royal cradle is proof that you do not suffer from the same barrenness as me. In a few short weeks, we will retire to Greenwich, and I will, again, bore you while we wait for your baby prince to come."

"This fascination with that sallow-faced maid sets me on edge. Henry insists that our daughter pleases him, but I don't believe it," Anne shifted uncomfortably, poking at her belly as if urging the child to move. "The further he moves from me, the more apprehensive I become, and you know how I behave when I'm fearful. It's as if I become powerless to stop myself." Anne's nerves had led to an increase of antagonistic words spoken between them, but the spats were always quickly forgotten. A passionate detente after an argument over His Grace's fondness for Mistress Ashley had resulted in her current gravid state. "He's still not moving," she continued with a frown.

A groan slipped from my lips as I rose from my seat by the window. The crisp, citrusy essence of juniper settled over the room as I plodded through the fresh rushes to the bed. "Come now; we need to get you from these torments," I commanded, pulling her to her feet. "I haven't yet shown you the mullioned windows His Grace had made in our lodgings. They offer a marvellous view of the park."

"I should have never given her those plovers from Lady Lisle. She has complained ever since," George declared as he gingerly removed the grey field mouse squirming under the sharp talons of his hawk. "The men at Dover assured me they were freshly slaughtered, but I had my doubts."

"George, that was weeks ago. Those birds aren't to blame for the trouble caused by His Grace's wandering eye. The onus will fall on him if your sister miscarries." I quickly clarified my comment at George's frown. "I meant that his wavering fidelity would be at fault. If she were certain of his loyalty, she wouldn't get so agitated."

George smiled at me, then sent his hawk off to find more prey. "Isn't she beautiful?" he asked with a satisfied sigh. "Lord Lisle's man procured her for me. I've just asked after a handsome destrier he sold for Master Highfield. I hope to bring it back with me when I return at the end of summer. He'll be perfect for the jousts held to celebrate the birth of our nephew."

"But our finances, George. Are you certain we can afford..." The taste of my husband's lips stopped my protestations. I rested my chin in the supple leather of his glove when his hand brushed my cheek; the dusty earthen notes in its scent comforted me.

"While we are on the subject of nephews," I purred when he finally pulled away, leaving me buzzing from his kiss. "My brother mentioned he wanted you to be the godfather if he and Grace have a daughter this time."

George broke into a grin. "Please tell him I would be honoured." I quickly stepped aside when I noticed the hawk out of the corner of my eye. The bird swiftly approached, and I narrowly avoided the brush of her wings as she landed on George's outstretched hand. "That's a good girl," he murmured while his fingers stroked her head. He worked quickly to replace her hood, before returning her to the mew. Once the cage was locked, he continued. "I'm pleased that your father has finally come around."

Of course, my husband thought the best of my father's New Year gift to his sister. His translation of *The Epistles & Gospels* had so delighted Anne that she made a show of using it every Sunday for the last year and a half. I felt less convinced of his generosity. "My father serves the king loyally. He will honour any woman His Grace commands him to, regardless of his affection for Catherine. He's a shrewd man, and he enjoys the favour of Cromwell. He'll do anything to keep it."

I had no doubts that the reformist leanings of the king's Lord Chancellor and recently appointed secretary, Thomas Cromwell, repulsed my conservative father. Lord Morley actively participated in the humanist ideals espoused by men like Erasmus, but he had his limits. The imprisonment of Sir Thomas More incensed him, yet he fully supported the Parliamentary Act that had put him there. My father would always do as his king told him. It was little wonder I found myself as biddable as he.

After the falconers had retrieved the cage, George and I wandered hand-in-hand back to the palace. The musky fragrance of the roses drew us into the garden, so we slowed our pace to admire the bursts of crimson and blush blooms. These quiet moments with George filled me with peace, but they were always short-lived. I tried not to resent George's growing importance. He had always admired his father's diplomatic skills, and I knew he was thrilled to find himself in the very same position. Besides, Wiltshire had spent most of George's childhood abroad; he knew no other way. Nothing would please me more than to have my husband home, but George was like his hawk. I could keep him tethered in his jesses for a short time, but eventually, he needed to spread his wings.

"A penny for your thoughts?" George asked, bringing my hand to his lips.

"If you keep spending money, you won't be able to afford them," I teased.

"I can always count on your probity, my love," George replied with a laugh. "Promise me that you'll be as forthright with my sister while I am abroad. I know her tongue often gets the better of her, but everything she says is subject to scrutiny. It is one thing for Norfolk to speak ill of the King's bastard with Catherine, but it's quite another when the anointed queen does it."

I winced at the memory of Anne's tirade against the Lady Mary. Her threats to starve the girl earned swift recriminations from both George and Wiltshire, but she said it in the presence of those still loyal to Catherine. Her harsh words were quickly reported to the Spanish ambassador and caused yet another argument between the royal couple. "I will try, George, but no promises."

"God's Blood! Do those birds ever cease their caterwauling? I can't even hear my own thoughts for the racket that they make! Send them to Cook and put them in a pie!" Anne's face flushed at the effort of her rage. I dabbed the sweat from her brow with my linen handkerchief, then brushed the hair from her face.

"Hush, Sister," I murmured. "The pain will pass soon; just continue to breathe through it."

"You lie!" Anne screamed. "This agony will never go away. You said so yourself. I must live with this forever." She shuddered when her spaniel, Purkoy, barked at the urgent squawking of the peacocks outside her window.

"Get that mutt out of here!" I commanded to the brace of maids who stood by staring nervously at the queen. I hated that they saw her at her weakest and in such disarray. Thankfully, Grace heard my voice, and rushed into the presence chamber to scatter the gawkers. She brushed away my words of appreciation as she grabbed the wriggling spaniel, and carried him from the room. I breathed a sigh of relief when the door slammed shut behind her.

"Be kind to my dog," Anne moaned between sobs. "He's the only one who cares for me."

"That's not true, and you know it. Quiet your mind, Your Grace. Your body must expel the child, or you will suffer irreparable damage. Grace will send for the midwife; she will help you." Anne's wailing continued unabated; the hot tears streaming from her eyes puddled in my lap. Her desperation reminded me of my own horrific miscarriages. I knew from experience that nothing I said could comfort her. I cradled Anne in my arms while my body instinctively rocked back and forth as if to sooth a child. It all happened so quickly. One moment she laughingly watched Purkoy skitter after a fly, then the next she doubled over in pain. I had suspected for some time that the child in her belly was dead, but I prayed that I was wrong. The midwife continued to insist there was hope, even though the baby never did move again. My fury at her grew with each moment my sister-in-law spent writhing in my arms.

"It is all the fault of that sorceress," she cried. "She wasn't telling prophecies; she was casting curses. She cursed me before she died. She cursed my baby."

The ravings and death of the nun, Elizabeth Barton, unsettled many at court. Before we went to Calais, she accosted the royal couple at Canterbury, proclaiming that the king would die a villain's death within seven months of their marriage. His Grace brushed it off as the mutterings of a mad woman until she attracted the support of Bishop Fisher and Sir Thomas More. In January, Parliament filed a bill of attainder against all three for treason. After the nun and five priests were dragged to the scaffold at Tyburn, the recalcitrant Bishop, and the former Lord Chancellor were locked in the Tower, where they still rotted. I didn't blame Elizabeth Barton for Anne's agony; I knew that miscarriages came without the aid of demonic affliction and yet, I said nothing against her oaths. She could fault anyone she cared to as long as it soothed her.

The radiant sparkle of Anne's eyes dimmed in the days following her loss. I stood by, helpless, as her usual vitality gave way to despondency. My losses were nothing like hers; at the end of my labours, God left me with something solid to mourn. Anne writhed in agony throughout the night, but she had nothing to show for her efforts besides a river of blood and a lump of flesh no bigger than my thumbnail. I begged the midwife for an explanation. Anne had every sign of a successful pregnancy: a burgeoning belly, unrelenting nausea, and the tell-tale fluttering within her womb. Where had the baby gone? The midwife offered me nothing in return but the shrug of her shoulders.

George's sense of triumph upon his return from France was quickly squelched when he saw the mournful state of his sister. She granted him a half-hearted smile when he visited us in her rooms, then they retreated to her bedchamber so she could tell him the news without the watchful stares of her ladies.

"Aren't you going to follow?" Grace asked as we watched the door swing shut behind them.

"I believe the queen deserves to have this moment to herself," I replied. My tone conveyed a sense of finality; I had witnessed the terrible event for myself and had no desire to relive it.

George appeared genuinely confused by his sister's loss. "Could she have been mistaken? Is that even possible?" he asked when we crawled into bed that evening.

I propped myself up against the headboard, then threw my husband a withering look; he had seen the bloated curve hiding under Anne's stomacher before he left, there was no mistaking that. "No, George, Anne conceived – I saw the evidence of it – but there was nothing to justify her symptoms. It's as if her desire were great enough to manifest them into being."

George snuggled closer to me, laying his head on my lap. "I wish that were possible," he replied with a deep sigh. I stared into the tangled dark locks of hair that fell across my thighs. I hooked a silken strand and twisted the curl around my fingertip, my skin paling against the inky colour.

"Me too, my love," I whispered. "Me too."

Anne's health had sufficiently recovered in time for us to join the king at Woodstock for the final days of the summer progress. While George hunted in the nearby park with the king and his father, I spent the balmy September afternoons sewing miniature frocks for Princess Elizabeth. I was in the middle of coaxing a violet into bloom when the sound of Anne's strangled laugh startled me. I unleashed a yelp of pain when the needle skidded across the silk fabric, anchoring itself in my skin. I brought my finger to my lips to suck away the crimson bead of blood before it stained the delicate fabric.

"Be careful, Jane," Anne admonished from her perch near the mullioned window overlooking the knot garden.

My caustic reply was interrupted by a brisk rap at the door. "I'll see to it, Your Grace," Margery Horseman said as she lunged from her cushion, eager to make an escape.

Anne shook her head, turning back to the window. "Well, we know it's not our husband because he is in the garden with Mistress Marchpane," she muttered under her breath.

"I thought he was hunting?" I asked, joining her in the embrasure.

"Oh, he is. He's found a pretty hind to stalk."

Margery appeared puzzled when she returned a few moments later. "Your Grace's sister, the Lady Mary Carey is here to see you."

Anne's faced brightened at the announcement. We had not seen Mary since she returned to Hever in the spring to visit her children. "Wonderful! Please see her in," she commanded, rising from her seat. I remained at the window, observing the king and Mistress Ashley below. They stood close together; her hands wrapped snugly in the crook of his elbow. Her head tilted towards him, and she appeared to be laughing at some marvellous joke. The king looked at her the same way he had looked at Anne in the early days; as if he wanted to possess her. I stared out the window until the waver in Anne's voice drew my attention away.

"When did this happen, Sister?"

Mary's face flushed as scarlet as the curls gracing the head of the young girl beside her. "I'm four months gone now," she replied. Her hand rested on the small mound protruding from under her gown. Anne struggled to remain calm, but I saw tears glinting in her eyes.

I wrapped Mary in a warm embrace, then knelt down to greet the child. "Mistress Catherine, I'm very pleased to see you again." Catherine offered me a tentative smile, but I saw fright dancing behind it. "Do you remember Purkoy?" I recalled that she had become attached to him when she visited court for Anne's coronation. Her eyes lit up when I pointed at the spaniel dozing next to the hearth. "How about we take Purkoy for a walk and see if we can't find your Uncle George?"

"Of course," Mary replied when Catherine looked to her for permission, then she gave me an appreciative nod. "Thank you."

Purkoy barked indignantly when I scooped him up from the cushion and handed him over to Catherine; she giggled at the wriggling mass of fur in her arms. "Mama said I could have my own pup after the baby comes."

"Well then, this will be excellent practice for you," I replied, ushering her out the door.

Catherine and I passed George in the corridor on our way to the garden. He appeared grim, but the sight of his niece elicited a bemused grin. She handed me Purkoy, then threw herself into his arms. "Anne's rooms, now," I mouthed while her face was buried in his doublet.

When they pulled apart, George knelt down to face her. "Don't leave without saying farewell," he instructed, placing a kiss on the back of her hand. He straightened, then dipped a bow to us both, before hurrying off in the direction of his sisters.

Catherine and I remained in the garden until the sun sank below the trees. I caught the king staring quizzically after the copper-haired girl playing in the leaves with his wife's pet, but he kept his distance for the duration of her visit. The girl may have carried the name Carey, but she looked every inch a Tudor. Perhaps he hadn't wanted to remind the woman clinging to his arm of his past affairs.

Mary's eyes appeared swollen, her face streaked with tears, when she arrived to collect her daughter. She squeezed me tightly, but gave no explanations as she bade me farewell. I watched them fade into the darkness before returning to face the turmoil behind the doors of the palace.

The tension filling Anne's privy chamber felt palpable. I kept my head down as I strode through the crowd of maids huddled together exchanging whispers, and made my way to the bedchamber. I found Anne on the bed curled into a ball and George aimlessly pacing before the window. "Catherine was very upset that you did not come to see her off," I chided.

"Mary told me to stay away from her," he replied as he continued to stare out the window. "She told us that we might as well be dead for all she cared."

"That doesn't sound like Mary. Why would she say such a thing?" I looked to Anne for confirmation, but she kept her face buried in her pillow; her body shook with the force of her sobs.

When George turned to face me I saw that his eyes were red; his lips set in a grim line. "She came to test our loyalty. She wanted to see if we would support her even though she married without permission. When Anne chastised her, she flung accusations at us. She informed us that her new husband believes that we've done nothing but use her."

"I've banished her. I've banished my own sister," Anne choked through her sobs.

I crawled onto the bed, sidling up next to Anne. Her hood had become unmoored and sat askance on her head. Her hair tumbled free over her shoulders, and when I brushed the strands aside, I felt the hot sweat soaking through her gown. Her body arched against me, but her face remained hidden. "What can I do, Anne?"

"Can you make everything perfect again?" she sobbed. "Can you make my husband love me again? Can you make my baby whole again?"

I looked to George for an answer, but he had turned back to the window. I couldn't fix any of the things that had gone wrong for Anne in the past year, but perhaps there was something I could do. Perhaps I could do something about Mistress Marchpane.

I hid my intentions from Anne and my husband to avoid putting them at risk. I had no plan to speak of, just hope that the right opportunity would present itself. The moment arrived a few days after we returned to London. The king held a private banquet at Greenwich to celebrate the death of the Pope. All of his favourites turned out, bedecked in their finery, to support the king in his joy. As I stared out into the dancing crowd of courtiers, I wondered if the conservatives amongst them chafed at their hypocrisy. Perhaps they justified it by telling themselves they celebrated not the Pope's death, but the hope that his successor would reverse the damage he had inflicted; that reunification with Rome was no longer a lost cause.

I observed the scene from my repose against the chilled stone wall. Mistress Ashley hovered near the table that held all of the sugared subtleties. Her eyes shined with glee when she pointed out a brilliantly painted confection of St. George's Dragon to her companion. The sight of her creamy neck thrown back in laughter caught the king's eye. While his wife was deep in conversation with her father and brother, he slipped away from the dais, and sidled up behind the two maids. When Mistress Ashley became aware of His Grace's presence, she fell into a curtsey so deep her nose nearly touched the floor. He gestured for her to stand, before leading her out onto the floor where I lost them in a swirl of damask.

"The king appears happy doesn't he?"

I turned to the source of the voice and found myself staring into the beady black eyes of Thomas Cromwell. His thick arms tightened around the rolls of parchment he held against his chest as he shifted closer to me. My fingers caressed the curve of his elbow when I plucked away a short grey hair that stood out against the severe black colouring of his sleeves. "My cat," he replied with a smirk when I held it up for his inspection. The intimate way in which I touched him should have shamed me, but it only made me bolder.

I watched the hair flutter to the ground, then turned my attention back to the dancing couples. The king and Mistress Ashley reappeared when the dancers formed their lines; their plump cheeks flushed from their exertions. "I doubt it would please the king to know that Mistress Ashley intrigues with the Imperial Ambassador."

Cromwell's sparse brows jumped in surprise. "Eustace Chapuys?"

"I saw her slip him a letter while we were at Woodstock," I tossed aside the remark as if I couldn't be bothered to explain her actions, and my mentioning of it was merely an afterthought. My accusation wasn't entirely untruthful. I never actually saw Mistress Ashley give Chapuys anything, but the ambassador had paid her an inordinate amount of attention while we were on progress; likely because of her previous service to Mary Tudor. Chapuys ardently supported the king's daughter with Catherine, and he served as her fiercest champion.

"Did you report it to the queen?"

I brushed his question aside with a flick of my wrist. "I didn't want to burden Her Grace after her troubles. Now that I think of it, I am certain it was nothing; please forget I spoke out of turn." I wrinkled my nose, before curving my lips into a broad smile.

"Indeed, Lady Rochford," Cromwell replied before excusing himself with a perfunctory nod. My stomach pitched as I watched the king's minister lumber towards the maid who had kept Mistress Ashley's company earlier in the evening. I had surrendered control the moment the accusations tumbled from my mouth. I pushed the image of Mistress Ashley walking through the stone corridors of the Tower from my mind.

I held my breath while I waited for the repercussions of my casual remark to unfold. My nausea subsided as the days passed by, uneventfully. I expected to be confronted by Mistress Ashley, but she treated me more deferentially than usual, and her dismissal from court did not appear to be imminent. The initial relief I felt at successfully avoiding confrontation gave way to annoyance that my gamble had not paid off. I felt so secure that the appearance of a stricken George in our presence chamber one evening, a week later, took me utterly by surprise.

"What is wrong?" I asked as I shrugged out of my cloak; my cheeks felt flushed with cold after a walk in the garden with Grace.

"You've made a grave mistake, Jane. The king has ordered you banished from court."

November 14, 1541
The Tower of London

LUCY'S FACE was ashen, her eyes stretched wide in terror, when Wriothesley herded her out of the bedchamber. Strands of hair, having come loose in her sleep, stuck out wildly around her face adding to the effect of disarray. "I– I – don't understand," she stammered. "The king – he sent me here. He said I could be with Lady Rochford. Where are you taking me?"

"Don't worry, you aren't going far," Wriothesley sneered. "You're to have your own accommodations. Someone will be sent along to take care of Lady Rochford." He stared at me as he said this last sentence, gauging my reaction. I flinched at his invective, but stood rooted to the floor. His eyes dared me to contradict him, but I felt too stunned to act. I realised in that moment that the king had played me for a fool. He led me to believe that Lucy's presence showed mercy, but now I saw he meant it as a punishment. The king had used her as a trick; he knew he couldn't hurt me if I had given up all hope.

Gage entered the room with two guards on his tail. He shot me an apologetic look as his henchmen crossed the floor to Lucy. "No! Please!" she cried, shrinking away from them in terror.

I dropped to my knees before the constable. The impact of my bones hitting the stone floor sent a jolt through my body; I clawed at Gage's legs trying desperately to steady myself, but my hands slipped on his silken hose and sent me toppling over into a heap on the ground. "Sir John, don't let them do this. She is innocent. Whatever they have said, she is innocent, I swear to it," I pleaded.

Gage knelt down and reached for my hands to pull me up. "Don't do this, Lady Rochford," he whispered. "Remember your dignity. You must keep your courage."

His words slapped me in the face. How dare he speak to me of dignity? Any sense I had of dignity died on the scaffold along with George. Ever since the life we built together was torn from my grasp, I had been forced to debase myself at every turn to survive. My humiliation began when my father told me to choke back my pride and be grateful that he and Cromwell had convinced His Grace to allow me back at court. I grovelled for the pale, meek woman who replaced Anne and watched her give birth to the son that should have been my nephew with a contrived smile on my face. I humbly accepted every gift and honour she bestowed upon me with grace even though I knew her guilty conscience drove her generosity.

When I thought I couldn't sink much lower, I further degraded myself when I agreed to ask Thomas Cromwell for help with my jointure. I shouldn't have been surprised when George's father refused to give me my dower lands; he wouldn't even help his own flesh and blood daughter in her penury. I hated fighting for it, but I had no other way of maintaining the opulent lifestyle required at court. I couldn't afford to keep up a household on the paltry pension he gave me. Ever the shrewd lawyer, Cromwell encouraged me to sue the king for an Act of Parliament confirming my settlement and His Grace was only too happy to comply. He even granted me two additional manors for good measure. I never knew if he did it out of pity for me or if he saw it as one more opportunity to punish the father of the woman he believed had unforgivably wronged him. I had devoured their offerings like a greedy child, and it had sustained, yet sickened me.

"Oh, I have long forgotten my dignity, Sir John."

I remained pathetically curled up on the floor as Wriothesley, and the guards dragged a sobbing Lucy past me. Gage waited until the door slammed shut behind them before approaching me again. "Come, Lady Rochford, let me help you."

"No, leave me be," I commanded, pushing away his proffered hand. I needed neither his assistance nor his pity. I felt all of the anguish and bitterness I had denied myself course through my veins, while a tempest of blind rage unfurled in my belly. I wound my fingers through the tangle of my hair, then yanked the strands as hard as I could, while unleashing an unearthly shriek. The physical pain offered a momentary reprieve from the pain in my soul.

My shrill demands to be left alone chased the constable from my room. I leveraged the nearby stool to lift myself from the ground, before launching it at Gage's receding figure. It slammed against the wall, splintering to pieces. I thought the effort would slow me, but it served only to fuel my rage; I felt powerful beyond measure. My eyes swivelled around the room for more items to destroy. Wriothesley's abandoned inkpot winked in the sunlight, drawing my attention. I wrapped my fingers around the bottle, then lobbed it hard against the window. It shattered on contact, sending rivulets of ink down the glass pane. I ran to the wreckage. *George...Anne...Norris...*my fingers traced their names in the sticky, black liquid. I failed to notice that a shard of glass had flayed my skin until I saw the scarlet streaks. By the time the guards arrived, I had filled the window with the names of all who had fallen victim to the king; I had memorialised their poor souls in my blood.

A dozen men, armed with halberds, stormed my chamber. Two of them gripped me by the arms and dragged me, flailing and screaming, towards the bed. I struggled against the bodies pinning my hands and feet to the mattress. The weight of them suffocated me, and my chest burned with each breath I gulped. The image of Gage's concerned face wavering above struck me as absurd. His lips moved, but I heard nothing through my sobs and manic laughter. I closed my eyes and found myself in my marriage bed. I had fought hard to reclaim it and all the memories it carried of George's love for me. After his fall it became my refuge, and I imagined myself there now. The stench of sweat and dread seemed to dissipate as I gazed up at the Rochford Knots worked into the canopy above me. A distressed voice called my name, but I dared not answer for fear of leaving my freedom and peace behind.

OCTOBER 1534 –
FEBRUARY 1535
BEAULIEU

AFTER YEARS of patient waiting to take full advantage of his appointment as Chief Steward of Beaulieu, George had wasted no time moving in our possessions the moment the king's eldest daughter departed for Princess Elizabeth's household. But that had been months ago, and we had yet to set foot on the property since, so I should have felt thrilled to repair to the extravagant palace. Beaulieu boasted every amenity for which we could have possibly wished. Our lodgings were sumptuously appointed with intricate tapestries and ornately carved furniture; rich carpets softened our footfalls, and a mahogany sideboard displayed the engraved silver plate George had commissioned after our wedding. The accommodations were luxurious, but I wasn't going to Beaulieu to establish our household, I was going there to serve my punishment. The carving of the king's arms above the gatehouse arch should have reminded me of the bounty he bestowed upon us; instead, it reminded me that his favour came with a price.

George said little on the journey; only the clopping of our horses' hooves on the packed dirt road filled the long stretches of uncomfortable silence. My impulsive remark to Cromwell baffled him. I had always demanded his honesty, why had I not extended the same courtesy to him? I tried to imagine the expression my poor husband wore on his face when he was dragged before the king and commanded to send his wife away for her misbehaviour. The picture that formed in my mind broke my heart. I saw anger in his furrowed brow; devastation in the dark pools of his eyes; betrayal in the downward curve of his frown. What I had done was not nearly so bad as how I had done it. The impetuous Jane of my youth had seemingly appeared from out of nowhere, and she was a stranger to George.

We arrived at the palace as the golden sun sank behind the trees. Candlelight danced in the gatehouse windows, but the courtyard appeared deserted. The desolate scene was a far cry from the bustling chaos we had witnessed at our last visit. When no one appeared to greet us, George hopped from his horse, and handed the reins to his page. "I'll be back," he intoned. "Stay here." He gave my knee an absentminded pat as he passed by and my heart leapt into my throat. His tenderness sharpened my guilt.

George returned to the courtyard a few moments later with a porter straggling behind him. "These are to go to the Rochford chambers," he said as he pointed to the cart attached to the page's horse. After the porter nodded, George pointed to my maid. "This is Lucy; she is not to be lodged with the servants. Her duty is companionship to my wife. See to it that Lady Rochford has another maid to perform menial tasks."

"As you wish, Lord Rochford," the porter replied before shuffling off.

George approached my palfrey, his hand held aloft to assist my dismount. "Welcome to your new home."

My husband stayed for the first night of my exile. We ate a light supper in the quiet of our presence chamber. George perused the books in the library while I packed away my cherished possessions: the white silk stockings I wore for masking, pearls I recovered when my lover's knot necklace from George broke, and my gilt-edged prayer book; all went into one of the iron bound coffers littering the property. After I settled in, we retired to the bedchamber. George's presence assured me, and I slept far better than I anticipated; in the morning we made love. He trailed kisses down my neck as we said our farewells, then he left me behind in the gilded bed draped in cloth of gold. The Rochford Knots worked into the satin canopy blurred through tears that dripped from my eyes and puddled in my ears.

My first days at Beaulieu were spent holed up behind the damask curtains of our bed where the scent of my husband remained. I wanted nothing more than to doze away my days in the dent he left behind in the mattress, but Lucy finally coaxed me out when the laundress came for my linens. I grudgingly surrendered everything but George's pillow, then allowed her to dress me for a walk in the gardens. The weather seemed to have turned crisp overnight. The russet leaves that had covered the trees lining the entrance to the property when we arrived now carpeted the ground. The flowers appeared to linger in a seasonal purgatory; their petals were faded and ragged, but they had not yet succumbed to their winter slumber.

Lucy and I trudged through the muck to one of the benches facing the parklands behind the palace. We sat there in silence while the birds twittered above us. I had just allowed my mind to wander into the void when Lucy tapped my hand. "What is it now, Lucy?" I asked with a deep sigh.

"A stag, my lady, behind that tree. Can you see him?" She pointed into the dim abyss beyond the tree-line. It took a moment for the outline of his rump to come into focus, but eventually I saw him. He sensed our gaze, and started backing away slowly, while his liquid eyes held us in his thrall. When one of the servants carelessly slammed the nearest palace door shut, the heavy thud startled the beast, and he fled without a backwards glance.

"Oh how I envy his freedom," I murmured to myself.

"May I speak plainly, my lady?"

Lucy appeared shocked by her own boldness, so I felt compelled to allow her the courtesy. "Please do, Lucy. Let's hear it."

"Am I mistaken in pointing out that you still retain a measure of freedom? It's true that you can't return to court, but it's not as though you are held prisoner here. I think any one of the pages would be more than happy to prepare your horse and take you anywhere you desired to go. Without a queen to serve, I'm certain you will find many empty hours to fill."

My maid broke into a grin at the sound of my laughter. It felt wonderful to find my humour again. "I didn't know you were so naughty, Lucy."

"Really, I'm not, my lady," she replied, covering her enflamed cheeks with her hands. "I merely hate to see you so sad. Perhaps this is an unexpected opportunity."

Lucy's words rattled around my mind. There was something I wanted to do, but I'd never had the courage to undertake it and every time I broached the subject with George, he rebuffed me. But George had returned to court, and I was the mistress of Beaulieu now.

When George left Beaulieu, he informed me that the king had requested he greet the Admiral of France upon his arrival at Dover. His journey to the port would take him south from the city through Dartford and Rochester; there would be no danger of passing him on the road. I waited until I felt certain that he had departed, then set off on my own pilgrimage.

"Cook has packed more than a week's worth of food. You'll want to go slow to save your horses, and always attend to your surroundings," the porter warned as he watched me climb into my saddle. "Lord Rochford would have my head if anything happened to you."

"Not to worry, Lucy and I are in Gilbert's capable hands. He will chase off anyone who dares to trouble us." I slid a glance at the rangy youth towering over the elderly porter. "In any case, should the worst happen, Lord Rochford would have my head as well so we shall be in good company," I continued with a smirk.

The porter heaved a great sigh. "I hope you find the peace you desire, my lady," he said with a shake of his head.

Our progress to Walsingham moved by slow stages. The early winter snow had not yet fallen, but the roads were icy, and the bitter wind chilled to the bone. I silently berated myself the whole of the first day. '*What have you done you, reckless girl?*' I screamed inside my head. '*Your prayers to the mother of Christ will be in vain if you die before you conceive.*' But by the time we reached Thetford at the end of the second day, I felt more at ease. Gilbert's imposing form seemed to have kept away any that sought to cause us harm, and his friendly nature earned us far more hospitality than we deserved. We arrived at the Chapel of St. Catherine on the afternoon of the fourth day. Like the pilgrims who came before me, I abandoned my shoes before continuing the final mile to the shrine on foot while my companions rode ahead with my horse on a lead.

The heavy sea air felt damp and fierce coastal gales tore at my woollen cloak. The soles of my feet throbbed with every step of the interminable walk. Violent shivers quaked through my body, but I pressed on against the pain. My discomfort began to drift away when the soaring stone walls of the cathedral finally rose into view. I offered up a prayer of thanksgiving before slipping quietly through its timbered doors. A dense fog of incense seemed to coat the inside of the church, and the air felt imbued with a solemn divinity. I held my breath as I padded slowly down the aisle to a small chancel holding the shrine of St. Mary. The canon who met me at the door held his hand aloft to receive my offering. He nodded his approval at the gold lover's knot pendant and coins I placed there, then he ushered me inside.

I moved wordlessly through the glittering riches strewn about, to the altar which lay beyond the flickering candlelight. I was struck by how unremarkable the statue depicting the Mother of Christ appeared. Our Lady needed none of the surrounding wealth; she held the only meaningful treasure in her lap, Christ, the Son of God. I humbled myself before the saintly mother, whispering my prayers beneath her serene gaze. I prayed for a treasure of my own; a healthy child of any sex that George and I could love and cherish. I prayed that Anne would be delivered of a prince to secure the realm. Finally, I prayed for the king; that he would show mercy and forgive me of my trespass.

I remained on my knees for as long as the canon allowed. When my eyes fluttered open at the tap of his hand, I saw that my tears had stained the floor around me. The canon guided me to a side door that led outside the church. Before I left, he gestured to the well of holy water where I could nourish myself a few paces away. A feeling of peace settled over me as I sipped the consecrated water. Prayer had purified my soul and renewed my hope. I had done everything in my power; if I failed to conceive now, then I knew it was never in God's plan.

We stayed the night at the monastery, rising at daybreak to head for home. The journey seemed less arduous in the face of my renewed spirits, and I found myself far merrier than before; I could finally spare a laugh for Gilbert's light-hearted jests. The porter met us with a relieved smile when our horses trotted into the courtyard eight days after our departure. "Praise be to God you've returned safely," he cheered. "You have a letter from your husband, Lady Rochford. You'll find it in your rooms."

"George was here?" I felt the joy drain from my face.

"Fear not, my lady," he assured me. "When his page brought the letter, we told him you were praying in the chapel."

"Not even a lie!" Gilbert exclaimed through gasps of laughter. I wrapped the stunned porter in an exuberant hug, then eagerly fled to my rooms.

My Dearest Jane,

By the time you receive this, I shall be at Dover awaiting the great Admiral of France. I pray that he sends fair words from the French King; for if His Grace's spirits are raised, I will be at greater leisure to sue for your pardon. These days pass painfully in your absence, and I look forward to the happy moment we are reunited. I shall send to you again at Christmas.

From the hand of one who loves you, George.

True to his promise, George wrote again at Christmas. I had dared to hope that it would be he who arrived through the gatehouse arch covered in a fine dusting of snow, but the king's mood had grown darker at the Admiral's insults, and my return was not yet meant to be.

My Dearest Jane,

It is with a heavy heart that I inform you of my abject failure. The Admiral's visit seems to have been blighted from the beginning. The king gave great feasts in his honour, but he turned up his nose at the reception. He rudely kept himself from the Queen for no other reason than his disdain, made all the more obvious by his suggestion that King Francis prefers to marry his heir to His Grace's bastard. This insulted the queen, of course. During supper, she burst into shrill laughter at the king's feigned attempt to introduce the Admiral's secretary to her. One of the fair maidens he brought for the entertainments caught His Grace's eye, and he forgot the whole thing. The Admiral took her to be mocking him and left in a great huff. Worse yet, I seem to have fallen into some disfavour with His Grace over a quarrel with my cousin, Bryan. Fret not, for it is of no great importance. I write of it not to worry you, but to explain why I've been remiss in securing your reinstatement. I do, however, ask one request of you. The queen is beside herself with grief over the loss of her beloved Purkoy. I'm certain she would take great comfort if you were to send her loving words of encouragement. We removed to Greenwich at Christmas. My servant, Atkyns, shall arrive soon with your gift for the New Year. Until then I send my love and prayers for a Happy Christmas.

Your loving husband, George

George's missive filled me with sadness. The wonder of Yuletide was tarnished without the company of my husband, and I felt guilty for abandoning Anne in her time of need. She never managed well under pressure; it always seemed to unleash her choleric humours. For the time being, there was nothing to be done but waiting. I would wait for His Grace's forgiveness; wait for George to return from court; and wait for Our Lady to answer my prayers.

"Lucy, it's blinding out there," I moaned. "Please shut the curtains."

After receiving George's New Year gift the previous night, I had fallen to sobbing. I retired to bed early, but sleep was elusive and only a few hours had passed since I drifted off with the gold lover's knot brooch my husband had sent clenched in my hand. Upon my rude awakening, my first thought was of the note that had accompanied it: *To match your necklace – Your loving husband, George.*

"My apologies, my lady, but I do think you will be pleasantly surprised when you come to the window." My grunted reply did nothing to sour the bright tone of Lucy's voice. "It's quite beautiful," she almost sang.

I pushed the thick counterpane aside, and then swung my feet to the floor. My body felt heavy, and my eyes gritty. I wanted nothing more than to bury myself back under the covers, but Lucy would find another way to drag me out. When I got to the window, I saw why it was so bright. The sky had split open during the night, scattering a flurry of snow over the world. A sparkling blanket of white powder carpeted the courtyard and beyond; even the tree branches sagged under the weight of it.

"A new world for a New Year," I breathed in awe at the sight before me. "It's as if God has covered up the ugliness of the last months and given us a fresh start."

"I'm pleased to hear a hint of enthusiasm in your voice finally. Perhaps we should take full advantage of this bounty?" Lucy's eyes twinkled in playful excitement.

"Oh, why not? I could use some merriment," I replied, after the briefest moment of hesitation.

Lucy ran to the closet and began pulling out every woollen layer of clothing she could find. Once she had me trussed up in my warmest, she set about wrapping herself up to accompany me outside. The heavy clothing felt so restrictive that our stroll to the courtyard looked more like a waddle, but I found myself glad of the protection it gave when the bitter air hit my face. The snow seemed to have muffled the ambient sounds of nature, yet I could hear the scrape of wood and the crunch of footsteps somewhere nearby. I brought my hand up to shield my eyes from the brilliant sun as I gazed out across the yard and caught sight of Gilbert's loping figure stacking firewood near the kitchen doors. I shot Lucy a sly look as I bent down to scoop up a handful of snow.

"My lady!" she teased, throwing her hands up to stifle a giggle.

I rolled the powder around in my hands until I had packed it into a dense ball, took aim, and then lobbed it in Gilbert's direction. I heard the dull thud as it hit its target, splattering across his cloak.

"God's Blood! Who in the…" he cried out.

Lucy and I ducked behind the wall, stifling our giggles into our gloves. We peered around the corner to watch Gilbert as he danced around whipping the snow from his cloak. We jumped back when he jerked his head around, scanning the courtyard for his attacker. "Don't move, Lucy," I whispered.

We waited until we thought we heard the scraping sound of the wood stacking resume before daring to sneak another look. When we finally got the courage to peek, Gilbert was waiting for us with his own frosty retribution. I felt the sting of the frozen snow on my face before I even realised that we had been caught out.

"Lady Rochford! My deepest apologies, I didn't expect you to be out here. Please let me help you." The sight of Gilbert's crimson nose and terrified eyes sent me into a fit of hysterics; my lungs burned at the frigid air I breathed in. I doubled over to wipe away the tears springing to my eyes and nearly tumbled into the snow. "Lady Rochford, please say something." The fearful pitch of Gilbert's voice sent another delicious ripple of mirth through me.

I shook with laughter until my stomach throbbed with the effort. Finally, I calmed myself enough to respond. "I'm fine, Gilbert; I'm fine," I sputtered. "The look upon your face was entirely worth the pain."

Gilbert's cheeks still flushed a brilliant crimson, but his lips were stretched wide in a grin. "I think you frightened a few years off my life," he exclaimed. "I thought one of the chamberers had played a trick on me. I did not expect to see you and Lucy around the corner. Can you ever forgive me?"

"I think I can forgive anything that gives me that much joy," I replied with a smile. "Lucy convinced me to come out and see the snow, and I am so glad I did." I turned to face my maid when I felt her insistent tap on my shoulder. "Yes, Lucy, I am..." My words trailed away when I saw what lay at the end of her pointed finger. I paid no heed to the cold wetness soaking through my shoes as I ran across the courtyard, nor did I slow when the hood toppled from my head. I didn't stop until I threw myself into the arms of the familiar form ambling in through the arched gateway.

George's visit was a welcome respite from the months of loneliness I faced in his absence. I felt deliriously happy to have him near, hardly daring to let him from my sight for the entirety of his stay. He brought with him good news from the court: my reckless remark had brought about Mistress Ashley's fall from favour. Shortly after my dismissal, Cromwell set one of his secretaries to following her; Ralph Sadler's reports of her meetings with Chapuys confirmed my accusations. It took Cromwell a month to convince the king of her duplicity and when he finally succeeded, His Grace became even more enraged that I had spoiled his fun.

"I didn't want to tell you," George lamented. "I knew his anger stemmed from the French Admiral's visit. You were merely an easy target for his bruised ego." The atmosphere at court still seethed with tension, but I had been granted forgiveness. I could return once the Shrovetide festivities were over.

"One last punishment," I quipped. "No banquets or jousting for me."

"At least you've been allowed to return; it could always be much worse."

An image of George's eldest sister ran through my mind. Her baby would be arriving in the coming weeks; I wondered how she fared. "Have you any word from Mary? Has her stubbornness abated finally?"

George rose from his chair, then sauntered over to stoke the fire before responding. He squatted next to the hearth and poked at the flames, their sputter and pop punctuating his silence. A soft groan escaped as he stood. "I feel wearier than ever. How is it that I've walked upon this Earth for over thirty years? The days seem so long and yet; the years slip by so fast."

I had entertained the same thoughts myself during my time in exile, but I wasn't in the mood to ruminate over my fading youth. "Don't change the subject, George. Where is Mary?"

"She's taken her daughter and gone to Calais with her new husband," George replied. He heaved a great sigh as he flopped back into to his chair. "I know you care for her, Jane, but it is best to just forget."

I crossed my arms as I stepped before George. How could he be so heartless? He had never been as close to Mary as he was to Anne, but she was still his sister. "How can you say such a thing? Surely she will return after the baby comes? What of her son? She won't abandon him?"

George shook his head. "No, she's not coming back. Even if I wanted to help her, it would be impossible. Rather than sue for our forgiveness, she threw herself on the mercy of Cromwell; Anne will never forgive her now." The increasing intensity in his voice displayed his underlying anger. "She used such spiteful words against us, even after all Anne's done for her," he spat. "Mary would have never thought of them herself. It's clear to us all that William Stafford used my sister to advance his fortunes, and Mary has shown herself naïve enough to swallow his fair words."

George appeared resolute in his denunciation of his sister, but I discerned a touch of sadness within him. Familial allegiance had always been imperative to my husband; Mary's disloyalty wounded him deeply. I plodded over to the chair and took my rightful place beside him. I rested my hand on his shoulder as we stared into the blazing fire. "Love makes fools of us all."

"Mary may believe she's in love, but I'm not convinced," George replied bitterly. "At least Anne and I can protect her son; we've kept him with his tutors; I just pray that my niece doesn't suffer for it."

November 18 –
December 2, 1541
The Tower of London
and Russell House
on the Strand

I HOVERED somewhere near the border between madness and sanity. My moments of lucidity were fleeting at first, but they continued to grow as my mania subsided. Those days were shrouded in a dark haze; my recollections of them muddled and distant. Snatches of memories fluttered through my mind: a crash of glass, icy fingers on my skin, and the pungent odour of sweat. When I came to, my clothing hung in tatters from my body; I had ripped the velvet to shreds.

Gage roused me on the morning of my seventh day of incarceration with news that I was to be moved to Russell House for my health. "Lady Russell will care for you," he informed me. "Have no fear; you will be in good hands." I winced when he gave my ink-blackened hand a tender squeeze; my skin had been scored by the shattered glass of the inkpot and still felt raw and tender.

Two chamberers arrived in the afternoon to pack my sparse belongings. I pilfered a beloved possession before they locked the coffer: a ragged grey cloak. I wrapped the worn velvet around my hands, clutching it tightly, as I followed the guards through the damp corridors and out into the fading light. We stopped just outside the doors to wait for Gage and, as I stood there, the unkindness of ravens I had watched from my room flocked to my feet. They bobbed and ducked in anticipation, as if they were eager to see me go. Gage's arrival scattered the birds initially, but they flocked back towards us, doggedly pursuing my steps, when we resumed our march to the river.

"If I were a raven, I would fly away from here and never look back."

Gage's rebuttal startled me; I had not realised that I said the words aloud. "We clip their wings so they can't," he replied tersely.

I stared at the ribbon of water between the stone steps and the boat remembering the moment I had contemplated taking my own life. Waves of regret washed over me. Surely death would have been preferable to this – life in a world without George or Anne; life in a world where even the ravens lacked freedom.

By the time we docked near the Strand, the sun had been gone long enough for it to be too dark for curious eyes to make out my identity. The few witnesses remaining on the nearly deserted streets were left to wonder which prisoner shuffled behind the Constable of the Tower to the home of the Lord Admiral. When Lady Russell met us at the door, she was accompanied by a young woman with olive skin and hair the colour of cinnamon. "Helena is my maid," she informed me with a curt nod. "She will take you to your room and serve you for the duration of your time here."

"The king thanks you for your service to him, Lady Russell," Gage said as he dipped a low bow. "His physician will be here at first light. I hope we haven't inconvenienced you too much."

"Not at all, Sir John; I expect that Lady Rochford shall be hastily amended."

My eyes shifted between the two; they spoke as though I were a naughty child, sent here to be trained up, perhaps even whipped. Helena, mercifully, drew my attention away. "Follow me, Lady Rochford."

The Russells gave me a chamber on the first floor; no doubt they worried that I would attempt to flee through the window. Perhaps they thought it would be easier to catch me than revive me. In any case, I had shown no desire to escape, only to die. The room was narrow, but long; the tapestries hanging on the walls seemed more for warmth than decoration. I saw only one small brazier and a rosary lying on the table next to the bed. *'At least I can pray for heat,'* I mused sarcastically to myself.

"It's not the finest accommodations that we have, but you can see the Thames at least," Helena explained. "Much better than the view from the other side of the house; nothing to see there, but the rubbish ditch."

I saw nothing, save my tired face, reflected in the darkened glass. "Thank you, Helena," I whispered. "Can you please help me to bed?"

Dr Butts arrived, as promised, in the early morning hours while I was still abed. He performed a cursory examination of my body, then shuffled off to his bag for leeches. I had become familiar with the routine in the days following my frenzy, so I knew to rollover before he returned. I buried my face in a pillow while the cold parasites writhed on my back, growing fat off my blood. I felt no pain, only a sense of detachment as the sedative in their saliva seeped into me. I drifted in and out of consciousness, hardly noticing when the physician removed the swollen mounds and replaced the quilt over my naked back. Snatches of conversation floated past me, but I paid little mind to it. Nothing of concern, merely orders of lavender for the rushes.

I moved through the next days as if walking in a dream. I ate meagrely, and tasted even less. If I wasn't sleeping, I fell to sobbing in relentless despair. I was free from the confines of the Tower, but I had been parted from George once again. The thought of Lucy, alone and afraid in an empty cell, clawed at me. I could never forgive myself if harm came to her. I alternated between raging at Kat Tylney for mentioning her to Wriothesley and myself for entangling her. I tried to keep her away when Culpeper visited the queen in my rooms at Lincoln, but Kat insisted she needed entertainment while she waited for her mistress, so I hid them both in a closet off my bedchamber with a pack of cards. Until that point, Lucy had no knowledge of what the queen had involved me in.

Dr Butts continued to visit me daily. He administered tinctures and potions, then occasionally, finished them off with a bleeding. I grew weaker rather than stronger in the face of my treatments, but that suited Lady Russell; I gave her far less trouble that way. When they had begun to believe that they had finally numbed me from my torments, they dared to inform me that the courts had found Dereham and Culpeper guilty; their executions were scheduled for eight days hence. Somehow I found the strength to hurl a book at Lady Russell's face.

MAY – OCTOBER 1535
YORK PLACE,
HAMPTON COURT AND
THE SUMMER PROGRESS

"JANE? IS that you?" I recognised Anne's voice, but I couldn't see her through the throng of courtiers surrounding her great chair of estate. "Please stand aside my lords, we have a guest." Suddenly, my sister-in-law's slight form emerged in the midst of the parted crowd.

"Your Grace," I replied, dropping into a deep curtsey.

I felt Anne's hand clasp around mine. "Come with me," she murmured under her breath as she gave it a quick tug. I followed her through the crowd of curious faces to the privy chamber. Once the door slammed shut behind us, she wrapped me in a warm embrace. When she pulled back, her face was shining. "Jane, you were very brave. How can I ever thank you for what you did?"

"No, Anne; there is no need for appreciation. I did something very foolish. I'm fortunate my punishment was not more severe."

Anne flicked my excuses away with her hand. I thought I recognised a flash of admiration in her eyes. "Nonsense, Henry knows you've done him a great service; he's just obstinate.

"She must not have been too dangerous," I scoffed. "I passed her in the corridor, and she shot me a most vicious scowl."

"Yes, well, she had a great many excuses; chief of which being her loyalty to his sickly bastard. I suggested that I would be more than happy to release her if she found her conscience so troubled in my service, but His Grace soundly reprimanded me." Anne edged into one of the embrasures, beckoning me to follow her.

"I'm pleased to see you haven't lost your spirit in spite of everything," I remarked as I followed her gaze to the gardens below.

"Jane, it's been awful; I can hardly bear it. Henry turned his eyes from Mistress Ashley only to alight them upon my cousin, Madge." Anne spoke in a low voice, but it sounded close to breaking.

"Madge Shelton?" The revelation took me by surprise, but Madge wasn't a terrible choice. I had always found her to be kind and loyal. Anne couldn't have picked a better object for her husband's attention even if she had wanted to. "She's harmless enough," I reasoned.

"Yes, but she's not me. I should have all of his love; just as he has all of mine. And there is something else." I silently waited while she cast her gaze about the room. Once she was satisfied that no one was near enough to eavesdrop, she tipped her head closer. "Henry often finds himself...unable."

"Unable to do what?" I arched a brow in confusion. The king had certainly aged, but I'd just seen him soundly beat Suffolk at tennis.

"You know..." Anne intimated with a huff. She stared at me, waiting for me to understand her meaning. Finally, she raised her voice in exasperation, "He has not the stamina." Her hands flew to her mouth in a panic, but it was too late. Both Lady Cobham and Lady Berkeley looked up from their sewing with interest at her outburst.

"Anne! Lower your voice!" I hissed.

"Henry can no longer please me like before," she gasped. "How does he expect me to conceive?"

Anne's words disheartened me; my prayers for Our Lady's intercession seemed to have fallen on deaf ears. "But – I prayed for you. I went to Walsingham even..." My voice trailed off.

"Don't let my brother find out," Anne cautioned. "Besides, those pilgrimages do nothing but serve the church."

Before I could respond, Lady Cobham approached. "Sir Henry Norris is here to see Madge, Your Grace," she informed us with a smirk.

Anne heaved a deep sigh. "Let him in," she commanded. She swept past, but threw an annoyed look over her shoulder at me as if to say: see how they pay her court?

George returned to our chambers that evening in the foulest of moods. "Get a chamberer in here to put out that fire," he barked at his page before slamming the door shut. He threw his cloak over the chair, then stomped off to our bedchamber without a further word.

I countered Lucy's fearful glance with a smile. "You've nothing to worry about," I reassured. "I shall call you when I am ready for bed." She nodded, and bobbed a curtsey, before scampering from the room.

I waited until the chamberer had extinguished the flames before checking on George. Outbursts were a rare occurrence from him. Whatever caused this one had upset him severely, so I didn't want to add to his frustrations. I expected to find my husband brooding at his desk, but I discovered him sprawled across the bed snoring softly. I moved to the edge of the bed and tugged his boots off, then I grabbed a quilt from the closet. The weather had not yet warmed enough to go without a fire overnight, and I didn't want him to catch a chill. I threw the quilt over his body, pulling it up over his shoulders. I caught my breath at the sight of the dark curls spilling over his eyes. I had never understood how someone as beautiful as George could love me. I planted a kiss on his bristled cheek, marvelling at the way the course hair chafed against my lips. The beard was a recent addition, and I found myself partial to it. I returned to the presence chamber and called Lucy to help me undress, before crawling into bed.

George had already dressed and gone for a ride through the park by the time I awoke; I found him taking breakfast at the table. The hearth remained cold and empty, but the sun cast a warming light through the windows. I tugged my robe tighter as I padded over to join him. "You appear well-rested this morning."

George mustered a half-hearted smile at my remark but shook his head. "I battled too many nightmares for that," he replied as he stood to pull out a chair for me.

I gulped from the tankard that had been set out for me, then tore a hunk off the manchet loaf before I spoke. "Might I ask what tormented you so?"

"I was at Tyburn with my father and uncle yesterday. The king's son, Richmond, came too. We were there to witness the executions of a few monks. Reynolds, Houghton, Lawrence and Webster they were called; there was a priest too." George stopped for a moment to consider his next words. He nervously drummed his fingers against the table. "I stood beside them, and I watched them suffer. They were hung by ropes while the executioner cut out their bowels and burned the flesh before their very eyes. I had to have the fire out yesterday because all I could smell from it was burnt flesh." He winced at the memory. "Afterwards, they were cut down, and their heads struck from their bodies. I can't wipe the scene from my mind."

His story extinguished my appetite. "Why would the king do such a thing?" I whimpered. "I'm very sorry, George."

"Don't be," he replied as he squeezed my hand. "It had to be done. They refused to swear the oath. We gave them every opportunity, and they refused."

I had sworn the very same oath upon my return to court the previous day, recognising Anne as His Grace's lawful wife and their daughter, Elizabeth, as heir to the throne. The words had rolled off my tongue easily, but I knew that others could never utter them. It hadn't occurred to me that their punishment would be so severe. "Surely you don't condone this?"

"I don't take great pleasure in carrying it out if that's what you mean," George spat. "I would gladly do anything else."

"You know I didn't mean that, please don't be angry with me," I pleaded.

George rubbed his eyes, then cleared his throat. "I'm not, Jane. Truly, I'm not. I just..." he sighed before going on. "I will do anything to keep my sister and her child safe; even if it takes extraordinary measures."

"I hate this, George. So many deaths…"

"I know, my love, but this will send a message. The people will know that the king is resolute; they must obey him. I also have further news." I waited for him to go on, preparing myself to hear the worst. "I am to go back to France to entreat the French Admiral. Cromwell was to go, but he claimed some illness. I've promised my sister that I will go with Norfolk in his stead and urge our niece's match with King Francis' son."

"But I've only just returned. I had hoped that we could try to conceive again."

"It will only be for a short time, Jane, then I promise; I promise we will try," he soothed.

George did return from France less than a week after he set off, but it was only to receive further instructions from His Grace. The French Admiral, furious at King Henry's temerity in not only pursuing the unfavourable match, but also insisting the young Duke of Angouleme be sent to England immediately, threatened to abandon the negotiations. Norfolk was at a loss to respond. George appeared winded when he arrived at Anne's privy chamber. He reported the difficulties to her first, before moving on to the king's rooms. Anne's fury towards the French King was palpable.

"After all I've done for that ungrateful, deceitful – How could anyone serve him better?" she fumed. "Does he believe that Catherine would have been friendlier to his causes? She's the Emperor's creature. She would do nothing to benefit Francis. The French King had himself a friend, but now he finds himself an enemy."

George stayed for as long as possible, but he was back in France during the first weeks of June. The Admiral's reticence made a foe out of Anne, but His Grace was not ready to concede defeat. Perhaps the Duke need only stay a year or less before his marriage to Princess Elizabeth; concessions could always be made. Unfortunately, the compromises were not enough and George returned before the end of the month under a cloud of gloom. Negotiations with the Admiral had broken down irretrievably, and there was to be no alliance. The deaths of Bishop Fisher and Sir Thomas More cast an even darker pall over the summer. While in the Tower for their complicity with the nun, Elizabeth Barton, both More and the Bishop had refused to swear the oath. Fisher was summarily cleaved from his head on Tower Hill two days before George returned from France. Thomas More followed him to the scaffold mere weeks later. London was in an uproar.

I was on progress with Anne and the king when a demonstration broke out at Greenwich in support of the Lady Mary. A crowd of women gathered outside the palace to greet her as she passed shouting words of encouragement and declaring their loyalty to her as Princess. The royal couple was in such high spirits, they brushed news of the event aside as a mere petty annoyance, even though two of Anne's ladies were imprisoned in the Tower for their role in it. I felt quite differently when I came to understand that one of the women present was my sister, Margaret. I sought an audience with Anne the moment I heard. She had just returned from the hunt with the king, and her cheeks were still flushed with joy. I hoped that her merry mood would aid my cause.

"I promise I knew nothing of her involvement, Your Grace," I implored, humbling myself before her feet. "Please don't punish her harshly. I've always known Margaret to be easily influenced, but I'm certain that she means little harm to you. Please, for the love you bear me, show mercy to my sister."

Anne looked down at me with interest. She tapped her riding gloves against the palm of her hand while she considered her response. "Jane, you need not prostrate yourself for this, please get up and we shall talk in private." Her words suddenly made me aware of the curious eyes turned our way; the entire room seemed to stand by in anticipation. Humiliation burned across my cheeks as I rose to my feet. I kept my head down and followed her to her bedchamber.

"How dare you ambush me that way, Jane? It is none of their concern whom I pardon and why!" Anne cried the moment the door slammed shut. "These things must always be dealt with in privacy. Haven't you learned that yet?"

My heart sank at her admonitions. How could I have been so stupid? "I'm sorry, Your Grace. My emotion overcame sense, and I reacted without thought." Hot tears pricked at the back of eyes. This was the way it had been my whole life: all of the effort I put into refining my behaviour obliterated by a moment of weakness. I always allowed my emotions to rule me.

"Make sure it never happens again," Anne thundered, but then she melted at the sight of my tears. "Oh, Jane, it is nothing to cry over. I'm not going to punish Margaret."

"But Fisher…More…the monks. People are dying for their support of Catherine and Mary," I sniffed.

Anne's eyes darkened as she shook her head. "I had nothing to do with their deaths, Jane; you know that. Henry has punished those men as he saw fit. Margaret's participation in this demonstration was misguided, but she did take the oath; she won't die for her actions. However, I can't speak for Lady Shelton. She may punish her wayward daughter-in-law, but have no fear that she will be put to death."

A wave of relief flooded through me. How could I have ever believed such ill of Anne? I felt ashamed by my reaction. "Please forgive me for overreaching. I know you would do the same for your own sister." I meant the words as a compliment, but I immediately saw that Anne took it as an indictment.

"Of course I would do it for you," she replied. "You are my only sister now, and it would be good for you to remember that the next time Margaret finds herself in need of my mercy. I thought that I could depend on your support, but perhaps I've been mistaken."

As Anne turned from me, I made a desperate grab for her hand. "I will always support you. Please don't walk away from me," I begged.

Her lips were set in a grim line when she turned back to face me. She pulled her hand away so forcefully that it caused me to flinch. "Lady Rochford, I am Queen, and I shall walk away from whomever I choose. Removing yourself from my presence at this time is the only thing that would help your cause. I will send for you tomorrow if my feelings have changed."

I had never heard Anne's voice so devoid of warmth. I swallowed hard before sputtering out a reply. "Yes, Your Grace."

Anne allowed me to return to her company the following day, but she gave me a noticeably chilly reception. She remained in high spirits despite our disagreement for the rest of the progress, but my confidence had faltered. I spent much of the summer on my own while George served in Dover as Lord Warden of the Cinq Ports. Worse still, Grace was in confinement against the coming of my niece or nephew. Anne was the only friend I had and she seemed to be slipping further and further away.

DECEMBER 3, 1541
RUSSELL HOUSE
ON THE STRAND

"LADY RUSSELL has instructed me to remove all of your books. She hopes it will teach you to recognise their value better. She said nothing of your embroidery needles, though. I would think she should fear them more," Helena snorted.

I giggled at the thought of chasing Lady Russell from the room with a needle. "Her face was a sight to behold," I replied. "She never saw that book coming."

Helena dissolved into a fit of laughter. "Lady Rochford," she groaned as she wiped tears from her eyes. "Thank you for giving me the most satisfying moment of my service here. I shall never wipe it from my mind."

"You're too kind, Helena. I really shouldn't have done such a thing," I sighed. "Over the years, I've found that I often behave far too rashly for my own good."

"I can't speak for your past, my lady, but I can say that, in this case, it was well deserved," Helena gave me a wink before she continued. "Now, before I remove your books, I am going to take these trays to the kitchen." She pointed to the table where my food remained, untouched, then she dropped her voice to a whisper. "I have not counted the books in your possession so, should you hide one or two before I return, I would be none the wiser."

I waited until Helena disappeared with the trays before slipping Anne's Bible beneath my mattress. Lady Russell could confiscate any book she liked, but she would never take that one from me. The maid returned a few moments later with the mistress of the house beside her. Lady Russell eyed me warily from the doorway. Her hand covered part of her face, but I could see the bright red gash beneath her swollen eye. I regretted causing her harm, but her disdain incensed me. How dare she treat me like a criminal? I had done nothing wrong and yet here I stood, jailed by this imperious woman.

"Helena?" I called, locking my eyes onto Lady Russell's. "When you have finished, would you please bring me my needles? I would like to continue my embroidery."

The heavy door to my chamber muffled most of the words coming from Lady Russell but as her indignation rose, so too did her voice. I heard the last sentence she uttered perfectly. "She's a complete lunatic, Sir John!"

"Now, Lady Anne," Gage's baritone voice trailed off, taking with it the words that followed.

I studied my hands as I slid down the rough wall. I'd hardly noticed the needle when it penetrated my skin, but I saw now that it had marred my palm with angry red pin pricks. I knew, even as I brandished the sharpened sliver of brass at Lady Russell, that what I was doing was wrong, but I had been powerless to stop myself. I had lost all ability to control my behaviour. My sanity had become like a slippery swatch of silk sliding away from the grip of my fingertips.

Gage's staccato rap against the door sent my heart racing. "Lady Rochford? May I come in?" His eyes peered at me through the crack between the door and its frame. I remained silent but scooted out of his way. My skirts dragged a clump of river rushes with them, wafting the floral fragrance of lavender into the air. The scent was supposed to calm me, but it seemed to have the opposite effect; instead, I grew irritated at the constant stream of chamberers strewing it about my room. Gage crouched down beside me. I noticed that he had recently trimmed his beard. The pointed shape elongated his chin, making his face appear very horse-like. I melted into giggles at the thought.

"This is no laughing matter, Lady Rochford," he scolded. "Your behaviour is unacceptable."

"I know, Sir John," I gasped, as I struggled to compose myself. My quaking laughter suddenly turned to sobs, and I crumpled at his feet.

"What am I going to do with you?" Gage breathed. I sagged limply in his arms as he carried me to the bed. After he had laid me down, I heard him call for a sleeping draught.

December 1535 –
January 1536
Eltham and
Greenwich

GEORGE RETURNED near the end of the progress while the court lodged at the home of Sir John Seymour in the parklands of Wulf Hall. He made little mention of my growing estrangement from Anne, preferring instead to wait until we arrived back in London before broaching the subject. "Anne is still quite upset about Mary," he admonished. "You should have known better."

"I made a mistake, George. I have not ceased apologizing to Anne, but she will have none of it. I know naught what else to do. Now she takes her diversions in the company of your friends: Norris, Brereton, Weston – they have all replaced me." Anne's increasing reliance on these new companions further emphasised my alienation. I felt like an intruder watching their merry pastime in Anne's chambers; I was no longer invited to participate in their dancing or games.

George ambled over to the bench where I sat with my head hung in despair. His hand slipped beneath my arm; I watched him entwine my fingers with his own. "I know of something," he murmured. When I finally looked up at him, he cupped my face in his palm, then used his thumb to brush away my tears. "Anne is with child again. Be there for her like those men cannot. Show her that you are her loyal servant beyond any shadow of a doubt. We must take care that she has a successful birth; we cannot risk another miscarriage." I brushed my lips against the palm of his hand and promised to look after his sister, but a storm of emotions swirled inside me.

His Grace was ebullient with cheer during the Yule festivities with all that he had to celebrate. His coffers were filled to bursting with the spoils plundered from the monasteries, and his queen carried the future heir to the throne in her womb. His belief that God's blessings were raining down upon him was further cemented by the news that Catherine languished on her deathbed. All of these pleasant tidings served to strengthen Anne's sense of security, and she softened towards me. Though I lamented Catherine's illness, I welcomed Anne's jolly mood and each day that I edged closer to regaining her favour.

Word arrived at Greenwich in the first week of January that Catherine was dead. The king's sobs quickly gave way to relief, then delight, when he realised what her death meant. "God be praised that we are free from all suspicion of war!" he cried in jubilation. He donned his sunniest yellow attire to go to mass, holding a giggling Princess Elizabeth aloft in triumph as he and Anne proceeded to chapel heralded by trumpets. The events of the summer kept me from vocalising my grief at Catherine's passing. I regretted that my rise had come as a result of her ill-handling, but nothing good would come of publically declaring it. Instead, I fixed a pleasant smile on my face during the raucous celebrations. During the secret hours of the night, I included Catherine in my prayers.

The heady celebrations came to an abrupt halt on the 24th of January when the king was thrown from his horse during the joust. Norfolk arrived at Anne's privy chamber breathless with fear. "Your Grace, the king has been knocked unconscious. The physicians are doing all that they can, but he will not awake."

Anne's hands flew protectively to her belly as the colour drained from her face. "Do not tarry here, Norfolk," she commanded with a wave. "Go see to my husband and don't come back until he is revived." She waited until Norfolk had vacated the room before melting into my arms. "What will happen to me if he dies, Jane?" she sobbed. "I'll end up just like Catherine! What shall I do?"

Anne's tears soaked through the partlet covering my chest as I held her close. "Everything will be well," I murmured, but I had little faith in my consolations.

Time itself seemed to still, each swollen minute reluctantly passing into the next, as we waited in strained silence for Norfolk's return. Most of the maids had gone down to the tiltyard earlier in the day to watch the jousts. The ones that remained behind kept their distance from us, but their droning whispers filled the room. Furrowed brows betrayed their secret questions. What happens when the king dies without an heir? I could see them working out the answer in their minds; considering the value of kindness to their queen. Would it help them or hurt them?

"Why hasn't my father come? Or George?" Anne's plaintive voice cut through my thoughts. "Don't they know that I need them?"

"They will be here any moment, Your Grace," I lied. Neither Wiltshire nor George would leave the king's side until he either revived or died. Though Anne felt abandoned, I welcomed their absence; it meant that the king lived.

Anne raised her head to respond, but her words were interrupted by the airy trill of the virginal. Her eyes swivelled to the corner where Marc Smeaton sat, hunched over the instrument. In one swift move, she ripped the slipper from her foot and whipped it at his head. "No music!" she shrieked.

"It would be in your best interests to make yourself scarce," I advised the startled musician with a glare, as I shuffled Anne to her bedchamber, where we could hide from the shocked stares.

Anne's nervous pacing had worn a path through the rushes by the time we heard the chamberlain announce Wiltshire's arrival. We both held our breath until the creaking of the door revealed the earl's towering form. His face was split wide with a smile, but I swore I saw a flicker of dread in his eyes. "Take comfort, my darling daughter; the king lives."

December 3 – 20, 1541
Russell House
on the Strand

The sleeping draught instantly tumbled me into the nightmarish world of my own memories. George often made appearances in my dreams, but this time I was haunted by those who loved him. I relived the moments when Wiltshire confronted me after the funeral ceremonies for the woman who replaced his daughter as queen.

"I can't even stand to look at you," he seethed through clenched teeth. "My son – my beloved George – destroyed and you left in his place. I made him a worthless marriage; you couldn't even bear a child to carry on his name." Wiltshire's voice dripped with loathing, but anguish contorted his face. I wanted so much to hate him for all that he made me go through to get my jointure, but the only emotion I could summon had been pity. His words had ripped my heart in two, but they weren't untrue. George had the potential for greatness, and his bright, flickering light had been extinguished far too soon. I had brought nothing of value to the Boleyn name in traits or deeds.

"I would give anything to take his place," I had whispered in response. It was all I knew to say, and it was true; even truer now than it had been back then. I would have taken George's place if I could have.

The dam that had held back Wiltshire's tears gave way then. He had covered his face with his hands and wept into them as a child would have. I had wanted to throw my arms around him and tell him that George would never be forgotten. I had wanted to weep with him and assure him that I understood his pain. I had wanted to do anything I could to comfort the man who had loved my husband even more than I could, but I never dared. He would never have accepted it anyway.

"The king should have paid your jointure," he had finally sniffed when his sobbing subsided. "He took your husband away. That was his debt to pay." With those final words, Wiltshire had shuffled out of my life. Any further dealings I had with the man had gone through Cromwell.

My dream of Wiltshire faded away, and I found myself in a corridor at Whitehall, the former York Place of my youth, staring into the guileless face of his granddaughter, Catherine. The news of her appointment had terrified me, for I was certain that she had been taught to despise me. I wasn't supposed to be the one to greet her when she came to court, but when I spied her peeking through the doors of the great hall, temptation overcame me. When she spun around to face me, I saw fear and distrust in her eyes, but I also saw a glimmer of pity. Those eyes were so much like George's, and they had compelled me to bear my soul. I couldn't burden my innocent niece with the horrors of my miscarriages; I hadn't wanted to frighten her before she had children of her own, so I told her only what I needed to in hopes that she could forgive me. I always wondered if she had. The Catherine who haunted my nightmares screamed that she would never forgive me.

When sobs wracked my body enough to awaken me, either Dr Butts or Helena quickly poured another tincture down my throat. I spent the next weeks this way: halfway between Earth and Hell with only the imagined fury of the Boleyns to keep me company.

January – March 1536
Greenwich and
York Place

"MY LADY," the whispered words seemed to float before me. When I reached out to capture them, another set of hands pulled me back. "Please wake up, my lady." I bobbed a moment longer in the sea of dreams before Lucy's frantic tugging dragged me to the surface.

"God's blood, Lucy," I gasped. "You've scared me nearly to death."

My maid waited for my breathing to calm before responding. "Mistress Horseman is here for you. She carries a message from the queen."

I looked over at George's sleeping form and considered whether I should wake him. He looked so peaceful; I hesitated to disturb his sleep if the matter turned out to be inconsequential. I quickly decided against it and directed Lucy to bring my robe.

Margery Horseman stood quietly in the shadows of my presence chamber. Her face appeared deathly pale in the light of the flames dancing upon the candles. "What is it, Mistress Horseman?" I hissed in a low voice.

"The queen's labour has begun," Margery replied, her eyes wide with fear. "The pain causes her to cry out for her brother. You must bring George to her."

"That cannot be; it is far too early for that." I tried to calculate the months of Anne's pregnancy in my head, but I hadn't yet cleared the fog of sleep from my mind. Regardless of how many months had passed, I knew that too many remained for the baby to survive the birth.

"Please, Lady Rochford," Margery pleaded. "We're wasting precious time."

The desperation in her voice suddenly spurred me to action. "Go Margery!" I called out as I turned back to my bedchamber. "I'll get George."

George groaned at my prodding, but the mention of his sister's name caused him to fly up in alarm. "Tarry not wife, let's go!" he cried as he struggled into his hose.

The cheerful illumination of Anne's presence chamber belied the terrible moans coming from the rooms beyond it. A brace of maids had gathered there at the first sign of trouble; by the time of our arrival, they had taken to the corners to gossip in hushed tones about the queen's distress. I trailed George as he followed the desperate cries to Anne's inner rooms. A lone yeoman guard barred the door to her bedchamber. I saw him noticeably relax when he caught sight of George.

"I've kept all visitors out, my lord. I have orders that none but you shall pass."

George nodded at the guard, then took a step towards the door.

"You can't go in there, George," I reached out to stop him.

My husband wore a mask of confusion when he turned to face me. "Why can't I?" he demanded.

"You are not allowed in if Anne is in labour. The rules are firm."

"But you heard Margery, she asked for me."

"George," I soothed as I took his hand. "Anne is in terrible pain; she is not thinking clearly. She will be very upset if we do not maintain her dignity at the birth of her prince. You wait out here, and I will tell you everything that happens."

George measured my words carefully. Brotherly instinct urged him to run to his sister's aid, but I knew he was cautious enough to heed my advice. After a moment's consideration, he relented. "Report back straight away and leave nothing out."

A ghastly sight awaited me inside Anne's bedchamber. The satin counterpane gracing the great tester bed had been tossed aside to expose the linen underneath. Brilliant red streaks marred the snowy white fabric that had been pristine only hours ago. I followed the sound of Anne's sobs and found her curled into a ball on the pallet next to her bed; blood soaked the bottom half of her nightshirt.

"Anne?" I asked tentatively as I knelt down beside her. I placed my hand on her back; it was moist with sweat.

Her response was muffled, but there was no mistaking what she said. "He's dead, Jane. My prince is dead."

I brushed the tangle of dark hair from her face, wiping the tears from her swollen eyes. "Let me help you up, Your Grace," I urged. Anne resisted my prodding, and when she finally rolled over, I realised why. Her arms were tightly wound around a tiny, blood-stained bundle containing the remains of her child.

"Please don't take him from me, Jane. Please just give me a moment longer."

She sounded so desperate, there was nothing else I could do but comply. "Of course, Your Grace," I soothed. "Hold him for as long as you like."

I wrapped my arm around her limp body and lifted her from the floor. After I had managed to settle her onto the bed, I tiptoed to the door to deliver the news to George. "Your sister needs a midwife, George. The child is no longer." George swallowed hard. He planted a kiss on my cheek before he hurried off to find help. I closed the door, then ambled back to the bed.

"The king is going to be very angry with me isn't he Jane?" Anne whimpered. "He might even send me away."

"Try not to worry, Your Grace. The king loves you; he would never send you away." My encouragement felt vacant. We were both thinking of the last woman who had miscarried His Grace's son. She had been laid to rest mere hours ago.

The king showed no emotion when Anne revealed her miscarriage to him the next morning. He merely stared at her in cold silence, impervious to her tears. Before he left the room, he fired a parting salvo, "I see now that God will not grant me male children. I will speak to you when you are up."

In the days that followed, His Grace removed himself to York Place for Shrovetide and the remaining session of Parliament. George was obliged to follow the court, but I stayed behind with Anne while she recovered.

"Once my sister is up and about, she will waste no time joining us. Don't look so sad; we will be together soon," he cajoled as he shoved a stack of books into his cedar trunk. "I'm certain you will be far too busy planning the May Day festivities to miss me."

I slipped behind him and wrapped my arms around his chest. I laid my head on his back, the heat from his body warming my cheek. "I miss you every time you leave."

George brought my hand to his lips for a kiss. "Take care of Anne. She is our greatest concern now."

The frigid wintry months faded away as the undaunted sun resumed its position in the skies. Anne grew stronger as the days grew longer and soon she found her way out of the bedchamber. Her body had not yet recovered enough to take part in dancing or other sports, so we spent our days in the privy chamber sewing or reading next to an open window. The sweet perfume of the early blooms floating in on the gentle spring breeze tickled our noses and enlivened our spirits. After begging Anne's forgiveness, Marc Smeaton was allowed to return. There was no denying his talent for music, and she had sorely missed the pleasant strains of his lute; he immediately took up residence in the corner with his instrument. Anne enjoyed Smeaton's company, but his presence bothered me. I often caught him openly staring at her and I found him far too familiar for his status.

"He's an artist, Jane, he behaves differently than we do," Anne remarked when I expressed my concern to her. She brushed aside my worries with a brusque wave, but I kept a much closer eye on him after that.

Towards the end of February, we moved on to York Place to join the rest of the court. Several of Anne's maids stayed behind; Jane Seymour being one of them. After Mistress Ashley had fallen from the king's favour, I had hoped that others would learn from her example. Instead, several others had sprung up to take her place, and when His Grace tired of Madge Shelton, he moved on to Mistress Seymour. The king's new amour was everything that Anne was not. Where Anne was slight and delicate, Mistress Seymour was statuesque. Anne's hair was the colour of mahogany, where Mistress Seymour's was the colour of straw. Anne was glimmering twilight and Mistress Seymour was the pale morning dawn. The two could not have been any more different if they were chalk and cheese. I didn't mind Mistress Seymour's meek countenance; she was always pleasant, always biddable, but I thought I sensed something treacherous beneath her compliant veneer. Nevertheless, I felt relieved to leave her behind at Greenwich.

I wasn't the only one growing wary of the parade of towheaded Seymours making their way into the heart of the court. When His Grace appointed the elder brother to the Privy Chamber, George fell into a mood. "The king has only promoted Seymour because he's charmed by that pale-faced sister of his. After he's had his fill of her, we will still have to stomach his presence. He's insufferable. Arrogant, and grasping…"

"I don't care for him either George, but others could have said the same of you. You become incensed when they insinuate your career has advanced because of your sisters," I interjected.

"That's hardly the same…" George's voice trailed off when he saw the look of disbelief I gave him. "You've been spending too much time with Anne," he finished with a laugh.

"Well, I would much rather spend my time with you," I replied, planting a kiss on his cheek before I sashayed out the door for another day of sewing in Anne's Privy Chamber.

By the time I arrived, an adoring crowd of courtiers had already gathered around Anne's chair of estate. They skittered about her feet like ravens, snatching up crumbs of her affection. She revelled in the attention, of course. Anne had always been partial to veneration, but I sensed by the rising pitch of her voice that she was becoming overwhelmed. Anxiety always seemed to bring out a shrill quality in her tone.

"Good morrow, Your Grace," I called out as I pressed through the mass of bodies. Both Sir Francis Weston and Sir Henry Norris ducked out of the way of my obligatory curtsey. "Pardon me, my lords." Norris dipped a bow in return, but Weston slunk off without meeting my gaze. "I passed the tailor in the corridor," I continued as I turned back to Anne. "He's coming to discuss the clothing you've ordered for the princess."

"At last," Anne exclaimed, breaking into a broad grin. "You may return to pay court to Mistress Shelton another day, gentleman," she said as she rose to her feet. "You had better cement your match Sir Henry before Sir Francis takes Madge as a mistress," she continued with a wink.

Weston muttered a reply under his breath, but it was loud enough for both Anne and me to hear, "It isn't Madge who Norris cares to see in these rooms."

Anne and I exchanged an uncomfortable glance. Thankfully, the chamberlain broke the silence. "Master Matte has arrived, Your Grace," he bellowed through the door.

After the meeting with the tailor, Anne joined us in the Privy Chamber for supper. She found me in an empty embrasure monitoring the kitchen staff as they set out the table. "George came when I was out in the Presence Chamber," she whispered.

My heart sank. "He didn't come in to see me."

"No, he was in a rush," she replied. "Henry wanted to play shovelboard."

"Oh, I see." George always seemed to be rushing off to entertain the king.

"Don't get morose," she warned, wrinkling her nose in disgust. "He only came to tell me that Cromwell offered up his rooms to that upstart Seymour and his flighty wife."

"Edward Seymour is hardly an upstart," I retorted.

Anne arched her brow, then indulged me with a giggle, "I'm not my brother, Jane. You have to be careful how to say things to me."

I crossed my arms and stared intently at her for a moment before flourishing a deep curtsey, "My apologies, Your Majesty."

"Only my fool gets away with such impertinence," Anne replied. I heard a laugh escape her lips, but when I straightened, I saw apprehension in her eyes. "Cromwell's lodgings have secret passageways to Henry's inner rooms. He's done this so that my husband can access Mistress Seymour without drawing attention."

"I thought Cromwell supported you?" I replied with a frown.

"As did I…"

December 20, 1541 – February 7, 1542 Russell House on the Strand

LADY RUSSELL took pity on me as time slid into the festive Yule season. Each day, the doses of bitter liquid administered by Dr Butts got smaller and smaller. During my waking moments, I took fresh air on the back of the property under the watchful eye of one of the male servants. Lady Russell had greatly reduced Helena's responsibilities after the incident with the embroidery needle. The poor maid had never intended to incite my naughty behaviour, and I felt bad for getting her into trouble. She still spent many hours of the day with me, reading the classics or gossiping about the neighbours. I had been surprised the first time she offered to read to me. I knew very few maids who could read beyond writing their own name, but Helena had an excellent grasp of the language.

"I taught myself, didn't I?" she replied quite proudly when I asked. "Lady Russell helped too. She can be very kind when she wants to be."

Lady Russell found my behaviour satisfactory enough to invite me to join the family in the hall for Christmas dinner; up until then, I had managed to control my worst impulses. Unfortunately, the commotion of the celebrations overwhelmed me and, in a fit of pique, I threw a fig tart at Lord Russell. I could not abide the stares of the Russell family and their closest companions; then the sight of the gaping hole where Lord Russell's eye should have been sent me over the edge. The hapless baron had merely attempted to straighten his eye patch.

I screamed at the servants as they dragged me back to my room, "Forgive me; I didn't mean to." That night, I cried until I grew hoarse. My mind had grown so strange that I was powerless to control it. I desperately prayed for God to return my sanity, but he ignored my pleas. I found myself living in fear of whatever might set me off next.

After New Year, I requested another bleeding from the king's physician. Dr Butts happily complied, then directed Lady Russell to adjust my diet: I could no longer imbibe wine or eat meat. The combination of both prescriptions resulted in a weakening of my body, and I lost all desire to do anything, but sleep. When I wasn't traipsing through nightmares, I stared at the blank wall next to my bed until the shadows dancing across it lengthened into night.

Most days, Helena sat quietly on a cushion in the corner, mending Lady Russell's gowns, while I slept, but today she seemed particularly sociable. I watched the animated way in which she spoke of the twin boys who lived next door and, for a moment, I felt like I was back in Anne's rooms, partaking in the daily exchange of court prattle.

"You can hardly tell them apart, save for the freckle one has on his nose. They are always playing tricks on the laundress; stealing the linen she hangs out on the line. When she finally recovers them, they are covered in sticky smudges. Worse yet, they smell like a pair of mouldy old boots," she clucked in disdain. "Their mother is run ragged caring for the household; no time to chase after them."

"Do you have children, Helena?"

The sound of my voice startled the maid. I didn't know whether the gravelly tone of it surprised her or if she was shocked by my participation. She took a moment to compose herself before responding.

"No, Lady Rochford. I've never cared for children. I've neither the patience nor desire to raise any of 'em," she scoffed. "And they stink," she finished with a wrinkle of her nose.

I couldn't help but smile at the look of disgust on her face. "Well, you've certainly done an excellent job of caring for me, and I probably smell as awful as those twins do."

Helena's cheeks flushed at the compliment. "Aye, I can't get the sweet scent of that lavender out of my nose; they spread too much of it in here. Not that it's done you much good."

I had no meaningful response, so I let the silence settle around us. Helena went back to her sewing, but I could see she still had something on her mind. "Go on, Helena," I finally said. "Ask your question."

Helena shifted uneasily as she considered her words. She opened her mouth once, before stopping herself. Just when I thought she had given up, the question fell from her lips. "Why did you do it, Lady Rochford?"

Everyone seemed to want an answer, but I had none to give. I should have known better. I should have been the one to tell Archbishop Cranmer what the queen was doing, but I couldn't bring myself to do it. I knew her meetings with Culpeper were wrong; the king had murdered my sister-in-law for the same offences. I should have been angry with the queen. Anne was innocent of her charges, but pretty little Katherine Howard — she was guilty. There wasn't any specific reason I had for helping her with her affairs. I felt lonely and abandoned, and her favour made me feel special. When it all became too much, I had no one to help me. Cromwell was dead, and when I tried to confide in my niece, Catherine, she became judgemental and indignant. I couldn't involve her anyway; I would never endanger her life.

Perhaps a small part of me felt righteous. Once I had been tempted to scream out at His Grace, *'Your precious queen has committed far more shocking acts than Anne Boleyn ever did. See how she flaunts it and yet you are blind!'* Instead, I bit my tongue as he limped by me, the stench of his infected leg causing the bile to creep up into my throat.

I may have helped Katherine because of the way she stared longingly after Culpeper. She looked at him the way I looked at

George; as if there were nothing greater in the world. George returned my heated gaze, but Culpeper didn't always appear to share her affections. I took pity on her. Life as King Henry's wife was difficult even in the best of circumstances. I imagined it could be like Hell on Earth for a vivacious and lively girl like Katherine to be married to an ageing, crippled tyrant. She had not been sufficiently prepared for the crushing weight of her position.

I thought of all the reasons I could give Helena to excuse my actions, but settled on the one that seemed the safest. "I thought the queen loved Culpeper, I acted as she bid me."

I anticipated news of my trial after the Christmas and New Year celebrations had drawn to a close. Though I knew in my heart that the trials for George and Anne and their alleged conspirators had been a farce, I still hoped that all was not lost for me. But, as each day passed into the next without word from the Constable of the Tower, I felt my faith slipping further and further away. During one of the few moments I had with Lady Russell, I plucked up my courage and asked her if the queen had been tried yet. She answered me with an instinctive shake of her head, but then she must have thought better of it because she followed with a contradictory reply, "My husband hasn't said. I'm certain it's already passed." Afterward, she hustled from the room, quick as you like, without giving me a second glance.

Lady Russell's evasiveness told me more than she intended. Even if my trial had been postponed due to the frailty of my mind, there would have been no reason to delay the queen's. The fact that she had not been tried yet meant only one thing: the king would use an Act of Attainder to convict us. Secretary Cromwell had gone in the same way in the days leading up to His Grace's marriage to the doomed queen. He had no trial, no lawyers, and certainly no defence. He went into a meeting with the Privy Council one day and, in a matter of minutes, he was stripped of his offices and carted off to the Tower. He didn't see the light of day until his walk to the scaffold. When Lord Russell had mentioned the opening of Parliament a few weeks ago, I paid little mind to it; now his remark seemed far more sinister. Parliament was meeting to give the king what he wanted: judicial murder. Perhaps my unprovoked launch of the fig tart had been driven by instinct at the hint the baron gave me at what was to come; I just hadn't known it at the time.

As the realisation of my imminent death took root in my heart, I became even harder to control. I vacillated between hysterical laughter and pathetic sobbing. After a particularly nasty outburst, resulting in two broken plates and a shattered vase, nearly everything small enough for me to lift was quickly removed from my room. Lady Russell even kept Helena away for fear I might injure her. The isolation held my reason hostage. My behaviour filled me with shame; I pored through passages in Anne's secreted Bible each time I recovered my senses, hoping to find anything that could ease my suffering. George had told me that the scriptures would teach me to die when the time came, but I found nothing in it of which he spoke. The words all seemed to run together and I could no longer make sense of anything. Eventually, I gave up.

On the morning of the seventh day of February, Sir John Gage arrived with the news I had been expecting. I was standing at the window overlooking the muddy Thames when I heard the knock at my door. The sun had just begun to rise above the horizon, and the sky seemed filled with every colour imaginable: sunny yellow, brilliant orange and rose all danced below a layer of the deepest blue. I pressed my hands up against the leaded glass and felt the frigid frost ice my fingertips. As I drank in the peaceful scene, I quietly asked God if He would grant me one more snowfall before my death. I continued to ignore the insistent rap at the door as if I could stave off the inevitable, but Gage burst through at last with Lord Russell trailing behind him.

"Lady Rochford," he admonished in a ragged breath. "I thought you were hurt. Why did you not answer our knock?"

"Would it matter if I was?" I asked, quickly brushing the tears from my eyes as I tried to make myself presentable. "I know why you are here."

Gage's body relaxed, and his lips drooped down into a frown. "Parliament has passed a Bill of Attainder against both you and Katherine Howard. Dr Butts has explained your malady to His Grace in hopes that your execution could be held off, but he is resolute that you go to the block the same day as Katherine. He's even put another bill to Parliament…"

"He's changed the law so that he can execute me regardless of my mental state, hasn't he?" I interjected before Gage could finish.

"Yes, my lady."

"Does he think this is all a show? Do you believe I am playacting? Have you all been amused at my misery?" The pitch of my voice grew higher with each question. I blinked hard against the tears pricking at my eyes, willing them not to fall.

This time, it was Lord Russell who answered me. "No, my lady, we do not." The mournful tone of his voice surprised me. I thought he, more than anyone, would be happiest to see me go. Perhaps pity had moved him to forgive my lapse in manners.

"When am I to return to the Tower?" I ventured after Gage broke the tense silence with a cough.

"I will come for you the day after tomorrow. In his great mercy, the king has said he would like to give you some time to prepare for your death. He anticipates a great crowd to gather at both your journey on the river and your execution. To lessen the risk of disturbing the witnesses, he is prepared to offer you something in return for your good behaviour."

"What could the king possibly offer me? My mind has already proved beyond my control," I scoffed.

"Dr Butts has told the king that it may be possible with the right incentive. If you can prove yourself worthy during your transport to the Tower, His Grace will greatly reward you."

I remained impassive. "There is nothing that could be of use to me after I'm dead."

Gage exchanged a cautious look with Lord Russell before he went on. Lord Russell responded with a nod of encouragement. "The king will allow you to visit your husband's grave."

After Gage and Lord Russell had left, I sobbed until I collapsed onto the floor. I wanted to wail out loud in desperation, but I swallowed it back with all of my might. If I was going to die, I required a pound of the king's flesh in return. It would torment his ego to allow me the small mercy of seeing George's grave, and I expected to collect on his promise no matter what. I was determined to harness every bit of strength that remained within me.

My stability following the news of my condemnation so impressed Lady Russell, she deigned to allow me the small comfort of Helena's presence more often. Few words were exchanged between us while the maid tidied my room and trimmed the wicks on the candles, but the silence was necessary for neither of us knew what to say. Once Helena completed her duties, she settled into her cushion, and we passed the afternoon just as we had every afternoon before my outbursts. There was no talk of death; no talk of the queen; no talk of regrets. We avoided any topic that might cause me disquiet or disrupt the tenuous peace I clung to.

I waited until Helena packed up her sewing for the evening before springing my last request on her. I slipped out of my bed while her back was turned and pulled out the two items I had hidden under my mattress: Anne's Bible and my grey velvet cloak. Her eyes widened when she turned back and found me standing up, but she quickly suppressed her surprise with a smile. "Can I get you something before I go, my lady?" she asked.

"Perhaps some absolution?" I replied with a weak laugh.

Helena's face split into a wide grin. "I'm not in the business of handing that out, but I will do anything I can to set your mind at ease."

"I'm probably asking far too much, but I need to return a few belongings," I said as I handed her the items. "The cloak belongs to a young man named Hugh Wynter. He gave it to me many years ago, and I've always treasured it, but I don't want it to become my shroud. I once told him that I had lost it and I'm hoping that its return will tell him that I've always treasured his friendship, even if I didn't always show it. I don't know where Master Wynter is now, but if you deliver it to Henry Parker at the king's court, he will know how to find him." After Helena had nodded her assent, I continued, "The Bible belonged to Queen Anne Boleyn, and it's imperative that it is returned to her family. The only one who remains is Mary Stafford. She can be found at Rochford Hall in Essex."

Helena carefully wrapped the items up in her sewing, then gave me a sly wink. "I will find someone discreet to deliver these before we leave for the Tower."

It took a moment for her words to sink in. "Did you say we?" I asked with a tinge of hope in my voice.

"Yes," she replied with a smile. "Lady Russell has given me leave to attend upon you in your final hours.

My brief moment of happiness gave way to a pang of guilt. "What of Lucy?" I whispered. I thought of her alone in a dark cell and felt myself tottering near the edge.

Helena set her pile of fabric on the bed and took my hands in hers. "Calm your fears, Lady Rochford. You must retain your composure." I felt my heartbeat slow as her thumbs stroked measured arches across my skin. "Secretary Wriothesley has released your maid," she continued in a low voice. "I heard Gage tell Lady Russell that they sent her home on the day that they brought you here."

When I released the breath I had been holding, I felt a heavy burden fall from my shoulders. My beloved Lucy was safe. My knees weakened, and I felt tears of joy prick at the back of my eyes.

"Don't cry, Lady Rochford!" Helena exclaimed as she struggled to hold me up. "Please don't cry. Think of what awaits you if you can maintain your sanity."

I gulped back my tears and willed my body to remain strong. "Thank you, Helena," I whispered.

APRIL 1536
GREENWICH

Springtime gales roared in like a lion bringing along with them the tumultuous winds of doubt and mistrust. Every act of reconciliation between Anne and the king saw a seed of discord spring up from the roots of resentment that had taken hold within the walls of the court. His Grace's anger with Anne over her miscarriage dissipated as quickly as it came, but the scar of Cromwell's treachery failed to heal.

"How dare he defy his anointed queen?" Anne seethed once her initial bewilderment subsided. "I would never countenance the surrender of his rooms to that family. His support of them is a disgrace, just as is his handling of the monasteries. Their destruction was not the purpose of this reformation. He overreaches himself in everything he touches."

"I understand your anger, sister, but difficult choices must be made to root out the vice and heresy practiced in those supposed houses of God. You must trust the king to act as he sees fit," George soothed, but I saw that his face was pinched in the way that it always was when Anne fell into one of her rages. The fits had been a rare occurrence in the past, but they seemed to come more frequently as the king's affections waxed and waned; the pressure to please the monarch could be crushing. "I don't believe Cromwell intended to defy you, Anne," he added. "Everything he does is for the king's benefit. You know, better than anyone, how vital that happiness is."

Anne humoured him at the time of their disagreement, but George's words fell on deaf ears. In the days following her brother's counsel, she lashed out at the Lord Secretary for his slights against her. So great was her fury, she went further than she intended. "I told him I had a mind to deprive him of his head," she wept later in her retelling of the scene.

"Anne, you must desist. You will anger His Grace if you continue down this path." If George had been unable to dissuade her, I knew I stood even less chance of success, but I had to try.

"I fear that the die has been cast, Jane. I no longer have Cromwell's fealty. I must continue my stand against him and prove to Henry that his guidance has been unwise," her voice faltered, but she pushed on. "Regardless of his niceties to those bloody Seymours, he makes a mockery of our reforms. The money from the dissolutions belongs to the care of those who cannot care for themselves; it is not meant to make my husband and his friends richer. Nor is it meant for their endless blood-stained wars. The very idea of it disgusts me."

True to her word, Anne enlisted the aid of her almoner in revealing the danger she felt Cromwell posed. John Skypp's sermon recounting the betrayal of King Ahasuerus by the evil advisor, Haman, created a stir that reverberated throughout the court. Anne made it known that she was the good Queen Esther; the only one who could root out the duplicity and greed surrounding her husband. To drive the nail in further, she displayed impressive generosity during the Maundy Thursday ceremonies; far above her already exceptional benevolence.

As I watched Anne scrubbing the calloused feet of the ragged and filthy poor haunting the streets of the city, I marvelled at the gentle way in which she handled them. She never rushed through the task; always taking the time to wash each foot like a mother would her child's. Her whispered words of encouragement always seemed to draw a tentative smile from even the most wretched soul. It felt impossible to reconcile the woman I saw on that day with the one I saw struggling under the weight of the king's expectation.

We waited with nervous anticipation for the dire repercussions of Anne's boldness, but they never came. The king spoke not one word against his wife aloud and, when the opportunity arose, he took great pains to force the Imperial Ambassador, Chapuys, to recognise Anne's position.

"If Chapuys fails to accept the gracious overture we have extended and refuses to meet Anne as queen, then other plans have been put in place to force his hand," George groaned as he wrestled a boot off his foot. He handed the pair to the chamberer, then stretched his legs as he rose. "I feel as if my body has aged a century during the last months."

"You still look as handsome as the day I married you," I replied coyly, as I crossed to the hearth where he stood warming himself before the flames. I wanted to ask my husband how he intended to persuade the ambassador, but the weariness on his face prevented me from raising the issue. Besides, I had far better things to discuss with him. Today, after my third morning of waking with an unsettled stomach, I realised I had missed my courses. In those initial moments of awareness, I panicked at the thought of telling him the news. What if I was wrong? What if it was too early? Then the idea of facing yet another loss without his support filled me with terror; I knew I couldn't keep it from him.

"I would counter with the argument that beauty is fleeting, my dearest wife, but I think it will stay forever on you." George pulled at a tendril of hair escaping from under my hood and wound it around his finger. When he released it, the curl bounced against my cheek, drawing a soft chuckle from his lips. "Oh, Jane, I'm not looking forward to another journey to France. These wars between us are never ending. The moment we negotiate one treaty, they break another, and the call to arms goes out again. The word of a prince, once stronger than oak, is no longer binding. At least, this time, my sister will be going so you will be by my side."

I brought George's hand to my lips, brushing them against the supple skin of his palm. "I won't be going to Calais, George."

My husband's brow arched in confusion, then I saw a light spread across his face as my meaning became clear. "Is it true?" he whispered. When I nodded, a great yelp of excitement issued from his mouth. He threw his arms around me and pulled me in close. I breathed deep his scent and allowed my body to relax into his embrace. I felt as though I had been waiting for this moment for such a long time; I would hold on to it for as long as I could.

"Jane?"

Grace breathed my name so faintly, I didn't hear it until the third time she repeated it.

"What is it?" I asked between clenched teeth. My brother's wife and I sat watch outside Anne's inner chamber while she and George discussed the meaning of Sir George Carew's election to Knight of the Garter away from the prying eyes of her household. Anne had put forth George's name and Carew's success in his place frightened them. Their relationship with Carew had been fraught with difficulty and everyone knew that his loyalties were bound to the Seymour family. This new preferment unsettled them after their success only days ago: with George and Cromwell's swift manoeuvring, Chapuys had been forced to pay reverence to Anne when she passed before him during the mass. That shining moment seemed to dull in light of the news from yesterday's meeting of the Garter.

"I must speak with you in private," Grace replied in hushed tones.

I searched her face for meaning, but she remained impassive as her needle dove in and out of the silk kirtle gathered in her lap. I shifted uncomfortably, turning back to the poem in my hand; it was a collection of verses George wrote for me on the night I told him of our conception. His fair words made my heart tremble with gladness, but I felt the glow slip away as I worried over what news Grace had. Her recent return to court had come after a long recuperation from a difficult childbirth. I hoped the child was well. "Come to my rooms tonight," I told her. "I have happy tidings for you as well."

After an afternoon in deep conversation with his sister, George was overcome with exhaustion and retired to bed soon after supper. The joyous gleam that had shone in his eyes over the last few days was replaced by the furrowed brow and pursed lips gracing his features now more often than not. He insisted he didn't want to worry me, so I avoided prying, but I felt my stomach sink as I watched him slip quietly behind the door to our bedchamber. I turned over the latest events in my head while I paced before the fire in anticipation of Grace's arrival. The king's vacillation perplexed me, and I felt at a loss to do anything to help.

"The Lady Parker is here to see you, my lady."

I looked up from the fire and nodded at Lucy. "Send her in please."

Grace's normally pale complexion appeared ghostly in the candlelight. Her eyes were wide, and she seemed to startle at every pop of the flames in the hearth. I tried to shake off her warnings, nothing she said made sense, but I couldn't ignore the panic in her voice.

"Cromwell has questioned you?" I repeated. "For what cause? What are his suspicions?"

"He has questioned several of the queen's ladies," she corrected me. "He believes that she has lived incontinently," she gulped, making a face as though she had swallowed something repugnant. "He asked me about George."

I blanched in disgust. "No, that's impossible. Cromwell has overstepped his bounds before, but he would never question Anne's fidelity; that's treason. He wouldn't dare impugn the line of succession. Not without..." I stuttered as I said it. "Not without the king's approval."

Grace's warning sent me reeling. Her allegations were fantastical; I couldn't bring myself to believe her. Why would the king do such a thing? God's Blood! He had broken with the church for Anne. He would never mar her reputation in this way.

"I know you don't believe me, Jane, but I swear to it. Cromwell has witnesses and a letter from Lady Wingfield."

I thought of the gentlewoman with whom we stayed on our journey to Calais. Anne and I had both mourned her death a few years after that visit, lamenting that her young child had such a short time with her. What could she have said about Anne that warranted such investigation? Nothing seemed strained during our time with her. "Lady Wingfield had no cause to speak against Anne. Who are the others?"

Grace hesitated, but the names finally spilt out, "Nan Cobham and Lady Worcester." My mind scrambled for any reason the women could have to besmirch their queen, but I could fathom no justification. Lady Worcester had even been granted a small loan from Anne mere weeks ago when she took pity on the woman after she unleashed a torrent of tears over her pregnancy. The baby's movement was faint, and she worried she might lose it. I knew not what the money was for, but Anne graciously granted it. "You must distance yourself, Jane," Grace continued. "You can't get caught up in this maelstrom."

"If there is a tempest coming I will weather it, Grace," I answered. "I will never forsake George or the queen." I wanted to be furious with Grace for even suggesting it, but I couldn't. I knew she said it only out of concern for me and I saw clearly my brother's hand in it. Harry was as pragmatic as our father; if he saw danger coming, he would always run from it.

Grace wiped away the tears dripping down her face. "I'm very sorry, Jane. I wish I could tell you that it is all a cruel joke, but I can't."

"It's not your fault. It took great bravery for you to warn me and, no matter what happens, I will never be able to repay you for that," I squeezed Grace's hand as I consoled her. "You must go now. I have to tell George."

George grew increasingly agitated as Grace's warnings sputtered out of me in a halting voice. When I parted company from my sister-in-law earlier in the evening, I spent an hour collecting my thoughts before waking my husband; I wanted to present a calm exterior. However, the wild look in George's eyes when he finally emerged from his sleep drenched dreams upended any serenity that remained.

"Spit it out, Jane," he bellowed. "Who did Cromwell question? What did he ask?"

"Please, don't yell at me, George," I gasped. My tears came hard and fast; I felt as if the air had been ripped from my lungs. I had never seen my husband this angry.

George leapt from the bed and began to pull on his hose. "I have to go to Anne. I must caution her of the treachery afoot."

I dragged myself across the bed and pulled at George's hand. "You'll only make things worse if you storm into her bedchamber in the dead of night. You must wait until morning."

George dropped the jerkin in his hand to the floor and stared at me, dumbstruck. "And what do you suggest we do until then? My mind is too harried to rest. How can I stand by while danger lurks in my sister's very rooms?"

I drew myself up to meet his eyes. "We plan; that is what we do. My own interrogation is assured, and I need you to tell me what to do." I fought off the panic constricting my throat. "I am weak, George; the pressure will be too great, and I'm afraid of what I may say. What if I lose the baby?" I rested George's hand on my belly, reminding him of the other life at stake; the life we had created together. I refused to sacrifice my child to the machinations of the king's advisors.

"I won't let that happen," he promised before crushing his lips against mine. When we pulled apart, he brushed my tears away with the pad of his thumb. "When your time comes, you must tell Cromwell the truth, Jane. Tell him everything you know about my sister. She has done nothing to deserve this stain on her honour, and there is nothing you can say that will hurt her."

"Even her secret about the king?" George appeared puzzled by my question, and I realised then that I had never told him of His Grace's difficulty in the bedchamber. "Anne had trouble conceiving the last time because the king…" My voice trailed off. I couldn't bring myself to say the words. Fortunately, George knew me well enough to understand my meaning.

"Yes," he commanded. "If anyone heard Anne tell you and they find out that way, they will suspect everything else you've said. Deceit surrounds my sister; the only thing that might save her is the truth."

The morning after our sleepless night, George rushed to his sister's side to prepare her for the oncoming storm. Having spent the earliest hours of the day vomiting into the piss pot, I arrived in the queen's apartments just as they emerged from the privy chamber. Anne's eyes were puffy, her lips set in a grim line. George kissed my hand, then hurried from the room while his sister called out for her chaplain. Margery Horseman scurried off to retrieve the sober Matthew Parker.

Anne continued to run her household as if nothing were amiss. She projected an air of confidence that fooled everyone, but me. While the rest of the women carried on with their usual vigour, I could see that, beneath the surface, Anne's shell was cracking. The breaking point came one sultry afternoon when Sir Henry Norris came to call on Madge Shelton.

"This game he plays with her has begun to tire me," Anne muttered under her breath as she watched Norris taunt her maid with a book of poetry that was making the rounds through the household. Mistress Shelton had written in it a posy of love Norris thought aimed at Sir Thomas Wyatt. Wyatt was a frequent contributor to the work, but many courtiers took part. Even George had a sonnet or two recorded inside.

"Let them be merry, Your Grace," I cautioned.

Anne paid no heed to my plea. "Why do you tarry in my chamber so often, Sir Henry?" she inquired, rising from her chair. The rest of us scrambled to our feet. "You've dallied too long in your courtship of my dearest cousin, and I've given up hope that you will ever marry her."

Norris' cheeks enflamed at the scrutiny aimed at him. "I've pledged myself to Madge," he stammered. "We will marry in good time."

"That's not true, is it Sir Henry?" I heard the danger laced through Anne's voice. Her words dripped with fury. The crowd of courtiers stared aghast at the change in their queen. We all stood by silently as we waited for the outburst to come.

"I don't understand," Norris tried to lighten the tension with a nervous chuckle.

"I understand perfectly," Anne spat. "You look for dead man's shoes, for if aught came to the king but good, you would look to have me."

The colour drained from Norris' face, and his jaw sagged towards the floor, while he took in the indictment his queen had lodged against him. My head suddenly felt light; a wave of nausea rushed over me. Anne's hasty words were treasonous. Not only were they rash and ill–advised, but they also imagined the king's death; a crime so heinous, others had been executed for it.

After a few moments of strained silence, Norris found his wits. "If I should ever have such thought," he replied carefully. "I would wish my head were off."

Anne shot him one last glare before she stormed off to her bedchamber.

I was the only one allowed into the queen's inner rooms the rest of the afternoon. I called for George when my efforts to calm her failed. She knew she had gone too far.

"Sir Henry must go to my almoner," she cried. "He knows I am a good woman; that I meant no treason."

"You must find a way to contain your emotions, Anne," he cautioned. "Until now you've done nothing in which they can find fault. Your hysterics put you in danger, and you will be your own undoing. Bite your tongue if you must."

"I'm afraid, George."

"Don't let them see," he replied. "The kitchen will send your supper soon. You must return to your presence chamber as if nothing has happened. Hold your head up, Sister. Show them that you are their anointed queen. No one touches you, but God."

Anne inhaled deeply, brushing the wrinkles from her gown as she straightened. She squared her shoulders and beckoned me to follow her. "Come, Jane. I must salvage my dignity."

The presence chamber had emptied while we were closeted and only the musician, Marc Smeaton, remained. He stood in one of the window embrasures, staring forlornly out into the garden. Anne cleared her throat to announce her presence. He started at the sound, then dipped a low bow. "Good evening, Your Grace," he simpered.

"Master Smeaton, why look you so sorrowful?" Anne's smile appeared forced, but she made an effort.

"It's no matter," Smeaton replied as he turned back to the window.

I watched Anne blink her eyes slowly and swallow back her displeasure. "You're far too familiar with me, Master Smeaton," her response was clipped; her tone irritated. "I cannot speak to you as I do to the others. You are low born, and such treatment does not belong to you."

Marc glowered back at the queen. "No," he remarked. "A mere look sufficed me."

"I think it's time for you to leave," I admonished. I felt the heat coming from Anne as she seethed beside me.

Marc twisted his lips into a smirk, before dipping into an exaggerated bow. "Thus fare you well," he sneered before he sauntered out of the room.

MAY 1, 1536
GREENWICH

THE FIRST day of May dawned clear and bright. A fair wind blew the sweet scent of the early garden blooms across the tiltyard where the court had gathered to witness the May Day jousts. An eager anticipation coursed through the crowd of courtiers sitting in the stands, but the atmosphere in the queen's gallery was thick with tension. Anne had always enjoyed the sport of the event, and the fact that George was leading the challengers should have excited her more, but the upheaval of the last few weeks had smothered her fire and yesterday's argument with the king put her on edge. Her body was rigid in the great chair of estate as she sat in stone silence.

Margery Horseman leaned into me as the men took to the field. "Where's Marc?" She whispered. "Shouldn't he be here?" I shuddered at the tickle of her breath in my ear.

"Do not ask about Master Smeaton," I warned. I glanced at Anne out of the corner of my eye to confirm that she had not overheard. "I don't think he will be joining us today."

I had not seen the young man since I dismissed him from the presence chamber. It was odd that he had not returned; he always managed to slither his way back into Anne's good graces. However, I was glad of his absence. It was one less thing for me to worry over.

I settled back to watch the tournament unfold while I kept an eye on the queen. Her stoicism faltered only once; when Sir Henry Norris' horse refused to run. She winced as the sleek black courser tossed its head wildly, dancing away from the lance Norris' page held aloft. When it became obvious the horse was too spooked to run, the king leapt from his seat and offered up his own so that the tournament could continue. At the end of the festivities, we followed Anne back to her apartments to await the king's return; we expected that he would come to sup with her as he always did. When the kitchen arrived with service for one, I saw it as a terrible omen.

"The king and Norris rode off to Westminster after the jousts," George explained later as we prepared for bed.

"What about the banquet?" I asked. "What of the other events planned for May Day? I thought you were leaving for Rochester with them?" My hands shook as I fumbled with the ties on my nightgown. I couldn't seem to calm the jittery sensations coursing through my limbs, and my stomach had yet to unclench from the knots that had formed at the king's abrupt departure.

Seeing my frustration, George brushed my hands aside and looped the silk ties for me. "There," he replied with a smile. He strode over to the window, propping it open, before returning to the bed. I waited until he settled in before badgering him with more questions.

"I have no answers for you, Jane," he groaned. "The only thing for certain is that the journey to Calais has been postponed and the king has not set a new date for our departure to Rochester. I will ride to York Place in the morning to see what I can discover. Now, please join me in our bed so that I might rest my hand on your belly to encourage our son to quicken." He shot me a smile as he patted the space beside him.

I slid under the thick counterpane and curled into George's warm body. He propped himself up on his elbow, then leaned in to kiss me deeply. "Good night, my love," he said before he settled against the pillow, draping his arm across my belly.

When I sleepily emerged from my dreams in the eerie pre-dawn darkness to kiss him farewell before he headed off to Westminster, I had no inkling it would be the last time I would ever see my husband again.

MAY 2–4, 1536
GREENWICH

ANNE KEPT calm when a messenger from the Privy Council presented himself in the gallery later that morning as we watched Sir Francis Weston compete in a tennis match, but when she returned to her rooms in the company of two royal guards, her ashen face betrayed the fear in her heart.

"Find George," she whispered urgently as she swept past me in the corridor. I waited until the guards dismissed us, then once I turned the corner into an empty hallway, I broke into a run. I needed to find George's page.

I found my brother, Harry, waiting for me when I skidded to a stop before the door to our apartments. "What are you doing here?" I demanded. "Have you seen my husband? Has he returned from Westminster?"

"Don't be alarmed, Jane. We need to speak inside."

My voice rose to a frantic pitch, "What is happening, Harry? They have just dismissed us from the queen's rooms. Something is terribly wrong."

Harry put his arm around me, guiding me through the doorway. "I'll tell you everything inside."

When Harry informed me of my husband's arrest, I slapped him so hard across the face, my palm burned from the force of it. I screamed at him until I grew hoarse; it took him and two other men to subdue me. I slammed my fists against them as they dragged me to the bedchamber. When I became lightheaded at my efforts, I allowed myself to sink into the oblivion. I awoke in the darkness several hours later to find the shadowed outline of my maid, Lucy, keeping watch at the end of the bed.

"Bring me parchment and ink," I commanded. "I must write to my husband."

"I'm sorry, my lady," she replied, despondently. "Your brother has instructed me to tell you that Lord Rochford is not to have any correspondence."

"Then I shall write to the constable, Master Kingston." My maid stared down at her hands. "Please say you'll find a way to get it to him," I pleaded.

Lucy finally raised her head to meet my gaze. "I'll try," she promised.

I had just signed my name at the bottom of the letter when I heard a knock at the door. I folded the parchment as small as I could, then slipped it to Lucy to hide in her gown. I pulled my robe tight across my body before I called out for my visitor to enter. The sight of Thomas Cromwell standing behind my brother stole the breath from my lungs. The moment I'd been dreading had arrived.

Cromwell's coal black eyes bore down on me. The cool, aloof man I'd only spoken to intermittently throughout my time at court was replaced by a wolfish inquisitor bent on catching any inconsistency in my story. He threw his questions at me like lightening, leaving me little time for a thoughtful answer. He wanted to know every word the queen had spoken to every man that ever came into her rooms. What did men do when they came to see her? How did they act? How did she act? Did she ever allow them to touch her? Had any of them ever been alone with her? Did I know of any plans she had to poison the king's daughter, the Lady Mary, or his bastard, the Duke of Richmond? He frowned at my frantic denials. "You spend more time with the queen than any other maid in her rooms. I do not believe that you, of all people, could be so ignorant of her activities," he snapped.

"I swear to it, Lord Secretary," I cried. "I've told you all that I know."

"No, there is something else. Something you are not telling me. I can see it – just there – hiding behind your eyes." He reached out to brush a tendril of hair from my brow. I blanched at his touch; he smirked at my disgust. "What do you know? What did the queen tell you?"

I hated to reveal Anne's secret, but I remembered George's guidance; I must tell the truth. I swallowed hard, then I answered his question. "The queen told me that His Grace had certain… complications… in their relations," I stammered.

"What sort of complications?"

"She said that he did not always have the vigour in which to bed her. She worried that she might not conceive due to these complications."

"When did she say this?" he demanded.

"I cannot recall the specific date, but it happened before her last pregnancy."

Cromwell's eyes narrowed. "So she conceived after these preposterous allegations against the king?" his response was more of a statement than a question. He didn't need my answer; he already had a vile thought in his mind.

"She appeared quite concerned, my lord," I heard my voice crack on the nicety.

"Oh I'm certain she was," he responded coolly. "I suppose she laughed when she told you. We've had many reports of the disdain in which she has treated His Royal Person."

"No, the queen would never laugh at His Grace!" I gasped. A cold sick dread spread through my belly. This was not the reaction I expected; I feared where Cromwell's thoughts were headed.

"Your husband spends a great deal of time alone with his sister, does he not?"

I found the question laughable, but this was not the time for amusements. "Yes, of course," I answered. "They are kin; George is one of her closest advisers."

"Were you with them? Did anyone witness these closed meetings?"

"They invited me occasionally, but I didn't expect to be there always. I don't believe anyone else attended them." I frantically searched my mind for any example to give him, but the most recent of their meetings took place in private.

"So, you are telling me that the queen complained to you about the king's inability to bed her, then after spending time alone with your husband, she became pregnant?"

"No, that's not... I mean yes, but..." His insinuation jumbled my thoughts. I couldn't make sense of his accusations. "All of that is true, but it didn't happen like you said. The very idea is an abomination! George is her brother!"

"Do you spend an inordinate time alone with your brother, Lady Rochford?" Cromwell appeared bemused by his own question. He seemed to find my flustered answers entertaining.

"I don't see Harry much at all, but I don't understand what that has to do with any of this," I replied. I had never felt so useless in my life. I wanted nothing more than to save my husband and my queen, but I was failing miserably.

"I'm rather surprised that you don't see the irony, Lady Rochford," Cromwell sneered. "You find the amount of time that your husband spends alone with his sister to be quite ordinary, yet you rarely speak to your brother. You also fail to question the queen's pregnancy after she tells you, in secret, that the king cannot bed her. Either you are the most naïve woman at court, or you're just plain stupid. So which is it, my lady?"

Instead of words, I replied with a gush of bile and vomit. Cromwell jumped away just in time to avoid being hit by the sick. "I'm sorry," I sobbed as the waves of nausea continued to break over me.

"Where is the maid?" Cromwell bellowed through the doorway.

Lucy barrelled in with a chamber pot and some rags. "Oh, you poor thing," she fretted. "This baby seems to make you sick at all hours."

Cromwell's face fell at the realisation of my pregnancy. His lip uncurled, and he regarded me with pity. "I apologise for distressing you, Lady Rochford," he murmured. "We can continue our conversation when you have recovered."

My body shook uncontrollably as the sweat chilled against my skin. I felt relief that the interrogation was over, but I couldn't stop thinking about Cromwell's accusations. What he said was not true, nor could it be possible. George could never have impregnated his sister. The very idea of it was monstrous. Certainly, the king could see through this? He would never believe the allegations, would he?

MAY 5 – 13, 1536
GREENWICH

THE DAY after my interrogation two more arrests took place. Our friend, Thomas Wyatt, was taken with Richard Page to join Marc Smeaton, Henry Norris, Francis Weston, William Brereton and George. Every raven that had flitted about Anne's chambers was now caged within the Tower. I began to wonder why the king spared me. Was my unborn child the reason? I may not have been held within the alabaster fortress of the Tower, but I too was a prisoner; my brother and his wife served as the gaolers outside my door. When I pleaded with Harry to let me out, he refused. "It's for your own good, Jane," he said. "We must protect you and the baby."

I had become so estranged from my family that I began to doubt their motivations. Were they truly concerned with my well-being or was this a passive form of torture? Did they hold me of their own volition or did they follow orders from a higher authority? These thoughts churned my mind as I drifted through my empty days waiting for an absolution.

My father arrived ten days into my captivity. When I asked him why he had come, he told me he was summoned to serve as a peer of the realm. He would sit on the jury that passed judgement on the queen and my husband.

"You must find them innocent, Father," I begged. "You know these are all lies."

Baron Morley frowned at my display of emotion. "The only thing I know is that I must do my duty to my Lord and Sovereign."

"You'd make your daughter a widow?" I retorted.

"If it means saving her life."

I aimed a glare at my father, then turned to walk away. I couldn't bear to look at the man anymore. "You just want to start again," I snapped over my shoulder. "You thought you had made an excellent match, but then Anne caught the king's attention and suddenly, my fortune came at the expense of his first wife. You told me then that if anything happened to the Boleyns, I would be on my own."

I couldn't see my father's face, but his voice sounded heavy and low. "You read far deeper into my words than I intended. I would never say such a thing."

"You didn't have to," I retorted. "Your meaning was clear enough." I tightened my arms around my body as if to protect myself, but thus far, I'd failed to identify the threat. Was it the king and Cromwell? Was it my father? Or, worse still, was it George and the Boleyns? I trembled at the thought.

I stared out the window until I heard my father rise to take his leave of me. "I will return after the trials," he informed me. "Only then, can we determine the future."

I turned back to face him with cold fury in my heart. "Do not, for one moment, deceive yourself into believing that I will ever marry another man."

FEBRUARY 9 – 12, 1542
THE TOWER OF LONDON

WE DISEMBARKED from the dock in the early morning hours as the rest of the Strand's inhabitants slept peacefully in their beds. The normal chaos of the street was gone, and all that remained was a deafening silence, hanging like a thick fog over the deserted cobblestones. The air was as cold as I had ever felt it and each inhalation burned deep within my chest. I tried to keep my breathing shallow as I followed Sir John Gage and Lord Russell to the bobbing boat waiting in the Thames for me, but I grew winded as I struggled to keep my balance on the thin sheet of ice covering the ground. I winced at each involuntary gasp that passed through my lips.

My journey back to the stone fortress bore no resemblance to the last one I took there. The vessel returning me to prison was much smaller and contained no yeoman guards to watch over me. My only companions were Helena, Gage, and the bony, grizzled boatman who rowed us down the muddy river. Lord Russell was left behind on the shore to stare forlornly at our receding forms. The unruly tide carried us quickly towards our destination, and we docked at the wharf near the court gate before the sun's rays unfurled from their nightly cocoon. Gage made no mention of my accommodations during the journey, so I blinked back tears of relief when he led Helena and me towards the royal apartments rather than the inner ward.

"The king would have preferred to house you in the Beauchamp Tower this time, but it's filled up with Howard relations," Gage explained as our feet crunched through the frost covering the ground. "His Grace has ordered them all detained because they knew of Katherine's prior misbehaviour. Even the Dowager Duchess of Norfolk is here. She spends her days lamenting her abandonment by her step-son, the Duke, and emphatically denying her culpability. She is the most wretched prisoner I've dealt with yet."

"Does the king want me in a cell because he's condemned me?" The question slipped out involuntarily. Gage's answer would make no difference, but I need to hear it. It was like a wound I couldn't stop poking.

Gage stopped to consider me with his clear blue eyes before pressing ahead; his words nearly lost in the frigid wind. "Yes, Lady Rochford."

Someone had tidied up my chambers since I last left them. The crisp scent of juniper wafted from the freshly laid rushes covering the floor and a cheery fire danced in the hearth. The bench had been removed from the window, and two plump cushions rested in its place. Helena immediately set to work unpacking the small trunk that held my belongings. It had preceded my arrival, having been delivered from Russell House the night before.

"Please let me know if you need anything, my lady," Gage intoned as he dipped a perfunctory bow.

When he came up, I asked the last question that remained in my mind. "When can I go to the chapel?"

"You've done well so far, Lady Rochford. The king is pleased with Lord Russell's reports, but I'm afraid that your greatest test is to come. I've been commanded to allow your access the night before your execution, so you must wait until that time. His Grace wants to ensure your decorum for the rest of your stay."

"My stay," I scoffed. "You make it sound as though I will be leaving; as if this is all just a pleasant diversion."

Gage shifted uncomfortably, but he maintained his gaze. "I'm not sure what you want me to say, my lady. I take no pleasure in the position in which I've been placed. When I close my eyes at night, I see the bloody and mangled bodies of those who have suffered within these stone walls. I shudder to remember the butchering of the piteous Countess of Salisbury. What were her crimes? Only the royal Plantagenet blood running through her veins and having children who refused to bend to the king's will. Each time I walk by the corner where the executioner hacked her to pieces, I say a prayer for her soul. I will live with those memories forever."

"I'm sorry, Sir John," I whispered. "I've thought only of my own pain. In truth, we all suffer in the king's service. In a few short days, I will be free of my burdens, but you will continue to carry yours throughout the rest of your life."

"That's kind of you to say, Lady Rochford," Gage replied with a wistful smile. "But I'm under no illusion that I suffer more than you. I see it as a command from God to show kindness to the condemned in my custody. I wish to provide nothing but comfort in their final days. Unfortunately, I am restricted by the king's laws. If you can show yourself well-amended, I assure you that I will escort you to the chapel myself."

"Thank you, Sir John." My voice wavered as the tears slid down my cheeks.

After Gage had excused himself to see to the other prisoners, I allowed Helena to lead me to the bedchamber. I had been unable to settle my mind during the night, and my body felt weary from the lack of sleep. It seemed strange to me that I could no longer comfort myself in the same way I had in the past. Before my arrest, I could always lose my worries in a deep slumber. Now that ability was gone. I found myself fortunate if I could manage a few hours of rest.

Helena removed my over gown and pulled back the thick counterpane so I could crawl into bed. "Just lie back for a bit," she clucked as she pulled the tapestry closed to shut out the light. "It will do you some good." I started to shake my head, but she put out her hand to stop me. "I took some when Dr Butts was otherwise occupied." It was then that I noticed the glass phial clutched between her fingers.

"Lady Russell would be furious if she knew you stole that sleeping draught," I admonished, but secretly I was pleased with her duplicity. A drop or two of that bitter liquid would help the long days ahead pass far more quickly.

"Lady Russell told me to do it!" Helena exclaimed with a grin. "I told you that she was kind when she wanted to be."

I felt a great laugh bubble up from inside of me and, for the first time in months, it was genuine. My laugh was not hysterical or acerbic; it was joyful.

Gage and a coterie of other nobles brought Katherine Howard to the Tower the day after me. I couldn't see her barge from my rooms, so I sent Helena to spy for me; I needed to know how she fared. There were times, when I tossed in my bed during the pitch black of the night, that I still heard her pitiful wails. I'd never forgotten the look of terror in her eyes when the yeoman guards filed into her chambers. I had hoped that telling the truth of my suspicions to Secretary Wriothesley would earn both Katherine and me leniency, but I suspected that my honesty had signed our death warrants instead. My conscience would not be unburdened until I knew that she was all right.

When Helena returned from the courtyard, rose-cheeked from the cold, she wore a smirk. "Quite the lady that queen is," she said with a laugh.

"What happened? How does she look?"

"Very demanding, she was! She regally trotted off the barge leaving all the nobles behind in her wake. She seemed a picture of health to my eyes. Her cheeks were nice and round, her figure plump; not frayed and thin like yours."

"Helena!" I exclaimed.

"Well, it's God's Truth. She's not starving herself as you are," the maid mocked.

"Never mind what I am doing," I replied with a dismissive wave. "Did the queen say anything?"

Helena jutted out her hip and rested a clenched fist there while she thought for a moment. "She said something to the constable, but I couldn't make out her words… Something about a block?" She shook her head as if clearing the thought from her mind before she continued. "Anyway, she appeared to be in good spirits."

"Thank you, Helena," I murmured before wandering over to the window. Katherine may have conducted herself bravely, but I knew her well enough to know that it was likely an act for the benefit of the witnesses. She could be haughty and imperious, she was a Howard after all, and it was in her nature, but she could also be vulnerable and insecure. If the king had not banned her from his rooms each time his leg plagued him, then perhaps she might never have given in to temptation. She made a valiant effort to avoid Thomas Culpeper when she first became queen, but her banishment during His Grace's illness scared her; after what happened to his previous wives, I couldn't blame the poor girl. Her mistake had been in going to a man for whom she still held deep feelings for comfort. Culpeper took it as an invitation to skulk back into her rooms, and it wasn't too long before Katherine went further than she intended. After that, there was no going back.

"Don't berate yourself, Lady Rochford," Helena called out over her shoulder. "You couldn't have saved the queen and her follies are her own. This mournfulness will only do your mind harm. Stay strong, and soon you shall see your husband."

I so feared the snapping of the tenuous thread of sanity I clung to, that I spent most of my remaining hours in a sleeping draught-induced haze. I surfaced long enough to take nourishment when directed, but I found the ritual pointless. What need did I have of sustenance when my head would soon be cleaved from my body? The meals delivered to my rooms tasted bland and felt like lead on my tongue. After each bite, I clamped my lips tight against the urge to regurgitate it. During my few lucid moments, I knelt at the prie-dieu and whispered every prayer I knew. All hope for a last minute reprieve had fled my heart, and I resigned myself to the darkness that edged ever closer with each passing day. My only concern now was the cleanliness of my soul. God's mercy was all that stood between George and me now.

I was on my knees, in this pose of contrition, when Gage arrived to take me to the chapel. When I heard the staccato beat of his knock on the door, I felt my heart drop down into my stomach. As much as I wanted to go, the thought of seeing the spot where he was so hastily buried filled me with dread. When I first arrived at the Tower I needed to visit George's grave to find closure for my grief, but my reasons had changed now that I was standing on the precipice of death. I no longer wanted to end my grief. What I wanted was to punish myself; for living while he died and for serving the man who murdered him. I needed to force myself to face the evidence of the king's cruelty.

After Helena let the constable in, she bustled over with a mantle. "You'll catch your death of the cold out there," she declared as she tied the fur around my shoulders, oblivious to the irony of her statement.

I carefully rose on quaking legs and followed her out into the corridor where Gage awaited me. His face was wan, and his eyes were puffy, but he offered me a tentative smile. "I always keep my promises, Lady Rochford," he said. "Now, let's go see your husband."

Timber and stone hid the other prisoners occupying the royal apartments from my view, but I heard the muffled sounds of life emanating from their barred doors. Quiet coughs and murmured words nipped at our heels as we made our way through the deserted hallway and down the narrow stone stairs to the courtyard. When we stepped through the doors, a glimmering night sky greeted us. A fine dusting of snow fell between the twinkling diamonds etched across the Heavens. I gave a small laugh when I turned my face up to feel the flutter of snowflakes. "He answered my prayers, Sir John," I said. Gage's face remained grim, but he gave my hand a comforting squeeze.

We moved through the craggy walls of the Coldharbour gate, carefully traversing the frost-crusted grass of the Tower Green to the modest chapel housing the remains of my beloved husband and sister-in-law. As I gazed across the open expanse, I found myself grateful for my ignorance of the site of Anne's execution. Because I did not witness her final moments, I spared myself from the reimagining of it.

"They wouldn't have wanted you here, Jane," Gage observed as if reading my thoughts.

"I couldn't bring myself to it," I shuddered. "I thought I might lose the baby if I saw it. It didn't matter in the end. The baby followed his father to Heaven; he didn't want to be left here with me."

Gage's voice dipped low in response, "You'll be with them soon." The constable linked his arm through mine as we descended the frost slicked steps leading to the entrance of the chapel.

The grey walls of the church were awash in the warm glow of candlelight. I slowly followed the line of flickering tapers from the door to the chancel. When I arrived at the altar, I sank to my knees and offered a prayer of thanksgiving. I opened my eyes when the final words passed through my lips and caught sight of a cluster of white blossoms lying on the floor beside me.

"Lady Anne rests there," Gage remarked. "I've brought snowdrops for George as well, but I thought it would be best if you placed them." He offered me his hand, and I struggled to my feet. "He's just on the other side of that wall." I looked past his extended finger to the stone arch beyond. "Wait, don't forget these," he advised as he pulled a matching bouquet off the altar. I grabbed the flowers, before stepping tentatively through the archway.

My mind conjured all manner of horrific images every time I thought of George's grave, so I was unprepared for how unremarkable it looked. The floor above him had settled back into position and appeared to have never been disturbed. I had not expected a monument erected in his honour, but I thought that perhaps there would have been something to mark his presence. I realised, almost instantly, my stupidity. Nothing marked Anne's grave either, and she had been an anointed queen. In the king's eyes, Anne and George were traitors, undeserving of any clemency. The snowdrops Gage had so kindly brought were likely the only tribute my beloved family members had ever, or would ever, receive. I stared down at the bare floor until tears clouded my sight, then I bent down to place the cheery white blossoms over my husband's body. There was so much I wanted to say, but the words refused to come. Instead, I touched my fingertips to my lips, before touching them to the cold floor. "I love you, George," I whispered.

My grief had so absorbed me, I didn't realise Gage had crept up behind me until I felt his hand on my shoulder. "It's time to go back," he breathed.

I pushed myself up and followed the constable back through the path of candles to the door, where a man I didn't recognise awaited us. Gage introduced him as Father John. "He will come to you in the morning for your last rites."

Father John met my gaze and granted me a benevolent smile. "Thank you," I quavered.

As we walked back to the royal apartments, I ventured a peek at the only window ablaze in candlelight. I watched the slight shadow figure behind the curtain waver, then dip down as if to bow.

"I see Katherine is practicing for tomorrow."

"What do you mean?" I asked. "What does she practice?"

Gage heaved a deep sigh before replying. "She asked for a block so she could practice laying her head upon it. I've never seen anyone greet death in such calm and measured fashion. Her composure is almost unearthly."

JULY 1536
HALLINGBURY

ON THE fifteenth day of May, my father and a host of the most eminent nobles of the realm convicted two innocent victims of the most abominable crimes imaginable. To add further insult, the victims received the sentence of death from no less a person than their very own uncle, the Duke of Norfolk. Not one soul stirred a foot to help them; even after my husband put forth a well-reasoned defence and wagers were made that the jury would acquit him of all crimes. Having done his duty by the sovereign, the king dismissed my father to his estates at Hallingbury. Before he set off from the city, he returned to the palace at Greenwich to collect me. Anne's household had been dismissed two days before her trial; there was no reason for me to remain at court.

I felt a sort of kinship with the brilliant summer sun warming me through the leaded windows of my childhood home. She had been there to mourn the fiery queen who set the world aflame and witness the deaths of the ravens who flocked about her feet, desperate for her attention. She had been there to comfort my beloved in his final moments when I could not. On the day that George's soul ascended into Heaven, a jagged pain tore through my belly. I took to my bed in hopes that I could save the child, but I awoke in the middle of the night, my nightgown soaked in crimson blood.

The only person I allowed to care for me during my recuperation was Lucy. She was the only one who didn't see my miscarriage as a blessing. My family denied it, but I suspected that they were thankful every last tie with the Boleyns had been severed. Better still, they didn't have to convince any man who had a mind to marry me to raise the child of a convicted traitor. The death of my child increased my value to any prospective suitor. My past failures to carry a pregnancy would make no difference at my age; I would not be chosen to produce heirs.

Everything George owned was forfeited to the crown; Hallingbury Manor was now the only home left to me. I steeled myself for the eventuality that my father would approach me with a proposition for either marriage or a return to court; it came much quicker than I expected. He found me in the orchard one sweltering afternoon, taking shade beneath one of our apple trees with one of George's books in my lap.

"One of the reasons I chose George to be your husband was his love of books."

I held my place with one finger, then used my other hand to shade my eyes. My father appeared more worn than I had ever seen him. Deep creases marred the thin skin around his eyes and his proud, square jaw sagged under the scruff of his beard. I didn't want to feel compassion for him, but he was still my father. I loved him even when I felt betrayed by him.

"Have you decided what to do with me, Father?" I asked.

Lord Morley crouched down to meet my gaze. He didn't offer me a smile, just a sigh of resignation. "I will honour your pledge to remain unmarried on one condition." He waited for me to respond.

"I'll hear it," I allowed.

"I've spoken to Lord Secretary Cromwell, and he has agreed to find you a position in the new queen's household."

"I will never serve that pallid, meek…"

He held up his hand to stop me. "To speak of Jane Seymour in such a way is now treason," he cautioned.

"What is the condition?" I sighed.

"The king and queen want experienced women from good families. You were always looked upon favourably in Queen Catherine's household and the king wants to show that he does not hold you accountable for your husband's misdeeds."

"George has no misdeeds," I shot back.

"Don't make this any more difficult than it needs to be, Jane. If you go back to court, Cromwell will help you collect on your jointure. I'm not a rich man; I cannot afford to keep you in the style of Dowager Viscountess. Besides, your husband would still be alive if his father had not been greedy. Wiltshire owes you what he promised."

"Wiltshire wasn't greedy, Father," I protested. "He never forced Anne to marry the king. That was a decision she made on her own."

"Regardless, those lands are yours, and Cromwell will see to it the earl honours his contract."

I would get my property, but I would have to sell my soul for it. My return would legitimise the king's actions against his wife. The court would believe that Anne must have truly been guilty for me to agree to serve the woman who supplanted her.

After a few moments of silence, I conceded my defeat, "I'll consider your proposal."

Lord Morley groaned as he rose up from the ground. "Grace will be there as well; I know she always admired you. Not that he would ever tell you, but Harry took George's death quite hard. What they had in common besides you, I will never know, but they had quite the partnership. That blond boy who used to come to fish in our pond always seemed to be carrying on some errand for the both of them. Your brother was always too busy to continue his studies."

As I watched my father amble away, I thought of George. What would he want me to do? The fact that I didn't know the answer saddened me.

When I returned to the manor, I retired to my room with a pot of ink and parchment. In the light of the flickering candles, I composed a letter to Cromwell. My father said the Lord Secretary desired me back at court, but he couldn't just give me his assistance, I had to ask for it. The moment the wax was sealed, I called for Lucy.

"Yes, my lady?" she asked from the doorway.

"Please inform the tailor that I will need at least three gowns of the deepest black that he can make. From now on, those are the only ones I shall be wearing."

February 13, 1542
The Tower of London

HELENA URGED me to take some rest when I returned to my rooms, but I couldn't bring myself to spend my last remaining hours of life in a draught-induced fog. I wanted to savour each moment left to me before the executioner ripped them from my grasp. Instead of sleeping, I curled up on one of the cushions and marvelled at the delicate snowflakes dancing outside the frosted window. Helena managed to find me a cup of hippocras, and the spicy sweet drink warmed me from the inside out. We said little during the hushed, dark hours, but I appreciated her calm and solid presence.

When the streaks of morning sunlight broke across the sky, Father John arrived to hear my last confession and administer the final rituals that prepared my soul for Heaven. After he bid me a kind farewell, I knelt at the prie-dieu to recite one last prayer. As my words died away, I noticed the clamour of the crowd filtering in through the stony tower walls. It was then that I realised all of these people had come here to watch us die. I wondered, for a brief moment, if any of my loved ones would be waiting for me on Tower Green. Would they come here in support or would they come here in disgust? Had my misdeeds further sullied their name? Did any of them love me in return?

Before I could linger too long on the questions in my mind, I heard the constable calling my name. "The time has come," he said. I rose to my feet, stepping slowly towards the door as if I could prolong the inevitable. "Katherine Howard made a good end, and she is with the Lord now," he finished as he slipped a small purse of coins to pay the executioner into my hand.

"Thank you for everything, Sir John. I have never deserved the kindness you have shown me."

"Everyone deserves kindness, Lady Rochford," Gage replied. With those words, I took one last look around the rooms that represented both the great triumphs, and the everlasting sadness, of my life. I linked my arm through his and, together we walked towards my death.

As we stood outside the Coldharbour gate, I heard the snap of the king's banners in the wind. The sound unnerved me, and I began clawing at my skirt, clenching fistfuls of velvet in my hands. I wore the same black over gown from the night before, and it was only in the bright and unforgiving sunlight that I realised how dirty the fabric appeared after my foray across the wet ground to the chapel. I nervously eyed the stained hem until the metallic screeching of the gate drew my attention. When I looked beyond the doors, a cold terror anchored itself in my belly. A hoard of bodies, rippling with anticipation, crowded around the scaffold. Standing just above them, on the platform itself, was the man who would end my life. His face was hidden by a black mask.

Gage parted the crowd and led me through with Helena following behind. When I reached the steps of the scaffold, she attempted to wrestle a coif onto my head, but her hands were shaking too much to tuck all of my hair inside of it; wild tendrils of my flaxen curls whipped in the wind. She winced at her fumbling and a wave a pity struck me. "It doesn't matter," I whispered.

Helena patted my hand. "May God bless you, Lady Rochford," she said.

I gripped my skirts and ascended the steps to the platform. When I arrived at the top, I found myself so fearful, I couldn't relax my hands. I searched the crowd for a friendly face, but they all seemed to blend together; then I recognised a pair of cool sapphire eyes staring back at me. Hugh Wynter had come, and he was wearing that battered grey cloak I had kept for so long. Standing next to him was my brother. Harry's face appeared ashen. I knew, by his swollen eyes, that he had been crying. I almost lost my nerve at the pitiful sight of my resilient brother so broken, but then a flash of copper hair behind them caught my attention. My beautiful niece, Catherine, stood there in a gown of the darkest blue. Her lips curved into a smile as she met my gaze, then she mouthed the words "I love you." She gave me just enough courage to loosen my fists so that I could place the bag of coins in the executioner's hand.

My eyes alighted on the chapel when I turned, and I saw a raven spread its wings in salute before it took flight from the roof. I thought of my husband then. George was that raven. He was dark and beautiful, brilliant and wise; yet his wit could snap you sharply like a beak, and he was far too concerned with the shimmer of gold. The other men who died with him: Norris and Weston, Brereton and Smeaton, they were Anne's ravens and together they formed an unkindness. Their legacies would be forever tarnished by the unkindness shown to them by the man who had once given them wings to soar. Anne could lay claim to the other men, but George, he was my raven, and I had been his widow for far too long. It was time for me to accept my own unkind judgement so that I could fly to him. Together, we would soar again.

The End

AUTHOR'S NOTE

JANE PARKER Boleyn, the Lady Rochford, was a shadowy woman. She has gone down in history as a "great bawd;" infamous for the role she played in the downfall of Henry VIII's fifth wife, Katherine Howard, and thought to have been the prime witness to accusations of incest between Anne Boleyn and her brother, George. But the truth is that we know almost nothing about her. How did she gain such notoriety? For centuries, Jane has been banished to the seedy Tudor underworld of naughty women, but is that reputation deserved? After all, the only certain facts about her are few and far between. Her parents were Henry and Alice Parker, she married George Boleyn at some point before 1526, she attended on all but the last of Henry VIII's queens at one time or another and she died February 13, 1542 within the confines of the Tower of London.

Jane's presence in the original documents of the time are fleeting and often up for conjecture. Did Chapuys get his information right when he says that she helped Anne in her quest to have one of the king's paramours banished? Is she truly the Mistress Parker listed in the retinue of Catherine of Aragon at

Calais in 1520? Even the documents of her jointure were buried for over 500 years. Now that they have emerged, we know the terms, but do we know why the king sealed the contract with a matching contribution?

What do we know for sure? Jane rode in the second chariot of ladies at the funeral of Henry's third wife, Jane Seymour, and attended his fourth wife, Anne of Cleves, while she awaited news of her annulment at Richmond Palace. We also know she exchanged gifts with the king's eldest daughter, the future Queen Mary I, but we have no idea if they were close. During the Tudor period, gifts often meant very little when given to royalty, as it was expected. If Jane had not given a gift to the king's daughter when she was in favour, there would have been a scandal, indeed. So, what do these tiny glimpses of Jane tell us about her? Well… pretty much nothing. Jane Parker Boleyn, as a personality, is almost non-existent.

When the traces of Jane's humanity are washed away, it's easy for later generations to demonise her actions. What could have been perfectly innocent behaviour is seen through the prism of her later behaviour and ultimate ending: death as a traitor to the crown. It is my goal in writing this novel to give Jane some of that humanity back. I want to put a face to a name that has been blackened by assumption for the last five centuries. I want to remind people that Jane wasn't some spectre lurking in the corner, plotting the downfall of others. She was a sister, a daughter, a wife, a friend, and a loyal servant. She had hopes and dreams. She had flaws and quirks. And to further muddy the waters, we have to consider her mental state. The choices she made may be hard to understand now, but at the moment that she made them, they made sense to her.

After all that I've said above, the most important thing I want you, Dear Reader, to remember is that this is a work of fiction. The interior worlds of Jane and George Boleyn and their friends and family members are created entirely out of my imagination. I've included snippets of dialogue that have been recorded and attributed to some of them, but for the most part, the dialogue comes only from my imagination. Any motivations I've attributed to the people in my novel have come from my interpretation of the research that exists on them and the period in which they lived. I do not claim any expertise and have made as many assumptions about Jane's life as any other historian, but the choices I've made in my poetic licence of telling her story are with the benefit of the doubt. I've interpreted the evidence available in the best possible light.

The Rochford marriage has been painted as extremely unhappy at best; tumultuous and abusive at worst. The truth of the matter is that we don't know how their marriage was. I've chosen to portray it like any other marriage of the time because that is how their contemporaries treated it. No one seems to have remarked upon it until at least a century after it happened. Those who offered an opinion relied on hearsay and family legends that had been passed down over time. There may be a grain of truth in some of the stories, but there are no concrete indications that the marriage was anything but typical of the period. For that matter, there is no evidence that George Boleyn was a homosexual or carried on illicit relations with either sex, consensual or not. Any conclusion that he was or did is drawn only from the words of a loyal servant to Cardinal Thomas Wolsey. George Cavendish's Metrical Visions has influenced historical opinion on George Boleyn and others who died with him since the 1500's, but it is important to remember that Cavendish had no love for the Boleyns and he blamed them for Wolsey's downfall. He may have been a contemporary witness, but we need to take his words with a pinch of salt. Was the marriage one of mutual affection? We will never know, but Jane was the only person brave enough to try to contract George after he was incarcerated. There has to be something said for that.

I've based my portrayal of George on the one and only unbiased biography of the man, written by Clare Cherry and Claire Ridgway. The primary documents show that he was liberal and witty. His intelligence and diplomatic skill earned him early appointments to Henry VIII's service and secured alliances with many in the French Court. His religious persuasion towards reformation is well-documented and a few of the books I've mentioned in this work did belong to him. One of the books, *The Book of Gladness,* is a rebuttal to an earlier translation by the same author, Jehan Lefèvre of a poem called *The Torments of Marriage.* While historians have been eager to point out that the latter makes a mockery of marriage and use it to support their theory of an unhappy union, it is often forgotten that the former praises women and exhorts men to treat them with dignity. It appears that George had a manuscript that contained both works. In it, he inscribed the words: *This book is mine, George Boleyn 1526.* At some point, he gave the book to Marc Smeaton and the musician added his own inscription: *A. Moi (and me/mine), M. Marc Sn.* No one knows why George shared this book with Marc, but I tend to wonder if he used it to inspire Marc to better behaviour towards his sister, Anne. Marc seemed unable to see the delineation between himself and the other courtiers of noble birth and he earned himself several recriminations from the queen as a result. My characterisation of the musician is based on analysis by Dr Suzannah Lipscomb in her book *1536: The Year That Changed Henry VIII.* It's unlikely that George could have prepared Jane for interrogation by Cromwell, but the fact that he was arrested at a different palace than Anne raises the theory that the events at court were deemed suspect enough that he took off after the king, either for answers or to try to fix things.

Henry Parker, Baron Morley, is an elusive man. What he thought of the events of Jane's life, we will never know. Jane's biographer, Dr Julia Fox, theorises that the artistic choices he made in the retelling of the story of Polyxena in his translation of Boccaccio's *De claris mulieribus,* can be seen as a veiled tribute to his daughter. Fox puts forth a reasoned argument and there is no reason to believe that the paternal relationship was fraught. It's likely that Morley mourned for his daughter, but never felt that he could openly voice his grief or anger. In this, he seems to have been a pragmatic servant; he did as his monarch bade him, but that doesn't mean that he completely abandoned Jane. In light of Jane's actions at the end of her life, it might be easy to believe that the apple didn't fall far from the tree. Jane may have helped Katherine in her affair because she was extremely biddable and very much like her father.

As for the woman at the centre of this story, Jane herself is an enigma wrapped in mystery. In this novel, she struggles with infertility. There are no records of miscarriages, but if the marriage was a typical one, there might have been one or two; perhaps even several. Certainly, no children were born of the marriage and there was no outward reason for that. The union was consummated and lasted for at least a decade. Jane and George cohabitated, however George was often on diplomatic missions so their opportunities to lie together had to be few and far between. I've gone on the assumption that several factors contributed to their lack of heirs: opportunity, infertility, and the general stress of living at court.

I've made a choice to portray Jane and Anne Boleyn as close friends and confidantes. Jane served her sister-in-law for many years and, in that time, she assisted Anne in her attempts to get one of Henry VIII's paramours banished, something she probably would not have done had they not got on. Jane suffered her own banishment as a result of her part in it and, if relations deteriorated between the two, it might have been as a result of this. The evidence that Jane took part in a demonstration against Anne at Greenwich is shaky at best and has since been dismissed by many historians. Jane certainly acted as a confidant to Anne on at least one occasion when the queen told her that Henry had trouble in the bedroom, an event recorded in the annals of George's trial. The true nature of their relationship is murky, but there is sufficient evidence to show that at least some form of mutual respect was there.

I've portrayed Jane's relationships with her brother, Henry Parker, and his wife, Grace Newport, as being affectionate if not necessarily close. The *Miscellanea Genealogica Et Heraldica* shows that Jane served as Godmother to two of their children. This same record shows that George served as Godfather their second child, Alice Parker. It is this evidence on which I have based the relationship between Henry and his brother-in-law. Jane does not serve as co-godparent in this particular instance so for George to have been named on his own, says a great deal. Also, Henry was chosen to receive a knighthood on the eve of Anne Boleyn's coronation. The middle Henry Parker does not appear to have shared either his father's or son's attachment to the Catholic religion and so I've aligned him with the reformers, though there is no evidence that he actively participated at this time. There is absolutely no evidence that Grace Newport gave any warning to Jane before her interrogation by Cromwell, but it's not outside the realm of possibility. Grace served in Anne's household in between her pregnancies and it's logical to think she and Jane were friendly.

I've shown the relationship between Jane and her sister, Margaret, as much more strained purely on the basis that Margaret seems to have been very loyal and supportive of the Princess Mary; understandable given that Margaret later married Sir John Shelton, the son of the women in charge of the princess' household. Three weeks after Anne's execution, she went with her parents to visit the princess at Hunsdon. Her role in the Greenwich protest is strictly fictional. These three siblings appear to have had two more in their ranks: sister, Elizabeth, and brother, Francis. Neither of them was mentioned with any consistency in the extant sources and so I've left them out for the sake of brevity. Elizabeth may have died early in her youth, but it appears that Francis was old enough to have been gifted property in conjunction with his father from the king.

The story of Jane's involvement with Queen Katherine Howard is told through Jane's perspective with the benefit of hindsight and coloured by the fragile state of her sanity. Jane is reported to have "gone mad" three days into her imprisonment at the Tower, necessitating a move to Russell House on the Strand. Her reasons for her behaviour died with her so I could only guess as to her motivations. Jane's interrogation on the matter exists, but it is a bit disjointed. Jane says little during her questioning, but accepts that the relationship between Katherine and Thomas Culpeper was indeed physical. The debate continues to rage over whether or not that is accurate, but since Jane believes it, I've portrayed it as a certainty.

I could fill my author's notes with reasons as to why I've portrayed Jane in the way I have, but then the notes would be almost as long as the book! The one and only thing that I can emphasise here is that *The Raven's Widow* is a work of fiction. Yes, there is plenty of evidence that *could* support the choices I've made, but that doesn't make my characterisations entirely accurate. If you are looking for a book that completely details the facts of Jane's life, please run to your nearest bookstore and buy a copy of *Jane Boleyn: the True Story of the Infamous Lady Rochford* by Julia Fox. Fox does a brilliant job of putting Jane's story in the context of her time and it is gorgeously written. I can't recommend it enough.

Finally, I want to point out that I've populated my novel with a few characters that did not exist during Jane's time. I based Hugh Wynter and Helena on two of my very good friends. Oswin Danvers was a bit of an Easter Egg. If you correctly guessed that I chose the name because I love Doctor Who, give yourself a gold star! His role may appear small, but Jane's failure to recognise him at the Tower serves to show just how much the inner workings of her mind had changed after the tragedy of George's death. One of the hallmarks of mental trauma is that it affects memory. It goes without saying that Jane's maid, Lucy, is also completely fictional, but we do know that Jane had maids. Katherine Tylney mentioned one of those maids during her interrogation. Apparently, Jane's maid entertained Mistress Tylney while the queen and Culpeper shared a private moment. If you are looking for further information on Katherine's life, including the ladies that served her, I recommend the biography *Young, Damned, and Fair* by Gareth Russell. This fascinating book is the most comprehensive one I've read so far on Katherine's downfall and confirmed everything I suspected about Henry VIII's enigmatic fifth queen.

ACKNOWLEDGEMENTS

I have a whole host of people to thank for offering their support and encouragement as I toiled through the research and writing of my second novel. First and foremost, I need to thank my immediate family for their love and understanding over the last few years of this "hobby" that I've picked up. Kyle and Logan Dillard, I love you up to the sky, down to the ground, and ALL around! I couldn't have done it without you both. Thank you to my parents, Judy Collum and Neil and Angela Swartz for always encouraging my love of books and history. Thank you for allowing me to read whatever my little heart desired and for the rides to the library; above all thank you for always loving me. Thank you to my grandmother, Dorothy Swartz for the many hours spent in the rocking chair while we "read a book." It's because of her and my dearly departed grandfather, Alden, that I fell in love with the written word. Though we aren't blood-related, I feel as though Derek Gilbert belongs in this paragraph. Of all the people that I know, he has by far spent the most time listening to me go on and on about the 16th century. He's not just my boss, but a true leader and a dear friend. Thank you for always telling everyone how awesome I am. Oh, and for your support and unnecessary positivity too!

Next, I would like to acknowledge the friends who've offered their ears for listening, their eyes for reading, and their hearts for support. Thank you to Jeff White and Elena Kuhnhenn, my Hugh Wynter and Helena, for your invaluable feedback on my early editions and for trusting me to infuse some of my characters with your best qualities. Thank you to the Osburn family (Nate, Jess and Erik) for the never ending enthusiasm and tea parties. Thank you to Olga Hughes for the enormously long emails, moral support, and beautiful discussions about Jane and the Parker family. I appreciate how much strength you have given me in taking on Jane's story and smashing through the shadows that surround her. You are my feminist icon. Thank you to Sandra Vasoli for all the chats, hugs, effusive encouragement, and candid feedback. It's because of you that I've grown as a writer. Thank you for taking me under your wing. You are definitely my "History Mom." Thank you to Wendy J. Dunn for all of the support and kindness; I'm so happy that our beautiful Catherine Carey brought us together. Our friendship is a prime example of how much more you can accomplish as friends rather than competitors. I'm thrilled to count you as my "History Sister." Thank you to Stephanie Young for your kind words and enthusiastic support. I'm so glad that we connected seven years ago through our September babies!

I'd like to acknowledge the wonderful people I work with in my "day" job. To my friends at Edward Jones, thank you all for all of your encouragement; for asking how my book was doing; for acting really excited anytime I talked about it. I would like to especially thank Jon Nicolazzo for taking an interest in my work and showing such enthusiasm. We have the best conversations about history. Thank you to all of my clients for all of your kind words and support. Oh and for always smiling and nodding patiently whenever my boss brags about my books; your tolerance is greatly appreciated! For Jolene, there are no words besides Thank You, Thank You, Thank You!

Thank you to Dr Catherine Helm-Clark for sharing with me her research on the Parker family and pointing me to the baptismal records for the children of Henry Parker and Grace Newport. It is rare to find a historian so willing to share their trove of research and I cannot even begin to enumerate just how much I appreciate your gracious generosity. Seeing George Boleyn listed as one of the Godfathers was a moment I will never forget. That record smashed any notion I had that Jane's family disliked her husband. A pure treasure.

My unending gratitude goes out to my Ravenclaw friend, Gareth Russell. He is a fine example of an historian and human being. I cannot begin to describe my appreciation for the trouble he took to send me an advanced copy of his brilliant biography of Katherine Howard, months before its publication. I don't think I have ever before been so thrilled to receive a package in the mail. His work was invaluable to me as I put the finishing touches on my manuscript and I am forever in his debt.

Finally, I'd like to thank my MadeGlobal Family. Thank you to my publisher, Tim Ridgway. He and his wife, Claire, are the Dynamic Duo and I couldn't have had any of the success I've had without them. Thank you for taking a chance on my first book and changing my life. Also, thank you for never asking me "Are you done with that next book yet?!" Thank you to my England family, Catherine Brooks and David Winter Ibbotson (Ozzie and Lucas too!) for being so wonderful and for all the fun times we had in London…and at Harry Potter of course! The vast ocean may separate us, but it will never come between us. Sarah Bryson and Beth Von Staats, thank you for your friendship; Clare Cherry and Claire Ridgway, thank you for bringing George back out into the light of day and your passion for setting his wrongs right again; and to Amy Licence for generously taking the time to read my manuscript and offer an endorsement.

For anyone I didn't specifically mention…thank you too! I'm so very fortunate to be surrounded by such wonderful people. I could never have accomplished writing one novel, let alone TWO, without all of encouragement and support I've received from everyone around me. I also have the best readers! Since the publication of Cor Rotto, I have been overwhelmed by your support and I've made some wonderful friends too – Mimi Cobb, Shauna Stone Johnston, and Carol Kettley Rushton, I'm looking at you! I am truly blessed.

Adrienne Dillard

Adrienne Dillard is a graduate with a Bachelor of Arts in Liberal Studies with emphasis in History from Montana State University-Northern.

Adrienne has been an eager student of history for most of her life and has completed in-depth research on the American Revolutionary War time period in American History and the history and sinking of the Titanic. Her senior university capstone paper was on the discrepancies in passenger lists on the ill-fated liner and Adrienne was able to work with Philip Hind of Encyclopedia Titanica for much of her research on that subject. Her previous works include best-selling novel, *"Cor Rotto: A Novel of Catherine Carey"* and the non-fiction *"Catherine Carey in a Nutshell"* for MadeGlobal's History in a Nutshell series.

When she isn't writing, Adrienne works as an administrative assistant in the financial services industry and enjoys spending time with her husband, Kyle, and son, Logan, at their home in the Pacific Northwest.

READING GROUP QUESTIONS

Adrienne Dillard would like to thank you for reading her novel, and has prepared these questions that might help to take you further in your understandings of this book.

» The Raven's Widow opens with a scene of Jane Boleyn, Lady Rochford's, first sojourn to the Tower of London as a prisoner. In this passage, she reflects on her experience during her last visit in the days leading up to Queen Anne Boleyn's coronation. She is relieved to find that she will be housed in the same accommodations, but what is different this time? What emotions do you think she felt? Have you ever experienced something similar, being in the same place twice under very different circumstances?

» Before Jane goes to the court to serve Katherine of Aragon, she seems to have lived a relatively simple "country" life at her home in Hallingbury. Certainly, there were relaxed diversions, such as fishing and ice skating, but what other skills would Jane be learning to prepare her for court life?

» If you are familiar with the history of the Tudors, what did you find the most surprising in this novel? If you are not as familiar, what did you find most interesting to learn? Did this novel make you want to dig deeper into the time period?

»   In 1520 Henry VIII and the King of France, Francis I, held a glorious summit in France termed "The Field of Cloth of Gold." The documents describing this summit indicate that Katherine of Aragon was accompanied by a maid named Mistress Parker. Since Jane's mother, Alice Parker, was also in attendance on the queen, it is assumed that Mistress Parker refers to Jane. If true, it would be her first appearance in the historical record. Going off that theory, the author portrays Jane's journey to France for this meeting. What did you find most interesting about this meeting and the protocol followed by the royal court? You can find a painting depicting this historical meeting online. As you look at it, do you see some of the things the author describes?

»   When Jane first meets her future husband, George Boleyn, she feels an initial attraction to him. However, when she learns of George's popularity, that attraction begins to wane and she finds herself questioning why he would be interested in her. What does that tell you about Jane? How have the assumptions made of both George and Jane influenced our perception of them? How have our own assumptions influenced perceptions of the people in our lives?

»   During her marriage, Jane struggles with several miscarriages and infertility. While there isn't any direct evidence of those struggles, we do know that she never had children. How do you think Jane's childlessness affected her in an age where the most important thing a woman could do was have children?

» One of Jane's biggest hurdles is overcoming her loyalty to Katherine of Aragon in order to support her sister-in-law. Have you faced a similar struggle in your lifetime? If you could give Jane advice, what would it be?

» Jane has always been viewed as a conservative Catholic because her father, Lord Morley was. That view has always been used as justification for the idea that her marriage to the Reformist leaning George was unhappy. While there is no concise historical evidence to support this view, there is evidence that her brother, Henry, was Reformist. Furthermore, Henry's son fled England during Elizabeth I's reign; proving yet again that the religious beliefs of one's parents did not necessarily wield that much influence. Is this true in your family? How are your beliefs and values different or similar to other members of your family?

» One of the things Jane finds throughout her incarceration is that kindness often comes in the most unexpected places. What kindnesses were granted to Jane? Have you experienced this as well? Have you also offered kindness to someone who may have thought they didn't deserve it?

» Of the finite amount of historical evidence existing for Jane, the dispatch from the Imperial Ambassador, Eustace Chapuys, indicating that she became "mad" after her third day in the Tower is the one that is most baffling. What do you think he meant by that? Do you think she was truly maniacal as depicted in the popular television series, The Tudors? Or do you think it was more of a mental "breakdown?" There is some question of whether she was faking it in order to drum up sympathy. Do you believe that to be true? What do you think of Henry VIII's decision to execute her in spite of her "madness?"

» In most historical novels and movies/television shows, Jane is depicted as being the villain in the downfall of both Queens she has served. The author of The Raven's Widow sought to portray her in a far more sympathetic light. Did these earlier portrayals affect your interest in reading this book? What was your initial view of Jane, and has reading this novel changed it?

» The historical genre has become increasingly popular over time and new eras and people are finally getting the attention they deserve. Which book/movie/television show has been your favourite? What era/person would you like to see explored?

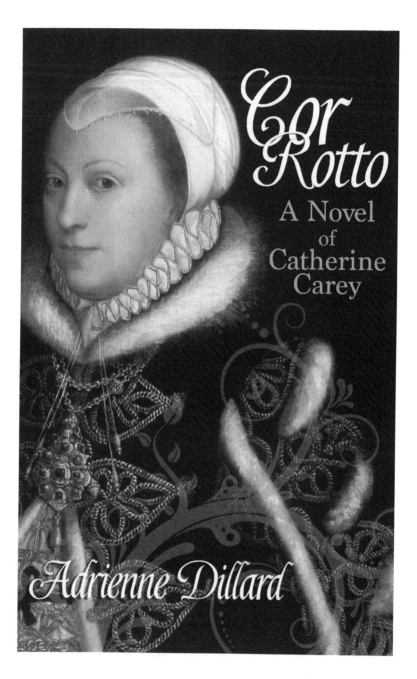

Cor Rotto
A Novel
of
Catherine
Carey

Adrienne Dillard

978-84-937464-7-6

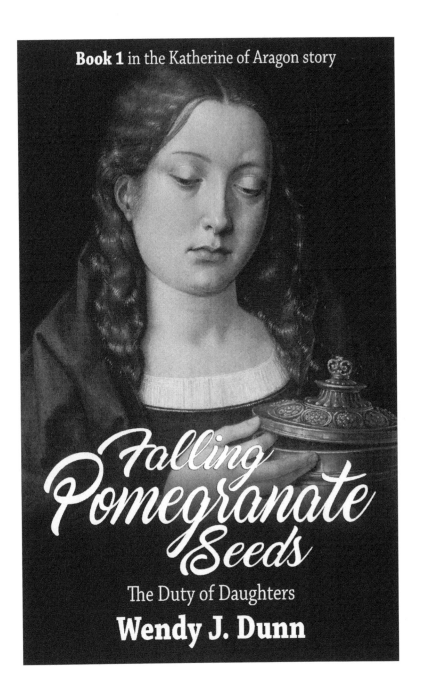

Book 1 in the Katherine of Aragon story

Falling Pomegranate Seeds

The Duty of Daughters

Wendy J. Dunn

978-84-944893-9-6

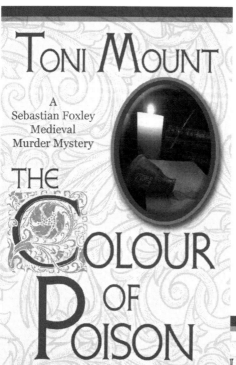

TONI MOUNT

A
Sebastian Foxley
Medieval
Murder Mystery

THE
COLOUR
OF
POISON

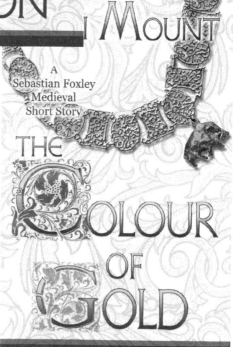

I MOUNT

A
Sebastian Foxley
Medieval
Short Story

THE
COLOUR
OF
GOLD

978-84-944893-3-4
978-84-946498-0-6

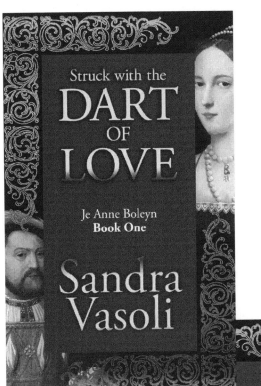

Struck with the
DART
OF
LOVE

Je Anne Boleyn
Book One

Sandra Vasoli

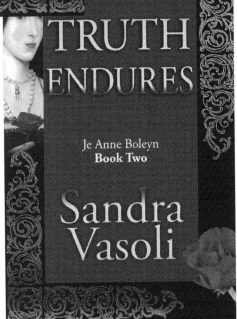

TRUTH
ENDURES

Je Anne Boleyn
Book Two

Sandra Vasoli

978-84-944893-6-5
978-84-944893-7-2

A NOVEL OF THE WARS OF THE ROSES

THE CLAIMANT

SIMON ANDERSON

978-84-937464-9-0

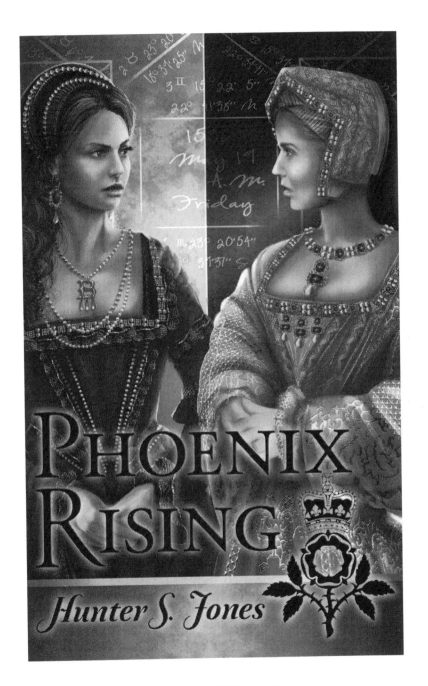

PHOENIX RISING

Hunter S. Jones

978-84-943721-4-8

Historical Fiction

Falling Pomegranate Seeds - **Wendy J. Dunn**
Struck With the Dart of Love - **Sandra Vasoli**
Truth Endures - **Sandra Vasoli**
Phoenix Rising - **Hunter S. Jones**
Cor Rotto - **Adrienne Dillard**
The Raven's Widow - **Adrienne Dillard**
The Claimant - **Simon Anderson**
The Truth of the Line - **Melanie V. Taylor**

Non Fiction History

Anne Boleyn's Letter from the Tower - **Sandra Vasoli**
Queenship in England - **Conor Byrne**
Katherine Howard - **Conor Byrne**
The Turbulent Crown - **Roland Hui**
Jasper Tudor - **Debra Bayani**
Tudor Places of Great Britain - **Claire Ridgway**
Illustrated Kings and Queens of England - **Claire Ridgway**
A History of the English Monarchy - **Gareth Russell**
The Fall of Anne Boleyn - **Claire Ridgway**
George Boleyn: Tudor Poet, Courtier & Diplomat - **Ridgway & Cherry**
The Anne Boleyn Collection - **Claire Ridgway**
The Anne Boleyn Collection II - **Claire Ridgway**
Two Gentleman Poets at the Court of Henry VIII - **Edmond Bapst**

Children's Books

All about Richard III - **Amy Licence**
All about Henry VII - **Amy Licence**
All about Henry VIII - **Amy Licence**
Tudor Tales William at Hampton Court - **Alan Wybrow**

PLEASE LEAVE A REVIEW

If you enjoyed this book, *please* leave a review at the book seller where you purchased it. There is no better way to thank the author and it really does make a huge difference!
Thank you in advance.

Made in the USA
Middletown, DE
27 May 2017